DRAGONESQUE

Other Anthologies Edited by:

Patricia Bray & Joshua Palmatier

After Hours: Tales from the Ur-bar
The Modern Fae's Guide to Surviving Humanity
Temporally Out of Order * Alien Artifacts * Were-
All Hail Our Robot Conquerors!
Second Round: A Return to the Ur-bar
The Modern Deity's Guide to Surviving Humanity
Solar Flare

S.C. Butler & Joshua Palmatier

Submerged * Guilds & Glaives * Apocalyptic
When Worlds Collide * Brave New Worlds * Dragonesque

Laura Anne Gilman & Kat Richardson

The Death of All Things

Troy Carrol Bucher & Joshua Palmatier

The Razor's Edge

Patricia Bray & S.C. Butler

Portals

David B. Coe & Joshua Palmatier

Temporally Deactivated * Galactic Stew
Derelict

Steven H Silver & Joshua Palmatier

Alternate Peace

Crystal Sarakas & Joshua Palmatier

My Battery Is Low and It Is Getting Dark

David B. Coe & John Zakour

Noir

Crystal Sarakas & Rhondi Salsitz

Shattering the Glass Slipper

David B. Coe & Edmund R. Schubert

Artifice & Craft

Stephen Kotowych & Tony Pi

Game On!

Dragonesque

Edited by

S.C. Butler
&
Joshua Palmatier

Zombies Need Brains LLC
www.zombiesneedbrains.com

Interior Design (ebook): ZNB Design
Interior Design (print): ZNB Design
Cover Design by ZNB Design
Cover Art "Dragonesque"
by Justin Adams of Varia Studios

ZNB Book Collectors #27

Kickstarter Edition Printing, June 2023
First Printing, July 2023

Print ISBN-13: 978-1940709529

Ebook ISBN-13: 978-1940709536

Printed in the U.S.A.

COPYRIGHTS

Table of Contents

SIGNATURE PAGE

S.C. Butler, editor:

Joshua Palmatier, editor:

Esther M. Friesner:

Madeline Dau:

Niall Spain:

Russell Hugh McConnell:

Grace Eliza:

Mike Jack Stoumbos:

Paul D. Smith:

Jean Marie Ward:

____

Gerald Brandt:

____

Gini Koch & Bebe Bayliss:

____

Larry Ivkovich:

____

Barbara Campbell:

____

Journey Sloane:

____

Em McDermott:

____

Auston Habershaw:

____

David B. Coe:

____

Justin Adams, artist:

____

Slay

Esther M. Friesner

Clutchleader Gehdreh rolled his fiery eyes in exasperation. The younger green-scaled dragon before him trembled. Jiryah was all grown up, but still just a wee bit terrified of the larger, more cantankerous wyrm. Part of it was respect for his aeons-older sire, part was the indelible memory of seeing Gehdreh lunch on one of Jiryah's fellow-hatchings as an example for the others.

Why does he have to be like this? Jiryah thought. *Why do* we*?*

Now Gehdreh slammed one massive forepaw to the floor. The marble paving shattered with a report loud enough to be heard three mountain ranges beyond the ancient dragon's palace.

"What is the matter with you, Jiryah?" The great wyrm tried and failed to maintain his millennia-nurtured air of *gravitas.* Sea-blue scales rattled with anger. "*Why* won't you eat? I went to a great deal of trouble to get you something this tasty."

Jiryah could not look Gehdreh in the eye. "My apologies, beloved clutchleader. I would like nothing better than to devour such a tender morsel as this—" He gestured at the human cowering before him in a shimmering crimson gown. "—but it would be wasted on me. My stomach would eject even the merest nibble of her leg or forelimb or even a teensy crunchlet of her skull. You saw what happened with the senator!"

Gehdreh uttered a low, grouchy rumble such as any elder—dragon or human—might voice when confronted by a young relative with the gall to be right. Reluctant to cede the point, the senior dragon snarled, "Are you certain your nausea didn't happen because your meal belonged to *that* political party? Even I have trouble stomaching them. They all taste so *fermented.*" His snout wrinkled in disgust.

The trembling human dared to look up and volunteer: "You should probably let me go. I belong to that party." This was said with such a degree of desperate, last-ditch hope as to make the animate entrée look even more pathetic.

"*Which* party?" Gehdreh asked coldly.

"Whichever one it takes for me not to be eaten."

Gehdreh's aggravated roar was not incendiary, but a few sparks did fly from his throat. The human shrieked and reverted to impersonating a terrified armadillo.

The younger dragon shook his head. "My digestive issues go beyond mortal politics. The culinary horrors of our time have slain my appetite. I think it began in that dismal age when my clutchmates and I often heard you and the other elders bemoaning the fact that princesses had become thin on the ground and even maidens of the proper ripeness had no shelf-life whatsoever!"

"Ah yes," Gehdreh said solemnly. "The Sixties."

Lifting his barbeled chin, he shook off those melancholy reflections and glowered at Jiryah. "And what of it? We adjusted! It takes more than virgin supply-train issues to daunt a dragon. Now you listen here, my fine drakelet: I am going out to stretch my wings and recover my patience. When I return, I expect to find your meal completely eaten or I will know the reason why!"

"I can tell you the reason why right now," Jiryah said sadly.

"Ohhhh, no you won't." The elder dragon waggled a monitory claw in the youngling's face. "You will eat what is set before you and if you *do* happen to unstomach your meal, you will eat it again, in whatever condition it re-emerges from your gullet, and you will continue to do this until you keep it down. Got it?"

Jiryah said nothing.

"I *said*, got it?"

"Mmrrrm*yeah*mm."

The mumbled concession wasn't loud or distinct, but it was enough. Gehdreh nodded crisply, satisfied, whipped his wings wide open, and soared out of the palace to the great world beyond.

Jiryah followed his flight with melancholy eyes, then turned to the human. "My apologies," he said. "I don't want to do this."

"You and me both." The human slumped in resignation. "Make it quick, will you?"

"Huh?" Jiryah tilted his head in the manner of a kitten who had just done something unspeakable to the living room carpet and was determined to blame it on the coffee table.

"Kill me. Eat me. Barf me up, if that's what happens, and snarf me down again. God knows, it won't make much difference to me after the first bite. Damn, your dad's a tightass bastard, isn't he? My mother was one of those 'How do you know you don't like it if you don't try it?' fanatics. So I asked if that applied to some, uh, alternative carnal recreational practices I picked up from *Collared* magazine, but I don't think you can use—"

"What are you talking about?" Jiryah said. "I'm not going to do anything like that."

"You're not?"

The dragon shook his head. "Why would I? You heard me: I can't stomach people. My dad—my clutchleader—refuses to believe me, but it's true, and there is nothing we dragonkind hold more sacred than the utterance of the truth!" He struck a heroic stance worthy of a Wagnerian tenor about to do something gloriously stupid.

"You—you'll let me go? I mean, you *could.* The main thing is for the big guy to believe you ate me, right? And if I'm nowhere to be seen when he comes back—"

Jiryah's *Siegfried Buys a Time-Share* pose crumbled. "It wouldn't work."

"Yes, it would! Look, I'm even willing to leave one shoe behind, even if it cost me a bundle to have these custom-made. You could gnaw on it a little so it'll look like—"

"No. When clutchleader Gehdreh returns, he'll ask if you were tasty and I can't lie."

"You could say I *wasn't* tasty. That'd be the truth, in a way."

Jiryah shook his head. "Even if I tried sophistry, he'd demand to smell my breath, whereupon he would know all! Then he'd hunt you down and devour you himself. Waste not, want not."

The human snorted. "So you're not going to eat me but you *are* going *let* me be eaten, and go boo-hoo-not-my-fault? Ugh. It is to gag. Which is what I hope I do to your stupid—what did you call him? Crotchleader?""

"*Clutch*leader. We dragons are born from a clutch of eggs laid by a single female and incubated by all the males who coupled with her. Whichever male is on duty at the time of our hatching becomes the clutchleader, responsible for our upbringing."

"Well, sucks to be him. Probably sucks to be you, too. I mean, how long can a dragon go without food before it dies?"

"I—I am not going *entirely* without food. I sneak feedings of the same things we were given in our hatchling days: humble mosses, seaweeds, assorted fungi, with a little lichen thrown in on our birthdays. The opportunity for us to savor humans was a promised reward, for when we would be old enough to appreciate the taste. And as for princesses—!" Jiryah's gaze drifted off to his dragonet days. "We're told you are an epicurean treat even better than eating an actual Epicurean."

"Great. I'm the dragon version of *escargots à la Bourguignonne.* Just the way I wanted to die, smothered in garlic butter. Kink-*kee.*" The human managed a shaky grin.

Jiryah stared, bewildered. *I will never understand these creatures,* he thought. *Jests, at a time like this? And yet... her jesting seems to have helped this damsel take heart. Would that I might learn her ways! Yet what jest would be great enough to help me face Gehdreh and tell him, unasked, the reason I refuse to eat—?* He sighed. *I am too afraid.*

"Hey! Earth to Puff!" The human's shout derailed Jiryah's melancholy train of thought. "Can we focus on *my* problem here? I've got an idea: If I can't run away, can I maybe get *disqualified* as dragon feed?"

"I do not understand."

"Your eggdaddy promised you a princess." The human raised one hand. "Not it."

"But—but your every aspect presents beauty, elegance, and the regal bearing of a king's daughter! Well, except for when you were cowering on the palace floor like a worm. And your garb! It dazzles the eye."

"Look, the only reason I'm wearing all this eleganza is I was headed home after the show and I was too tired to change out of my work clothes at the club. We had *three* bridesmaid mobs, and those ladies are big tippers. I'd done pretty well, but I was so damn tired that I wanted to go straight home and *maybe* untuck before I kissed the sheets. Dumbass me, I took a shortcut down the wrong street, came face to face with what I thought was a bear, and the next thing I know, I'm being gripped in a set of claws Wolverine would die for and whisked through the skies to wherever *this* little pied-à-terror stands. I wanted a nap, I got a kidnap." Jiryah's rejected meal waited for a reaction, but the dragon was dumbstruck. "Uh, hello? Scaley McScalerson? What's wrong, basilisk got your tongue?"

"I—I am merely astonished to learn that there are still cities of men, in this day and age, that harbor bears and wolverines."

"Ohhhhh."

(Here followed a brief tutorial on alternate meanings of some animal names in contemporary culture, with a sidebar lecture teaching Jiryah more about the Marvel Universe than he had ever wanted to know.)

The human concluded this little talk by saying: "The one thing I don't get is how a dragon the size of your old man, er, reptile, could lose enough bulk to cosplay a person, even a big, brawny one. Talk about impressive!"

"It's no great accomplishment," Jiryah replied, a trifle testily. Given the imbalance of power between him and Gehdreh, anyone's admiration for his clutchleader made his tail spikes itch with annoyance. "It's a minor bit of our inborn magic, less impressive than breathing fire or being able to fly with aerodynamically insufficient wings. Even I can do it. The result is temporary. What *I* don't get is how a princess like you can speak of work clothes. Princesses don't *work*! Not unless you count needlepoint and singing to squirrels."

"I get needled enough onstage. Besides, weren't you paying attention? I told you: I'm not a princess. *I* am a *queen*!" The human dropped a curtsey. "Akmi Anville, at your serv—"

"*Your majesty*!" The green dragon's bellow made the palace walls shake. He bowed his head until his chin brushed the floor. "Forgive my failure to recognize your true rank, O royal lady. This is an honor! If you but knew how highly valued one of your regal status is counted among our kind, milady Anville, it would knock your silken hose off. By the Flame, when Clutchleader Gehdreh finds out his error, he will be shamed for his failure to treat you with the respect your stature demands."

"Because you don't eat queens? What are we, a protected species? Like, the same reason we humans don't eat panda fajitas?"

"Oh, we eat queens. That is, the other dragons do. Or would, if there were more of you, these days. Queens are a legendary delicacy, so much more succulent than common humans or even princesses. But your kind are beyond rare in this unhappy world, much like the glorious beauty and grace of—" His voice dropped to a wistful shadow. "—unicorns."

"So he *will* eat me?"

"Unless he decides to use you for breeding purposes." Before Akmi could respond to this, the young dragon's expression hardened. "He'll probably just gobble you up the moment he learns what you are, the selfish old toad." Jiryah stamped his foot, though with less effect than his clutchleader's earlier display of temper. "No. I will not allow it. There is little enough beauty in this world. I will protect you, milady Anville. I will save you!"

"You mean you're going to fight the big guy?" Akmi's eyebrows rose sharply.

"What? No! He'd slaughter me. But he cannot slaughter what he cannot find."

* * *

Suddenly light.

* * *

Suddenly Manhattan.

* * *

"What—what just happened?" Akmi said, while fighting for breath. A swift glance took in quite a different scene than the clutchleader's lair. Instead, the bustle of a city street surrounded human and dragon—

No, not dragon. Not exactly.

A slender young man clad all in green stood before Akmi, grinning like a used car salesman. He executed a bow worthy of a cartoon Prince Charming. "Your Majesty, it is my honor to have transported you out of peril…for the nonce."

"Yeah, right, thanks." Akmi spoke as one distracted by the rush of pedestrians plowing their way around the pair of them. None of the harried passers-by seemed to have noticed the abrupt irruption of two new people in their midst, not even those who didn't have their noses an inch from their phones. "That was—was a lot better than flying. Not as talon-y."

The transformed dragon smiled. "I wouldn't dream of subjecting you to such a brutish mode of transport, milady Anville. *I* know how to respect royalty, even if my clutchleader does not. A transport spell takes precious little power, but you know Gehdreh: he must have his moment of drama."

"I know the type. But even if you didn't fly me here, why isn't anyone losing their shit over our big entrance?"

"All part of the spell, milady."

"So, when you leave me here and head home, no one's going to notice that either?"

Jiryah raised one eyebrow. "I'm not leaving; not until I have rendered you *completely* and *ultimately* safe from a fate worse than—er, *equivalent to* death."

Akmi glanced up and down the bustling street. "I think I'm safe enough. We're not that far from where I was when your clutchleader nabbed me."

"I know. I backtracked your scent trail." Jiryah's face fell. "But this is not enough to assure your safety. It is only a matter of time before Gehdreh returns to his lair and finds us gone. He will not let that pass unchallenged. He will pursue us. I brought you back to your own realm, in hopes that here you will be able to rally enough of your loyal knights and plenteous peasant cannon-fodder to give my clutchleader strong second thoughts about devouring you or forcing you down *my* craw."

Akmi looked uneasy. "I…don't have any knights or peasants. The most I've got on my side are my sisters."

"No knights? No peasants? What sort of queen are you?"

"Yeah, about that…" Akmi patted the dragon's very human-for-the-moment shoulder. "There's a *little* something you need to learn."

* * *

Jiryah stood under the glare of a single spotlight on the otherwise vacant stage of Club Soirée and rocked nervously from foot to foot. The ghosts of used cooking oil and stale beer in the dormant nightclub gave him the shivers. If he squinted past the bright light into the audience, he could just make out the glow of four pairs of eyes peering at him intently. For an instant he wished he were not blessed, cursed, or otherwise saddled with a dragon's power to perceive other creatures in even the darkest, deepest shadows by the soulfire in their gaze.

He'd been raised to believe that humans always viewed dragons with awe or terror, but ever since his queen had led him to her place of employment and introduced him to the ones she called her sisters, he'd been on the receiving end of stares that embodied neither dread nor amazement, but rather...dissection.

Out among the unoccupied chairs and tables, a heated conversation was in full swing. Jiryah's hearing was keen; he wasn't spared from a single word.

"Girl, are you for real? How is *that* a dragon?" came the baritone demand. It was the third time that question or one similar to it had been posed, and for the third time Akmi reacted with a put-upon sigh.

"*Yes*, Idaho, that *is* a dragon, and I'll have him prove it to you stubborn-ass bitches in a minute. He's onstage so he'll have enough room to change to his original shape. You've got no idea how big he gets."

"That's what s*he* said!" came a third voice.

"Shut up, Pastelle."

"Does that light have to be on?" Jiryah whined.

"Yep, it does." Akmi's friendly words came to him out of the darkness. "We can't help you if we can't all get a really good look at you."

"Help *me*? But I'm the one who rescued *you*," the dragon protested.

"Help *us*, then; you and me. You said your clutchleader would hunt me down. He's a fire-breathing dick—shut up, Pastelle—"

"I never said a word." Pastelle sounded equally affronted and guilty.

"Consider it a pre-emptive strike. Anyhoo, is there any hope he'll give up and stay home when he sees we've skedaddled?"

Jiryah hung his head. "None."

"And will *you* escape punishment when he confirms that you were the one to whisk me out of his lair?"

The dragon shook his still-human head, but there was already the faintest hint of scales shadowing his face, unmistakable under the merciless spotlight. The transformation spell's temporary nature was beginning to make itself manifest.

"All right then." Akmi sounded satisfied. "That means we need to plan and plan quickly."

Yet another voice, this one deep and gravelly, cut in: "Speaking as one of Akmi's stubborn-ass bitches and the only one here with any military service record, it'd help if we had a better idea of what we're dealing with. Because I, for one, have zero experience slaying dragons."

"I—I hope we can keep it that way," Jiryah said. "I would rather avoid slaying my clutchleader, if at all possible."

"And I'd rather avoid being collateral damage when he comes for you."

Akmi clicked her tongue. "Jesus, Tori, Rambo much? It's been ages since you served, so unless you've got a souvenir bazooka under your corset—Pastelle, *do not even*—we are all in the same boat as Jiryah when his eggdaddy shows up." There was a pause. "Unless you girls want to get the hell out now. I wouldn't blame you."

Cries of protest arose from the other three. "Bitch, please, we're your *sisters*," Idaho said staunchly. "Give us a little credit. Didn't we get Mark to let us have the club to ourselves the *second* you got in touch, so we could have a secure meeting spot?"

"Although to be honest, he only agreed because we told him we needed an emergency rehearsal," Tori said. "Mark's a good club owner-manager but he's no saint."

"You've got to admit, this whole story about dragons, for God's sake, is a lot for us to swallow—shut up, me—" Pastelle chimed in. "—but you've never been the shady type, Akmi. We'll believe you until we've got a reason not to."

"I believe you," Tori grumbled. "But you're the only one who's seen dragons *as* dragons, Akmi. I want my own idea of what we'll be up against." There was the rapid clack-clack-clack of high heels across the nightclub floor and a tall, heavily tattooed man in partial drag climbed onto the stage beside Jiryah.

"Nice to meet you, Smaug." A hand offered in friendship, or at least peace, closed firmly on Jiryah's transformed forepaw. "The name's Tori de Force and I'm from Missouri."

"I beg your pardon?"

"Show me. Show us all. Can we see what you *really* look like?"

Jiryah obliged.

"Happy?" said the dragon.

"Uh." Tori stared. "We're gonna need a bigger…everything."

Jiryah's original form left precious little space in the spotlight, but that didn't stop Idaho and Pastelle from scrambling their way onstage for a closer look. Three pairs of hands ran over the green dragon's flanks, made bold to touch his wings, even stroked his pointed muzzle as though he were an outsized palomino.

"Ooh, look at how his scales shimmer," Pastelle said, enraptured. "I would love a gown this color. And those eyelashes! They're much more glamorous than any of mine, and I paid top dollar. I never *dreamed* dragons had such awesome lashes. Unicorns, maybe."

"Unicorns?" The word wobbled from Jiryah's lips and worked a startling effect on the young dragon. Golden teardrops brimmed in his eyes, streamed down his cheeks, and splashed onto the stage. "*Unicorns!*" His voice ached with misery and his harsh sobs set the spotlight swaying.

Jiryah's unexpected breakdown staggered the four queens even more than his transformation. One moment he'd been a man, then a monster, then a curiosity, and now he was simply the essence of suffering vulnerability. It was not at all what the best legends of dragons had led them to expect.

Instinctively they threw their arms around him, even though they could not do more than hug him piecemeal. Akmi herself joined the supportive swarm onstage and attempted to take some control of the situation.

"Jiryah, honey, what's wrong? What is it about unicorns that's got you so upset?"

"I took a course in medieval lit when I was at Vassar," Idaho said. "I think I remember reading how a unicorn's the only creature that can kill a dragon."

"Is that it, baby?" Tori asked, stroking Jiryah's neck. "Did a unicorn kill your mom or something and you want revenge?"

"Noooooooo!" Jiryah wailed. "It's just—that is—I mean—" He took a deep breath. "*I want to* **be** *a unicorn*!"

The dragon's declaration dropped a weighted blanket of silence over the four queens. Akmi was the first to recover.

"Have you told your eggdaddy?"

"I'm still alive, so what do *you* think?" Jiryah replied bitterly.

"Even after that spiel you gave me about dragons always telling the truth?"

"He never asked so I never told."

"Boy, *that* takes me back," Tori the veteran muttered.

"You mean a *real* unicorn, right?" Pastelle asked. "Not the slang for a—"

Akmi clapped one hand over Pastelle's mouth and blurted, "Yes, he means a real fake legendary mythological horn-headed horse and shut up, Pastelle, I don't want to have to teach baby about *that* sort of unicorn. I had one hell of a time explaining queens, bears, and wolverines to him not one hour ago."

Pastelle slapped Akmi's muffling hand aside. "Do not touch the face," she snapped. "*Some* of us are ready for work. *Some* of us would like to get this whole dragon thing sorted out so we can actually rehearse for tonight."

"*Some* of us would also appreciate not getting devoured," Idaho said. "Why the fuck would I want to put on full makeup if I'm only going to end up lip-syncing 'Cover Girl' inside a dragon's gut?"

"No." Jiryah drew a deep, shaky breath. "I will not let that happen. O my queens, you may not be the sort I was taught about, but you are truly noble beings nonetheless. You must not sacrifice yourselves on my account. It's true, I've known that I wanted to be a unicorn ever since I was a mere hatchling. For centuries I cherished it as an impossible dream. I would not eat meat. I entered the respite of Long Sleep to escape a life that pressured me to be what I truly was not. I hoped my clutchleader would leave me to my misery, but he was determined to change me into what *he* thought I should be. If I had simply eaten a cow or two, a few wildebeest, even a single hamster—!"

"How *could* you?" Pastelle cried.

Jiryah laid his cheek against her shoulder. "Indeed, I could not. That was why Gehdreh tried tempting me with the savory flesh of a princess."

"Queen," Akmi said automatically.

"I will not wait for him to find us," Jiryah went on. "I will return and tell him everything, even my dread secret shame. Then I will yield up my throat to him and invite the one who gave me life to give me death. He will feast upon me and be satisfied." The young dragon's head drooped. "It's the only way."

"Oh no." Tori shook her head emphatically. "Oh *so much* no. First of all, you rescued our drag sister and I'm allergic to martyrs." The other queens loudly affirmed their own dedication to Team Jiryah.

"Second, how is wanting to be a unicorn a *shame*?" Idaho said. "They're at least as magical as dragons and ten times as glam. No offense."

"I know, I agree. They are even more magical than we. They breathe and feast on enchantment!" Jiryah sighed. "Even if Gehdreh would accept my desire, there is no transformation spell I could work that would make me appear half so lovely as a unicorn. There simply isn't that much magic in me. It was a stupid dream." Gently he rose from the stage. "I choose to give it up, along with my life. May all of you remain safe and happy."

The four queens exchanged a look.

"Hold it right there, girlfriend." Pastelle grabbed Jiryah by the barbels. "I know we can't stop you if you really want to leave, but we owe you one for bringing our sister home safe."

"One?" Akmi echoed. "Hell, *I* owe you a billion!"

"Exactly," Tori said, folding her arms. "I say you wait here, dig in, secure a solid defensive position, and let the enemy come to you."

"Who knows?" Idaho shrugged. "He might never show up. Even dragons have to say 'Screw it, this shit isn't worth my time' *sometimes*, yeah?"

Jiryah shook his head. "Dragons invented grudges. He will come."

"And we will face him if—when—he does," Akmi said decisively.

Pastelle sighed. "I just hope he doesn't pop in during the show. I would never live it down if my Cher medley got upstaged by an overgrown gecko."

"You're worried about living *that* down at a time like this? Do you even *listen* to yourself, Pastelle?"

"Chill, bitch." Pastelle snapped glitter-tipped fingers. "I'm just trying to distract myself from what's coming, okay? If we're just gonna wait around for the big, bad dragon to come calling, the tension will kill us before he does."

"She's got a point," Idaho said. "No sense brooding. We've got a show to do—if we live to do it—and I'm not even tucked yet."

"And I'm still in yesterday's drag," said Akmi.

"*And* we've got a dragon to hide before Mark and the waitstaff come in. It's almost that time." Tori sized up Jiryah. "You mind turning yourself human again?"

"Oh, where's the fun in *that*? I've got an idea." Pastelle turned her impish smile on the dragon. "You were in a rush to die for us, doll. Why don't we help you live a little first?"

* * *

Gehdreh burst into Club Soirée just as Tori was performing the big finish of her tribute to Britney, Barbra, and Beyoncé. It was a showstopper, but nothing compared to the effect the invading dragon had on the audience.

Except he wasn't in dragon form. Once again, he'd taken the shape of a burly human male. Gehdreh deemed it more prudent to keep a low profile—or in his case, a somewhat rugged and hairy one—until he sussed out the site to which he'd tracked his prey.

(Gehdreh hadn't survived the centuries of gung-ho knights errant by taking foolish risks. Swords, lances, battle-axes, and the like had done for many of his birth-clutch companions, but the latest body counts among dragonkind included the victims of bullets, flame-throwers, and in one case, a massive hit of pepper spray to the eyes when the dragon in question surprised a lone female hiker. The spray didn't kill him, but the cliff's edge he plunged over did.)

The clutchleader swaggered to an empty table, leaving the club hostess stumbling after. He roared an order for meat—his exact word—and grabbed a nigh-denuded steak bone from the plate of a neighboring diner, crunching it to slivers. If his rudeness didn't distract the audience from Tori's brilliant interpretation of "People," shattering a hefty rib in a single bite sure as hell did the job.

"What?" Gehdreh snarled at the array of shocked faces. "He was done with it and I don't like waiting when I'm hungry."

On stage, Tori took her bow and ran to spread the word that their unwelcome guest had arrived. "You sure you want to do this, Jiryah?" she asked.

"I was never more sure of anything in my life," said the dragon.

"Are we sure *we* want to do this?" Akmi asked nervously. "This is like fighting a fire with buckets of kerosene. When he sees Jiryah, he'll go ballistic!"

The other queens were unfazed, or at least good at putting up a front that didn't call for boobie bibs.

"This is the *plan*, Akmi," Idaho said. "We talked this through, remember? He sees Jiryah, he blows up, Mark calls the cops, and they take out the trash for us."

"And how many of us will the trash take out first?" Akmi murmured, but it was too late. This was the best—the *only*—plan they'd been able to construct, short of running away. She faced the inevitable with a smile she didn't mean. "Fine. Let's do this."

"Okay, baby." Pastelle patted Jiryah's neck. "Don't forget your cue, and do not step on my lines or I will end you." With a final fit-check of her floor-length blonde wig, she strutted out to claim the spotlight and launched into her song.

A s*ong*, not a lip-sync. A song done live, without so much as a note of accompanying music. Small wonder: Peter and Gordon's hoary hit, "Lady Godiva," wasn't exactly the stuff of which drag show dreams were made. Pastelle belted it out *a cappella* and danced in a cinched and padded iridescent bodysuit while the audience shouted enthusiastic approval and Mark-the-Owner/Manager lost any illusion of control in his own club.

Then a second player stepped onstage.

What is Lady Godiva without her horse?

And what is a fabulous drag Godiva without an equally fabulous steed?

Drag queens thrive on competition and every competition is a challenge. Akmi and her sisters had stomped this challenge into the ground in a hail of stiletto heels. Jiryah's initial shape-shift attempt left the young dragon merely on the *brink* of unicornhood. The queens shoved him over the edge with every transformative trick in their arsenal. He sparkled, from gilded hooves to silvery mane and tail extensions. Pastelle donated four whole palettes of twinkly eye shadows. Tori de Force parted with her entire stash of Poetry in Porcelain foundation and concealer to give Jiryah's coat an extra boost of pale radiance. Idaho contributed three jars of body glitter. Ever the completist, Akmi sacrificed one of her favorite pageant tiaras, bending the headband so that it was now firmly anchored on the unicorn's brow.

Gehdreh was dumbstruck. He knew he was looking at Jiryah—the young dragon's scent could not be disguised—but he refused to believe what he was seeing. As the audience thundered their appreciation, the elder dragon's jaw dropped and a pile of steak-bone splinters landed in his lap.

Then his eyes narrowed. His mouth snapped shut. Rage flared in his eyes and countless cracks zig-zagged over the surface of his human guise. He sprang from his seat, toppling the table, and sucked in the breath that was destined to become a flaming roar monstrous enough to immolate not merely his wayward hatchling but the entire club and everyone within.

He never got the chance. A cascade of opalescent radiance engulfed him, holding him like a peach chunk in a 1950s Jell-O mold. Indeed, the entire population of Club Soirée was similarly suspended in gelatinous time.

There *were* a few exceptions.

"What happened?" Idaho asked in a hoarse whisper from where she, Akmi, and Tori were huddled behind the wing curtain. "Pastelle? Jiryah?"

"Um, I think you ought to see for yourself, hon," Pastelle replied.

What they saw left them breathless: three unicorns were gracefully picking their way forward between the frozen club tables. The resplendent creatures mounted the stage and slowly circled Jiryah, who bowed his horned head before them.

"If I have offended you, O beauteous ones—" he began, voice quavering.

"Shh," said the tallest of the three. The unicorns extended their muzzles and daintily sniffed the transformed dragon. "Wow," said the first. "So it's true."

The second unicorn uttered a melodious whinny. "Told you so. You know I've got the gift for scenting major enchantments seventy-seven realms away."

"Yes, I'd say this definitely counts as major." The third unicorn gave Jiryah a piercing look. "Would you care to tell us what this is all about, dragonling?"

Jiryah poured out the whole story. He did his best to keep talking in a rational manner even though he was emotionally overwhelmed by the proximity of his idols. When he finished, the unicorns looked at one another.

"Is that why we find you like this?" said one.

"This was certainly not what we were expecting," said the second with a shake of their pearly mane.

"We sensed such a surge of magic that we naturally assumed a new unicorn had been born. We are attuned to receive such messages from the

Great Out There," said the third. "It is our duty to welcome the newcomer to the world. Gosh, are *our* faces an extremely becoming shade of red!"

"I've got some base that'll cover that right up!" Pastelle volunteered.

"And yet…" The first unicorn grew pensive. "And yet we cannot deny the presence of great enchantment at work here, even if it could stand a bit of post-production tweakage."

The three nodded as one.

"With your permission?" The tallest spoke gently to Jiryah. Nothing was explained; everything was understood.

"Oh. Oh, yes. Please." The young dragon's eyes shone with fragile hope.

Three horns touched tips over Jiryah's head, and the four queens became witnesses to wonder.

* * *

Later that same miracle, the three original unicorns did a thorough job of forensic site clean-up. After they left and took their stasis spell with them, the ordinary patrons of Club Soirée never knew what they'd missed, though some of them did puzzle over the round of complimentary cocktails before them, accompanied by *Thank you for your mortal time* notes that smelled of spring meadows.

Gehdreh found himself backstage in the dressing room, his still-human wrists bound with a whisper of cobweb. *Unbreakable* cobweb. He was seated on the ancient sofa the queens used at break time. A unicorn stood before him. There was nothing familiar about its appearance or scent, but when it spoke, Gehdreh gasped in recognition.

"Yes, it is me, my clutchleader," Jiryah said with confidence. "Me as I have always been, and now truly am. I am going to release you from your bonds, but first you will swear by our sacred ancestors, the Aforegone, that you will never take revenge on those who helped me realize my dream." The unicorn indicated the waiting queens, who were regarding Gehdreh's helpless indignation with different degrees of glee. "While you're at it, I also want you to swear you'll stop eating humans. The cholesterol in those things will kill you one day."

Gehdreh struggled with his bonds; it was useless. He ground his teeth. "All right. I so swear."

Jiryah smiled and touched their horn to the spiderweb, which melted away. The elder dragon rubbed his wrists, cursing. He only stopped in order to glower at Jiryah. "I am free to go?"

"As you wish."

"I won't be back!"

"That would sadden me. You are still my clutchleader, the one who raised me. I have many good memories of our time together."

"You are a horrible disappointment!"

"Not to myself. My clutchleader, you raised me with the knowledge that dragons value, honor, and cherish the truth. Is that not so?"

Gedreh's truculent, "Yes," was barely audible.

"Well, this—" Jiryah turned slowly, showing off the exquisite beauty of their new form. "—is *my* truth. As it has always been."

Jiryah's cool serenity damped down the great dragon's wrath. Gehdreh slumped against the sofa cushions. "I understand none of this," he said in mournful tones. "You have taken a path beyond my power to comprehend. *Why?*"

The newly made unicorn frowned. All that they had dreamed of, wanted, done to reach their dream, their *truth*, seemed so obvious, so natural, nothing needed explanation. But finding the right words to communicate this? That was a struggle.

"Here, baby, let Mama try." Akmi knelt on the cushion beside Gehdreh and patted his hand. "It's like this: sometimes you've just got to *become* who you are."

Pastelle leaned in from the other side: "And who you are is someone you've got *every right* to be."

"Your words...it will take me time to fathom them," Gehdreh said slowly.

"It'll be easier if you actually *want* to understand. Do you?" Idaho asked.

Gehdreh's human face assumed a determined expression. "I do. Yes. Jiryah is my hatchling. Nothing changes that."

"Well, how about you think it over during the second show? If you can keep up your human drag that long, I mean."

"As our guest," Akmi added. "We'll even comp your drinks. Er...dragons do drink alcohol, right?"

"Without it turning into a fire hazard?" Tori asked.

"No promises," Gehdreh replied.

And that was how one dragon's heartfelt choice became their truth, and likewise how—after downing a tidal wave of tequila—Gehdreh revealed a truth of his own:

Dragons tip *much* better than bridesmaids.

Avarice and Vengeance

Madeline Dau

I smell him long before the door opens—sharp Italian crocodile leather and cigarette smoke masked with pricey Parisian bergamot cologne. For a brief moment, I consider ducking into the kitchen, but the odds of fancypants wannabe antiquities collector Charles Soleil Alarie showing up at Shane's Beer and Wing Emporium for a lukewarm light beer and microwaved frozen buffalo tenders is fairly slim.

Though I'm expecting it, the door's electronic chime triggers an unpleasant jolt along my nerves. The legion of iron-dipped bracelets on either wrist clink reassuringly as I grab a pint glass and scrub at a stubborn lipstick stain with a damp cloth.

Charles sweeps into the sports bar like an Oscar-winning actor emerging from a limousine and parading on a red carpet. He'll have to cope with peeling wood laminate and green felt doormats repurposed from old billiard tables. He sweeps a hand through his blond hair as he settles his designer shades on top of his head.

I spare a glance at the rain lashing the windows, haloed by the neon sign advertising $5 BEER BUCKETS.

"What a tool," I grumble to the glass.

Charles' smokey quartz eyes find mine and he smiles as he approaches the bar. The tang of copper fills my mouth as my teeth prick my tongue. The glass creaks in my hand.

"You're a tough one to track down, Layni." Charles leans against the bar, not a single raindrop clinging to him. A muscle in his jaw twitches and he pulls away from the counter, frowning at the sticky residue on his palm.

I never claimed to be the best bartender. Not even a good one.

"That should've been your first clue," I drawl, tossing my hair over my shoulder. "You're the last person I want to see, Chaz."

He wrinkles his nose. He despises that nickname almost as much as he hates flying business class. "You don't mean that, Layni."

"I do, actually. The last time I saw you, I spent a weekend trapped in a dog kennel as a Yorkie. The only reason you're here is to recruit me for a job, and I can already tell you I want no part of it."

"That kennel thing was the goblin's fault."

One of the regulars perched a few barstools away glances at us, a confused frown etched between his brows. I can imagine his thoughts: why would two normal-looking adults be blaming something on a goblin? What a couple of weirdos.

Charles leans closer, careful to avoid the bar's dingy faux wood surface. "This haul is worth your while, I promise you."

The towel squeaks obnoxiously against the glass as I stare down at him, lip curled. Even without the boots, I'm a few inches taller. The last time someone suggested I wear flats, I *accidentally* jabbed his finger with a wickedly sharp pair of jeweler's forceps. Luckily for Charles, he possesses the rare gift of learning from other people's mistakes, even if he has to pay cash for everything else.

"Perhaps this will change your mind?" He reaches into his pocket with a changeling's feral leer.

"I seriously doubt anything in your pants can change my mind."

Charles ignores me as he withdraws a softball-sized bundle swaddled in cream silk. With a gentle swish of fabric, he reveals the medallion. Even with a cursory glance, I gauge its worth on par with the entire city block. Unable to help myself, I lean closer.

An icy diamond flashes beneath the ugly fluorescent bar lighting, cut so that it radiates with the fire of the sun. A golden faerie-hammered elethril setting spirals around the central jewel in delicate whorls set with blood droplet rubies.

Iara the Relentless' Heart. One of a kind. Exquisite. Lost to the ages.

Saliva floods my mouth. Every muscle in my body coils into compressed springs. I don't smell Charles' entourage. He's just one man, a frail-boned changeling with the barest whisper of Old Magic that he desperately bleeds into eternal youth. Nothing is stopping me from swiping a razor-tipped claw across his throat. If I desire, I could just *take it.*

It's mine it's mine IT'S MINE

"Careful. Your greed is showing."

The nictitating membrane sweeps across my eyes and my vision clears.

"Where did you find this?" I grind out between gritted teeth.

"So, it *is* genuine." Charles' triumphant grin makes me want to rip into his milk-pale neck with my teeth. "Fantastic. I'll expect you—"

"Sorry I wasn't clear before—get lost, Chaz."

"You know..." Charles trails off delicately, twisting the elegant ring—opal set in platinum—around his finger. "Rumor has it that a certain Yvrir the Starving is tearing through the veils between worlds searching for a Layndri Blazeheart for looting the Couronne in Paris. Any relation, *Layni*?"

The pint glass cracks in my hand. Iron hisses, sublimating into fumes as magic burns through the fae bane to heal the cut slashed across my palm. The skin around my wrists is calloused from years of tamping down my powers with iron-dipped jewelry.

Charles smirks at the broken glass. He scratches his carefully cultivated stubble, as if we're holding a casual conversation between friends. "Couronne was a minor hoard, sure, but to a dragon? I've been told even a single stolen copper coin is met with a gruesome death. I'm sure Yvrir would pay handsomely for an opportunity to recoup his loss. Ha, but why am I lecturing *you* about this?"

"Are you *threatening* me? Listen here, you narcissistic son of a—"

"Easy now." Charles grins, his polished veneers flashing like bleached bone. "Don't want to startle the grubby little humanfolk. Wouldn't want to shatter the sultry barmaid illusion—very convincing transmogrification, by the way—and reveal our existence."

"If you honestly think a couple of measly humans will stop me from ripping your heart out through your mouth, you're mistaken."

"I suppose that's true," Charles says mildly, peeling my fingers from his lapel with a surgeon's precision. I don't remember grabbing him. "But I'm expected to meet the crew I've assembled. If I don't return, they have explicit instructions to broadcast your location to all of the Fair Folk."

The glass rattles as I set it on the counter, a single shard falling to the ground with a delicate plink. Gold glints through patches of dull iron on my bracelets. I'll have to dip them again or risk my nature boiling free.

"Look, everyone profits from this job," Charles says. "*I* stand to make a fortune. Our target will be supremely weakened, which benefits everyone on this side of the Oblivion Veil. And you get to disappear once and for all, if that's what you desire. My brilliant fence also deals in forging new identities."

I run a finger along the thin pink sliver dividing my palm, considering.

"Well?" Charles draws out the word like a song. "Can I count on your expertise, Layni?"

"Get the hell out of my bar."

"It's a pleasure doing business with you, ma chérie. I'll introduce you to the rest of the crew after your shift ends. See you at the Cerulean Horizon Hotel in a few hours."

* * *

My blood seethes with every floor the elevator climbs. The receptionist barely glanced at me before calling security, but as the towering slab of human packed into a dull navy uniform lumbered toward me, the phone rang. The spacey twit with the pencil skirt gushed apologies like a bloody nose and steered me to the private elevator leading up to the penthouse. I comb my fingers through my hair, using the glass wall as a mirror. The tight T-shirt emblazoned with Shane's logo across the front has certainly seen better days.

Maybe I should get a new job. Maybe Charles' fence could help with that.

Through the glass, the lobby shrinks to a toy set, decorated with crystal icicles and glittering ornaments. The elevator pings, and my fists clench as I steel myself for the doors to slide apart.

My bootheels click against the marble entry, a rich concoction of ivory swirled with navy veins and gold leaf. That, at least, is authentic. The thousands of crystals dripping from the chandeliers are convincing counterfeits, beautifully cut glass but nothing more. I bite my tongue to hide my smile; either Charles doesn't know he is surrounded by glass or he's posturing. Both ideas fill me with a sadistic joy.

The entry leads into a large receiving room featuring a massive window hidden behind a heavy drape. Three other people occupy the crushed velvet upholstery of various chairs. A mortal Seer sits alone on a couch fit for three. Her bony arms wrap around her shins, her chin resting on her knees. Eyes glazed with milky film dance over my general direction. She frowns and tilts her head, brushing her fingers over her collapsible white walking stick as if reassuring herself it's still there.

Poor kid. She's too young to have gotten involved in one of Charles' idiotic schemes. Maybe she'll have access to better jobs if this goes well.

Molten bile creeps up my throat. I recognize the pair tangled on the loveseat.

Azaris the Razorwing with the woman he left me for, Sierra Neverisle.

Charles scuttles from his post at the wet bar, rattling the square ice cube in his Baccarat crystal tumbler. He sweeps my hand to his lips, saving me from small talk with two of my least favorite Fair Folk while condemning me to an unending moment of profound disgust as his saliva dries on my skin.

"Layni, so glad you could make it." Charles beams, his eyes glittering maliciously. "How was the rest of your shift?"

Azaris snickers into a fist. He's never held an honest job in his long, lonely existence. *Shifts* are for mortals and pathetic Fair Folk, scrambling to accumulate enough money to survive.

"Now, for introductions. Here on the loveseat are the sorcerer Azaris and—"

"I've met your fence before," I reply, with a jerk of my chin. "She's not quite as talented as you advertised. And I know you're aware I used to sleep with Azaris, so spare me the charade. Now you…" I turn toward the Seer, ignoring Sierra's pretty fae face twisting into a sneer. "You, I haven't seen before. Chaz, has your reputation suffered so much with your shady dealings that you need to hire children?"

"I'm nineteen," the Seer replies serenely, her voice aged beyond her years.

"Rest assured, Adelaide is the best of the best," Charles says. He claps his hands, sloshing hundreds of dollars of whisky onto the carpet. "Well, now that we're all here, let's begin! I've enticed you all here with promises of wealth and whatever else your hearts desire. I'm sure you're on the edge of your seats waiting to see our target."

"I'm not sitting," I mutter.

Adelaide smiles and whispers. "And I can't see anything."

Sierra's ear twitches, her myriad of crystal droplet earrings catching and reflecting the light. She definitely heard us, even if Charles didn't. Oblivious, Charles sweeps the drapes aside with a flourish, revealing doors to a balcony instead of a window.

Outside, silhouetted by the setting sun, the Obelisk Resort and Casino towers over everything, even the Cerulean Horizon. Its black mirrored windows reflect the surrounding city lights like a sky of stars. Music from the casino fills the room as Charles throws the balcony doors open. He raises his glass to the building in the distance, that lethal needle piercing the heavens, haunting my dreams. Everyone hiding from mortals behind the veils knows who owns the resort.

Yvrir the Starving.

Azaris' smug façade cracks. His widened eyes shift to me and quickly back to the view. Even if we despise each other now, we didn't once. He knows my history with Yvrir. Azaris was the one that crushed me in his arms like he could piece me back together himself with tears and bargains with indifferent gods. He was the one who took care of me in the months it took my legs to regenerate.

"You're not serious." I cross my arms over my chest like armor. "What are you playing at, Charles?"

"It's exactly what it looks like, Layni," he says, gesturing for me to join him on the balcony. Headlights and taillights decorate the ground with moving baubles of light. Intermingling laughter of humans and Fair Folk alike drift from the casino's open doors. "We're going to clear out Yvrir's grandest vault, the Pearl."

"The Obelisk is a fortress," I reply dryly. "What you're suggesting is impossible."

Charles smirks. "Perhaps, *if* we were walking in unprepared. I cashed in some favors and stumbled across the most delightful information. We'll know precisely what we're walking into."

"You're saying you have floorplans?" Azaris asks, frowning.

"That and more. Adelaide?"

The Seer's white cane sweeps side-to-side against the ground until she reaches the balcony railing. She grips the marble with her small hand. "My mother wove the glamours protecting the vault. I know of every floor and hallway. The Pearl is a multi-room compound cloistered in the Obelisk penthouse. The vaults branch off a central round room, and alchemight bars every door, each lock unique and complicated." She leans against the railing, squinting at intricate spellwork that the rest of us can't perceive. "The penthouse is only accessible by an elevator, like the one in this building. The glamours woven around the top floor are designed to make it blend seamlessly into the glass windows below, but they're actually walls made of vanguardrium, so we can't break in from the outside."

"And Yvrir the Starving just lets someone who knows his vaults walk around freely?" I shake my head. "I don't buy it."

"Yvrir threatened my father to ensure my mother's compliance, then he ate them to ensure her silence. He doesn't know about me—that I'm a Seer, that my mother could show me her work through her eyes."

"Our secret weapon," Charles says, smoothing Adelaide's collar where it had flipped. A stranger might misconstrue the action as affection, but the dragon in me recognizes the gesture as possessive. Adelaide is one of Charles' new belongings, a tool like a pair of wire cutters. If she doesn't know it already, she will soon.

"The glamour concealing the building is intricate," Adelaide notes, distractedly tapping her cane on the balcony. "It will take weeks to unravel."

"You have one." Charles turns to the rest of us. "I have it on good authority that Yvrir is building another vault. We need to empty this one before he divides the hoard. Adelaide will unravel the glamours and guide us around vault traps with her Sight once we break into the penthouse. Naturally, I recruited a sorcerer well-versed in alchemight to disable security wherever needed. Ma chérie Sierra will obtain uniforms and badges for us to seamlessly blend in with the staff."

"That's all?" I ask. "The crowds in the casino move about as well as solid brick, and the security will be outrageous."

"Well, that's not very constructive. I don't see what Layni offers the crew besides negativity." Sierra rises from the loveseat with the grace of a paper lantern, stretching her lithe legs. The petulance in her voice leads me to think that I've been the root of a recent argument with Azaris. "What exactly do we need a washed-up appraiser for, anyway?"

Definitely some kind of argument. A ruthless smile curves my lips.

"Yvrir is notorious for commissioning forgeries and hiding the valuables amongst the fakes in his vaults," I reply as Charles takes a delicate sip of his Old Fashioned. "Any halfway decent fence would know that."

"I can distinguish between reproductions and originals just fine." Sierra crosses her arms, a practiced motion to draw attention to her cleavage.

"Of that I have no doubt, ma chérie." Charles smiles indulgently. "But you are to study my private copy of Yvrir's suspected artifacts and compile a list of the pieces you will have the most profit fencing. *Layni* will find the original pieces and anything else that her exceptional taste deems valuable."

"Yvrir would be a fool to rely only on glamours and traps," Adelaide says. "What about the security guards inside?"

Charles drags his eyes to mine, that infernal smile dripping with malice. "If memory serves, as long as she's not trapped in the transmogrification of a lapdog, Layni also serves as an excellent shield to hide behind."

* * *

Seven days later, Sierra and I follow Azaris, disguised as an Obelisk usher pushing a wealthy patron in a wheelchair through the throngs of people inside the casino. Adelaide resembles a doll, hair curled and woven into an elegant updo fastened with pearls. The only sign of her nerves is how she can't stop running her hands over the tops of her thighs, palms rustling against the satin flounces, which I can hear despite Charles nattering at Azaris over her head. The financier himself is posing as Adelaide's uncle, and he dug his ostentatious disguise out of his own closet.

Meanwhile, a starchy high-collared shirt chafes my neck and a pair of high-waisted slacks bite into my gut. Sierra must have gotten a size too small on purpose. Obelisk employees aren't permitted jewelry, so iron chainmail cinches around my shoulders and chest. It's all I can do to resist clawing my skin off.

"Need to review the catalogue again?" Sierra asks, her voice like venom dripping into my ears. "Wouldn't want you to mess up your incredibly easy job that I could do without any help."

I shoot her a sidelong glance. "Are you serious? I'm a dragon. How many times do you think I need to look at a list of treasure?"

"If you're so great, why did Azaris leave you? Hm?" Sierra's glamour shivers, images flickering between rounded human ears and delicately pointed fae ears. "You're not nearly as perfect as you think you are—that's not even your real face."

A lazy smile lifts the corners of my mouth. "He likes his women young and dumb, I guess, of which I am neither."

"Dumb enough to get dragged into one of Charles' schemes. If I understand correctly, if Yvrir finds you here, you're dead."

"You do, and don't get any bright ideas."

"And what's stopping me from walking right up to the pit boss over there and telling him who you are?"

My teeth grind together as I imagine what her faery wings would look like, gossamer threads of monarch orange and black trailing from my talons like streamers.

"Do that, and I'll tell Charles you swapped his chandelier crystals for glass."

Sierra's face blanches. "How—how did you know?"

How naïve. Confirming a vague suspicion without even trying to hide her involvement.

"It wasn't hard to guess. A Neverisle owns a rare quartz mine and her wife is a renowned glass sculptor. You have the connections to unload the crystal and a means to convincingly replace it."

The faery recovers her composure with a sneer.

"Look, we don't have to like each other to complete this job. Charles promised me a new identity, which is apparently one of your specialties. Forge me a convincing one, and I can forget all about crystals and chandeliers."

"Very well."

As if summoned, Charles drops back behind Azaris and Adelaide, adjusting his cufflinks. "Ready? We're breaking into the elevator now."

"Of course. Sierra?"

She nods, a curt jerk of her chin.

"Oh, I do so love that you two are getting along, despite, well, everything." Charles joins Azaris and Adelaide beside the elevator. He smiles and pushes the call button as the bones in Sierra's fists groan with how hard she's clenching. I wonder if she's imagining her hands around his throat. Probably mine, too.

The elevator doors slide open and the porter inside pulls the gleaming golden grate aside. He starts when he sees Charles and smiles, straddling the line between obsequious and courteous. "My apologies, sir, miss, this is a private elevator. It would be my pleasure to escort you to the public elevators on the other side of the casino."

Charles slams an open palm against the man's mouth, shoving him against the back wall. Azaris pushes Adelaide inside, and Sierra yanks the grate shut. I jam the door close button with my thumb as the musty stench of death magic clogs the elevator. The porter tries to pry Charles' hand from his face, but he's not strong enough. The opal on Charles' finger glows a wicked violet as wrinkles crease the man's face. Gray ripples through his hair, then white. The porter crumbles to the elevator floor in a tangle of desiccated skin and bone and excess folds of stiff clothing.

"Thank you," Charles says, nudging the drained corpse with his foot. A golden nameplate flashes up at us. "Walter. Thank you for the extra thirty years."

Azaris chuckles darkly, throwing an arm around Sierra's shoulders and pressing a kiss fiercely against her temple. Her eyes catch mine in the mirrored door, and her lips quirk into a cruel, feline smirk.

The frantic patter of a racing heartbeat draws my attention to Adelaide. Her eyes are scrunched shut, her fingers locked into claws on her armrests. I brush my fingers reassuringly against her shoulder and she relaxes the tiniest bit.

Charles waves Sierra's forged keycard in front of the sensor and the elevator climbs. I can't believe it works—this is where I would have gotten stuck trying to loot the Pearl alone. Trapped in a vanguardrium box with no way in or back out. I had my doubts, watching Sierra smacking bubblegum as she meticulously adjusted wafer thin magnets of spellbound lodestone, but I'm old enough that I'm occasionally proven wrong.

Sierra giggles about her ears popping, the others chorusing in agreement, but even entombed in this small, soft, fleshy form, my body is designed to plummet from the clouds to the ground and soar back up into the sky.

As soon as we step into the penthouse, I shuck my horrid shirt and waistcoat and rip the chainmail off. It clatters against the floor like metallic rain. Painful welts cover my skin, despite the undershirt. The thin material hardly prevented chafing, let alone the fae bane burns.

But no time to worry about that.

Adelaide raises her hands and rips through the glamours with a blinding pulse of light, revealing the trap tiles exactly where she said they would be. "Azaris, the wires are hidden right there."

Azaris severs communications with the rest of the Obelisk, his eyes glowing an electric blue as he slams his palms against the wall, melting the panel beneath. Twenty-two guards, one for each door, pour into the elevator hallway in a flooding menagerie of gryphics, faeries, and merfolk. A cyclops waits in the central room hefting a double-sided axe, too bulky to fit into the hallway.

Without the iron chainmail, fire coils around my arms, seeping from my mouth and eyes. My hair undulates with flames like I'm submerged. I sprint through the hallway, wreathed with white-hot fire that drips and spatters against the marble tiles. My muscles contract with joy, breaking through their human-shaped prison.

The vicious traps set into the corridor destroy any Fair Folk that my fire doesn't melt. As I reach the end of the hallway, I launch into the air and curl into a ball. The cyclops' stomach offers as much resistance as a pool of pudding to a cannonball. I land on my feet in the central round room, shuddering as I try to rein the flames into submission.

The floor vibrates as the halves of the cyclops hit the tiles. Soot covers the marble and walls like fine silt. The stench of charred hair and scorched meat lingers in the air.

Charles scoffs. "Layni, when you incinerate people, I can't siphon their life forces."

"Your stolen life forces aren't my priority," I manage through clenched jaws. Ebony scales emerge through a fissure along my bicep like a molting scorpion. I try pressing it down, but it's like trying to stop a volcanic eruption with my tiny human hands. The last thing we need is for Yvrir to scent my magic and interrupt our little heist.

"Here." Adelaide climbs from the wheelchair, revealing the treasure trove of iron she'd been hiding beneath her skirt. She hedges around the trapped tiles, pushing the chair. I hurriedly grab a fistful of iron bracelets and slip them onto my forearms.

The blaze recedes and I recast my transmogrification. I heave a sigh, tinged with acrid smoke. The other three join us in the central room where twenty-two rounded vanguardrium doors wear alchemight locks like rounded shields. Gears, studs, and coils cover their surfaces, with no indication of which features are functional or decorative.

Or deadly.

Charles claps his hands, rubbing them together. "Azaris, if you would be so kind?"

The sorcerer crouches in front of the first door. He maneuvers his fingers like a puppet master, trailing sparks. Gears turn, ticking like little clocks. Pistons shift and levers snap into position like resetting broken bones.

Finally, the door creaks open an inch with a guttural hiss. Azaris sits back on his heels, wiping the thin sheen of sweat from his forehead.

"Nicely done," Charles says as he shoves the vault open.

Azaris nods gravely. "I'll move on to the next door. They won't all be this easy."

The merriment dies in Charles' expression as he glances at the rest of us over his shoulder. "Get to work."

Sierra darts into the vault behind him, giddy as a hummingbird. I follow at a more measured pace, arms crossed tightly over my chest.

The air inside the vault is cold and dry. Loose jewels arranged by color and size glitter within the glass cases stacked from floor to ceiling. My nails prick my sides as I cringe away from a wall of crowns, fighting the urge to sweep the lot into my satchel. Obsidian mannequins crowding the center of the room display larger pieces—a dress forged entirely of sapphires, an emerald necklace that cinches around the throat and cascades to the waist.

Biting my tongue, I sidle over to the rings decorating the fingers on a shelf of model hands. Up close, the obsidian is slightly translucent, revealing the barest hint of ivory bones. Hm. Maybe not mannequins after all.

With a quick glance, I spy counterfeits scattered throughout the shelf. Luckily, the rings on the list—the Oracle's Eye, the Titan's Wedding Band, and Charis' Diamond Ring—are all authentic. I drop them into the bag and join Sierra by the crowns where she's squinting at a jeweled concoction set in rose gold though a jeweler's loupe. The tip of her tongue juts between her teeth.

"It's authentic," I say.

"Look, I don't need—"

"Let's not get into this now," I interrupt. "Just get what we came for and get out before Yvrir eats us."

"I've got another vault open," Azaris calls from the common room.

"I'm coming." I glance over my shoulder. "That Menestroth's Helm is a forgery, and it looks like the Crown of Winterreach is authentic except for the central diamond—it looks different from the others. Check the drawers of loose diamonds for a match."

Sierra growls, making an obscene gesture with her fingers. With an unbothered shrug, I leave the vault. Adelaide stands in the center of the room, twisting her hands as she faces the door opposite the elevator hall. Cool air eddies from the vault next to Sierra's. Azaris kneels in front of the lock beside it, blood dribbling from a thin cut across his cheek.

"Careless with the lock," he says when he feels me looming over him.

"There are twenty locks to go," I observe.

"Worried about me?"

"Worried that if you kill yourself on a trap, we won't find everything on Charles' list. Then he won't honor our deal."

Azaris grins. "I've missed your brutal honesty."

I consider telling him that I haven't missed him at all. "Don't hurt yourself."

The vault door opens with the soft sweep of a brush on canvas. The smell of conditioned leather feels like a punch to the nose. Inside, light filters from domed fixtures set into recesses in the ceiling. An armory of blades fills the room. Swords arranged by size and origin, hunting knives with smooth and serrated edges glistening with poison. Daggers whose blades glimmer with the oily sheen of mother of pearl. Weapons with pommels of giant, flawless gemstones, their scabbards shimmering with gold inlay.

Charles has a long-dead hero's bow on his list, but no blades, which is surprising considering the rarity of some of the specimens. I'll return to comb the vault for valuables if there's time. I turn and nearly collide with Adelaide.

"Sorry," she mumbles. "I can see swirls of your aura trying to escape the transmogrification, but I didn't realize I was so close."

"Don't worry about it."

By now, Azaris has managed to open the fourth vault door and moved to the fifth. His fitted black jacket is tied limply around his waist, and his waistcoat flaps open. Sweat rings drench the white shirt beneath his arms, and his sleeves are rolled to his elbows.

Charles storms from the first vault, Sierra nearly treading on his heels. "What is taking so long? You're supposed to be a master sorcerer. We didn't account for you taking this much time at each vault."

"You gave me a week to prepare," Azaris snarls, jabbing a finger at his bleeding cheek. "There is a reason only a handful of sorcerers know alchemight—because even simple spellwork mistakes are fatal and most sorcerers die before achieving any sort of mastery."

"There are more glamours inside that vault." Adelaide's voice is a dry whisper, like reeds rustling together. She points to the vault door she had been facing earlier, the one across from the elevator.

"So?" Sierra snaps.

"Yvrir might be hiding something more valuable inside," I say. "It's what I would do."

Charles rubs the carefully cultivated stubble on his chin. "You may have a point there. All right, Azaris. Take a break from that one and open this door."

Azaris' expression is a mask of murder as he climbs to his feet and stalks to the vault. He brushes past me, streaming a litany of curses under his breath. His fingertips trail light, flickering like sparklers. Charles' cologne and Sierra's fruity lipstain pummel my nose as we edge closer to the door. I can smell each staticky hiss of the lock burning Azaris' fingers, each foul release of mercury and sulfur vapors. After a few minutes, the lock splits and falls to the floor.

"That seemed too easy." Sierra glances anxiously around the group. "Didn't it?"

"I…I think there's another alchemight lock inside," Adelaide says. Her fingers brush lightly against the back of my shirt. She has the manners not to say anything about the sweat and grime.

"If there is glamour *and* another alchemight lock inside, maybe he didn't see the need to emphasize the vault door." I shrug. "Yvrir's odd like that. One way to find out."

Azaris opens the door and we surge forward. Charles because he's thrilled at the prospect of finding the rest of his list within, Azaris and Sierra because Charles practically shoves them inside in his haste, and Adelaide because she's clinging to the back of my shirt.

"This …this isn't a vault…" Charles trails off, spinning in a slow circle.

Scarcely before the words escape his lips, the door slams shut behind us with the finality of an executioner's axe. I only have a second to take in the shelves of rare books bound in all species of skin from dragon to cyclops to human before a hulking shape rises above a marble writing desk.

"Yvrir…" I breathe.

Yvrir the Starving uncoils from behind his desk, his tail lashing an expensive set of balancing scales. He looms at three times my height, his scales the brilliant red of arterial blood. Sierra shrieks and shoves me aside in a desperate sprint back to the door. If Adelaide had not been gripping my shirt, Sierra would have knocked her aside.

"Let me out!" Sierra pounds on the door with her fists.

"Don't!" Adelaide cries, but it's too late. Sierra triggers some trap woven into a glamour on the door. Bony fingers clench against my back and yank, just enough for me to dive backward and avoid the barrage of spikes raining down from the ceiling.

Sierra isn't so fortunate.

She collapses, anchored to the floor with gleaming vanguardrium pillars, without so much as a whimper.

"How did you get in here, little mice?" Yvrir's voice is the deep, terrible rumble of an avalanche. His bloodshot eyes land on me, pupils narrowing to slits. Massive leathery wings whip the air into a frenzy. "Layndri Blazeheart. I am going to enjoy tearing you apart until you tell me what you've done with my irreplaceable Iara."

Adrenaline sears through my veins. Blood thunders in my ears with each heartbeat, drowning out Azaris' vengeful roar and Charles' goatlike bleating.

"There's a chink in his transmogrification—two inches beneath the right eye," Adelaide whispers behind me, stripping the bracelets from my right wrist with a sharp tug. Power rages through every muscle fiber, hungry as a devouring wildfire. She presses a bar wrapped in satin into my palm. Not a bar. A hilt, one that burns my palm through the fabric like pure capsaicin oil. It can only be one thing.

Dragon's Bane, the legendary hunting knife used to assassinate the dragon tyrant Uzil the Eternal centuries ago.

"Heard." Strength flares through my arm, unfettered by the iron, and I hurl the dagger at Yvrir's cheekbone.

The blade hits home. The old dragon screeches. Azaris sags to the floor on his knees, hands pressed against his ears. Blood trickles between his fingers. Yvrir's transmogrification shatters, splintering into thousands of lethal fragments that pelt everything in the room. I throw my hands up protectively. The shards of Yvrir's magic vaporize harmlessly against the blazing shield protecting Adelaide and me.

Charles has never shielded against such a powerful spell breaking. He falls back onto his backside, clapping a hand over a deep gash on his upper arm. The opal on his ring glows as he siphons his extra years to heal himself. It will take several minutes at least. I can't rely on him or Azaris. If I want to make it out of this tower unscathed, I must confront Yvrir myself.

As the smoke clears from the ruined transmogrification, I dart toward Yvrir. Fire seeps from my fingertips, bubbling from beneath my talons as they break through my own glamour. The old dragon pulls himself to standing, his true form revealed. He's hardly twice my height, stooped with age and old injuries. Muddy red scales stretch over withered limbs.

Yvrir controls his subordinates through fear, not strength, and no one has challenged him for eons. He snaps his alligator jaws at me, teeth shredding my sleeve as I slide to the marble floor, seizing Dragon's Bane. Its hilt sears my hand and I bite back a scream. With a wild slash, I manage to bury the blade into Yvrir's bloated stomach.

If the hilt hurt my palm, it is a guttering candle flame compared to the searing sun that Yvrir is experiencing. He bellows, curling around the wound left by the mythical blade. The roar dies to a low rumble that rattles the study. Flesh disintegrates, scales contracting around bones. A bloody ruby glimmers, trapped within a frail ribcage.

Dragons can't play dead like other fae.

And Adelaide isn't saying that Yvrir is casting a glamour to trick us. Relief feels like falling into a sweet, cool pond after trudging through the desert for a thousand years. My knees buckle and I nearly spill to the ground. I did it. I finally did it.

"Beautifully done, Layni," Charles says, glancing up from his wound with a grimace. "Too bad about Sierra. At least you don't need that new identity after all."

I stalk across to the fancypants wannabe antiquities collector in three steps and slam my boot into his face.

"Spare your fake condolences for yourself. You didn't think to question your luck finding a dragon you could blackmail working at a sports bar? Really?" Charles gurgles wetly as I press my heel into his throat. "You're a thousand years too young to threaten me, you pathetic little insect."

His skull cracks like an ant's exoskeleton.

Azaris groans, his eyes flicking wildly between me, Charles' face, my boot, and back to me. "Layni? What is going on?" His voice creeps higher in fear as I stalk closer.

"This was my heist all along. I owed Charles for humiliating me during our last job. All it took was a few rumors and planting Iara the Relentless' diamond heart, and the fool fell for it. Vengeance on *you* is an unexpected bonus."

"I didn't leave you because of Sierra." His back bumps against the wall. "It was Yvrir—I was afraid that since he wanted to destroy you, he'd get to you through me. I was a coward, I know that, but now he's dead and we can be together again."

"So you can flee at the barest hint of trouble?" I draw close enough that our chests nearly touch. So close that his panicked breathing stirs my hair where it isn't plastered to my forehead with sweat.

"I'm sorry, Layni—I didn't mean to hurt you, I swear!"

I tilt my head inquisitively. "Hurt me? How could you? You aren't gold or silver or even bronze. You're nothing but a pretty sack of skin containing muscle and bone and blood. A lot of blood."

"You always were a self-important shrew," he snarls, palm glowing blue with alchemight. I catch his wrist before he can strike me with the spell.

"And you were always so shortsighted."

His bones crunch in my grip, distracting him from the razors tipping my other hand. He doesn't even feel the scarlet line open along his throat, and as he slides to the floor, his final expression is locked in anger rather than fear.

I flick blood from my talons and turn to loom over the Seer, frowning. "I'm not pleased that you lied to me."

Adelaide frowns.

"Your age. You didn't tell me you were a child."

The Seer smirks. "I didn't *lie.* You just assumed without ever seeing me. Besides, any mortal will seem a child to you."

"Fair point. What will you do now, Seer?"

"Well, now that the foul beast that discarded my parents like trash is an oily scorch mark on the floor, I have no idea." Adelaide shrugs. "But I have my whole life to figure it out."

"Careful with that foul beast talk." Smoke steamed with sulfur gushes through my nostrils as I blow a smoke ring and grin.

Adelaide giggles, the only music I've heard that makes her sound her age. She bends to retrieve Dragon's Bane. I had smelled it as soon as Azaris opened the second vault. It was right inside the door, so easy to mark for Adelaide to find and hide within the folds of her doll-like disguise.

"What will you do now, Blazeheart?" she asks, turning the knife over in her hands.

I cross the room, shoes squelching in the crimson puddles growing from Charles' cooling body. Yvrir rolls over with a gentle nudge, clearing the way to his chair. Bloody leather squeaks against wood as I prop my feet up on Yvrir's desk—well, I suppose it's mine now. I turn my new favorite treasure, an opal set in a glittering platinum ring, around my thumb. Thank you, Charles. Thank you for the extra four hundred years. Not that I need it.

"I hear there's a vacancy in the Obelisk penthouse." I survey the room, littered with limbs and slick with blood. "If the cleaning crew are halfway decent, perhaps I'll move in."

The Princess Network

Niall Spain

Between killing a dragon and planning a wedding, it was a busy week for Kaile. Not that he was deeply involved with the wedding decisions—that was beneath him, of course—but with his bride-to-be missing, hopefully not dead, he was still the only one his army of wedding planners could reach out to when their imagination failed them.

What color flowers? He didn't know. Something that would make his bride glow and that would go well with white. They hadn't seemed happy with that answer, but at least they'd left him alone for a spell. Honestly, he didn't know why he was paying them a small fortune. He was doing practically all of the work, signing off on venues and picking colors that you imagine would be obvious to a so-called professional.

He'd already picked out her dress, too, to be tailored to her body once he had her in hand. Maybe he'd only give them partial payment. That would show them, make them put in more effort the next time a gentleman in need came by. A civic service, really. Besides, what could they do? He was a knight, from a good family.

They'd take what he paid and be *pleased.* That, or Father would deal with them.

Either way, it didn't bear thinking about. He'd left his butler in charge while he was gone. At least *he* knew that if things weren't handled well there'd be a whipping. Kaile almost felt sorry for him, but that would involve thinking of the man when he wasn't there and Kaile wasn't in the habit of that. Besides, there was something of importance he needed to focus on.

The dragon he was set to kill later that evening.

He came down the stairs in full armor, the wood beneath his feet creaking alarmingly. The whole inn seemed a belch away from caving in around him. He might have to have his butler whipped after all. It wasn't fitting for a man of his station—not at all—and surely there had to have been more than one inn out this direction.

"My lord," the innkeeper said. She made a shambles of a curtsey. He winced watching it. He'd rarely seen a commoner be so, well, *common.* "I hope you enjoyed your stay."

"Well, the walls remained intact, against all odds." She laughed. He didn't. "Farewell." He couldn't see his men outside with the horses, but they damn well better be ready considering he'd sent them down over an hour ago.

"Um…My Lord." The innkeeper came around the counter, almost standing in his way. He eyed her. "You've yet to, um, give me the gold for your stay. I'm terribly sorry, maybe one of your men was supposed to, I just…"

He smiled and leaned towards her a little. Women liked his smile. Liked him near them, too. He'd asked plenty and they all agreed. "Well, here's the thing, I thought I'd do you one better."

"My Lord?"

"People like me. They listen to me. I'm a man of influence, as I'm sure you know."

"Mmhmm."

"So how about this: I'll spread the word when I get back, far and wide, that this is the best establishment out this direction. Anyone who finds themselves traveling this way, well, I tell you…they'll heed my words."

"But, my Lord, we're the only inn for miles."

He winked. "That's exactly what I'll say."

He headed for the door, taking no care of his scabbard and letting it clip her in the knees as he passed. Small punishment for obstructing him. He wouldn't breathe a word about this place—gods forbid someone found out he'd stayed here—but she didn't have to know that. She could rock herself to sleep with peasant dreams of being fully booked. Not that her little inn could handle that.

His squires were ready with the horses, just a few feet down the road. He motioned for them to bring the mounts nearer. He wasn't about to trudge through the muck to get to them, even if it was near solid in the cold.

"Good luck with the dragon," the innkeeper called out from behind.

He smiled. So easy to deal with these rubes. She wasn't worth a response, so he climbed on his horse and began the long ride up the mountain.

* * *

Nikita needed a husband. At least, that's what everyone was telling her. Her father: at the breakfast nook and over dinner. Her brothers: when they came back from training with the men-at-arms, plastered in sweat and oh-so loud. Her maids: when they combed her hair in the morning and before bed. Even the other ladies—most already claimed by some man or other—agreed.

It was curious; some of the ones most vocal about her need for marriage were the ones who'd complained about their upcoming nuptials only weeks prior. She wanted to believe that they had found their perfect mate and, thus, happiness. They didn't smile when they were with their husbands though, not unless they knew someone was watching.

So Nikita lived in fear.

There were men lined up, vying for her hand. She could hear them, through the walls, making promises and boasts to her father. She could hear them, too, threatening each other beneath her window as they left, all pretenses removed at the door. She'd even met a few, against her wishes—the ones who'd made it past her father and gotten permission to view her.

There had been seven, in total. Lately, however, there was only one remaining. She knew why the other six hadn't returned. After all, she'd heard his threats.

Today, her suitor was to ask for her hand. The maids knew, and they'd tugged and fussed at her hair for hours before they'd deemed her acceptable. Now, she sat at the window, staring off at the mountains, wondering if there was anything she could do to stop the process. She needed a husband; everyone else had decided. They were about to get their wish.

The door opened behind her.

She frowned. Father wouldn't come in for fear of seeing womanly business, and the maids knew to knock. That meant…

She whirled, expecting her brothers and some form of prank—the day of her betrothal would be like *catnip* for them—and was surprised to see her mother standing there, a white box in her hands.

Of everyone, she was one of the few who had remained quiet about the whole affair. It hurt. The only one to remain mute, but the one most likely to understand the situation. Why then, was she here now?

"My lovely daughter," Queen Dionne said. "Come here, sit with me."

She joined her on the bed. "What is it?"

"I know you've been…having doubts. I understand. We all did, when we were your age."

"Even with Father?" This surprised Nikita. Her father was a lovely man, the two of them nigh inseparable. She couldn't imagine that ever not being the case.

"Not exactly." The queen sighed. "Look. My mother had this chat with me, as did her mother, and her mother before her. Sometimes you just have to—" She passed over the white box. It was absurdly heavy. "—take matters into your own hands." With that, she left.

Nikita was confused, but she opened the box. There were a number of things inside, although none of them did anything to explain its sheer weight: dried flowers, little jars of dirt, vials of liquid, a large glass container, and a note with instructions on it. It looked like a recipe. At the top of it, the princess read the words *Love Potion.*

Trust me was written right below.

A love potion? She wasn't fool enough to believe something like that. Her mother was a practical woman though, as was her grandmother. They both had happy marriages, too, the only ones in Nikita's existence that had ever given her hope for the institution. *Trust me.* She did.

So she started following the instructions.

Leave the castle by the back gate. Make your way past the wildflowers until you reach the great oak.

There were no guards posted by the rear gate for the first time Nikita could remember. No one saw her as she left and made her way towards the large oak, the tall grass swishing against her bare shins. Mother must have arranged it for her.

Her heart had picked up by the time she moved on to the next step. It was simple. *Mix the ingredients, swirl, and set the container down on the ground. Step away.* That last one seemed worrying but, hey, she'd left the castle already. She couldn't face going back and seeing her future husband without at least trying.

So she set that heavy, heavy box down on the ground and got to work. She didn't know if the dried flowers went in whole, so she broke them up between her fingers and sprinkled them in the bottom of the container. The different colored dirt followed: gold, red, and black. She felt like she was doing something wrong, even though there was no order listed on the instructions. Finally, she poured the liquid over it all.

Then she stepped away.

For a second nothing happened and she wasn't sure what she felt. Disappointment? Relief? Then the potion started fizzing. Something crackled in the container and the mixture began to bubble. A love potion, she thought as she watched the mixture start to foam red. Was it for her future husband? She didn't know if love was the answer there. Was it for herself?

That thought was almost more horrifying. The thought that her mother, and her grandmother, had poisoned themselves, made themselves love the men they married magically, instead of naturally… She refused to believe it. What was the point of this potion, then?

Abruptly, there was a pop. Red smoke started to billow, violently, creating a large, thick column. Nikita stared, alarmed, as the cloud grew skyward. Had she done something wrong? This didn't look like a love potion to her. She scrambled backwards so she didn't accidentally inhale the smoke. It looked poisonous and she refused to be the one to fall in love. Not this way. Not unless it was real.

After a minute, the castle bells started to ring out. Damn. They probably thought someone had lit the fields alight. She didn't know what her mother was playing at. Maybe she'd finally allied with her brothers and joined in on one of their pranks. She was frantic, looking for something to cover the container with, when she heard something. A loud, heavy swooshing.

A large shadow moved over her and she glanced up to see the real reason the alarm was tolling. A reason with two huge wings, a long, barbed tail, and talons that were reaching for her. She screamed, and then the dragon had her.

* * *

"Prepare my spear, boys," Kaile proclaimed, standing outside the dragon's lair.

They didn't pause when he asked them that anymore. His "spear" was twice the size of a normal one, but he refused to call it a lance, and he had his servants whipped if they insisted on doing so. Lance was his older brother's name, and his brother was a jackass. He didn't deserve to share his name with a knight's weapon, so Kaile simply wouldn't let it happen.

If Lance ever found out, the knowledge would probably crush him. Kaile hoped so anyway. If it didn't, seeing his younger brother become a dragon slayer certainly would. All icing on the cake of his wonderful, busy week.

He'd managed to discover the dragon's lair quickly. People talked when they saw a giant flying lizard—sadly they were rare, or he'd have killed one already—and he could charm a stone into giving him information. If he wasn't so talented on a horse, he might have been quite the spy, or the diplomat.

He strapped his weapon to his arm and gave a few practice thrusts, his horse solid as a rock beneath him. He liked this horse. Maybe when this was done, he'd ask this one's name. Or not. He'd probably just have to change it anyway. A legendary knight deserved a legendary mount, after all. By the end of the week, he'd have it all: title, wife, legend, and horse. If the creature survived the battle, that was.

If not, no matter. He had a whole stable's worth.

"Stay out here," he bade the men. They sagged in such relief that he was half tempted to order them to come and watch him instead. They'd probably get in his way though, or alert the creature, and he knew from experience that having an eyewitness didn't mean much when it came time for the bards to start singing. They went with what they thought best, not what actually happened. Unless you paid them to sing what you wanted, which was always the safest route.

Never leave something to chance, not when coin would do it for you. That's what Father always said and Father was always right.

"No matter what you hear inside, don't come after me." No harm in a little theatrics. Maybe they'd spread it to some peasants who couldn't afford to listen to a proper bard. He fluffed out his cloak, raised his spear. "I shan't be but a minute."

Then he entered the cave.

Almost immediately he was stopped, his spear raised too high to allow him to progress. He lowered it, edged his mount to the side, and proceeded. His horse's hooves clopped against the stone, but there was nothing he could do about that. If the dragon heard him coming that was alright. He just needed to be quick once it had him in its sight. Close the gap and strike for the throat. He'd read the books—well, he'd had them read to him—and he knew that a dragon couldn't breathe flame immediately. They took some time to gather it, time that lesser fighters spent frozen in fear before the great beasts.

Well, fear hadn't stopped him from slaying bears, large hunting cats, and even a pair of minotaurs up near the mountains. It certainly wasn't going to stop him here.

He had to light a torch after two twists of the passage. The air had already gotten noticeably cooler. He'd very much expected there to be more heat. The walls closed in as he progressed and he was worried for a moment that the cave would get too narrow for his mount, but it quickly opened up again, like he knew it would. Dragons were big, after all, and so were their hordes. That was the real reason he'd made the peasants stay outside. He'd get his choice of the gold and none of them would be tempted.

Imagine. A handful of gold and they'd be uncontrollable. Disgusting. He imagined one showing up at a city ball and sneered. He'd seen it happen before, new money parading around like they deserved to be there. *Ugh.* What he didn't claim for himself he'd send Father's men to gather. It was the thing he was looking forward to most, this week, just above slaying the creature. His future wife had the honor of coming third. If she was suitably grateful, maybe he'd even let her choose something for herself.

The cave widened the deeper he went until the walls to either side of him were no longer visible by the light of his torch. He hesitated. Maybe he should get a squire after all, send him ahead until he found the creature; just in case. Finally, he saw something farther on: a glint of cold light.

He moved towards it, slowly, until he was certain. Daylight. Of course, the dragon had to get in here, too. It surely had its own entrance, some crater in the roof of the mountain. He snuffed out the torch. It was near. He'd need to be quick.

Kaile came around the bend into a gigantic cavern with his spear at the ready. Two things stood out. Most importantly was the gold. Mounded in a heap taller than even he was, it shone in the light let in by a ragged crack in the roof. It was a lot. Even Father might have appreciated it, and his many vaults were no joke. Next to the gold, in an iron cage, was the second thing of interest. His future wife.

She didn't look great. Her hair was artless, undone, and she wore a plain white shift. She'd spent some time in the cage; she could have at least braided it. Still, she'd learn. He moved his mount forward, out of the shadows, and he saw her notice him. Her eyes widened and she leaned forwards. "That's…that's him." Her voice shook.

Kaile was confused. Was she speaking to herself? He noticed that the cage door was slightly ajar. Of course, how would a dragon close it? Was she simply too scared to leave? What a useless creature. He beckoned to her before he noticed that deep in the cavern behind her, the cave itself was *moving*.

Silently, sinuously, the walls were unfolding. No, not the walls. Scales so reflective as to act like camouflage. Now that it was moving, he could see it clearly; wings, those small, taloned arms, sharp, glinting eyes, and its maw, ringed with vicious teeth. He was already spurring his horse towards the thing, spear erect. He could see the nape of its neck, his target.

The creature was gigantic. All the better for his legend. It didn't take to the air—he'd caught it by surprise, clearly—opening its mouth instead as it turned to face him. In seconds he'd be awash with flame. In half that time, the thing would be dead.

His mount surged beneath him, hooves clattering on the stone. He tensed his arm, angled his spear, and wondered how the bards would sing of this moment. Maybe the song would be ready by the time they wed, even. Father had enough sway to make it happen.

Then there was a sound. Horrible, high pitched, like a knife through the skull. Kaile barely managed to keep his spear aimed at the thing, fighting the urge to clutch at his ears. His mount stopped though, rearing beneath him, whinnying in distress.

He tried to hold on, but a second later he hit the ground.

* * *

There was a metallic thud as the small knight hit the floor.

Atraxi flapped her wings, once, surging forward and landing on him. There was a large, wet crack. She stayed put for a second, just in case—even though it sounded like he had broken, those metal human shells could do wonders these days—but she didn't feel any squirming beneath her. He was gone.

She scraped her claw along the ground, hiding the worst of the gore behind a large boulder. A red smear remained, but she'd learned over the years that humans were far less upset by the sight of blood than by shattered bone and ripped skin. So peculiar, but she'd learned to cater to them.

The horse was still shrieking, backing away in a frothing, wide-eyed stumble. Atraxi couldn't do anything about that. One of her clients had begged her to spare the horse, decades ago, and it had become a service she included naturally these days. The women she worked with rarely wanted to see the horse perish too, and it wasn't much more work to achieve. It was a simple matter for her to upset them enough to toss their rider—sometimes just the sight of her did it; more often than not she had to make her little scream—but calming one down was beyond her talents.

It would flee, the princess would tend to it, or it would die from fear. Atraxi hated when that last one happened.

"You can open your eyes now," she said.

She swung her head back to regard the little noble sitting in her cage. Nikita was already staring at the ground where her suitor had met his end. That was rare; usually they still had a hand in front of their eyes. There weren't any tears coming though. Atraxi thought she might well like this client.

"Thank the gods," the princess said.

"I'm no god." Nikita looked at her, wide-eyed. Atraxi snorted. The woman didn't even flinch. Yeah, she was a good one. "It's a joke."

"Oh, yes. Of course, I just…"

"It's fine. Seriously. Now, can you talk to the horse? I'll make us some tea."

As the bewildered human left her cage, Atraxi made her way to the large copper pot she'd had painstakingly installed years prior. It was a work of marvel: twice as tall as a person with one large spout for herself and a number of smaller, wooden handles nearer to the ground for humans. It had been a thank you gift from Queen Malia of Thrassus after her wedding, a nice bonus considering what she'd already paid.

It had changed Atraxi's life. She'd never known what tea was before, other than the fact that most princesses asked for it after their ordeal. Well, that or "whiskey," but Malia had been curiously quiet when Atraxi had inquired after *that.*

There were small sacks stacked neatly in a box nearby, pre-stuffed by her human friends. She hooked one with a claw and dropped it into the pot. It took a few moments to gather flame. She felt the reaction inside her foremost stomach, that familiar, comforting burn. Then, gently, she breathed out fire against the edge of the copper.

Within a minute the water was bubbling. She breathed in deeply. The comforting aroma of black tea and cardamom filled her cave. Carefully, Atraxi turned back around. It was all well and good stepping on those who deserved it, but she lived in fear of accidentally tail-swiping a client into oblivion.

Nikita was standing by the horse, stroking it. The creature was still looking at Atraxi with eyes as wide as they went, but at least it had finally quieted down. Maybe it, too, would like some tea. She'd leave that in the princess's hands though. "Shouldn't be more than a minute," she said. "There are some golden goblets, well, everywhere. Take one; just rinse it after if you don't mind."

"Thank you."

"Are you doing okay?"

The princess nodded. "Better, actually. I was…" Living in fear. Atraxi already knew. They always were. The little woman changed the subject. "So you knew my mother?"

"Back when she was looking to wed, yes. Your family have been clients of mine for centuries."

"I just find it so hard to believe."

"This hoard didn't gather itself, sweetie." Atraxi's newest additions—some platinum bars and a golden book-cover that had been secreted in the bottom of Nikita's box—had pride of place atop her pile. "You're not the only family, either. If you'd be so kind as to let your daughter know, someday, too…"

Nikita shook her head. She smiled in one of those weird human ways that didn't mean she was happy. "Well, first I've got to wed."

"I can help with that, too, actually. Same price as before."

"I…but *how*?"

"The opposite service, really. You pick a gentleman you're interested in and I'll have my friend Trinity—she's a princess, too, but she gave it up—send them a letter from you. The usual stuff: 'Oh, a bad dragon has me, please come save me.' This time I'll fly away in fear when he arrives though. He gets to save you, you get to marry him. Simple."

"Sorry, she just *gave it up*?"

Atraxi sighed. Humans were great, but they tended to be slow on the uptake. Especially after watching things get killed. It was a strange evolutionary feature. She wondered how it was helpful.

"Yes, she runs the nearby inn. She brings me my tea. It's another service I offer, if you're interested. All we need is some fire and a lump of meat that's roughly your size and then I can fly you anywhere you like. I've little ex-princesses all over. I will tell you, though, this one is a little more expensive. More work, for one, as well as more danger. Kings don't love it when their daughters get 'roasted,' although the queens in the know usually manage to talk them down while I lay low. It does also mean that I lose some customers. Non-noble daughters usually don't need me." The woman was staring at her. "Although sometimes they do. Tea?"

The woman nodded. Atraxi nudged the large, wooden handle and the steaming hot liquid gushed out, filling the small trench in the stone below. She slurped it up immediately. It cooled her throat nicely, after the flame. Nikita poured some from her own little handle but didn't drink it. Princesses, she knew, needed to wait until it was practically cold.

"So, what do you think?"

"With Kaile out of the way…I think the others will return. They're not as bad."

"And if they are…"

She smiled. This time it was one of the good ones, Atraxi was sure of it. "If they are, I know where to find you."

"Exactly." Atraxi sniffed the air. Past the wonderful smell of tea and the less-wonderful smell of horse and scared princess, she could smell the unmistakeable scent of men. Two of them, at least, and another pair of horses. "Your dearly departed has some friends outside. Would you care to leave for your home with them or stay a while? One of your predecessors has laid what I'm told is a comfy bed in a smaller cave in the back. That, or you can stay at the inn free of charge."

"I think I could take a day or two. The men outside though, what will—"

Atraxi slurped the rest of her tea from the trench. "No, no, don't fret. I'll do a flyby and they'll flee. Even from here I can smell that they didn't really care for their knight. Any excuse and they'll be gone. Besides, I usually recommend this course of action."

"You do?"

"Definitely. The squires will flee home with tales of the knight's death. If you don't take too long, they won't have time to send more. You'll look like a daring adventurer returning from an ordeal even *such a hero* couldn't surpass."

"Oh. I hadn't thought of it that way. It does sound quite fun."

"We'll brainstorm over dinner," Atraxi said. "Trinity is a wonderful cook. Have you heard of *seasoning*?" She blinked in appreciation as she got to her feet and spread her wings. "Honestly, you humans can be remarkable. Now, tuck yourself in the corner there. There's a bit of a downdraft."

Atraxi launched herself upwards, out of her cave, and into the sky. She'd be back before the tea cooled.

Cold Fire of Manhattan

Russell Hugh McConnell

Checking in, checking out, Broadway tickets, off-Broadway tickets, off-off-Broadway tickets, directions, bus tours, birthday arrangements, lost children, lost jewelry, lost luggage, wrong luggage, forgotten toiletries, child care, pet care, packages, conferences, wine recommendations, taxis, limos, discreet female companionship, discreet male companionship. Every day is different, but the dance is always the same. Your needs are my responsibility.

I'm a damn good concierge.

The Wyvern Hotel is the best place to stay in New York City. I was there when it was built, and I imagine I will be there when it falls down. I remember the Great Depression. I remember when this city was called New Amsterdam. I remember before that, when it had a name no one could write down. My kind is famous for getting attached to places and I feel at home here.

It's a day like any other until he walks in. He's lean and tanned and difficult to age, his long hair and short beard both bleached blond by the sun. He looks like a boat captain. His dark suit fits his body but not his spirit; it's obvious that he's monstrously uncomfortable in formal wear. Over the years, I've met thousands of people who were here for job interviews and I know the look. This man belongs on the sea. He even smells like the sea: a faint whiff of salt spray and seaweed clings to him, despite the exhalations of the city. There is an intensity to his gaze that is strangely familiar, but which I cannot quite place. From across the room, his eyes meet mine and in that moment I know with absolute certainty that he can tell what I am. This could be disastrous.

I take a step towards him, bracing for whatever comes next, but all that happens is that he turns abruptly and strides back out through the revolving door and into the brisk autumn morning.

And so I fall back into the concierge dance. But he is in my thoughts now, and I am sure that some kind of trouble is afoot.

* * *

I stand on the roof of 432 Park Avenue, looking down on the vast carpet of lights and lives that stretches out below. My human form melts away and I expand to my true size, my wings stretching out towards the night sky. It is always windy at the top of a skyscraper—so deliciously cold—and it's getting colder now that it's early November. I drink deeply of the wind, feeding the cold fire inside me. Traditionally, dragons spend a great deal of time asleep, sometimes curled up for centuries on a gleaming gold-hoard, but since taking the cold fire, I no longer sleep at all.

Guion is also a sleepless New Yorker. There are over a thousand gargoyles in the city, but most of them are not alive. More than once I have offered a friendly hello to one of them before realizing to my embarrassment that it was merely a statue. Guion is one of the few live ones. He claims to have been imported illegally from an old French manor house back in 1912, although his vagueness about the details makes me suspect that he may really be American-born. He does, however, speak with a strong French accent. If it is an affectation, it is at least a consistent and authentic-sounding one, and I am hardly in a position to criticize anyone for self-reinvention. Apparently Guion used to live on the Croisic Building, but now he roams freely from place to place. When we met about a century ago, we were both enormously relieved to find someone to talk to.

When I tell him about my encounter today, he does not share my surprise. "Think about it, Mark," he says drolly. "New York City gets over sixty million visitors every year and you work in the main lobby of one of the biggest hotels in town. If you were hoping no one would ever recognize you, you picked a very odd profession and you practice it in a very odd place."

"You know why I work in a hotel," I say, a little more defensively than I mean to.

He nods, no longer jocular. "*Oui*, I know. It is just that, in the long run, it's not really all that unlikely, is it?" Seeing my expression he adds, "Are you worried?"

"I don't know what to think. Maybe nothing will come of it." I do not actually believe this.

"Do you think he might be…?" Guion is reluctant to finish the thought.

"A dragon-slayer? Or an ambitious hopeful? It could be." I take another large gulp of cold wind. "If so, there will be trouble."

Guion glances nervously at me. "If we get that kind of trouble maybe you could warn me, so I can get out of town. I mean this person might just be a loser. An *amuse bouche* for you. But if he is actually dangerous—I mean, if he's a sorcerer or a disguised daemon or something…if there's a real fight…" He shudders a little, and it's not because of the cold wind. "*Mon Dieu*, Mark. After that, there might not be much Manhattan left."

Again, I gaze down at the lights below. My city. "I won't let that happen," I say.

"If you can help it," Guion adds in a low voice. I cannot dispute the comment; I was thinking the same thing myself.

* * *

The sailor returns to the hotel the next day. He has the same intense gaze as before, but not the same clothing: now he's in blue jeans, a flannel shirt, and well-worn hiking shoes. He's also wearing a smile—not a grim or threatening smile either, but one that looks genuinely friendly, if a bit wary. It is late morning and the hotel is quiet, with just a few people hanging around the lobby. He approaches me and raises his hand, which wavers uncertainly through a series of partial gestures: a wave, then a salute, then a proffered handshake. I quickly reach out and accept the handshake before he can change his mind again.

"Captain Stanley Nelson," he says, by way of introduction. "Or, you know, just Stanley."

"Mark Robinson," I reply.

"Mark Robinson?" he says. "Okay, if you say so."

There is no one within earshot, so I get right to the point. "Very few people in this world can see a dragon, and no one is supposed to. Even in old times, this might be thought ill luck for both of us."

"Ill luck?" he says. "I hope not, man."

"You recognized me yesterday. I saw you recognize me. Why didn't you speak to me then? I have been wondering about your intentions."

"Why didn't I just waltz over and start talking? Did you see the look on your face? My very first time seeing a dragon and you looked at me the way I imagine Fafnir looked at a thousand screaming Norse peasants."

I try not to sound sniffy when I reply, "Fafnir was not a real dragon. He was a transmuted dwarf."

"You don't say? Well anyway, I got one look at you and then I went outside and threw up in a trash can. It took me this long just to work up the courage to come back."

This gives me pause. It has been so long since anyone really saw me—anyone other than a sardonic gargoyle—that I forget how I might appear to a mortal. I am unsure of what is appropriate conduct in this situation, so I fall back on the ethic of the concierge. "I beg your pardon, sir," I say, and I mean it.

"Hey, don't worry about it, buddy," he says, seeming genuinely sorry to have distressed me. He gestures down at himself. "As you can see, I didn't bother with the suit this time. I thought I should be dressed up to meet a dragon, but as soon as I saw you I knew it wouldn't make any difference. You're not the kind of guy who's going to be impressed by a Brooks Brothers three-piece." He takes a deep breath and stands up straight. "The truth is, I've come for your help."

"Certainly, sir. Perhaps you would like tickets to a Broadway show? Restaurant recommendations? I could get you into Manny's, even without a reservation. I have known Manny since he was born."

"Come on, man," he says, but I can tell that the gentle teasing is making him relax a bit. As I said, I'm a damn good concierge. He leans in closer and I see that the intense look in his eyes is due to the fact that they are glimmering with a silver light.

"You have the Shine," I say with surprise. I already took this guy seriously, but this is really something special.

"It had to be done," is all he says in reply.

"Who did it?"

"The King of the Otherworld, of course. Manannán mac Lir."

"You met with the Sidhe?" I say, astonished. "*And* you made it back alive?"

"You know anyone else who could do a shine job these days?"

I think for a moment. "No," I said. "These days, no, I suppose not. That must have been dangerous though, in more ways than one."

His gaze is earnest, and the Shine lends it a compelling force that I am not used to. "I did it to find you."

Then he does it. I had a feeling something like this was coming, and I suppose it's just as well that he gets it out of the way. He raises both hands and curls his fingers into a very specific interlocking shape. Goodness knows what musty old book he found that in. I haven't seen anyone even attempt the Eye of Vritra for over four centuries, and even then it wasn't done properly. It must have been a proper quest for him to learn how to do it, and I don't have the heart to tell him that it doesn't actually make any difference. What does make a difference is that he says formally, "I call upon the Warden of Hecate. I call upon the one who took the Vow of Service."

This guy has good information. I wonder if the Sidhe helped him out with that, or if he's got his fingers in other pies as well. Dangerous business for a mortal.

"What do you need?" I ask.

He looks slightly surprised and I realize that he did not assume that his appeal would work. "You will honor the oath?"

"I have to. If you know about the oath, then you know I must honor it."

He nods and looks at me intently, the Shine gleaming around his irises. "I need the cold fire."

* * *

"What are you going to do with it?" The neighbor is shouting. He is short, graying, and sixtyish, with the kind of impenetrable self-assurance that you only ever find in immortals, or in people with metropolitan New York accents. "I mean how are you going to get it down? That's what I'd like to know. How are you going to get it down?"

Captain Stanley and I are standing on the roof of a squat, brown brick apartment building in Brooklyn. Most of the roof space is taken up with a large wooden framework: the skeleton of what will clearly become a fine sailing ship. Evidently, this project has been causing consternation to Stanley's neighbor. The man stands about fifteen feet away on the roof of the next building, perched on the edge, apparently totally unconcerned about his own safety. It is true I like to stand on the edge myself, but then I have wings.

Stanley obviously wants to ignore the guy, but experience has taught him that sometimes ignoring things doesn't make them go away. "Don't worry about it, Frank," he says. "Go watch TV or something."

"You," says Frank, gesturing animatedly to me. "You talk some sense into him. I mean he's building a ship on the roof. Who builds a ship on a roof?"

Stanley looks ready to start shouting, so I turn to Frank and offer a pre-emptive bow. "Sir," I say, "you are surely right to be concerned. Your neighbor has called me to consult on this very matter. I will endeavor to 'talk some sense into him,' as you say."

Somewhat mollified, Franks replies, "Thank goodness! And tell him not to do his hammering so early in the morning," before heading through the heavy fire door and back downstairs.

I stand at the edge of the building and look down. "It's only eight stories" I say.

"It's the highest launch point I could get."

"You sailed to Emain Ablach and got Manannán mac Lir to put the Shine on your eyes, but you couldn't get roof access higher than eight stories?"

"Eldrich sailing is one thing. New York real estate is something else entirely."

"I could have helped; I know some people."

He laughs. "Of course you do. You're a damn good concierge."

I gesture towards the half-built ship. "It looks like she'll take a long time to finish."

"Not so long, actually. I already built her in miniature down at my place in Punta Gorda, so there's no real design points to work out. She'll be done by mid-December."

I'm not an expert in skyships, but I've seen a few in my time and I can't fault the design. "How are you going to power it?"

"Hey, I told you, man."

I look at him curiously. "The cold fire? You don't need that to power the ship. With respect, that would be like putting a jet engine on a rowboat."

"Let me show you something." Stanley disappears down the stairwell for a minute before reappearing with a battered cardboard box. "It's not just to power this ship. It's to power this." He opens the box and pulls out a crystal sphere about the size of a baseball. I can feel the magic radiating off it like heat from a blast furnace.

"What is that?" I ask, recoiling slightly.

"Don't you know?" He looks surprised. I can hardly believe he's just holding the thing in his hand. The Shine will enable him to see the magic rolling off of it in waves, but he must not be able to feel it. "Manannán mac Lir called it a sféar." He puts it back in the box.

"Okay, you've got my attention. What are you going to do with it?"

"Look, man, I know this might be a sensitive subject, but I've got to be direct. Magic isn't what it used to be, is it?"

"That's true," I reply quietly.

"No more pixies in the forest. No more wizard duels. Not very many dragons left. That's how you're able to work out in plain view in the lobby of a New York hotel. I mean you've been living in this city for decades and I'll bet I'm the first person who's recognized you in a long time."

"That is true also."

"The moon used to have a Shine all of her own, you know. Things looked different by the light of the moon. That was the time to see the pixies, to watch the wizard duels, to find a dragon. It used to be that the Shine happened every night, for anyone who cared to look."

"There were dangers to that."

"There sure were. But there was also magic in the world. I mean properly *out* in the world, not lurking in corners, not buried in tombs. And, with respect, not hiding out in hotel lobbies."

I am quiet for a long moment. Then I say, "Show it to me again."

He draws out the sféar; the wave of magic hits me, but I am ready for it this time. I look hard and my vision plunges deep into its impossibly pellucid depths, which curve in more directions than there are. An impossible sphere—a sphere that has been sphered into the fourth dimension. "Filled with the cold fire…" I murmur, half to myself and half to him. "Could this put the Shine back on the moon? I suppose it just might. I doubt anyone has ever tried." I glance up at him. "There is no guarantee that it would work, and certainly no guarantee that you would ever make it back again."

Captain Stanley's tanned and weathered sailor's face is as earnest as I have ever seen it. "But that's still the mission, man. Together, you and I are going to put some magic back into this grubby old world."

* * *

A cold Atlantic wind blows from the east, carrying tiny flecks of snow through the air. A perfect December night. I let my human form melt away and spread my wings skyward, but I do not inhale as deeply as I do on the high rooftops. The eighth floor is too close to the car exhaust.

Captain Stanley is bundled up in an old navy coat, the classic effect of which is somewhat spoiled—or perhaps made perfect—by the addition of a bright orange bobble hat. We have a bit of time before we can launch, and I can tell from Stanley's manner that he wants to chat.

"My dad had a thing for birds," he says. "He named all of his boats after birds. Skylark. Swallowtail. Sparrowhawk. He also had a thing for the letter S I guess." He gestures proudly to the finished skyship, and can I see the Shine gleaming around his irises. "This is the Silvereye," he says with a wink.

"Good," I say. I hadn't thought to ask about the name, but of course it's bad luck to launch a ship without one.

Then Stanley changes the subject. "Why did you do it? Why take the Oath of Service? Don't tell me you just always wanted to work at a hotel."

"It wasn't altruism, or love of man. It was self-interest. I needed the cold fire. A life of service was the price." I sigh. "Why Hecate cares whether or not I serve humankind I cannot imagine. I've always suspected that she got something else out of the deal that I never knew about." I can tell he's going to ask more questions, so I get to the point. "Dragonfire was fading. Dragonkind was imperiled." It has been decades since I last told this story. That was to Guion, on New Year's Day in 1925. "The others said that the waxing and waning of the hot fire was normal. They said it would return to its former strength soon enough. They said that I was a fool to sacrifice my autonomy in exchange for the cold fire. It seems they were wrong."

Stanley is silent for a long time, just as Guion had been when I told him. Then he says, "So is it just you now then?"

"As far as I know, I am the only one that took the cold fire. A few of the others may have found other ways to survive."

We spend the next ten minutes gazing wordlessly up at the moon and stars, and at the flecks of snow falling softly through the universe.

After a while, Captain Stanley checks his watch. It's perfect: a nice big silver pocket watch on a fob. A digital watch would work at least as well, but the aesthetic would be all wrong. This watch makes a statement. "Okay," he says. "Let's do it."

The sféar is mounted on its own steel pillar next to the big ship's wheel, covered with a towel. Stanley pulls off the covering and I feel the now-familiar magic aura radiating from it. Still standing on the roof, I lean over the edge of the Silvereye and put my mouth right up against the smooth crystal of the sféar. I cautiously exhale just the tiniest wisp of cold fire

The sféar flares with an icy blue light. So far so good. I let out a thin, steady stream of cold fire, which pours readily into the sféar.

"Looking good, man," he says. "It's all going in. I think it's safe to turn it on full."

"Avert your eyes." I pause and look to make sure he does. I take a deep breath, feeling the energy stirring and roiling deep inside me. Then, to use Stanley's phrase, I turn it on full.

I do not believe there is a viable unit of measurement to compare magical energy with those energies described by modern science. Magic is not really "energy" in any precise scientific sense. Although joules, calories, and other such conceptualizations might be able to measure some of its products and consequences, magic itself is different. Nevertheless, if I had to try to describe this unrestrained release of cold fire, I would have to say that it has something of the quality of a nuclear explosion. I try not to roar, but I think I do emit a low rumble as I discharge a tremendous blast into the heart of the sféar. This kind of power could raze cities, obliterate armies, or break mountains down to dust. The sféar does not get much brighter, but its icy white-blue light acquires a certain indefinable intensity. Most mortals would probably find themselves transfixed by it. The sféar now resembles a star, burning with an inexhaustible freezing light. I pour in as much as I dare, then toss the towel over it and fasten it firmly in place with a leather strap, so that there is no risk that Captain Stanley might look at the sféar by accident and become mesmerized.

I slump backwards, sitting down on the rooftop, and feel a profound dizziness and disorientation that I have not felt in a long time. The cold fire is theoretically inexhaustible, but I am not sure I have ever spent it so lavishly. After a few deep breaths I say, "Launch time," and only now does Stanley uncover his eyes.

"Hey ho, let's go," he says. He's trying to sound breezy, but I can hear the tension and emotion in his voice. He grips the wheel and immediately the Silvereye lurches about six feet off the rooftop. "Woah," exclaims Stanley. Then he laughs. "This is the only way to fly!"

A skyship cannot simply levitate straight upwards; it has to gain height gradually, which means that Stanley needs to keep sailing around the air of the city, rising higher and higher with each turn. In addition to powering the ship, the sféar is also shielding him from view of most mortal eyes. For eight minutes or so he sails steadily, gradually gathering speed as he becomes more confident with the vessel. I just watch from the roof, hoping my head will stop spinning soon. Despite my condition, I can see sharply enough to tell that Stanley is grinning hugely. He's piloting his ship with joyous enthusiasm, tiny snowflakes beginning to accumulate on his orange hat. The cold air is doing me some good, but I feel it will be some time before I am up to normal function.

Then my eyes narrow.

Just a few blocks away, there's a dark cloud swirling amidst the buildings. I'm still extremely dizzy, but I furrow my brow and do my best to focus and peer through the night. Then, to my horror, the blast of smell hits me: frankincense.

"Evasive maneuvers!" I roar. Stanley looks up, startled, and I realize he hasn't even seen them yet. But to his credit, he takes my word and veers sharply starboard. I flap my wings and hurl myself towards the black cloud. My best chance is to strike fast and hard before they can disperse, but in my current condition I'm horribly slow; I'm also struggling to fly in a straight line.

I can see the cloud getting larger already, thinning. With no time for proper delicacy, and at too distant a range, I take a quick, shallow gulp of air and let out a wide, thin burst of cold fire, attempting to sweep it through the central mass of the swarm. In the eerie quiet, I can hear the almost musical tinkling of flesh freezing instantaneously and bursting into a mist that rains down on the streets below.

The most famous account of the drakontes occurs in Herodotus and to be fair to the man (and to the Egyptians he interviewed) he does get the facts mostly right: they are venomous winged snakes. They do not present a serious threat to me, but even just a few of them could be a major problem for Captain Stanley, particularly given that he's already trying to pilot a skyship through the New York skyline. So I hurl myself into the midst of the widening cloud, hoping that they go for me instead of him.

The drakontes are not large, but they are alarmingly fast, wriggling like water snakes, agile on their batlike wings. The smell of frankincense is almost overwhelming. Several of them latch onto me with their sharp teeth, and although they cannot penetrate my scales, they attach firmly. I carefully veer left and scrape dozens of them off my back against the edge of a glass and steel office building. But in my disoriented state, I am unable to maintain a clean flying line and feel a steel girder buckle against my spine amidst an explosion of shattering glass.

Next, I dive right, smushing another ten or so against a metal fire escape, but in doing so I snap the structure clean off the brick wall of the apartment building it belongs to, sending it clattering down to the street below. There will be a gruesome mess for someone to clean up tomorrow—bent and twisted iron smeared with dead snake—but there's not much I can do about that at the moment. I angle myself so that I'm flying more-or-less straight upwards, then tuck my head so that I can send a quick cough of cold fire down my chest and belly, destroying fifty or so more.

It's all going reasonably well, despite the property damage, until one of them—operating on instinct, rather than any calculated strategy—sinks its fangs into my right eye. I lose flight trajectory, and feel my rear left foot collide with something that breaks and crumbles apart. I grab at my face, and the sudden movement, combined with my dizziness and obstructed vision, causes me to lurch sideways. My right shoulder drives through someone's corner office, shards of glass and chunks of concrete flying in all directions. I try to keep flying straight upwards as much as possible, to minimize collisions, and blink hard, but the stubborn snake will not be dislodged. Another opportunistic attacker darts towards my left eye but I am able to swat it aside with my left front claws; my elbow hits something and I hear more smashing glass. All I can think of is that Stanley might be getting ripped apart by drakontes at this very moment.

I spread my wings fully, halting my upward flight, then reverse direction, diving straight downwards. When I have accelerated enough to feel a proper hurricane wind, I belch out a mouthful of cold fire that blows back in my face, obliterating the stubborn snake. I blink vigorously, then pull up just in time to avoid crashing into an apartment block.

I blink again. Fortunately, my nictitating membrane is approximately as tough as carbon steel, so there's no real harm done and, although I still feel nauseatingly dizzy, seeing out of both eyes properly is a decided improvement. Anyway, I'm not the one I'm worried about right now. Wheeling around, I scan urgently for the Silvereye and, to my relief, I see it scudding along amongst the buildings. It's flying a little erratically, but it's still airborne. Then I see there's something moving in the air around the ship—something bigger than the drakontes, nearly human-sized.

I zoom up towards the Silvereye, ready to attack, and realize that the flying creature is Guion. He's clutching a snake in each hand and is crushing the life out of them, doing an accidental impersonation of the infant Herakles. Stanley has lost his bobble hat and his hair has come partway free of the ponytail, whipping all around his head in the freezing wind. He's clutching the ship's wheel, wild-eyed and harried, but he seems to be uninjured. Guion sees me first.

"Hey, Mark," he cries, "can you believe this? Talk about the neighborhood going downhill. These things smell like pinewood and oranges. Phew!"

"Mark?" says Stanley, barely daring to glance in my direction. "I don't know who this guy is, but he just stopped a flying snake from eating my face." He wipes his brow with his sleeve, sweating despite the cold and his lost hat. "Thanks, man," he says to Guion. "Those damn creatures—"

"Stanley," I interrupt. My head is spinning and my stomach is roiling. I don't like having to keep pace with the Silvereye when I'm flying so badly. With an effort, I pull myself back into human form and land stumblingly on the deck. "Stanley," I bark again, "where did you really get the sféar? And where did you really get the Shine? None of that crap about the Sidhe."

Stanley is silent for a long moment, gripping the wheel and gazing straight forward as he continues to steer the ship. "I told you the truth about the Shine," he says. "Manannán mac Lir did it. But the sféar…" He sighs. "The Sidhe were the ones who told me it existed. I only know their name for it; no doubt it has others. But they didn't have one anymore. I got mine from, er, someone else. I did a deal."

Guion has landed on the deck. He's scanning the sky for more flying snakes, but he's clearly listening to the conversation, too.

"A deal?" I say. "You made a deal for the sféar?"

"Um, no. No, I made a deal for a scarab amulet. But when the time came, I took more than what was promised."

I shake my head sadly. "Stanley, I could refuse to help you now. You called on the Vow of Service and I answered. But you deceived me. This violates the terms."

Stanley blanches. "Is—is that true?"

"It's a gray area. But the way I see it, I don't really have to help you with this. This is a whole other scale of problem. It's not just about skyship launches and moonshot missions. It's not even about clouds of drakontes. You've put the whole city in danger. *My* city."

He slumps and suddenly looks much older. "Look, Mark, I get it. If you want to bow out, I'll have to just make the run as best I can. At top speed—"

"Speed won't matter. If there's more drakontes, you won't outrun them. And it's not just them. You know who else must be here. If you are very, very lucky, she will only kill you."

"Oh God, you think she came here herself?" Stanley blanches and slumps even further.

Guion looks worried, casting me a sidelong glance, but he doesn't say anything.

"This isn't about vows any more, Stanley. This is about believing in your mission. And it's about friendship. Guion will stick with you for now. I'll go talk to her."

Stanley perks up and nearly smiles. "Really, Mark? You would really—"

"No time for that, Captain. You can hover, right? Anchor here. Count to a hundred. If I'm not back by then, shoot straight for the moon as hard and fast as you can and don't look back." Without waiting for a reply, I vault over the side of the skyship and resume dragon form, flapping my wings and soaring upwards.

I don't know exactly where she is, but I know how to find her. I just sniff the air and there she is, unmistakable amidst the cold Atlantic wind and the odors of the city. It's been two thousand years, but I'll never forget her scent. It's hot wind sifting through ancient sand; it's cool, silent crypts and deep memory. But most of all, it's secrets.

Within moments I have found her. Her feline body reclines comfortably on the roof of Central Park Tower, her feathery wings elegantly folded. Her ageless face regards me with a smile which is neither friendly, nor unfriendly, and her eyes burn with the same cat-green flame that I knew in ancient times. People talk about the Mona Lisa's inscrutable smile, and with good reason, but Leonardo da Vinci never met the Sphinx.

She says my name: fourteen guttural syllables that I have not heard spoken for a thousand years. For a moment I am surprised that she knows it, but then immediately feel a fool. She knows the location of Atlantis, the designers of Stonehenge, and every word of Homer's lost epic. Of course she knows my name.

"I thought Oedipus killed you," I say.

"Did you really?" she replies purringly. "Did you really think that?" I realize nothing has changed in two millennia. There's no point trying to be clever with her.

"No," I admit. "Not really. I guess I was just trying to sound cool." Then I add, "I suppose you knew I was going to turn up."

"Oh, darling," she replies, "I appreciate the compliment but I'm not actually omniscient. If I knew that brave Captain Stanley had a dragon bodyguard, don't you think I would have brought more aid than a few hundred drakontes?" Her eyes narrow and a rare flicker of emotion crosses her impassive face. "Particularly if I had known it was you. You are not in full fighting trim just at the moment, but we both know that doesn't fundamentally matter. If two such as we do battle, even I cannot know who will win, or even who will survive. If this is to be our battlefield, I expect the casualties will number in the millions. I've never been deeply concerned with human life, but if we destroy the Met I'll never forgive myself."

"What will it take for you to let him go?"

Slowly and majestically, she shakes her head. "No deals. He robbed me. I have sworn an oath."

"As have I. An oath no less binding than yours, made to an authority no less terrible."

She shakes her head again, a gesture which she makes look incredibly impressive. "Your vow hagrides and limits you. I can hardly imagine such a humiliation as being forced to serve humans. But I do not believe your vow extends to this. You have no cause to help this foolish man."

"Do you know what he intends to do with it? He will put the Shine back on the moon and try to reverse some of the damage that has been done in recent centuries. It is in all of our interests to bring magic back into the world. You and I have survived the Fading, but even we cannot last forever the way things are."

"Interesting," she says. "I suppose he might actually be able to do that. But I still cannot permit the theft. As long as it is possible for the sphere to be recovered, then I must pursue it."

"Don't you miss the old days? Don't you remember the way the desert used to look by moonlight? The way the air was alive with mystical presences? The way men came to you with praise and worship? Don't you miss—"

"You have no gift for poetry," she interrupts. "My memories are infinitely richer than your feeble descriptions, and they are in any case irrelevant. My hopes for the future are likewise irrelevant. I still need to get it back. Your friend still needs to die."

"If we do battle," I say, trying another tack, "the sféar will almost certainly be destroyed in the process. Even if you win the fight, you will not recover it."

"All the more reason for you to stop obstructing me." Then she stands up and I know that I cannot delay her any longer with words. She steps forward, unfurling her wings, which gleam a brilliant, sparkling white, even at night.

I am feeling a bit less dizzy now. Good.

I rear up to my full height and spread my wings wide, drawing in a huge breath of the deliciously cold night air. On the exhale, I expel just the thinnest mist of cold fire, enough to drop the ambient temperature by a few dozen degrees and surround us both with a pale blue glow.

The Sphinx recoils slightly, nearly showing some emotion again. "Oh really," she says. "There's no need for theatrics."

Her tone is faintly sardonic, but if you know her then you know that you must not take her unflappable manner at face value. The Sphinx is a great bluffer.

"I am a concierge. Captain Stanley's needs are my responsibility, as are humanity's in general."

"How can you serve humanity's needs by condemning millions of them to death and destruction?" she demands, and there is a hint of panic in her voice.

"Because you will submit. There will be no battle. You are a calculator and a survivor. I, on the other hand, am a servant."

"This is—" she begins, and I unleash a torrent of cold fire up into the air above our heads. This time, I also emit a proper thunderous roar that shakes the air around us and makes the building vibrate under our feet. The dizziness returns and I drop back down to all fours. The Sphinx recoils, her green-fire eyes widening, another flash of emotion momentarily breaking through her impassivity. I said there was no point trying to be clever with her, and that includes trying to bluff her. It's just a bad idea. But even if she cannot be bluffed, she can be backed into a corner. She opens her mouth and bares her fangs, but I am by no means certain whether she will actually fight me or not.

I think of my city, of the vast carpet of lights and lives that stretches out below the skyscrapers. I think of the way the world used to look when the moon had a Shine.

The Sphinx is just lunging forward when Guion lands on the edge of the roof. "*Un moment, madame*!" he says. "It is over. Captain Stanley is gone."

With eerie speed and smoothness, the Sphinx's look of combat-ready rage flicks back to smooth calm. She turns her gaze to Guion, who flinches.

"Please, *madame*," he says, "it is all over now. Captain Stanley has completed his launch and left the Earth behind. He is gone, and the sféar is gone with him."

She says nothing, just keeps regarding us with that unnervingly blank countenance. I decide that I might as well jump in. "Well, that's that. The battle is off."

"I am not satisfied," says the Sphinx.

"You have no obligation to fulfil," I say. "Your job was to stop Stanley and recover the sféar, not to avenge his success. Now that he is gone, it's all over. There is nothing to fight about."

The Sphinx neither objects to my claim nor concedes it. She just turns, flaps her wings once, and steps off the edge of the roof, swooping silently away into the night.

"I hope you enjoyed your brief stay," I call after her. I do not add my usual next sentence: "You are welcome back anytime." If I am very, very lucky, we will not see one another again for another two thousand years.

I do not tend to think of myself as very, very lucky.

* * *

Checking in, checking out, Broadway tickets, off-Broadway tickets, off-off-Broadway tickets, directions, bus tours, birthday arrangements, lost children, lost jewelry, lost luggage, wrong luggage, forgotten toiletries, child care, pet care, packages, conferences, wine recommendations, taxis, limos, discreet female companionship, discreet male companionship. Every day is different, but the dance is always the same. Your needs are my responsibility.

I'm still a damn good concierge.

I continue to fulfil my vow of service every day in the lobby of the Wyvern Hotel. At nights I stand on high skyscraper rooftops amidst the falling snow, chatting with Guion and breathing in the icy wind, feeding the cold fire that sustains me. I often gaze up at the moon and wonder about the fate of Captain Stanley. I do not know whether he made it to his destination or whether he will one day return. If he does return, I do not know if that will precipitate another visit from an old frenemy—a visit that might not end so well this time.

I cannot know any of this...but on these nights the moon does look remarkably large and bright. According to Guion, one might be tempted to say that it has a Shine.

Duck, Duck, Dragon

Grace Eliza

The Shimmering Mountains spoke to Lueetha of home and belonging. She felt it when a cool breeze lifted her wings and when the flavors of salmon and berries danced on her forked tongue. She knew she belonged when the lake reflected her sinuous, emerald body. It was good that the mountains spoke to her, since practically no one else did. She had human visitors once every five years and all they cared to speak of was that blasted covenant.

She watched the procession of knights, banners, and horses winding up the steep incline through narrowed amber eyes. One of the knights waved his gaudy purple and gold banner, likely hoping she would fly down to meet them. She turned her tail on them, replacing the procession with the much-preferred view of a lake nestled between pine-covered mountains.

Staying up here wouldn't stop their visit, but she didn't mind making them sweat for a few more miles.

The men reached Lueetha hours later, interrupting a perfect cloud-studded sunset. One of them stepped forward. He unfurled a piece of parchment and puffed out his chest like a griffin looking for a mate, not that she'd seen any griffins for decades.

"Dragon Lueetha, we come on behalf of King Reginol the Third to review the terms and conditions of the covenant between—"

"Yes, yes, I know why you're here." She swished her tail. A couple of the horses whinnied but the man continued to look her in the eye.

"So even the dragons have heard about my promotion." He smirked.

"What? No. I didn't mean *you* specifically. I just meant—never mind. You can tell your king that I've kept my end of the covenant; I haven't eaten humans or livestock or burned towns or farms or caused any strife. Now, you can help keep his end by leaving me alone."

"You're forgetting one thing."

"I'm not," she said, huffily. She was avoiding, not forgetting. There was a difference. "I know the covenant backward and forward. I was here the day it was formed and will be here long after it's dissolved when the mountain chooses a new keeper." The day her kin and friends would return and she would no longer be the lone dragon protecting the Shimmering Mountains from human hands.

"Yes, but until then, any dragon that lives in these mountains is obligated to dedicate themselves or their hatchling to a decade of service to the knighthood."

Lueetha exhaled a cloud of smoke.

"You have twenty years left to comply," said the man, taking a step back and looking at the parchment. "And, uh, if you don't, then you forfeit your home in the Shimmering Mountains to the reigning king..."

"You've delivered your message," said Lueetha, head spikes raised. Smoke followed her words like they were the most beautiful thing there. "Begone."

The men left with much less dignity than they had arrived and, with their absence, Lueetha felt herself deflate. It'd been eighty years and the mountain still hadn't chosen a new keeper, and it would be foolish to hope that it would choose one anytime soon. Except for her, Mati, and Herb, everyone had left. There was no one that could be the new keeper. She sighed. It was time to accept that in the next twenty short years she either had to give up her home or commit to a decade of service in the knighthood.

Continuing to fret, she stretched out her wings and glided to the outcropping of rocks where the river met the lake. The sun slipped away as if it felt the burden of Lueetha's troubles and wanted no part in them. The moon came out and, with it, Mati. She flopped onto the rocks, splashing the distracted dragon with clear, almost snow-cold water.

"Wanna fish?" asked the river maiden. Her scales glowed a soft purple in the moonlight.

It was difficult to say whether she was asking if Lueetha wanted to fish with her or was offering her an already caught fish. Either way, Lueetha was in no mood for the salmon that tinted her soft spots, like her throat and belly, pink. "No."

"No fun." The maiden pouted.

"It's the humans' fault. They require my service or my departure and both are repugnant to me."

"Or you could have a child."

"That's even worse. The whole process of finding a partner and creating and caring for a hatchling…tedious is the only word for it."

"Romance isn't supposed to be a process. It's supposed to be fun."

Lueetha sniffed. Before either of them continued the conversation, something rippled the smooth water of the lake, disturbing the reflection of the mountains and moon. Mati slipped under the water. When she resurfaced her eyes were wide.

"Poachers. At the north side of the Fungi Forest."

Mati scrambled onto her back and Lueetha unfurled her wings. As the only dragon left in the Shimmering Mountains, the responsibility of ensuring the humans complied with their side of the deal fell to her.

They found a group of people dressed as hunters and carrying a bundle that was too large to be a beaver or fox but also too small to be a bear or moose.

"It's Herb," Mati yelled at her.

"So it is." Lueetha floated towards the group.

"They're taking our wizard!" said Mati with more urgency.

"He's not a wizard."

"But his beard."

"Lots of humans have beards. Look at the one carrying his feet." It was easy to see the feet carrier's beard as he was looking up at them and yelling at the others to run.

"Remember that time we saw him flying?" asked Mati.

"He was falling." Lueetha half-flapped her wings, keeping up with the men below. "He broke his foot."

"But it healed so fast."

"Because the Witches of Windswept Wood treated it."

"So you're going to let them take him because you don't believe he's a real wizard?"

"Of course not. Even if he's just a weird old man, no one gets away with kidnapping weird old men from my mountains." She landed in front of the would-be kidnappers, crushing a whole swath of ferns as she did so. She opened her jaws to tell them off, but they had already dropped Herb and scattered.

"Are you alright?" asked Mati, slipping off Lueetha's back and untying Herb's bare and leather-like hands and feet. A few of the wildflowers had fallen from his braided beard, and his gaze was a little unfocused, but then his gaze was often a little unfocused.

"I am what I am," he said, which was as close to a real answer as they were going to get.

"Hey, there might be something you can help Lueetha with," said Mati.

"The mountain's chosen keeper," he said.

Mati looked to Lueetha, eyebrows wriggling. Lueetha knew that the ridiculous facial expression meant "See, he is a wizard!" just as she knew that anyone could have guessed her problems today. The knights came on the same day every five years.

"Your dad's vision," said Mati. "When will the mountains choose? Is there anything we can do to hasten it?"

"It will happen when the time is right."

"And when will that be?" asked Lueetha.

"When the mountains sing again and the adopted becomes the caretaker."

While Mati muttered, "So wise," Lueetha frowned at the non-answer. It was just vague enough that if and when the mountain chose a keeper, it would most likely apply. Herb's choice of words gave her a different idea for fulfilling the covenant, though.

"Mati, can you send a message to my sister?"

"Sure."

"Tell her I need a child. There must be an excess of those in the Caterpillar Hills since that's why the other dragons moved away."

"You're going to give someone else's child to the knighthood?" Mati frowned.

"It can be one that no one else wants."

Mati's frown deepened.

Yes, it was a little cruel to sacrifice ten years of another dragon's life to the knighthood, but it allowed Lueetha to stay in the mountains protecting them for as long as she lived. The trade-off was well worth it.

"I'll prepare them," she said, trying to appease the river maiden. She knew little about combat, but that's why books existed. "They'll be fine."

* * *

In the Caterpillar Hills, Polanna pondered the message she'd received through the riverfolk network. Lueetha needed a child and well, there was one sure way to find yourself with a hatchling. After years of protests, Lueetha finally wanted her sister to set her up on a date. Polanna took flight, pulling her mate from a game of duck, duck, dragon with their children. She needed information about his single friends.

* * *

Nickloss's heart skipped a beat as he soared through the Shimmering Mountains for the first time in 80 years. He'd agreed to Polanna's unexpected request because he'd needed a fresh start and because he remembered Lueetha's emerald scales and her passion for protecting the mountains.

Scales shined to a brilliant amber, he landed outside her cave. "Hello?" he called, wondering how she wanted to be courted.

"Come in," she invited, which probably meant less formal.

He found her in a cozy cavern with books along one wall, a thick rug on the floor, and a blazing fire in the hearth.

"I've got a few tips for you," she said, peering at a book.

Very informal then. Heat filled his belly.

"So you don't die," she continued.

Nickloss opened his mouth and then closed it and then opened it again. He blew a few blue sparks her way, rising to the challenge.

Lueetha twisted her head to look at him. "Nickloss?" She eyed the blue sparks. Her nostrils flared. "There's been a misunderstanding. I'm not looking for a mate."

"Oh." Oh no. He slunk backward, wishing the shadows would consume him and his embarrassment.

"It's not *you* specifically. My sister misunderstood. Let's go outside."

* * *

There was an old saying: Ask the riverfolk to deliver a message and prepare for a dozen angry turnip farmers at your door. Nickloss wasn't an angry turnip farmer but his presence was just as disappointing. Judging by the way he rested his head on the ground, he also found the situation disappointing.

Lueetha finished explaining that she'd wanted her sister to send her a child, not the means to make one, and waited for him to leave. Mati, curious and more sympathetic, stroked one of his head spikes.

"You can leave now," said Lueetha, giving him a nudge. Mati glared at her.

Nickloss sighed. "I was nervous about coming here, but when I flew in this morning everything felt right."

"Of course," said Lueetha, matter-of-factly. "This is your home."

He shook his head. "Or it was just the relief of leaving behind my crumbling life in Caterpillar Hills."

"You don't have to go back there." Now it was Lueetha's turn to sigh. "You came to help. Stay here. You can watch over the mountains when I get kicked out."

"I…appreciate that."

Mati jumped out of the way as Nickloss raised his head and spread his wings.

"You're leaving?" she asked.

"I'll be back, but not until I've found a child."

* * *

Nickloss returned a week later, swooping through the cloud-studded sky with glee. He didn't seem to have another dragon with him, but he had to have good news. Lueetha paced the ground as he descended.

"So?" she asked.

He twisted his head and pulled off the pack that had been snuggly settled between his shoulder blades. Gentling setting it on the ground, he nodded for her to open it.

Her breath caught as a beam of sunlight glanced off a smooth white and brown-speckled surface. "An egg?"

"Yes! When no one would give up their hatchlings—"

"You stole one?"

"What? No! I asked the riverfolk if they'd heard of any abandoned children."

Lueetha was only half listening. She stared at the egg. "What am I supposed to—how am I—how do I care for this thing?"

"What thing?" asked Mati, popping out of the lake. "Ooo, pretty."

Lueetha swung her tail out, wrapping it around the maiden to keep her from putting her cold, wet hands on it.

"Look at those motherly instincts," said Nickloss.

"Instincts? You expect me to ferry this young dragon from the precipice of life and death that it so precariously teeters on with something as ill-defined as *instincts*?"

"That was the plan, yes."

She glared at him.

"Maybe the other woman here can help?"

Lueetha unfurled a wing, blocking his attempt at a hasty departure. She turned her gaze to Mati.

"Riverfolk don't make babies like this."

"Okay, here's what we're going to do," said Lueetha, realizing she needed to make some decisions. A tiny life and her home were on the line.

"We?" asked Nickloss. "But—"

"You brought this thing here, you're going to help."

"Yes." He bowed his head. "Of course."

"Take it inside. To the chamber with the hearth, where we interacted last time." She turned to Mati. "You're going to send a message to the Witches of the Windswept Wood and I'm going to craft it very carefully to make sure it can't be misinterpreted on the way there."

* * *

Lueetha survived the next days only because the witches sent her potions and advice, and Mati and Nickloss visited often. As the days turned into weeks, the others became anxious for the egg to hatch and Lueetha became anxious that it would hatch. Taking care of an egg wasn't so bad.

At least that's what she'd thought until she woke up to find it a few paces from where she'd left it and with a crack in it.

Her heart raced. She'd broken it somehow.

Without a thought for the wildflowers, she flung herself at Mati in the meadow.

"Wanna fish?" asked the river maiden.

"No," moaned Lueetha. "I've doomed myself and you and these mountains. The egg. I must have knocked it in my sleep. It has a crack in it."

Mati's expression of concern turned into a grin. She laughed and ran to the lake. Lueetha dug her claws into the dirt. She'd injured the egg *and* caused her friend to have a nervous breakdown. Mati returned and pushed ineffectively on Lueetha's hind leg.

"Come on," she said. "We should be there when the hatchling breaks out."

* * *

"Ooooo," said Mati, as a part of the hatchling—it was difficult to say which part—broke free.

"Oh?" asked Nickloss as another part of it emerged.

"Huh." Lueetha stared at the small creature that stumbled away from the broken pieces of shell. She'd imagined that the hatchling would look just like an adult dragon but about twenty times smaller. It did not. "It's kind of ugly."

"Shhh," said Mati. "He's adorable."

"He? How can you tell?"

"It's obvious."

"It is?" asked Lueetha, feeling very out of her depth.

"Can I hold him?" asked Mati.

"Sure."

"No, you don't." Nickloss flicked his tail, knocking the wind out of Mati as she sprung forward. "His mother gets to hold him first."

They stood there for a moment.

"Oh. You mean me." Lueetha approached the hatchling with caution. She encircled it, just as she had when it was an egg, close but not quite touching it. It was wet with egg goop. She wished it was cleaner.

"What are you going to name him?" asked Mati.

The small creature stumbled and fell against Lueetha, smearing the goop across one of her legs. She suppressed a shudder. Holding him away from her with one claw, she breathed a stream of warm air at him. Cleaned and dried to her satisfaction, she released him. He nestled against her. Fluffy and mostly white, he looked even less like a dragon than before.

"Awww," said Mati and Nickloss in unison.

"You need to give him a name," Mati insisted.

"Fine," Lueetha considered it. "Cloud."

* * *

"Mom," said Cloud, wiggling around behind a tapestry covered in a geometric jewel-toned pattern. They sat in a chamber deep within the cave, tucked away from the snowstorm outside. She was glad to have a break from Mati and Nickloss, if only because it meant they didn't have enough players for duck, duck, dragon. The game was Cloud's favorite but it was becoming a bit awkward to play as it became more and more obvious that Cloud was not a dragon.

"Hmm?" Lueetha looked up from a book recounting the history of the knighthood.

"Can I paint on the walls?" His long white tail with grayish-black spots swished out from behind the decoration.

"Absolutely not."

"Why not? Someone else painted here."

Lueetha sighed and pulled away the tapestry, revealing the marred wall and a very ruffled Cloud. He shook himself, fluffing his light pink feathers and his fur.

"This painting is…" Lueetha wasn't sure how to explain what a prophecy was to a small child. "Special."

"Why?"

"It was painted by a wizard. It tells a story."

"What story?"

"Take a step back and you can see it."

He stepped back, then she pulled him a few more paces away.

"What's happening here?" asked Cloud, stretching out his wing to brush the spot that depicted a flock of griffins leaving the Shimmering Mountains. "Who are they?"

"Oh, hmm," Lueetha hemmed and hawed. "That's the middle of the story. Let's start at the beginning." She pointed to the first painting on the wall. "Many years ago, these mountains were full of people. Riverfolk, rockfolk, flowerfolk, gnomes, humans, dragons. These people lived in relative harmony with each other and the mountains."

"Where are all those people now?"

"I'm getting there. Back when everyone lived here there was someone called the keeper." She pointed to a depiction of a griffin. The griffin on her wall had brown feathers. Cloud's feathers were mostly pink with a black band spanning his eyes and the tips of his wings. "The last keeper was…a small dragon. As was the keeper before."

Lueetha paused, waiting to see if Cloud had questions about why the small dragons looked so different. When he only looked at her expectantly, she continued the story. Someday he would realize that he looked more like the griffins in the paintings than he did Lueetha or Nickloss. When that happened, it'd be best if he thought of himself as a small dragon. She wanted to make sure he felt like he belonged and was willing to dedicate a decade of his life to the knighthood when the time came.

For the rest of that winter, Cloud loved nothing more than the story of the chosen keeper. He loved to reenact the discord that had broken out when the last keeper had died before naming a new one. The humans had tried to claim the mountains for their resources and the dragons had tried to claim them for their home. The other peoples had wanted to avoid a war. They'd gone in circles trying to determine the new keeper. Eventually Herb's father, a verified wizard, had seen a vision. The mountain would choose a new keeper when there was someone worthy of the title. Until then, the peoples agreed to the covenant. It avoided war.

When spring came, Cloud and Lueetha spent their afternoons at the highest peak, where the next keeper was supposed to be chosen. While Cloud talked about how the mountain was waiting for the perfect person—someone that was patient, good at peacemaking, and loved the mountains more than anyone else—to be the next keeper, Lueetha enjoyed the breeze and the bright green of new grass and leaves.

That summer, the knights came for their usual five-year visit. She left Cloud with Mati while she and Nickloss met with them. They pretended to be mates, because otherwise, Nickloss would also need a child to sacrifice to the knighthood, and they sent the knights back with a request. Lueetha wanted it in writing that an adopted child could enter the knighthood and fulfill that part of the covenant.

* * *

"Mom," said Cloud, now eight. "When will I breathe fire like you and Uncle Nick? I want to burn something until it's dead."

"Cloud, what have I told you about killing?"

"I'd eat whatever I burned."

Lueetha shook her head. She didn't know where this violence was coming from, but wherever it was, she gave thanks every day that griffins didn't breathe fire. "You won't be burning anything until you can show that you're more responsible."

When it wasn't fire, Cloud pestered her about scales. "When will I get them, Mom?"

"Some dragons don't."

"Oh," Cloud hung his head.

"What do you need scales for?"

"To protect me when I fight evil sorcerers!"

Lueetha stayed up that night melting a few pieces of metal from her hoard. She supposed his desire for scales was a good thing. That kind of attitude would certainly make him a good fit for the knighthood. She formed the hot metal into a chainmail of silver scales.

Cloud loved it. He refused to take it off to fly up to the mountain peak or take a bath, and Lueetha let him have his way.

* * *

A few months before Cloud turned ten, the knights came to visit again.

"Can I talk to them?" he asked, leaping from the cliffs by the lake and unfurling his wings. "I want to know how many sorcerers they've exploded."

"Probably none," said Lueetha. She sighed, snatched him from the air, and placed him by the cave's entrance. She wanted to keep him away from the knights until she had a written statement that an adopted child could satisfy the covenant. "You stay here, Cloud."

"But—"

"This isn't up for discussion." With a flap of her wings, she soared down the side of the mountain to meet the knights halfway. Pebbles and dirt went everywhere as she landed hard in front of them.

"Dragon Lueetha, we come on behalf of King Reginol the Third to review the terms and conditions of the Covenant between—"

"Yes, I know all that. What about the question I asked last time?"

The lead knight clapped the back of a wispy man beside him. "Notary, you're up."

The notary opened a hefty book that must have weighed half as much as he did and pursed his lips. "There are requirements."

"Such as?"

"The adopted child must join the knighthood willingly. They must be at least sixteen years of age. They must be healthy. This includes good eyesight, hearing, and mobility. They must not be prone to illness or moodiness. It's preferable if the child is male, but a strong female is acceptable."

"Is that it?" asked Lueetha, trying to keep a straight face. Cloud fit those requirements. "Can I get an official statement in writing?"

"Upon completion of a thorough physical examination, yes."

"I see," said Lueetha. That was a problem. "I'm afraid that today won't work. My son is out hunting with Nickloss."

"No, I'm not. I'm here!" said Cloud, leaping out of the bushes behind them. Leaves stuck to his feathers.

Lueetha let out a deep breath and wrapped a tail around him before he bounced into the lead knight and started bombarding him with questions about evil sorcerers.

"This is your child?" asked the notary.

"He's not a dragon," muttered one of the knights.

Lueetha stilled, watching for Cloud's reaction.

"Sure I am," chirped Cloud.

"Let's go," shouted the lead knight.

"But you haven't examined me," said Cloud. "I'm all the things you listed. My eyes and ears are great, and I never get sick."

"Yes, well, you're lacking in a few other areas. You're not cut out for the job."

"That's not fair! You don't *know* that. Give me a trial."

"That could be arranged," said the notary scribbling notes.

The lead knight frowned at him. "But we're supposed to—"

The notary shut the book with a clap and addressed Lueetha. "Five years from now we'll send the requirements of the trial. Your son will have five more years to prepare. If he proves himself worthy of the knighthood, you can stay in the mountains. If not, you must leave."

"Fine," said Lueetha, knowing the notary had just sealed the fate of the mountains. With Cloud still wrapped in her tail, she flapped her wings, leaving the humans behind. She took her son to the place where the river and lake met. They only had ten years left to enjoy the sunbaked rocks and the cool breeze floating down the valley.

"Are you angry?" asked Cloud.

"Not at you." Lueetha sighed. "But there are some things you should know."

Lueetha started as cold water splashed her.

"Hey," said Mati, flopping onto the rocks next to them. "Wanna fish?"

"Are you offering us fish?" asked Cloud. "Or are you asking if we'll go fishing with you?"

"Both. But also neither."

"Hey," said Lueetha before they got sidetracked by whatever that meant. "I'm trying to have a serious conversation with my son."

"Just pretend I'm not even here. I'm just a rock." Mati pressed her lips together, pulled her knees up to her chest, and rested her chin on them.

"Cloud—"

A dark shadow crossed over them and Lueetha groaned as Nickloss landed beside Mati. "How'd the meeting go?" he asked, folding his leathery wings against his sides.

"She's trying to have a serious conversation with her son," said Mati.

"I thought you were going to be quiet." A little smoke wafted from Lueetha's nostrils. "I need you two to either be quiet or leave."

"We'll be quiet," said Nickloss, chin tilted in curiosity.

Lueetha held her breath for a moment and waited to see if anyone else was going to pop from the ground or something. She let it out. "Cloud—"

"What's up?" asked Herb, strolling out of the nearby glade.

"Herb!" cried everyone except Lueetha. She gave them all a look that made them hang their heads.

"No one has time to hear about your dreams," said Lueetha before the hermit started blabbing. "Sit down and be quiet with the others."

He took a cross-legged seat next to Nickloss.

With all of the inhabitants of the Shimmering Mountains quiet and expectant, Lueetha proceeded. "Cloud, you're adopted."

Herb's eyes widened, Mati sputtered something unintelligible, and Nickloss said, "You've never been one for delicacy, have you?"

Trying to tune out the others, Lueetha watched her son.

"I know," he chirped.

"Yes, well that's not all. You're not a dragon, you're a griffin."

"I know."

Lueetha paused with her head tilted to one side. She'd expected to be answering a lot of questions at this point in the conversation, but instead, she had a bunch of questions. First and foremost on her mind, "You know?"

Cloud's wings fluttered. "There may not be any griffins here, but there's plenty in my books."

"Then why did you suggest a trial?"

"Because I want to protect our home from the humans. No offense, Herb."

"None taken, little guy," said Herb, plucking a flower from his beard and letting the breeze whisk it away. "Men believe they're meant to conquer nature or it will conquer them. It's difficult for them to set aside that fear and live in balance with the natural world."

"So wise," whispered Mati.

"They haven't learned how to feel the truth here." Herb pressed a hand to his chest.

"*So* wise," repeated Mati.

"Okay," said Lueetha. "Do you two need to leave?"

They shook their heads.

"I'm glad you want to protect our home," she continued, "but they're not going to take you now that they know you're a griffin."

"They agreed to a trial. They have to take me when I complete it."

"*If* you complete it. They plan to make it impossible for anyone but a dragon."

"But I am a dragon," said Cloud sitting up straighter and pressing his beak to his chest. "Here."

An unexpected warmth ran through Lueetha. If she had been forced to identify where it was coming from, she would have reluctantly pointed to her chest. She clenched her jaw.

"I know I'm not as big as a dragon, but I'm going to train," said Cloud jumping to his feet. "I'll get strong, and I'll be the best swooper ever."

"Very well," said Lueetha. The test would still be impossible, but her son didn't have to learn that today.

* * *

Lueetha threw aside another biology book and slunk through the caves. She reached the entrance and breathed in the fresh air. For the most part, she felt that she'd been a good mother to Cloud, but there was one area where she sorely lacked the knowledge to properly guide him. She could read all the books in the world on anatomy and biology, but what she really needed was a griffin.

"Greetings."

Lueetha started. Two figures stood at her feet, a human woman in armor and a griffin with brown-gray feathers. She blinked.

"Are you a fully grown, adult griffin?" she asked.

"Yes?"

"Good. I need your help."

"What's going on?" asked Cloud, joining them. Over the last years, he'd gone through a transformation from a cuddly ball of fluff to a sleek, mature griffin. "Are you knights?"

"Yes," said the woman. "We're here with the requirements for the trial, but if you need aid—"

"Aid with what?" asked Cloud.

"You," said Lueetha.

"Me?"

"You've matured over the last year. Not just mentally and emotionally, but also physically. There are probably new feelings and urges stirring in you—"

"Mom!" said Cloud, ducking his head behind a wing. "Now is *not* the time."

"Yes, it is. We never get other griffins up here." She turned to the adult griffin. "Please, go ahead."

"Ah, hmmm," he said, feathers slightly ruffled. He looked at his partner.

The other knight's lips were a tight line with one corner curving up. She nodded at him to continue.

"Well…um…"

"Shouldn't we talk about the test?" mumbled Cloud.

"This is important," said Lueetha.

"It is," said the adult griffin. "But um…it's also important that your son is comfortable with the conversation. If you don't mind, my aunt and uncle have wanted to visit the Shimmering Mountains for ages. I'm sure they'd be happy to answer any questions that your son has."

"That sounds great," said Cloud quickly.

Lueetha thought the sooner he knew about these things the better, but she saw the embarrassment in his stance and supposed it could wait.

The knights described the requirements of the trial, which included setting various things on fire, transporting several knights at once, and flying through oncoming volleys of arrows and spears. All of these things fell within Lueetha's expectations of tasks that dragons could easily perform but would be impossible for a griffin.

Lueetha and Cloud sat in silence as the knights glided away into the deep blue of twilight. She sighed. She was going to miss this place.

Cloud got up. Instead of going to the cave, he walked towards the lake.

"Where are you going?"

"I want to see how many of Mati's sisters I can carry." Cloud faced her. In the moonlight, his long light pink neck and black eyes were regal and full of confidence. "I have a lot of training to do if I'm going to become a dragon knight."

* * *

Once Mati and her sisters heard about the trial, word spread quickly. Not necessarily the word that Cloud would be participating in a trial to become a dragon knight, but various words about him and fire and feats of strength. People started journeying to the mountains to see if the rumors were true. Many stayed to help Cloud.

The griffins that came taught him about flight feathers and how to care for his plumage to reduce drag. His skill at flight improved significantly. When the Witch of Windswept Wood— there was only one these days—came, she made him fire potions. A team of gnomes and dwarves made him gauntlets to shoot the fire potions.

The potions and the gauntlets made Lueetha's stomach twist. Not only would the trial be difficult, but it would also be dangerous. She commissioned healing potions and armor to protect Cloud. She pushed him to train with any visitors that were experienced in battle, knowing they would have the best advice to help him stay safe.

Spectators filled the mountains when the day of the trial came. More than a hundred riverfolk bobbed in the lake and griffins soared above. Both groups seemed to be trying to outshout each other in encouragement. The team of craftspeople that had worked on the gauntlets and armor stood in the meadow. Even Lueetha's sister Polanna had brought the dragons of the Caterpillar Hills to watch. Mati, Nickloss, and Herb flanked Cloud, as he went to meet with the procession of knights. Lueetha lagged behind.

The knights gave a lengthy review of the requirements of the test and then, with the sounding of a trumpet, it commenced. Cloud soared through the sky, letting arrows clink off his armor and dodging larger projectiles. He carried five knights on his back while weaving through obstacles and lighting straw targets on fire. He performed with grace and strength that would make any dragon or griffin or any other people proud.

When he finished, the lead knight clapped him on the wing. "Welcome to our ranks."

The valley rang with cheers.

"Your first quest," said the knight as the noise began to lower, "will be to join us against a rogue sorcerer at Withering Hollow. Please make your goodbyes brief."

Cloud made his way around the crowd, thanking everyone who had helped him and cheered him on. At the end of each brief conversation, he bent his long neck towards the ground in a bow. Lueetha's belly felt cold as he approached her.

"I did it, mom," he said, head held high.

She nodded.

"I know you don't want a sappy goodbye so I'll keep it short. I love you and I'll make sure to send you messages as often as possible." He started to turn away.

"Cloud—" She cleared her throat. "You don't have to do this. I don't want you to feel pressured into—"

"I know." He trotted over to her and briefly leaned against her front leg. "I'll miss you, too."

The chill in her belly spread to her chest as she watched him go. Polanna landed next to her.

"I know it's hard, but you're doing the right thing," said her sister.

"It doesn't feel right." Lueetha sunk to the ground, letting her whole body from the tip of her tail to her chin rest against it.

Polanna shifted her haunches a little. "You know, I thought Nickloss was crazy when he decided to stay here even after you rejected him, but I can feel it now. This place is home, and I believe that many of the others gathered today felt it, too. You and Cloud are doing the right thing by protecting this place until the next keeper is chosen."

Polanna sat with her in silence well after everyone else left.

* * *

A few months after Cloud's departure, Lueetha lay on the rocks where the river met the lake. An orange leaf drifted on the water until Mati popped up. It stuck to the river maiden's head.

"Wanna fish?" she asked, but there was no real conviction behind the words.

Lueetha shook her head. "Any word from Cloud?"

"He says he's doing fine."

"And?" asked Lueetha. When Cloud had first left, he'd sent long messages home detailing his adventures. As time went by those messages had gotten shorter and shorter until Lueetha found herself relying on gossip from the riverfolk network for the most up-to-date information on her son.

"Sounds like he's being sent to Tess's Hollow. He's supposed to lure out someone either called Rotting Ham or Trotting Lamb or maybe it's Rotting Lamb. Apparently, this guy has a vendetta against griffins."

Lueetha curled in on herself. Cloud had only been a knight for a few months and he was being assigned the most dangerous quests. "This isn't right," she said.

"Maybe the mountain will choose a keeper soon," said Mati, trying to be optimistic. They'd had this conversation a hundred times. If the mountain chose a keeper, then the covenant would be null and Cloud could come home.

Lueetha snorted. "It's been a hundred years. The mountain isn't choosing another keeper anytime soon. I mean really, the perfect leader? It's a fairytale. My son is in danger, doing what has to be done to protect the mountains while we sit around waiting for a fairytale to come true. It's not right. I should be taking care of him not the other way around… Oh."

"What?" asked Mati.

"Do you remember what Herb said?"

"About not trusting beavers that claim to know where the best mushrooms are?"

"No."

"About feeling the truth here?" asked Mati, raising a hand to her chest.

"No, something about the mountains choosing a keeper when the adopted becomes the caretaker."

"Oh," Mati's eyes went wide. "I'll start spreading the word to meet at the summit."

* * *

The word that the mountains would choose a new keeper spread quickly. Seven days later, a crowd that was bigger than the one that had come to see Cloud's trial met at the highest summit. Lueetha scanned the orange-colored sky for her son. She'd requested permission for him to be here and it had been accepted.

Nickloss nudged her, pointing to a small speck on the horizon.

Warmth blossomed in her chest as Cloud glided into view. A little of it cooled as she noticed the dents in his armor and the three knights on his back. He landed and she let out a hot stream of fire, quieting the crowd.

"Cloud, please come here." She pointed to a spot in front of her. It was the place where the paintings on her cave wall depicted the new keeper being chosen.

Cloud complied, standing at the center of the summit. Only the slightest ruffle at the black tips of his wings betrayed his confusion. Otherwise, he looked confident and majestic with the sun glinting off his armor.

Lueetha cleared her throat again, more for herself than anyone else. "For the last hundred years, there has been a covenant in place between the dragons and the king. Only one thing has the power to dissolve this covenant and that is the mountain's choosing of a new keeper. I propose that my son Cloud is worthy of the title."

Cloud twisted his head around to stare at her with one wide, black eye, and whispers broke out among the crowd. Lueetha plowed on. "The last three keepers were griffins, and no one cares about this place more deeply than Cloud. It's evident in the way he's trained over the last five years and his willingness to dedicate a decade of his life to the knighthood."

"But doesn't the mountain have to choose him?" asked one of the griffins.

"Well, yes." Lueetha had hoped that while she spoke the air around Cloud would start sparkling or something.

"How do we know if that's happened?" asked a knight.

"Um...well..." Lueetha looked at Herb, and everyone turned to him. He said something in his soft-spoken voice that most people couldn't hear.

"He says you'll know it when you see it," said Mati, loudly.

"Does anyone see anything?" asked a gnome whose view was blocked by a dragon.

"I don't," said one of the knights. "This is a waste of time. Let's go."

Head down, Cloud stepped towards the knight. Lueetha hadn't noticed it before, but not only was Cloud's armor dented, his feathers were a paler pink than usual, and scar tissue ran down the side of his right haunch.

"He's not going anywhere," said Lueetha, curling her tail around her son and pulling him behind her.

"Mom," he squawked. "It's fine."

"No, it's not." Smoke wafted from her snout. "I won't allow this to go on any longer."

The knight that had spoken before folded his arms. "Does this mean you're forfeiting the mountain to the king?"

Everyone fell quiet. A soft breeze swept over the summit, bending blades of grass, fluttering feathers, cooling hot jaws, and ruffling hair. It touched every person gathered in one way or another.

"No," said Lueetha softly. Then with more conviction. "I'll take Cloud's place."

"That technically goes against the agreement," said the knight.

"Then we'll make a new one. Are you really going to turn down the opportunity to have a dragon working for you?"

"Hey," said Cloud.

Lueetha turned to him. "I don't mean to belittle your talent. You're better than I ever expected, but you also deserve better."

"No, look." Cloud stared at her tail, still wrapped around him.

The scales pressed against him shimmered a soft blue. The shimmer traveled up her tail and spread over her legs, then her spine and sides. She lost sight of it there but felt the cool tingle at the tips of her head spikes.

"I don't understand," she said.

"The mountains choose you."

* * *

Lueetha belonged in the Shimmering Mountains. She felt it when she soared with the dragons of Caterpillar Hills, welcoming them back to their home. She knew it when she saw the riverfolk fishing or gnomes searching for berries and when griffins called out to her from their new nests in the cliffs. It was good having so many people to speak to these days, even if she'd rather have a little more time with her son. He was as busy with the newcomers as she was, but he was happy and safe. They both were and that, more than anything else, made the Shimmering Mountains feel like home.

Sheep Rarely Wear Gold

Mike Jack Stoumbos

A sudden clanging cuts through the dull, resonating dome of my stone encasing. Hardly worth opening my eyes.

I feel no signs of precious metals between my rough skin and the smooth floor. I am still shielded from the sun, and no food is being presented to me. My stone shackles have not expired with time. No reason not to return to sleep.

The clanging sounds again, this time closer, hard to pinpoint along winding staircases. But something else…not just the urgency of heightened breathing, but new footsteps. Listening, I pick out distant shouts along with other sounds of impact, but many layers of earth away. I have heard reports of weapons fire before; perhaps this is no different. But the timbre of some voices strikes me as distinct from those of my current jailers or previous captors. Voices unlike any I've known for several revolutions of this planet. Though not altogether unfamiliar…

However, that symphony fades before I'm fully conscious. Perhaps it is just the remnant of a dream, an old trace or echo, concocted by a mind that has not yet changed to stone itself.

I am tired. Better to dream anyway.

* * *

I barely feel I've closed my eyes a wink before the clanging jars me again.

I squeeze my eyes shut tighter. I clench my foreclaws—old habit, older than the civilization that keeps me—but a bad habit, for it pains my wrists. I try to relax my grip, which is under *my* control. Silently, I will my interrupters to leave my door closed and go away. Not under my control.

The lock rattles; the door opens.

I feel my nostrils flare in frustration, but that alone won't tell them I'm awake.

The jailer opening my door is tittering something unintelligible, but another party suddenly forms the sounds, "Oh my God."

My eyelids fly open, and my gaze falls upon the shocked expression frozen on the face of a species I have not seen for a very long time, but one which I could not forget.

I twist my neck to get a better look at the newest visitor with both my eyes. My foreclaws are pinned in place, and the figure stands well beyond their reach anyway.

It is bipedal in form, wearing a new kind of bulky armor that is not metallic in appearance, with a cap on the head and no fur on the face. I could easily swallow it whole, suit and all, and am hungry enough to do so.

It must've been less than a quarter the mass of one of my captors, who walk on four legs but also have two manipulating arms. One such giant, hairy arm holds the door open for the comparatively spindly biped, who boldly approaches me. The captor has its bulk planted in the doorway, as if expecting me to attempt escape—a laughable concept for many reasons, were I in a laughing mood.

I stare at the newcomer. An intruder, yes, but with countenance nobler than a jailer, a voice more serene and melodic than that insufferable chittering. I see in its eyes—which, compared to the oaf at the threshold, are very like mine—a most inviting sense of wonder. There is fear, and confusion, and that capriciousness of short-lived beings. Regardless, I am immediately charmed by the wonder.

The newcomer speaks more words in that comforting timbre, a combination of musings spoken to itself and then to the being behind it—its words to my jailer filter through some manipulation installed in the armor, before a speaker emulates their translated chitter sounds.

Wer emerges from my long memory. Then another name they called themselves: *Mann.*

"Mann," I say, my deep voice rattling out through my lately unused throat.

Even poorly vocalized, my utterance startles the newcomer.

It regards me, its face twisted into emotions I have not considered in far too long to discern. Its lips move before it replies, as if trying to find the right word. It looks down to a rectangle fitting in the palm of its hand—more likely a tool than a weapon—then back up to me.

It says some words I do not place, some syllables difficult to imbue with meaning in my tired and depleted state.

Then, in a sure display of wisdom, it indicates its torso and slowly says, "Human," for my benefit.

"Human," I rumble in echo. I cannot move my arm very far, but I can tip my chin toward my long neck to indicate myself. Straining to recall, I ask, "Ormr? Wyrm?"

Human gasps and places gloved hands in front of its mouth. The glistening eyes strike another familiar note within me, slough away another layer of dust in my recollection. The vocalized, chopping gasps represent elation. Apparently, it is a laughing matter, though not in irony or derision. Human removes hands from bared teeth—an open-mouth grin—and dubs me, "Dragon."

Dragon. Yes, that sounds right. Perhaps some had already begun to use this word by the time we left.

Though separated by eons and stars, more than enough reason to speak different languages, I behold a kindred spirit, a traveler and a scholar.

This is how we make our second *first contact.*

* * *

I do not understand the majority of its words—perhaps my memory is fading, but I believe it an entirely different language than when last I knew their kind. I do not understand everything that is said, but I interpret the open palm to mean, "Wait."

So I shall wait.

I do not have much choice. There is not strength enough in my system to break through my stone cuffs, else I would have done so countless days ago, perhaps hundreds of this planet's years.

No, within the cavern that is too cramped for my wings but which has become permanent home as well as unwanted cell, I am already resigned to wait. But I can choose my demeanor. If I wait with bitterness or anxiousness, perhaps it could damage my impression on the human and rob me of my chance to work with them. To entreat them. If I remember their behavior correctly—that is the most tenuous *if*—the presence of the human could be my salvation.

I resolved to wait with dignity.

Again, the human does not leave me alone for long.

I recognize its voice, growing in volume and excitement as it approaches my door, then by its footfalls down the stairs. But not just one set, several, wearing similar boots, with similar gait. I would guess at least four, in addition to the harsher clicking claws of my jailer.

The jailer unlatches and opens the door, but I only have to observe its grotesque face with the compound eyes briefly before the human pushes past, accompanied by five others.

I am even more certain now that they are human, from the green blue world in that distant system. They have subtle variations in height and the skin tone of their faces. Their suits—a kind of flexible and probably adaptive armor—are identical, save for the occasional difference in color patches in the right breast or shoulder. One wears a face plate and I judge by the bulky neck guard that the rest of their suits can deploy the same protection.

When the greeter speaks, I'm certain it is the same one I observed before—maybe a day ago, or maybe only the space of a few breaths. "Hello, Dragon."

I press down onto my elbows so I may raise my chest and take on a regal posture with my neck. I attempt to pitch my voice similarly to theirs, to sound full without shouting—though, I admit, I am out of practice. "Hello, Mann."

Another human speaks, then another, using words I don't understand—their current language.

My jailer remains at the door, its upper torso partially in the doorway, the head tilting, the mandibles twitching. It makes some comment with its unpleasant screeching and clicking. Then, one human turns around and addresses it, again through a filter, turning the pleasant human speech into the high-pitched alien language.

This exchange sounds harsh, but I am biased. Either way, the jailer retreats and allows the humans to remain, leaving the door open. The door isn't even big enough for my head, let alone my shoulders, but so rarely is it left open that this, too, is an odd treat.

The human that shooed away my jailer turns back to me. This one is not the tallest, but I understand in its countenance authority. It is in charge. And though it does not use the old language of their people, it repeats the same phrase slowly, three times, to be sure I will retain it. "We come in peace."

I can't help but perceive this positively, regardless of the true meaning, for I've noticed something else: the insignia on this leader's right breast glows with an unmistakable luster. The perfection that is gold.

The first greeter still stands in front, and faces me fully to translate the repeated words, a declaration of peaceful intentions. This human is the shortest of the group of six, with neither the palest nor the darkest complexion. It does appear to have the widest eyes, although that could be a temporary condition, even an affectation. The greeter holds a small object I've seen before, partially transparent and rectangular, which illuminates its face with a pleasant blue glow. It refers to this object before and after speaking. A visual translator. These humans have taken pains and preparations to speak with other species.

The greeter identifies the group, seemingly as part of a larger organization of either explorers or conquerors—some of the vocabulary is imperfect without context. The proper nouns assigned to the individuals are accompanied by rank and hierarchy. I can interpret their word for "Commander" to refer to the leader. I also understand the role of what they call a "first contact specialist," which the greeter assigns to itself before adding the proper noun designation, "Georgia Ballantine."

That name I make a point of remembering. Though it does not wear any visible gold, I shall benefit most from the value of this relationship.

I close my eyes and nod my head low, a formal bow.

Georgia Ballantine asks, "What is your name?"

With my head still lowered, I return, "What name do you give me?"

Silence. I keep my eyes closed, I show patience. I can be patient and still for ten of their lifetimes or more—though I am uncertain of how long their lifetimes are now.

I crack one eyelid when I hear voices again—in their language, to each other, not to me. Confusion.

The greeter sees that I have opened one eye before I can shut it again. Georgia speaks haltingly, having to consult the transparent translator tool. "We would like to call you by your name. What do you call yourself?"

I consider telling them the usual lie, that they could not possibly pronounce it, but I imagine this greeter would attempt to emulate any growls I produced. So I pay with the truth. "My name is not for me. My name is what *you* address me."

Georgia relays this to the commander, and one of the other humans laughs. I do not recall humans ever laughing at or even questioning their naming of a dragon—or anything else they encounter.

"What do the Sk'vesh call you?" Georgia asks. Stubborn, but informative. I had not even known my captors' species name—unless that is their national name, or the alien word for *jailer.*

"They never named me." I hear my despondency and wish to withdraw and change it as soon as the sound passes over my teeth.

Georgia looks down to the device then back up to me.

One human calls out the sounds, "Space Dragon."

This is addressed to me, and I can hear by the tone that it is a title, albeit an adjective designation before their word for my species—but most names bestowed on me and my kin have been similarly uncreative.

The laughing human laughs again. The commander shushes them. The one with the faceplate seems to sense urgency—and draws a rifle from its back. I have not seen the specific weapon in these hands before, but I am certain it is a weapon, probably the one I heard on the surface.

Are they worried they have offended me? Do they perhaps suspect some violent nature because my jaws are capable of snapping them in half and swallowing them—even though I am imprisoned more than neck's reach away? I wonder what the Sk'vesh told them about me, if they highlighted danger, ferocity—even though the faction of Sk'vesh currently residing above the surface and serving as my jailers were not those who originally captured me, even though I have not had strength to attempt escape or any offensive strikes since they assumed control. Besides, the Sk'vesh people do not seem to value individual life or resent past violence.

I maintain my calm throughout the humans' conversations, some of which is a reprimand for—if I've concluded correctly—mocking my plight.

The greeter speaks with sincerity, again seemingly observant with those wide eyes. "Would you like to be called Space Dragon?"

"That is your name for me."

Thus, I adopt the mantle of Space Dragon and effect initial understanding of the greeter named Georgia.

* * *

Shortly after the initial exchange, the commander leaves, called away to another task—after giving the greeter some verbal directives and summoning two of the six to follow.

I am glad that Georgia remains.

Georgia explains that the other two humans are going to scan me for their research, that they are scientists. And then Georgia asks my permission, respectfully calling me "Space Dragon."

I am…charmed by the notion that I, a prisoner, am asked. I see that one scientist is wary about approaching within my striking arc. They have some sense of distance and precaution. The second scientist stands farther back, with a device ready that might not be a weapon, for it is aimed at its fellow, rather than me. I fear I will never be able to see how it is used.

I graciously allow them forward, using the word "Mann" to refer to the first human.

The greeter corrects me on this, saying to address its kind as "human." Georgia adds, "In fact, I am a woman. Not a man."

That's right! I remember now, these bipedal beings have two sexes for their reproduction. Georgia goes on to tell me that the feminine pronoun is "she," and I feel fortunate that she has not heard me say "it" about any of the others. I further recall that when I last visited, their species displayed a great deal more sexual dimorphism, and hair, clothing, and makeup, as well as body shape. I can observe no difference in the armor they wear now, but

I accept it when she tells me that multiple genders serve on her crew, and I retain that first contact specialist Georgia Ballantine is a woman.

Again, I receive this correction graciously. I do not imagine it will be the last.

During our first day's conversation, several other humans descend the dungeon stairs and enter through the door to see me. Many gasp. Several use similar transparent rectangular devices that make flashes at me—sometimes they do this with their backs to me, so the flash may shine on their faces first and then mine behind them. One kneels, displays a series of orthogonal hand gestures, and recites phrases in another human language I've heard before, but with markedly different pronunciation.

Georgia explains that the other language is Latin, and that the prayer was not to me but a God hundreds of stars away. The human first contact specialist also informs me that several humans have taken pictures of themselves, a souvenir of their proximity to the Space Dragon.

The visitors become less frequent, however, as time progresses. Though they do interrupt somewhat, Georgia is able to tell me a great deal about the current exploration efforts of the human people and how they arrived in a ship to survey this planet. She explains that the Sk'vesh—species name—appear to be divided into warring factions, and that during their arrival conversations, this fortress was attacked.

I only have a vague recollection of the surface, but I do recall natural crags and crater being morphed to serve as the outer walls of a large encampment. I mark the information for future use. Upon the surface is a fortress. And, before the humans ventured down to my level, I must have heard them engage in battle.

"So, you defended this fortress of Sk'vesh," I say, filling in the implication.

Georgia's large eyes narrow slightly and her brow twists as she considers the response and the translated words. "Our landing party defended itself against an assault that didn't care if we were allied with this group or just visitors. It was within an hour of us touching down, so we acted according to protocol." Georgia pauses. She glances in the direction of the other scientist, the only other person who remains down here with us, who cannot understand her anyway. "That seemed to earn us some good will. They invited us below the fortress to see you."

To see *me*. What am I to the Sk'vesh? A trophy, a pet, a resource they had not yet figured out how to tap? Certainly I am not a deity on this planet. Or maybe I am just a prisoner, though I wonder if the humans have earned enough good will to have me set free. I say none of this out loud. Not yet.

The scientist, who has set up various scanners and monitors, some of which shine low intensity, high frequency lights in my direction, approaches Georgia and asks something.

Georgia replies in her negotiating voice. She has specific pitches for calming the fellow humans. I am not offended that she uses this on me; I do not deny that I do the same.

To me, she says, "He's wondering if he can take a scale. To study."

I bend my neck so my teeth can reach my forearm, just behind the solid stone cuffs holding me in place. I grip and rip out a scale, wincing as I do so, smelling my own blood open to the air. I then extend my neck and release the scale onto the floor of the cavern, as close to the humans I can manage. I see that the fresh scale does indeed shine red with a few drops. The scale itself is not nearly as lustrous as it once was, more like aged copper than anything brilliant or robust.

The scientist says something which the greeter translates to "Thank you."

Little do they know, if I'd shaken my neck hard enough, I probably could have dislodged some loose and dry ones.

This is how *I* establish good will.

* * *

The questions turn toward me on the second day.

I had assumed this might have been their style—either because they are being polite and offering information first, or are arrogant and like to talk about themselves. Georgia disabuses me of this notion by letting me know that she was more rapidly able to translate the standard greeting protocol and had waited for their captain in orbit to send down questions to translate for our second meeting.

Georgia has brought with her two thermoses, one of which releases rich and bitter steam, and seems to help rouse her from her recent sleep. The other I assume is sustenance rather than stimulant, and I mark the container in my mind.

After she has finished sipping, she says, "We would like to know about you. We—that is, my species—have stories about dragons, but up until yesterday, most people would have assumed you were…"

She seems worried about offending me. "Extinct?"

"Mythical. Imagined. That's why everyone's reacting this way. Everything about you—your species," she corrects, "comes long before recording technology. We have had no reliable new information for at least eight centuries."

I do not remember how long a human century is, if I had ever known such a detail, but I would theorize that the human generation is shorter than their century.

"You're not native to this planet, are you?" she asks, referring to her device and most likely paraphrasing a prompt from the captain in orbit.

They display more intelligence. "No. Like you, I am a visitor here."

"Imprisoned," she says.

"Yes, unfortunately."

She appears torn on returning to her list or following up on this theme. For the moment, the list takes precedent. "How do you travel between planets?"

"That is difficult to answer."

"We…" Georgia looks at her device and appears to double check or even mentally practice what she's about to say. "We are much more advanced than the last time you knew us. We can make sense of very complicated science."

As evidenced by her device and her armor, not to mention her presence on this planet. I do not doubt this testimony. "We do not like to share these means with others."

"Is it because you're worried they'll be stolen? Or that someone will take advantage of them?"

I say nothing.

"Your kind went to Earth before. How did you get there?"

I say nothing.

"I have to assume you have some means of travel," she says. "How can I earn your trust enough for you to tell me?"

"If I tell you, you'll tell your commander."

"I—" Does she consider lying, or is she merely realizing the accuracy of my statement? "True."

She does not press the point. She moves on to the next question. For now.

"If you can't tell us how you got here, maybe you can tell us why."

"Exploration."

"Is that it? Weren't you looking for something, some end goal?"

"It is the same as what you do," I say. "Is it not?"

She raises an eyebrow at me. Perhaps she catches my meaning.

I have not explored for exploration's sake alone. Neither have the humans, and she knows it as well as I.

"All right. How about how you came to be a prisoner. What happened?"

Here we have gone in the right direction. I exaggerate my exhale so it sounds like a sigh. I wait long enough that Georgia moves in response, taking a step toward me, in intrigue and impatience.

In truth, the difficulties began the moment I entered the atmosphere.

I could not see much through the clouds. I could sense my quarry, yes, but that is not a product of visible light. Any refraction patterns that might indicate a toxic layer were not apparent to me until I was within them. The lightning had stung on my descent, but it was the noxious fumes that disoriented me—even more so because I had traveled so far through vacuum without a breath and had filled my lungs with the first atmosphere that contained oxygen.

The layer broke before the ground. The lower atmosphere close to the surface—and apparently underground—was not nearly as bad, but I crashed with a mighty impact. I split open in several places and bled, and had to use my internal reserve to heal my cells. Which meant that when I was beset by their grotesque warriors, I was not at my full faculties, though still clearly strong and ravenous. They tasted far worse than they looked, I remember, and their spears pierced me in several places. Worse, those spears had been laced with a liquid form of the same atmospheric toxin, which eventually rendered me unconscious.

I had woken to the blinding pain of molten rock being poured over all four limbs and my tail, attaching me to the ground of this cavern. I managed to kill one before the fumes once again knocked me out.

By the time I found consciousness again, they had sealed the entry to the surface behind me, presenting the choice between full capitulation or death.

That is the full truth.

I say, "The upper levels of atmosphere make me drowsy. The Sk'vesh found me sleeping shortly after I arrived. I defended myself, and, yes, I did kill some of theirs. That is, the warriors of the previous faction who held this fortress. They captured me and trapped me here. And here I have remained. My fault was in lack of preparation." All true, but certainly not complete.

It seems Georgia has also expected me to tell the longer tale. As soon as I have begun, she sits and reaches for the second thermos, the one which certainly smells more savory.

When she drinks what I imagine to be marvelous soup, I growl deep in my throat.

I do not imagine it is on her list of questions, but Georgia asks, "When do you eat?"

"My jailers do not feed me."

Her eyes widen. Georgia looks behind her at the open door, then says, "Excuse me."

She exits my cell, and I hear her calling for one of the jailers. They have a brief high-pitched exchange, in which it sounds like Georgia is levying some kind of accusation. At least one more human joins the conversation. The volume and confusion increases. I wait and listen.

This is how I invite her pity.

***

I make a great show of voracious hunger. The performance is based in reality and therefore not difficult.

First contact specialist Georgia Ballantine waits patiently for me to finish swallowing any of the huge platters of food that are brought to me before asking the next question.

In between time, she tells me that her captain has arranged negotiations for my release but admits that they do not look promising. The host of this fortress—my prison—refuses on some grounds that do not translate well. The group of humans has to split up and send a smaller party to another faction and speak with their leaders, possibly to corroborate my story about how and why I was captured. They will not find me a liar.

When I am done with what has been provided, I indicate that I am still hungry, and Georgia calls for more food. Human food, based on nutrients of planet Earth, and far more delectable than anything I could hope to be served here. Richer than what I could find on most planets, in fact—not that I share this with her.

"You'll have to tell me how you were able to survive so long without food," she says, when I request a third helping.

"It is a sort of hibernation," I explain. "My species can exist for a long period of time with nothing. Although, we prefer to eat." And drink. And breathe. And keep the company of other dragons or at least a cohort of worshippers. "We can do far less on an empty stomach and without—" I stop myself.

"Without?" she asks.

The third helping arrives. I resume eating.

Georgia accepts that matter as paused for now, but her eyebrows indicate her impatience is growing. Still, she goes on to explain more about the human assumptions of dragons. She admits she had always found it perplexing how many cultures had similar stories of dragons. Giants, flying reptiles or possibly serpents, many of whom were described as capable of speaking, who were proud and hoarded treasure, along with rituals and secrets. When she says this, she squints, as if to gauge my reaction.

I continue eating.

"And keep in mind, this was before the discovery of dinosaurs, which means that the closest thing that they had to compare were actual lizards, snakes, and crocodiles. The fact that you—your kind, I mean—were there on Earth explains so much of our lore but creates so many unanswered questions."

I swallow a large mouthful. The nutrients are already having some effect. Not enough to execute my plan, but progress nonetheless.

Seeing I have swallowed, Georgia takes the opportunity to ask, "How many generations ago, for you, were the dragons on Earth?"

I pause to consider, genuinely. In my moment of consideration, I hear more footfalls coming down the stairs toward me and a human's voice. I am not certain, but I take a guess as to who will arrive.

I stretch my head toward Georgia, close enough that she could reach out an arm and touch my snout. "Can you keep a secret?" I whisper.

The commander arrives and calls, "Ballantine!"

Georgia jumps, startled, but quickly recovers and addresses her commanding officer.

I wait and listen. I think I understand more of the modern human speech with each exchange, though I have not yet tested my own replies.

Even with more energy at my disposal to control my reactions, I stare at the commander's gold insignia. I can't help it.

At least in front of me, Georgia says nothing that indicates she might betray my confidence. This is not full proof, but perhaps it is enough.

I can tell Georgia's disappointed. Bad news about my release, not that I am surprised, but I consider how I should react to show my own disappointment when she tells me.

The commander gives me a nod and a kind of salute, declaring me "Space Dragon" once again before turning and leaving.

The humans trust Georgia to remain with me, and I suppose they trust me not to eat her. Even the jailers leave the door open and do not intervene, even if they will not release me.

Georgia faces me once again. Slowly, with, I believe, sincerity, she says, "I'm sorry. It seems the Sk'vesh—"

I hold up one hand—or, rather, I try, restricted though it is by my solid manacle. "Let's not discuss that now. I have enjoyed this supper and our conversation far too much."

She grins—that enviably effusive human gesture. "Me, too."

She sounds as if she believes this, even though she is merely responding to my sentiment out of politeness, social decorum. In truth—at least in deeper truth—she had been growing frustrated with me, but all of that disappears after a single positive sentiment.

I take a gamble and try to move one step further. "You asked me a question. I think you have worked out the answer."

She considers and recalls—but for no more than a few seconds. "You were there!" She whispers this, does not yell to match her level of excitement. "You, personally, were on Earth, weren't you?" She rushes forward, beyond the line that my original captors had drawn on the stone, the radius of my reach. "That means you know—you know firsthand what we were, how our societies worked, what we wore, and even how we—

how we smelled." She laughs in giddy anticipation of my stories. "Please, you have to tell me. I—" She must have realized her over-eagerness, for she pauses and straightens her posture. "As a first contact specialist, as someone who studies other cultures, this is the most groundbreaking find. You are the most groundbreaking contact for the people of Earth. These kinds of stories, firsthand, are the Holy Grail for a human explorer."

"Very well. I trust you." I take a deep breath, but I do not begin telling the long saga she wishes to hear. "I trust you to understand that I do not intend to remain here. And if you cannot free me by negotiation, there is something I need to free myself by force."

She hardly flinches at this. "What is it?"

"Gold."

This is how I achieve my salvation.

* * *

She does not understand, so I tell her a little more. I remind her of the story she told me about dragons hoarding treasure, and justify the truth behind it. Our systems process oxygen, like theirs. We also use proteins and other nutrients. Most importantly, however, our systems are designed to use gold.

She calls for the commander to help procure it, and the commander explains that they don't have nearly enough on hand for the quantities I specify.

So I tell them where to procure it, that there is a mountain on this planet with more than enough, many of the veins exposed to the surface, where the humans can easily melt it down to extract. I do not doubt that they have this kind of technology available, and I do not mind contaminants. I have to tell them that I could sense it from beyond the atmosphere. I have to tell them that, yes, I can survive in a vacuum and travel much farther than they would have assumed. Perhaps I am too desperate. I shall have to beg forgiveness from my kind later, but at least I will be among my own kind again.

Scientists and engineers are eager to help, fascinated by the prospect of an organic being that consumes gold as fuel. The captain in orbit apparently cautions that many human parties cannot all gather for such long periods of time without making their hosts suspicious.

So the information is relayed through Georgia Ballantine, the first contact specialist who has already established a desire for long conversations with me that have not led to incident.

Georgia confides in me that the hosts are already suspicious. "But they're willing to work with us, because they think we can give them something they want."

The inevitable selfishness of sentient beings. "What have they bargained for?"

"You," Georgia says with a wry smile. "Specifically, they want you to fight other factions for them. Apparently, on this planet, they can effectively domesticate most beasts through long periods of isolation, and then retraining after the creatures have forgotten their pack connection. Because *we* can talk to you, the Sk'vesh have accepted that you're from a different place and that you might need a different handling method."

"Did you tell them you could manage this for them?"

"I told them we were working on understanding you better and that we discovered you were not more likely to submit if you were deprived of food."

So she hadn't lied.

* * *

The food continues in smaller quantities, but the organic matter is no longer important. Even before biting into the next morsel delivered, I can tell what's encased within. Several nuggets of gold.

The moment I bite through that outer layer, I feel the metal begin to break down, to corrode in my saliva, to suffuse into my system.

After I'm finished with my first Golden meal, Georgia asks, "How does it work?"

"This is not often something we share," I say, and I can see her begin to slouch before I continue. "When the gold is absorbed into our system, it heads toward a core chamber, not far from our hearts. This chamber manufactures the gold into the energy that we need for the kinds of feats your ancestors would have called magic. We can heal ourselves and, yes, fly out of the atmosphere. The travel from there, once in the vacuum, is harder to explain without much longer conversations and words you do not know."

"You heal yourselves?" she asks, seemingly missing the commentary on deep space travel. "You're already at least a thousand years old, aren't you? If you have enough gold, could you live forever?"

Though she has seriously underestimated my age, I do not deny her conclusion. "Are you beginning to understand why there are stories about my people hoarding treasure?"

"Yes. What happens to the gold after it's processed?"

"It changes. During the transformation, it becomes iron, which we pass quite easily in small quantities."

"You turn gold into iron?" She considers this. "Were dragons responsible for inspiring the study of alchemy?"

I laugh, though I do not deny the connection. I cannot be certain, but it is possible that, knowing the reverse is possible, a human on ages-old

Earth might have decided to try to form gold from iron leavings. "I fear I cannot provide grounds in reality for every story."

"There are also stories of frightened kingdoms sacrificing princesses to your kind. Are those true?"

"Yes."

"And you ate them?" she asks, with some concern.

"Yes."

"But they're other sentient beings. Why not just eat dumb animals, like sheep?"

"Sheep rarely wear gold."

Any verbal argument ends there, though I suspect she continues it in her mind. I suppose I could have spared her that information, but I doubt it would have done me any good.

"We must seem very different to you now." I wonder if she says this more to herself than to me. Then, something occurs to her, more interesting than the thought of deaths that occurred many human lifetimes ago. "Can gold make you breathe fire?"

* * *

After the humans have said their goodbyes and exited the fortress, I wait a day for the jailer to feed me again. The grotesque alien seems to resent this task, but it is motivated by the idea of having a powerful beast on its side.

This platter of food is not interesting, but I take a bite as we have planned.

Then, I draw my head back and let my chest open and fill with a warm glow. The reserve in my core is full of molten gold, and some of that energy processes forward into my windpipe, of my neck, toward a gland that ignites.

I spew a jet of flame through my mouth for the first time in a long time, completely missing but intimidating the jailer that had come to feed me.

Will they really think it was their fault and they delivered the wrong food? I do not care either way.

I clench my hands and feet. I strain the stone that contains them. I bash my chin and then my forehead into the first one until I feel something crack. If it is my own skeleton, the gold will heal me. I breathe fire at myself until the stone loosens. Then, I wrench my foreclaw. One limb free makes the others easier.

The Sk'vesh are not sure of whether to flee from my fury or to gather and contain me. I make sure not to kill the first jailer, not directly, so it may relay what happened, rendering the humans harder to blame.

Once my tail is free, I start on the wall they erected behind me. Partially caved in, partially mortared shut, but recent, and not structurally strong enough to resist me.

I swish my tail and create small gusts of wind with my cramped wings, hoping to disorient my enemies so none will have a chance to poison me.

I ram the wall simultaneously with a burst of flame.

When I crash through, I know my forehead is bleeding. I have left many scales behind, a few broken claws, but I am outside with enough room to spread my wings once more.

The landscape, hideous when I first encountered it, is now beautiful for its openness. My eyes strain against the light, but I start toward a rendezvous point, where the humans mined the vein of gold.

Their ship waits for me, a large enough vessel to have a cargo bay that can envelop me.

The last part of our bargain has begun. Safe passage through the toxic atmosphere of this planet toward open space, in exchange for my knowledge. A small price to pay.

By the time I reach the cargo bay, I am tired and in pain, but I am elated. I land amidst cheers from the humans, and the cargo bay door seals behind me. I breathe heavily, after having exerted myself for the first time in a long time.

I am so giddy that I do not initially register a noxious smell, but I do quickly notice that humans are not in the cargo bay with me. Some watch on a higher level, behind thick transparencies, including Georgia. She wears a uniform made of fabric rather than her armor, on her right breast sits a pin with a golden insignia.

While she stands at attention, I slowly sink. I am aware that I am being poisoned, or, more accurately, sedated. I suspect the effect is stronger and faster than when I flew through the atmosphere. Impressive humans, concentrating the gas.

I collapse entirely and strain to keep my eyelids open.

From behind the partition, Georgia says, "Sorry, Space Dragon. As soon as they found out you could change gold on an atomic level, they…*we* determined it would take more than a few days to learn your information."

I feel for my gold reserves, but they are too drained for fire, and the heavy gas flooding my lungs is not oxygen-rich enough to support it—a clever touch. It seems the gas also contains a euphoric agent, for I hear myself chuckling, more in amusement than rue, and maybe a touch of misplaced pride. I do not witness Georgia's reaction as I drift toward a chemically-induced sleep, a tacit acceptance of my new prison—however temporary it may be.

This is how I discover the true progress of humankind, not just into the stars but into a realm of control that even their former kings could rarely grasp, no matter how grand the golden crowns on their heads. They are no longer mere sheep.

The Exposé

Paul D. Smith

"'Ey, Ig, you got a hottie here to see you."

Ig turned away from the pot of chili to see Haskins sticking his head around the door to the kitchen. Haskins had that shit-eating grin on his face that Ig knew all too well.

Ig smiled and said, "What're you up to this time, man?"

"God's honest truth; there's a hot girl in the office askin' to see you. Can't imagine why she's here looking for you."

Ig faced Haskins, arms extended, flexing his pectorals and biceps under his form-fitting, navy blue, FDNY t-shirt. He simply said, "This?"

Haskins shook his head. "How is it you don't work out, eat whatever you want, and still look like that? I gotta hit the gym three times a week just to maintain this dad-bod o' mine."

Ig slung the kitchen towel over his broad shoulder. "What does this girl want?"

"Damned if I know. Just go talk to her, if you even remember how to talk to a girl."

Ig snorted at the comment and turned the flame down to a simmer. As he passed through the lounge of the fire station, he saw the boys watching *Breaking Bad*.

"New episodes?" he asked.

"Yeah, season three just started," someone answered.

He made a mental note to catch up on the episodes later. As he turned the corner to the hall, he found himself adjusting his pony tail and wiping his hands on the towel. "Stupid," he said to himself, then he turned into the office and saw her sitting at the desk.

She couldn't have been more than twenty-five, with thick raven hair pulled back and into a braid. As soon as she saw him enter, she pushed up her glasses and sat up a bit straighter. "Are you Mr. Tulipalo?"

"Call me Ig." He held out his hand. She shook it without getting up and he seated himself in the ratty office chair behind the desk. Her green eyes met his, but she said nothing for a couple of beats. Ig held out his hands to his sides and asked, "What's this about?"

She cleared her throat, and thin, well-manicured fingers opened a laptop. "Sorry. I'm a journalism student at NYU and I've been assigned to write a biographical piece on Congressman Rainsford who—"

"Who just passed. Yeah, I know."

"So, you two knew each other?"

Ig felt a slight pang in his heart. Mr. R. had only died a couple of weeks ago. The loss was still fresh. "Yeah, the guy kind of took me under his wing when I was new to the city."

"His will was just read a couple of days ago. He left a sizable sum of money to the New York Fire Department."

"Makes sense. He was a huge supporter of the Department after 9/11."

"Did you know he made some specific mentions in bequests? The commissioner, a couple of captains, and then you."

Ig paused. He actually didn't know. He narrowed his eyes and said, "Didn't catch your name."

She looked down to her laptop, straightened her glasses again, and said, "Sorry. Brittney."

He sat back in the chair and folded his arms. "Got a last name, Brittney?"

She looked down again. "Stephens. Sorry…my last name is Stephens."

"Well, Brittney Stephens, you've apologized three times in as many minutes. It seems like interviewing a stranger is something you don't do often, which seems a bit odd for a journalism student. And you keep breaking eye contact with me, which tells me you're hiding something."

"I'm…slightly intimidated being here. Some of these fire stations have a reputation for being, well, inhospitable to women."

He felt a bit embarrassed. "Haskins say something?"

"It's more like how he looked at me."

Ig rolled his eyes at the all-too-familiar complaint. Haskins was a friend, but could be a real dick, too. "Okay, Brittney Stephens, let's try this again. You want to know about Congressman Rainsford and why my name, some schmoe at the FDNY, is showing up in his will."

She nodded. “Correct.”

He saw her shoulders relax a little. “Back when I was just a newbie in the department, we got dispatched to a call at his apartment building. It was going up pretty quick. He and the missus were out at some politician thing. I went in, got his son and the baby sitter out, and there were no lives lost. Mr. and Mrs. R. kinda took me under their wing after that. They were grateful they didn’t lose anyone, and I got a mentor and someone to make me a home-cooked meal once a week.”

She was tapping away at her keyboard and then asked, “So he was your mentor?”

Ig smoothed his wavy hair and tightened the elastic keeping it back. “Eh, mentor’s not really a good word. More like a close friend. Not quite a dad. Maybe more like an older and smarter uncle.”

She nodded. “Sounds nice. Having someone like that.”

“Yeah, real nice,” He wondered where this was going. He’d expected something a bit more articulate from a journalism student than “Sounds nice.”

“So that’s why he mentioned you in his will?”

“Yep.”

“But then why weren’t you at the funeral?”

Ig didn’t expect that. The question was like a slap in the face. “Now how would you know something like that, Brittney Stephens?” He leaned forward in the chair, clasped his hands together, and laid them on the desk. He saw her swallow hard.

“I was assigned to attend the service,” she gestured at the laptop. “It was part of my graduate work.”

Ig purposefully took a few moments to let that answer just hang in the air. Something was off about all this, but he hadn’t quite figured out what. “Had to work a shift. Comes with the job, ya know? Sometimes you gotta miss the important stuff when you’re a public servant.”

She nodded and tapped the keys again. “Umm, they wouldn’t let you off for something like that?”

“Half of the department was at the service. Someone has to be at the station, and I’m a low man on the ladder.”

“Still, your name was in the will, so…”

“So, what?” As she lifted her eyes again, he let warmth flow through his body as he focused his eyes on her round glasses. The anti-reflective coating on her lenses created a mirroring effect and he could see what was on her screen. There were no programs open on the monitor where she was taking notes. It was time to shut down this conversation. “There ain’t anything else to say. We were friends, I had to work, and I missed the funeral. I don't know what else you're looking for, Brittney, but you ain't gonna find it here."

She raised her eyebrows and he could see her eyes dart back and forth. "That's it?"

He splayed open his hands. "'Fraid so. Besides, I got a pot of chili on the stove that needs a few scorpion peppers so…" He gestured to the door.

She closed her laptop, thanked Ig for his time, and followed him to the firehouse exit. He shut it behind her and made his way back to the kitchen. As he passed through the lounge, Haskins asked, "How'd it go?"

"Boys, I'd like to tell ya, but I gotta finish this chili."

"That bad, huh? Par for the course for Ig. Means you ain't gettin' any tonight, right?"

The other guys in the room jeered cheerfully. Ig ignored them as he tried to deduce what Brittney Stephens was really after. Still, the whole encounter served as a somber reminder that he needed to pay someone a visit. Someone he should have visited right after Mr. R. died.

* * *

When he left the firehouse the next morning, it was a rainy, dreary day in the city. Ig took the subway to Central Park, then walked along Central Park West until he came to 81st Street. From there, the brownstone was only a few doors down. As he climbed the stairway to the front door, he chided himself for not having done this sooner. Ig took in a deep breath and let the familiar warmth settle him as it always did. But it still didn't feel like enough in this circumstance.

He rang the doorbell and noticed the Rainsfords never installed the security doorbell he gave them last Christmas. This part of the city was fairly safe, but one could never be sure. Their kids had all moved out west and Ig had been the only one left in town to keep an eye on the couple.

He heard the deadbolt turn and the door gently swung open. A small, silver-haired woman with oversized glasses peered back at him. Her pink velour tracksuit hung loosely on her frail frame.

The smile that came across Mrs. Rainsford's deeply wrinkled face was genuine, but tired. "Well, as I live and breathe, Ignatius! I've missed you so much." She shuffled forward as quickly as she could and embraced him. Ig's muscled arms wrapped around her and he concealed a frown at how fragile she felt.

"Good to see you, too, Mrs. R." He held her out in front of him. "You didn't install the security camera and you just opened the door for me. I could have been anyone."

Mrs. R. waved a dismissive hand. "For such a strapping young man, you are quite the nervous Nellie. Come in, come in."

Ig followed her into the dark but tastefully decorated home. There was a museum-like quality to the residence. The Rainsfords were multi-generational New Yorkers and over the decades they had collected an impressive number of artifacts that were native to the area. A set of original blueprints of the Empire State Building hung in an Art Deco frame on one wall, while a collection of fire helmets from departments across the five boroughs were displayed on another. Pictures of the Rainsford family with a who's who of New York's movers and shakers were arranged for all to see. There was even a display of photos and other signed memorabilia from a house concert that an up-and-coming Billy Joel performed at their old apartment in the Essex House.

She led him to the kitchen table and, without asking, put on water for tea. He hung his head while she puttered about the kitchen, putting cookies on a plate before sitting across from him. He finally met her eyes.

"I..." he began. "I'm sorry that..."

She reached across and patted his forearm. "You know I understand, kiddo. It would have been too risky."

"I feel like shit, Mrs. R."

"Language," she gently corrected.

"Nah, I think shit is the right word in this case."

"Listen to me, Ignatius...or perhaps I should call you Ignyss today."

His gaze hardened. "You know..."

"He told me before he passed. He felt someone on this planet, besides him, should know your true name. He told me that names have meaning, and knowing someone's real name means you know them. Now, I'm not sure what this all means, mind you, but Mr. R. told me to make sure you didn't feel alone after he...well...moved on."

"I actually don't feel alone, Mrs. R. I kinda enjoy solitude. But Mr. R. was the only one—" He paused and reconsidered his words. "—well, he was the only person who knew what my real name was all about."

He barely felt her squeeze his forearm. "He knew that the two of you being seen in public at the same time could cause problems. He also knew that you would try to come regardless, which is why he called in a few last-minute favors to make sure the fire station was understaffed and that you would be called in to fill the shift."

"I..." He let out a small laugh. "I shouldn't be at all surprised that he did that."

"Even now, these tired old eyes of mine can see that you haven't aged a day since we met thirty-five years ago. There are pictures that exist from the day of the fire, pictures of you, and someone could easily put two and two together."

"I'm afraid someone may have already done that," he said, and he filled her in on the visit from Brittney Stephens.

The tea kettle whistled and she was immediately up and fixing their beverages. "Sounds like she was fishing for information more than anything. You put on that icy exterior of yours and didn't give her anything."

He smiled at her choice of words as she set a mug of his favorite concoction in front of him: chai tea with cinnamon creamer. She cautioned him that it was too hot to drink, but he took a deep sip and let the flavor wash over his taste buds. "Yeah, seemed like she was just wondering why a guy like me was mentioned in the will."

"Mr. R. told me quite a few years ago that you could—how do I say this?—become someone else if you needed to. Could you do that?"

"I could, but he also told me that I shouldn't just change who I am when life gets difficult. He told me that if I can't even settle on who I am, I'll never find any kind of peace in life. Wise words."

"They were," she said. There was a long pause before she said anything. "Would it be that bad for someone else to know about you?"

Ig was confused. "Mrs. R., I was going to tell you…"

She held up her hand to stop him from talking. "Ig, I'm not too far behind Mr. R. And if I'm being honest, I'm ready. My children are grown and have their own children. And as much as I would like to see my grandkids grow up, they have their own lives that I am less and less a part of. This place—" She waved her hand around the room. "—is just a collection of memories in a frame of brownstone. You, young man, are far more than just a memory, and definitely a memory that shouldn't die with me and my husband."

"There are others like me, Mrs. R."

"Oh? When was the last time you saw one of them?"

He did the math in his head. "I think we were watching the Boston Tea Party together. Wasn't much of a party, really."

She smiled. "So just a little while ago, eh?"

"You bustin' my chops, Mrs. R.?"

"I believe the term you are more familiar with is that I'm giving you shit."

"Mrs. R.?!? Language!"

They shared a laugh and she brought his head to her chest in an embrace. He felt her kiss the top of his head and smiled as he took in a warmth that didn't come from within himself. "All I'm saying, kiddo, is that it may not be that bad for someone else to know your secret when we are gone. My husband did a lot to help you hide through the years. Maybe it's someone else's turn to help with that."

They finished their tea, spent some more time catching up, and Ig got up and headed for the front door. As she held it open for him, he bent down and kissed her on the cheek. She asked, "Ig?"

"Yeah?"

"Are you, you know, human?"

"What do you think, Mrs. R.?"

She thought for a moment. "I think you are like a son and that is all that matters."

"That's good enough for me." He turned to walk down the front steps to 81st Street.

* * *

A week passed and Ig thought he was in the clear. It was baked ziti night at the station, and the large pan of pasta was in the oven while he chopped up vegetables. His back was toward the kitchen door when he heard the knock on the frame.

"Yeah?" he said.

"Mr. Tulipalo?"

He cursed. "You here to ask me about where to get take out?" He turned to face Brittney Stephens.

"Is it good take out?" He could hear the sarcasm in her voice.

He inhaled sharply. "How did you get in here anyway?"

"It's not like you lock your door, and no one was around, so I just came in. It's a public building, you know."

"Doesn't mean you get free access."

"I was in the area, so I wanted to follow up with you."

"In the area? You live around here? I can't imagine a graduate student can afford an apartment in this part of town."

She sighed. "No, I live way uptown. A building called the Havershire."

"The Havershire? God, you'd be better off homeless. Do you have to bribe the rats just to let you sleep through the night without being disturbed?"

She smiled. "I order traps by the dozen."

"Whaddaya want, Brittney? My ziti is almost done, so you have until then."

She reached into her backpack and withdrew a folder. She slipped a photo out of it and laid it on the table. Ig felt the heat intensify in his chest.

"I remember what you said about the fire at the Rainsford apartment, so I looked it up. Amazing story, really. The picture taken at the scene is really interesting." She laid a picture from the *Times* on the table. He saw the familiar photo of the Rainsford son and babysitter resting in the back of an ambulance. He was standing next to the door. It was like it happened yesterday, and it was the photo he wished had never been taken.

"What is so interesting about it?" he asked, already knowing the answer.

"This was quite a few years ago, and you look exactly the same."

"I don't know what you want me to say. It's a crappy photo and I got good genes."

"Ig, you really expect me to believe that?"

"I don't give a shit what you do and don't believe. Besides, why don't you be truthful with me? Ain't no journalism student is gonna pursue something this trivial so aggressively. Plus, you should be living in student housing instead of a deathtrap like the Havershire."

Her cheeks blushed. "Fine. I'm an investigative reporter and I've been assigned to Congressman Rainsford. He had his fingers in so many pies in this city, it can't possibly be all altruistic. Then we see someone like you mentioned in his will and we wonder if you were a beneficiary of more than just a firefighter's salary."

"So…what? You think he was skimming off the top to line my pockets? For what?"

"He gives you money, you invest it, the investments get paid out to offshore accounts that happen to be owned by him and members of his family." She paused and glanced around the room. "Is it getting hot in here?"

Ig focused for a moment and slowed his heart rate. "So because I'm mentioned in his will, you think that means I'm laundering money for him. What rag do you work for?" The timer on the oven went off. He pointed to it and said, "Your time is up, so you better find a way to make this worth my while."

"It's…an up-and-coming publication. We seek to expose the truth. And yes, I thought this was money laundering, but then I found this picture." She pointed to the table. "And then I dug some more and I found THIS picture." She slipped another photo out of her backpack. "Westchester County, 1957. There was a fire at a textile factory. The firefighters miraculously rescued three migrant workers from the conflagration. This fireman," she jabbed her finger down on the black and white, "looks amazingly like the one in the picture of the Rainsfords."

Ig swore under his breath and went to the oven, trying to come up with a cover story. He was drawing a blank.

Brittney continued and produced a third photograph. "Rochester, New York, 1934. An Eastman Kodak film processing center. There was a chemical fire and several departments came to the scene. Nasty things those chemical fires. *The Democrat and Chronicle* reports one very brave fireman miraculously pulled five people out. Managed to catch a photo of the guy. Guess who he looks like?"

Ig opened the oven door. The heat hit him and he inhaled it deeply. He needed some kind of excuse. How did she uncover all of this?

"And here's the coup de grace," she continued with a copy of a very old photograph, "Chicago, 1871. A picture of one of the fire brigades that fought that awful fire. Guess who I see there?"

Ig whipped around. "What do you want from me?" he shouted. He saw her looking back at him with wide eyes. Her glance flicked from his eyes to his hand and then back to him. Ig looked down and saw he had unconsciously taken the ziti out of the oven. He wasn't wearing any oven mitts.

"I…what…?" she stammered. He could see fear in her eyes.

Ig gently set the pasta on the stovetop and pinched the bridge of his nose. As he tried to think of how he was going to explain this, he muttered, "Ziti's done."

"Are you an alien?" she blurted.

"What? You go from me grabbing a hot pan to me being some kinda little green man? I'm from this planet, just like you."

"So—" She swallowed hard. "—you're human?"

Such a simple question with such a complex answer. He answered, "I didn't say that."

"I don't understand," she said. "I thought you were just a scammer of some sort."

"That's what you get for digging into holes that you can't get out of."

He kicked himself for what he was about to say, but he couldn't think of any other choice. "Here's what is going to happen next. Option one is you publish whatever story you think is happening here. When folks come looking to talk to me to verify your story, I'll be gone. No one will ever see this face again." He pointed to his own face. "And all of your colleagues will think you're full of shit."

"I don't like to be full of shit."

"I don't blame you. Option two is you meet me at the Metro North kiosk at Grand Central Station tomorrow and I show what is really happening. I will be there at this time tomorrow. If you don't come, I'll assume you chose option one. So, leave now. Don't say a word. Just leave. You have a big decision to make and I have to finish a tossed salad."

Her mouth opened to say something but closed again. She packed up her pictures, slid them into her backpack, and left without a word.

As soon as he heard the door to the station close behind her, he let loose a string of profanities as he finished chopping the carrots.

* * *

She met him the next day. Ig was leaning against the busy kiosk when she approached. He said, "I gotta admit, I was fifty-fifty on whether you were going to show up or not."

"You left me on a bit of a cliffhanger there."

He jammed his thumb over his shoulder. "Get a ticket to Beacon. We'll ride the train and I'll take you to our destination from there."

She began digging through her bag for her wallet. "You aren't buying tickets?"

He wrinkled a nostril at her. "This ain't a date. You wanna know, you pay your fair share."

The two were soon on the Hudson River line of the Metro North railroad. About an hour later, the train stopped in the small town of Beacon. Ig led Brittney to an old minivan parked in one of the most distant spaces in the large parking lot. Another half hour in the van down Interstate 84 brought them to the small town of Shenandoah. A short drive down Shenandoah Road took them to the Bethel Baptist Church, where Ig turned onto a seasonal road. A pothole-laden fifteen minutes later, they pulled up to an old barn where Ig finally parked and shut off the van.

Brittney said, "You're giving off serial killer vibes here."

"You're the one who started all of this, remember?"

She acknowledged him with a nod as they stepped into a small glade of evergreens and Ig proceeded to the large double doors. A hefty chain and padlock secured them shut and he produced a key to allow them entrance.

The inside was mostly a large empty space. A loft was at the far end, accessible via a rickety ladder. Ig flipped the light switch and four old half-dome light fixtures buzzed to life overhead.

Brittney pointed to one of the corners. "What's with the shed?"

Ig walked to the plastic gray utility shed he had installed a few years ago. The green roof was coated with a fine layer of dust, but it was the only modern-looking thing in the structure. He pulled the doors open to reveal a small computer desk with a MacBook sitting alone on the surface.

Brittney looked at it and then went back to him. "You don't strike me as a computer guy."

"I'm not, but this is my way to do what I do. At least since records became computerized."

"I don't understand. What is it that you do?"

Ig sighed. "Okay, look, kid. I haven't hurt you or even threatened you up to this point, right?"

"Y-y-yes," she stammered.

"That ain't about to change, but you need to remember that what you are going to see is still me. Still Ig. Got it?"

"You're totally freaking me out."

"That's cause this is the part where people usually shriek and scream." Ig walked to the middle of the barn and closed his eyes. He felt the constant warmth that was in the center of his chest and focused on it. It blazed to a raging fire and blistering heat coursed through his body. It was an ecstasy to him. The energy dug past his cells, past his molecular structure, even past his atoms, into the quantum foam of existence, and his body mass started to increase. Mass that was stored somewhere incomprehensible but waiting for him to summon it. His body began to grow, to change. Clothing ripped and fell away in seconds as limbs sprang from his shoulder blades and a tail extended from the end of his spine. He could hear Brittney screaming at the sight of him shifting, but Ignyss didn't care. It had been far too long since he inhabited his actual form and he reveled in the power that flowed into his true body.

The transformation complete, Ig's head towered thirty feet above Brittney, horns scraping the roof of the old barn. He held up a foreleg and took in the sight of his deep red scales while twitching his tail, using muscles that hadn't been used in years.

Brittney's screaming filled his auditory canals as his mind returned to the present. Ig sat back on his haunches and gestured with his foreclaws. "Easy, easy. Like I said, this is the screaming part, but it's still me," he said, his gravelly, deep, booming true voice speaking in the now very full space of the barn.

"Jesus Christ! You're a fucking dragon!"

"Yeah, to be specific, I'm a flame dragon. I breathe fire, the whole nine yards."

She was hyperventilating as she tried to speak, but couldn't get any words out. She fell to her knees and vomited on the wood floor.

"Ech. That's the first time I made anyone puke."

There were several seconds of retching before she could speak. "Oh, God, I got it on my shoes."

"Yeah, you should've turned your head to, you know, the left a little more."

She finally stood up and slowly looked him up and down. "Can I…" she made a gesture toward him.

"Sure. Take a look around."

She spent a good five minutes walking circles around his body. He gave her permission to feel his scales, his talons, even the spines along the ridge of his tail. "I have no words. You definitely aren't human."

He pointed one toe to the ceiling. "But I am an earthling, just like I said."

"So you can turn into a person whenever you want?"

He nodded. "Not all dragons can."

"There are more of you?"

“A handful of us are still wandering the planet. I know of one who’s a teacher in the Midwest, and another living on some island in the South Atlantic. That’s all I know that are active.”

“Sounds like there are more that aren’t active.”

“That’s a long story. There was a war 700 or so years ago. A dragon war. There was some demigod that had a beef with our ancestors and he decided to take his vengeance on us. We defeated him, but he laid down a curse that put almost all of us into a sort of suspended animation. We’re all over the planet in some magical sleep, but hidden. I don’t know how, but those of us that could shape change, and were in human form at the time, were unaffected.”

Brittney eventually flopped down onto the wood floor and exhaled deeply. She looked up at him. After giving him another once over, she looked at the shed. “So, what’s with the computer?”

“Mr. R. set that up for me a while ago. If this were a hundred years ago, and I needed to adopt a different human shape, changing my identity was pretty much a piece of cake. These days, not so much. Mr. R. pulled a lot of strings and set up a backdoor into the Social Security Administration database for me. If I ever need to change my identity, I can do it from here.”

“Have you ever had to do that?”

“Not yet, no. Seems that a fireproof dragon made for a good firefighter human. Believe it or not, I kind of like the little life I’ve set up for myself and I really don’t want to change it.”

“Ig, this is all so…incomprehensible. It’s going to make an amazing story.”

“No, it isn’t.”

She motioned around the barn with her arms. “This…all of this…for the first time we have proof that we aren’t alone, that there is another sentient, intelligent, self-aware species on this planet. Why shouldn’t the world know about that?”

“You ever seen those movies when aliens come to earth? How does that usually work out for the aliens?”

She dropped her head. “But that is just—”

“It’s a reflection of reality. Kid, you humans can’t even figure out how to share this planet with each other. Hell, even here in the U.S., you argue over water, farmland, oil. Shit, you even fight over internet speed. What do you think will happen when news gets out that another intelligent, powerful, non-human species seeks co-existence? I brought you here because the only other person on this planet who knew what I was just died. For some insane reason, I decided to trust you, Brittney Stephens.”

“Ig, I’m beyond flattered, but I can’t keep this quiet. This is monumental! You’re a literal myth come to life. And it turns out everything about you is superior to us. I mean, you're a critically endangered species. You won't be touched, you'll be protected!"

"Like hell we will, we'll be hunted to…" He stopped and inhaled deeply, calming himself. This was a bad idea and now he was left with minimal options. "Clearly, I've made a mistake. I'll bring you back to the city and we can go our separate ways. I'll change my look and my identity and no one will be the wiser. This thing—" He gestured back and forth between the two of them. "—will be nothing but another sasquatch encounter."

"Ig, I'll never mention you in my exposé. You can stay…"

He held up his claw to silence her. "There's a duffel bag in the shed with a spare set of clothes. Please turn around while I transform and get dressed, okay?"

She did as he asked and, as soon he was dressed, they were on their way back to Beacon. The return journey was spent in silence. Ig couldn't shake the thought that he had followed Mrs. R.'s advice and it didn't work out. He didn't want to take the next steps, but he knew they were necessary. As soon as they arrived back at Grand Central, he gave her a weak smile and a simple wave and disappeared into the crowd.

* * *

Ig cleared his throat and Brittney startled awake. At first, she was disoriented. He could tell she had no idea why he was there and why she couldn't move her limbs. As she took a few moments to reorient herself, she exclaimed, "Ig? What the hell? Why are you here in my apartment?"

He sat back in the chair by her kitchen table. "You're a very deep sleeper, you know?"

She started to thrash and realized her arms and legs were bound to the bed frame. "Am I tied up?"

Ig nodded. "Yeah. It's just garden twine, but pretty tough to break. Like I said, you're a deep sleeper."

"I don't understand any of this." He could see the tears starting to trickle out of her eyes. She was realizing what was happening but she didn't want to verbalize it.

"To sum it up kid, you can't keep your mouth shut and I don't want the world to know about dragons."

"Hey, look, I…I won't publish the story. Right? I can keep a secret, you know?"

He took in a deep breath and let it out again. "I have to admit it was a perfect storm of bad circumstances. Mr. R. was recently passed, Mrs. R. talking about death and finding someone else to confide in, and then you. You show up, and I gotta admit, after all this time living as a human, I've come to appreciate the allure of a pretty face. A pretty, human face that is. So I made the erroneous assumption that you were going to be the person

I could trust." He pointed to his temple and wiggled his finger in a circular motion. "Your human physiology and hormones really make your thought processes malleable, particularly by emotions. Something I've never quite mastered."

"I…I'll scream for help," she stammered.

Ig smiled a sad smile. "Kid, there are at least three domestic disputes happening in this building, right now. There's a handful of parties going on as well. You screaming for help will just fade into the background."

He could see her eyes darting around the room, looking for something to help her, until they fixed on the three objects he'd brought in with him. "What's with the three garbage bags?"

"Leaves, furniture stuffing, oily rags; stuff that produces a lot of smoke when it burns."

"You're going to burn me to death?"

"Kid, this place is a firetrap. I'm going to bring the whole building down."

Her eyes became even more wild. "But there are fire alarms and a sprinkler system. It's the thing I made sure was up to code before I moved in."

He pointed to his chest. "I'm a firefighter and a fire inspector, too. I've already closed off the supply to the fire suppression system. The alarms will go off, so people will be able to evacuate, but I disabled the detectors and the individual sprinkler in here. This room will be the source of the fire, and they will find one casualty. That twine will burn away and it will look like you died from smoke inhalation."

"Ig, please, I swear, I won't publish the story. I'll keep my mouth shut. You don't need to do this."

"You have family, Brittney? Parents, siblings, nephews or nieces?"

She nodded curtly, tears streaming down into her hair.

"You see, you won't be able to help yourself. It may take a few months, or even a year, but you'll publish it. Someone will take your story seriously and will offer you money. A lot of money, Brittney. And by then, you'll be tired of living in this god-forsaken hell hole, living on ramen noodles and boxed mac and cheese. But you may still possess your convictions at that point and refuse to give me up. Then the threats will come. Parents or siblings losing jobs. Kids humiliated on social media. You won't be able to stand them being in pain because of you. One way or another, kid, you will be manipulated to tell someone what you know. Not just about me, but about my kind. It'll all go to hell for us after that."

She started to plead and scream and struggle against her bonds as he unpacked the garbage bags and surrounded the bed with the trash. Besides the internal fire that he always felt, his heart was breaking. When he had to do this back in Chicago all of those years ago, he swore he would never allow this to happen again. The Rainsfords were different. They were mature adults and knew the value of keeping a secret. As much as he liked his life as a human, he cursed the vulnerabilities of the human condition.

He faced her. "The smoke all of this shit will produce will knock you out well before the fire catches. You'll cough, lose oxygen, and pass out. Almost no pain." He doubted she could hear his reassurances through all of the screams and cries for help and mercy, but he felt the need to explain anyway. After it was laid out, he crouched down and focused on his internal fire. His dragon fire. Ig exhaled.

The dry leaves caught first, followed by the oily rags, which were the main fuel. He stood up and locked the door from the inside. As she screamed and started to cough, he quickly stepped to the window and pushed it open. The drop to the alley below was four stories. Perfect.

Ig turned to Brittney one last time and said, "Sorry, kid." He summoned his dragon strength and dropped out of the window. Landing without pain, Ig jogged out of the alley and away from the Havershire as quickly as he could. The fire wouldn't be noticed for a few more minutes, and he had to start a shift in a few hours.

Lord Bai and the Magic Pirate

Jean Marie Ward

Nanjing, 1421

"What do spells, copying, and writing have to do with pirates?" Lord Bai, White Dragon of the West, whined—no, *repined* in a light baritone befitting his human form.

It was a reasonable question for a gathering that billed itself as China's First Imperial Conference on Magic Piracy. But he could have misunderstood the conference's keynote speaker. Professor Yeoh was orating at the front of the hosting restaurant's second floor banquet hall, while Bai hid among the sorcery students at the back.

"Not 'copying and writing'—copy rights," whispered the student beside him. "Like Professor Yeoh said: All magicians are endowed as creators with certain unalienable rights, including the right to profit from all original spells, amulets, and charms."

"Even if somebody else does the copying?"

"Exactly."

But didn't writers pay printers to publish their work? Or was it the other way around? Who knew with humans? The longer Bai spent at the conference, the more at sea he felt.

Based on the invitation sent to Master Lao, Bai's self-appointed human teacher, Bai assumed the conference concerned pirates and magic treasure—subjects dear to every dragon's heart. When Lao forbade him to attend under threat of several exceptionally creative dooms, Bai had grown even more excited, certain it was one of *those* conferences—a four-day, Mandarins-only orgy of dim sum and dancing girls. But Bai had searched the venue from foundation to rafters and found no pretty women, no pirates, no treasure.

No food.

None for the students anyway. The attending scholars lounged around capacious tables, feasting at the Emperor's expense on every delicacy on the restaurant's menu. But between the professionals' gourmet paradise and the students' hellishly hard benches lay a wide aisle patrolled by waiters more vigilant than soldiers on the Great Wall. Bai couldn't even savor the aromas thanks to the mages' fondness for patchouli and the absence of anything resembling a breeze. The sliding doors to the loggia had been shut for "security reasons." *In the middle of summer!*

Concealed within his perspiring human form, the spirit of Bai's dragon tail thrashed irritably. He was experiencing a growth spurt and overdue to molt, magnifying his discomfort. He longed to depart, only he couldn't risk drawing attention to himself. Lao didn't look like much, but his sorcery could boil a dragon's eyeballs in their sockets.

That's when Bai saw it: the answer to his unspoken prayer. A fat red centipede—his favorite treat from the time he was a little wyrm—wriggled into the aisle.

Another steam basket-laden waiter barreled toward the door. Caution fled. Lunging off the bench, Bai snatched his prize from under the very shoe of doom. He popped it into his mouth.

It tasted like paper. He spat it into his hand. The centipede *was* paper—cheap red paper covered in smeared black ink. What was a paper magic centipede doing crawling around a magicians' conference? Was it some kind of joke?

Bai glanced at the students. As far as he could tell, they were all enraptured by Yeoh.

Could it be a message? Bai scanned the tables for a likely sender. Officials of the Department of Rites, their blue-violet robes emblazoned with the embroidered panels of their respective ranks, fanned themselves with painted silk paddles. Shaven-headed Buddhist monks traded superior looks with Daoist priests in crimson coats. Women physicians from the Imperial Palace held court behind latticework screens. At the foreigners' table, Arab scholars and Delhi astrologers scribbled notes with reed pens instead of brushes. No one was looking at the back of the room, not even Lao. The scrawny old reprobate rested his cheek on his upraised hand. Faint snores ruffled his wispy moustache. From the platters and wine pots massed around him, he had, as usual, consumed enough for three.

"That's the least of what we can expect if this deplorable state of affairs is allowed to continue," Yeoh warned. The silver gilt designs on his wide purple sleeves flashed as he thrust a pearl-ringed forefinger overhead. "The criminals engaged in the unlicensed reproduction, distribution, and sale of our spells, philters, and talismans are pirates as surely as the Wokou marauders of the Eastern Sea. Magic piracy is not a victimless crime. These spells are our livelihood. Every unauthorized copy is theft and should be punished as such. By stealing our intellectual property, they steal the rice from our mouths, strip the altars of our ancestors, and beggar our children. They must be stopped!"

Applause thundered in the closed room. Conferees jumped to their feet, including several at Lao's table. Lao jerked awake. Bai lowered his head and clapped furiously.

Another red centipede crawled into the aisle.

"Thank you, Professor Yeoh, for your brilliant summation," the master of ceremonies boomed as the centipede inched across the floor. "Friends and colleagues, the issues are clear. The stakes couldn't be higher. Now, let's hear some solutions!"

A wizened scholar jumped from his seat. He jerked a brass wand from his sash and sliced the air in a wobbly arc. "There can be only one!"

Everybody ducked, including the students. Bai bisected the centipede with a discreetly extended claw, hoping to learn its origin. The halves reverted to paper. Each scrap sported the partial outline of a centipede and the characters of a basic animation spell, which only established it wasn't made by Lao. His perfectly scissored paper servants needed no ink.

"Close the printing presses!" the old scholar bawled.

The crowd shifted. The papers skidded away on the draft. *Not good.*

"Professor Deng," the master of ceremonies soothed, "we want to protect legitimate printers, not close them down. We need printers to publish our books. More importantly, we need them to print the money for our salaries."

"Paper money! Bah!" Deng flapped his wand. "Silver was good enough for my daddy, and it's good enough for me."

"I hope your daddy's silver was good enough," Lao drawled. "He ran the Imperial mint."

Deng squawked as laughter burbled across the room. The master of ceremonies bleated, "Gentlemen! Gentlemen...and ladies!"

Phantom spines rippled uneasily under Bai's human nape. Paper servants had no will of their own. Someone directed those centipedes his way. But who? The why was easy. Many magicians coveted a dragon's abilities—to fly, to summon storms and disperse them, to speak any tongue—and the medicinal value of their individual parts.

Maybe he owed his tutor an apology. Maybe Lao's threats were a misguided attempt to protect him. *From paper centipedes? They were spelled for motion, not poison.*

Besides, how would anyone know there was a dragon to find? Other than a faint smoky tang to his perspiration, practically imperceptible amid the patchouli-pickled primates, there was nothing to distinguish Bai's current guise from that of a young human man. Unlike lesser species, dragons transformed completely, including their shadows. A powerful mage might detect the subtle difference in his aura, but only if they concentrated. But who, other than Lao, was strong enough and knew to look?

Engrossed in a quarrel about the cost of astrology manuals, none of the assembly seemed aware of his presence. Then again, anyone using something as inconspicuous as a paper centipede was trying hard *not* to be noticed. They wouldn't reveal themselves if they thought anyone was looking. Bai needed to act oblivious.

He pretended to stifle a yawn and slumped forward. Several overlong moments later, a russet-robed wizard with a fat topknot of white hair eased a bamboo tube from his sleeve. Shielding his face with one hand, he angled the tube under his mustache and inflated his cheeks. A red pellet dropped to the floor, unfurled into a centipede, and crawled toward the aisle.

The dragon waited until the centipede was a hairbreadth from his shoe before "accidentally" grinding it into the floor. The wizard's shoulders fell. Color drained from his face. One of his companions mouthed a question. Bai retrieved the centipede and snuck across the aisle.

He hadn't realized the aisle acted as a metaphysical barrier as well as a physical one. Once he crossed it, a dozen powerful magical auras blazed in his dragon sight like New Year fireworks. *Crap.* That changed everything. If the owners of those auras trained their occult senses on him, magic centipedes and Master Lao would be the least of his problems.

He was considering a strategic retreat when Deng hoisted his wand again. Suddenly everyone was too busy dodging the professor's swings to notice the dragon in the middle of the room. Bai hurried to the wizard's table. There was something odd about the group's magical auras—not strong, not bad, just…musky.

Bai could handle musky. He bowed.

"Did you lose something?" He dropped the centipede on the table.

The wizard squealed and sprang from his seat. The master of ceremonies called for order, Bai peered at the wizard's incongruously delicate hands. He didn't smell like an old man, either. Bai seized the wizard's whiskers. Beard and mustache came away in his grasp, revealing a smooth, sweetly rounded face with lips too pink and ripe for any man. The wizard was a woman. A very pretty woman.

All thoughts of danger and centipedes fled from Bai's head. "Hel-lo," he purred.

The young woman screamed. Her voice rang like a giant bronze bell, vibrating through muscle, bone, and brain. Bai's vision blurred. Humans rocked in their seats. Some lost control of their bladders.

Hoisting her robes over her shapely legs, the woman darted toward the paper-screened doors to the loggia. Bai gave chase, muscling aside the dazed magicians staggering from their seats. The woman burst through the latticed panels and leapt onto the railing overlooking the street.

He lunged. She jumped. Her robe grazed his fingertips as she plunged out of reach.

Hair spilled from her topknot, darkening to black as the strands swirled around her shoulders. Her robes billowed. For an instant she seemed suspended midair. Then she vanished. Her garments crumpled against the road in front of the restaurant. A three-tailed fox scuttled from under the pile. She dashed between the feet of the nearest sedan-chair driver, lashing her tails against the man's bare legs. He started. The poles on his shoulders pitched dangerously.

The woman was a fox? That made no sense. Foxes were masters of illusion, but even the strongest was no match for a dragon. Why tease him with centipedes, then run away?

Behind him, Lao yodeled, "Baaaaaaaaaaaaaaiiii—"

No time like the present to find out. Lao couldn't curse someone who wasn't there.

Bai vaulted over the rail and landed cat-nimble on the street. The fox woman's discarded clothes spun into a cyclone of twigs, dead leaves, and dust. The chair driver stumbled, tipping his cab and passenger into the dirt. By the time the leaves settled, the road was packed with stalled traffic. Everyone was shouting. Bai could barely hear the dogs caroling one street over. *Wait, dogs only bayed in the daytime when they hunted fox.*

He forced a path toward the sound. The closest cross street was backing up fast. Luckily the building at the corner was only one story tall. He launched himself at the eaves and clambered over the tiled roof. Flying would've been better, but he didn't dare flaunt his dragon self around so many adepts. If they weren't in league with the fox, he didn't want to give them any ideas.

The fox and its growing entourage of yapping dogs and outraged humans headed east, toward the Qinhuai River and the sprawling mansions on the opposite bank. Bai thought he saw a way of cutting her off before she reached the bridge. But pursuit by rooftop was harder than he expected. His heart hammered and his soft human legs burned. His next leap fell short. Sweaty hands skidded down the roof tiles, unable to find purchase.

He crashed through the awning of a noodle shop and landed awkwardly on a table. Customers screamed and scattered as he pitched forward into the street. He lurched to his feet.

The damn fox ran between his legs. The dogs hurtled after it, knocking Bai on his ass just as the noodle cook recovered his cleaver.

Now it was personal.

Yipping merrily, the fox scooted across the Qinhuai River Bridge. The dogs and Bai pounded after it, losing the cook along the way. The vixen led them past the elegant, red-roofed residential compounds fronting the river into a warren of narrow streets and foul-smelling lanes. Bai skidded on the mud outside a butcher shop and nearly landed in the muck. By the time he recovered, the last of the dogs had disappeared down an alley to his right.

Bai followed—and promptly smacked into a clothesline hung with wet linens. He ducked under it and blundered into another. And another. By the time he reached the T-intersection at the end of the alley, he didn't know which way to turn. The smell of washing soda and bleach had purged the reek of offal from his nostrils but made it impossible to scent any trace of fox. In contrast, the din of frustrated dogs seemed to echo from everywhere at once.

Bai shook the sweat from his eyes. He wasn't used to running so long in human form. His head ached, he had a blistered heel, and his sweat smelled smokier than usual. Stupid fox. He only wanted to question it. Now he'd have to make an example of it. *An extra crispy example.*

Wisteria frothed over the whitewashed wall of the compound facing the alley. A solitary seed pod dripped from the end of a bare vine. That wasn't right. The pod should have been nestled among the fronds, not dangling like a jade pendant from a single thread.

Something heavy crashed inside the compound. A woman yelped. A deeper voice cursed.

Bai grabbed the ropy trunk vine and hoisted himself partway over the wall.

Green crickets peppered the air over the courtyard within. They ricocheted from an overturned bench to the irises bordering a small pond, narrowly avoiding the maws of several hopeful carp. Beside the pond, a short middle-aged woman wearing a broad-brimmed hat and sapphirine gown wrestled a ginger cat almost as wide as she was. A much taller man clothed in a faded tunic and trousers swatted the crickets with his kerchief as if trying to emulate the legendary tailor who smote seven flies with one blow.

Bai instinctively caught one as it rocketed toward him. It crumpled like the centipedes at the conference. He opened his hand. A pair of limp wisteria leaves nestled in his palm.

"Fox magic!" he exclaimed.

The spell animating the crickets collapsed, swirling wisteria leaves across the yard. Glugging their disappointment, the carp returned to the depths. With a heartfelt sigh, the big ginger cat oozed through the woman's grasp, then picked his way through the shards of a broken tea service to a sunny rock overlooking the pond.

The woman fixed her beady gaze on Bai. In a voice as imperious as any at the conference, she demanded, "What did you say?"

"Fox magic. I'm chasing a magical three-tailed fox. For the authorities," he added mendaciously. "Turning leaves into crickets is the least of its tricks."

"There are such things?" Her hand stirred the air.

"Yes," meowed the cat.

The woman ignored it. Since her shadow appeared no more than human, chances were she didn't understand Cat. Bai added his "Yes" to the chorus.

She sagged in relief. "Merciful Buddha, I thought I was seeing things."

A loud bang echoed down the alley to Bai's left. In the narrow slice of street visible from his perch, he glimpsed the tangled wreck of two sedan chairs. The drivers bawled for the watch as a throng of bystanders descended on the scene, shouting contradictory orders.

The door to the lead sedan chair flopped open. A dazed, black-capped scholar tumbled onto the street. The rumpled cap and battered face of a second scholar appeared over the roof of the other chair. Bai recognized them as two of the Mandarins from the conference. What were they doing on this side of the river?

Looking for him! Bai flattened himself against the vines.

"Trouble?" the woman asked.

"An accident. I'm sure it was the fox, but I don't see her. She must have escaped in the confusion. Are there any temples in the area where she might find sanctuary?"

"Just her?"

Phantom spines and short hairs stiffened along the back of his neck.

The woman's lips twitched as if she sensed what she couldn't possibly see. "I thought so. Luckily for you, I never could resist a scamp. There are three joss houses in the neighborhood, but they're always crowded. The girls can be so superstitious. What about an abandoned kiln?"

He could have kissed her. *He* could hide in a kiln. Not that he needed to. *He hoped.* "Is there one nearby?"

"There's one on the grounds of the Nanjing Iron and Metal Company. Tell the foreman Lady Iris sent you."

* * *

The iron works' pug-faced foreman hurled his apron and thick leather mitts to the ground. He snarled at the furnace crew, "Don't get any ideas. I won't be long."

Bai's temples throbbed from the effort of restraining himself. The only thing that kept him from flash-frying the shrimp was the need to remain undetected. Just because he hadn't sensed any pursuers since leaving Lady Iris didn't mean he was safe—though the foundry's equally surly gatekeeper and resident dogs considerably improved the odds. Odds which would worsen in an instant if Bai delivered the set-down the foreman deserved.

"You're too kind, but I wouldn't want to take any more of your valuable time." *Surely there's a hellfire in need of your attentions.* "Surely one of your assistants—"

"Ha! Did you hear that?" the foreman boomed over the clamor of hammer and fire. "Our 'honored guest' wants a volunteer to show him the kiln."

The heat-reddened faces of the tenders paled. Fresh beads of sweat popped from their foreheads. Arms as thick as Bai's human thigh—arms hardened by a lifetime of heavy labor—trembled.

The foreman snickered. "No one in their right mind goes anywhere near that place."

Why, Bai wondered as they approached a derelict brick building shadowed by the city's massive ramparts. It looked deserted and felt inert. The broken top of the beehive oven cradled an untidy stork's nest. Storks were kin to phoenix. They would never cohabit with an evil spirit. Scuffed trails leading to the collapsed firebox indicated other animals also sheltered there, possibly including his three-tailed quarry.

The condition of the kiln's attached workshop, however, suggested the building wasn't as forsaken as it appeared. There were no gaps in the walls and no missing slats in the bolted shutters. The side door needed painting, but it fit snugly in its jamb.

Bai glanced over his shoulder. The iron works blocked the view to the street. Pyramids of coke blocked the view from the furnaces. A fugitive—fox or dragon—couldn't ask for a better hiding place.

A padlocked rear door faced the city wall. It echoed oddly when tapped. A rain-bleached paper rectangle clung to the lintel. Whatever magic the talisman might've possessed would've faded with its ink, yet he sensed no infernal aura seeping through the door. No spells, either. *Curious.* He took a deep breath, hoping for a whiff of fox. All he smelled was smoke, ash, liquescent metal, and the nervous sweat of his companion.

The foreman's left eyelid twitched. His gaze drifted westward, toward the sun-gilded roofs of the South Wall's Gathering Treasure Gate. "You done yet? The foundry closes at sundown."

"Really?" Perversely cheered by the foreman's fear, Bai strolled to the side door. "When was your last exorcism?"

"Are you kidding? You couldn't pay an exorcist to come here."

Bai lifted the vines shrouding the top of the door. He suspected any talismans there would be better preserved than those out back, but he never expected to find a Mandarin-grade, government-issued, demon-suppression charm, complete with Imperial crest. He was so shocked it took him a moment to realize he couldn't sense any magic. *That was odd.* Government exorcists were hardly the strongest mages around, but all their talismans carried an echo of the Emperor's heavenly mandate, even the denatured ones displayed at the conference.

"What the hell?" the foreman sputtered. "The Rites Department wouldn't send an exorcist without letting us know. It's too dangerous."

Bai gave himself a mental shake. The implications of the dud talisman could wait. "What about after dark, when you're closed?"

"Never happen. Those hacks quit earlier than we do, and even if they didn't, they wouldn't come here. Not after last fall. We found three dead kids by the oven." He grimaced. "It was bad."

Bai liked the part about government officials avoiding the place. But dead children? That didn't sound like a fox. Foxes protected children. "How did they die?"

"Hell if I know. They weren't strangled, but their faces were blue and covered in sores. The watch said they were burned. As if I don't know burns."

"What did the coroner say?"

"It isn't plague. Get back to work."

Translation: the coroner had no idea. "I see. I'll take it from here."

The foreman's scorn raked him from topknot to thick-soled shoes. "Where's your backup?"

"I've just come from the First Imperial Conference on Magic Piracy. I can handle it." Bai looked down his nose and defied the human to argue.

The foreman shook his head and stomped away. Once he was out of sight, Bai hardened his skin and extended his talons. He suspected the talismans only served to deter people from entering—or to alert someone if they had. But it never hurt to be careful. Human flesh scarred so easily, and Bai was vain in every form.

He slid a claw along the edge of the charm. The paste beneath smelled like rice. Satisfied it was safe, he broke the lock and pushed open the door.

Hinges screamed. Piercing whistles and ululating wails rose from deep within the building. The gatekeeper's dogs howled in protest. The smiths hammered faster, as if trying to drown out the noise.

Bai grinned. There was nothing uncanny about the sounds or the coolness that slithered over his hide. The anteroom was dark, with thick walls and floor-to-ceiling shelves. The voices were human. There was no mistaking the fug of human habitation, albeit salted with ink, paper, the distinctive musk of fox, and a whiff of...patchouli?

At the other end of the room a doorway opened into the workshop proper. From where he stood, the view consisted of stacked wooden planks and buckets of sand. Human footsteps retreated across the workshop floor. The moans acquired an echo, as if the performers had decamped to the oven. *"Leeeeeeeave now or shaaaaaaaare ourrrrrr faaaaaaaaate."*

A harsh, froggy voice took up the chant: "Leave now leave now leave now."

Bai was hot, winded, and (much as he loathed admitting it) worried. But with an entire foundry between him and any stray dragon-hunting mages, he wasn't leaving until he determined whether the fox he smelled was the one he sought. If it was, he'd make her pay for every itch and injury.

In a quavering tenor he commanded the spirits of the place to depart. Not surprisingly, the cries grew louder. "By Heaven," he shouted, "this kiln really is haunted. I'd better get my master."

He jogged a few steps in place to mimic flight, slammed the door, and waited for his eyes to adapt to the dim light from the workshop.

A peddler's pack stowed near the door reeked of the same musky smell as the fox's table. Crouching to examine it, he noticed something else. Lines of a dark, syrupy substance crisscrossed the floor. They didn't appear to form a pattern, but neither did some spider webs. Or clotheslines. He carefully stepped between them.

Dealing with the kiln's ersatz ghosts demanded equal care. He wouldn't repeat his mistake with the fox. He'd wait until he could surprise them. Meanwhile, he'd reconnoiter. The shelves were stacked with bundled charms, amulets, loose pages from various arcane texts, more government talismans, and ink-stained printer's blocks.

What was going on here? None of the books or talismans were illegal. They exuded no dangerous magic. Like the charm on the door, they exuded no magic at all. In fact, Bai couldn't sense any magic in the entire building, not even a fox-based illusion, which added to the mystery. Why employ a magic fox in a mundane printshop? *Why secrete it in an abandoned kiln?*

Because the texts were counterfeit, purloined—pirated!—and printed without permission from the authors or the government. But he bet they weren't sold that way. Talk about a sweet racket. It was like printing money—only minus the death penalty attached to counterfeit currency. *Oh, this was what they were talking about at the conference, and why they were so upset.* It also explained the bogus haunting. It was cheaper and safer to scare Imperial officials away than to bribe them. *Especially if you were pirating their work.*

But why did the fox lure him here? With his mind no longer clouded by his species' instinctive compulsion to hunt, he saw her actions in a new light. She deliberately aroused his curiosity with her centipedes and fled to guarantee his pursuit. Instead of diverting him with illusions, she led him to Lady Iris to ensure he found the kiln—and probably connived the scholars' crash to ensure they didn't. But bringing him here carried a terrible risk. One healthy dragon sneeze and the building would erupt in flames.

Could that be the goal? Revenge for the dead children?

He peeked into the workshop. Light seeping through the shutters illuminated a chamber three times the size of the anteroom. Low shelves spanned the front wall beneath the windows. Cabinets flanked the doorway to the kiln. A battered wardrobe blocked the back door, explaining the echo he'd heard earlier. A bedroll and trays of movable type filled the space between the wardrobe and the planks. A large table occupied the center of the room. Dust-spangled bands of sunshine striped ink trays, sponges, print blocks, and stacks of the same thick, ivory-colored paper used in the Department of Rites' most expensive charms. Ink, and only ink, splotched the floorboards—confirmation, if any was needed, that the syrupy trails of goo on the anteroom floor were some kind of trap.

"Froggy's" performance ended in hacking coughs. The wailer fell silent. Bai retreated deeper into the shadows. Someone hissed, "You can't stop. It's too soon."

"My throat hurts," Froggy responded. "Besides, he left."

"You don't know that. You'd better check."

"Yes, Mom," Froggy answered in a sarcastic sing-song.

A skinny, barefoot boy emerged from the oven. He looked about twelve in human years. Bai rolled back the scales from his head and hands. He wanted to talk to the children, not scare the piss out of them. He'd smelled enough of that today.

The boy checked the print table and the shutters but barely glanced at the anteroom. "He's gone. I told you he ran away," he rasped.

He pulled a pair of cracked leather mitts from under his shirt. The gauntlets swallowed his forearms. He re-entered the oven. "Hand me the goo."

Metal scraped against brick. Something *thunked.* The boy flinched. He reached into the darkness. Shoulders bowed by the weight of a heavy iron kettle, he shuffled into the workroom and lowered his burden to the floor.

A shorter, marginally cleaner little girl scampered after him.

"Don't put it away," she said. "We need to moisten the ink."

"We can use water. Master Sorcerer will never know."

The girl planted her mitts on her bony hips. "Xie Xiaoliang, that's not the point. If we don't feed the Golden Silkworm, we'll be stuck here forever."

"Shumeng, the smell makes me sick."

Her lips quivered. Her face puckered. Bai feared she'd start blubbering.

The boy opened his arms. "We can always run away."

"And go hungry again? Or have Master Sorcerer feed us to the Silkworm? No, we stick it out until we get our share of the gold. That way nobody gets hurt."

Not "goo." *Gu*—the legendary poison the Emperor feared more than death. The penalty for possession of *gu* was the Death of Ten Thousand Cuts. The penalty for actually using it... *Was that the syrup poured across the anteroom floor?* An angry growl rolled up Bai's throat. Shumeng and Xiaoliang jumped.

"Get back," Bai ordered as he strode across the room.

Rescaling his hands, he carried the kettle to the nearest window. The stench of turpentine and rust assaulted his nose as he lifted the lid. Eyes watering, he held his breath and tilted the kettle to see inside. The bloated carcass of a snake, a scorpion's stinger, and half a dead centipede bobbed in the thick sludge at the bottom of the pot. He shut the lid, pressed his face against the shutters, and cleared his lungs.

The pirate running this operation was a monster. It was one thing to use the legend of the Golden Silkworm to keep his minions in line. It was quite another to make them work with poison, especially one as lethal to breathe as it was to drink. Bai remembered the foreman's description of the dead children and tasted bile.

The girl yanked his tunic. "That's ours! Give it back!" A small fist connected with his scale-hardened back. "Ow! No fair! You're wearing armor!"

"Good thing, too," Bai said. The girl's eyes widened as a wisp of smoke floated between them. *So much for remaining incognito.* But she backed off. He pointed to the sand buckets on the other side of the room. "Over there. Both of you. Now."

Shumeng's chin jutted forward. "No."

"Don't be stupid. This stuff will kill you."

Her answer was to grab for the kettle. Bai lifted it out of reach. She jumped after it like a puppy.

"Put it down, you big thief. The Golden Silkworm belongs to us!"

"There is no Golden Silkworm. It's a dead snake."

"Is so a silkworm. It's too fat to be a snake. Master Sorcerer said—"

Bai snarled. "Let me guess: he told you he put a snake, a scorpion, and a centipede in the kettle. They fought to the death, and the winner turned into a Golden Silkworm which would spin money all day—as long as you fed it right. I don't suppose 'Master Sorcerer' explained what it ate."

Xiaoliang clenched his mitts. His gaze flicked from the girl to Bai. "Golden Silkworms eat *chi*," he admitted. "But he said if we mixed the *gu* with the ink, it could feed on lots of people at once. Nobody would get hurt, and the charms would be stronger."

"Wrong. All you get is poison." *Poison to kill you before you're tempted to betray him.*

"Prove it," Shumeng said.

"I don't have to. I'm bigger than you and..." He couldn't say "I've got scales." "No, you prove I'm wrong. Show me the money the silkworm spun."

"You'd just steal it," Shumeng spat.

"Would not!"

"How could he? We don't—" Xiaoliang began.

"No! Don't tell him!"

Shumeng's cry almost drowned out the muted thud of something striking the wardrobe doors. They sprang open. (*As if by magic,* Bai thought sardonically.)

He expected a flash of foxfire—an illusion to protect the many flammable objects in the workshop. But he underestimated the "Master Sorcerer." Patchouli-scented smoke gushed into the room. Professor Yeoh emerged from the cloud an instant before it cleared.

Enhanced by the opalescent gleam of the pearl ring on his right forefinger and the silver trigrams on his heavy purple sleeves, the effect was extraordinary. But there was no power behind it. The professor possessed no magical aura. None. The only glimmer of magic on his person were the faint emanations of the chestnut-sized pearl on his ring. *No wonder he became a pirate. No wonder he sent his fox slave to lure me here. This so-called Master Sorcerer has no magic of his own. He wants to steal mine.*

"Enough!" Yeoh commanded. The word resonated impressively in the small space.

Xiaoliang tried to drag Shumeng behind the type wheels. She twisted free and flung herself at Yeoh's feet.

"Stop him, Master Sorcerer!" she cried. "He's stealing our *gu*!"

Bai lowered his arm. "I am not. I'm getting rid of it for your own good."

"Silence, dragon!" Yeoh roared.

Bai winced, then froze as the kettle rocked on its handle. His human skin was as vulnerable as a child's.

Shumeng yelped, "Dragon? Him?"

The three-tailed fox shot from under the alchemist's robe. She grasped Shumeng's tunic in her teeth and dragged her toward the oven. Taking it as a warning, Bai hardened his skin.

But instead of squirting him with dangerous chemicals or blinding him with smoke, Yeoh threw a paper at him. It stuck to Bai's perspiring forehead. As he snatched it away, the alchemist slashed the pad of his left thumb with the sharpened nail of his right. Yeoh smeared a bloody yin–yang on his right palm and thrust it at Bai.

"By the powers of Earth and Air," he boomed. "*Om mani padme hum! Om mani padme hum!*"

Bai's gaze darted between the paper and the alchemist's hand. The yin–yang symbolized a thousand things in Daoism and nearly as many in alchemy. But he couldn't see any connection to the Six Treasures Mantra—in Sanskrit, no less—or the paper, which appeared to be a leaf from a Sanskrit version of the Heart Sutra.

"*Om mani padme hum! Om mani padme hum! Om mani padme hum!*"

Yeoh acted like he was intoning a spell. But neither mantra nor sutra had any effect on dragons. Maybe he didn't know what they were. From the way he butchered the syllables, Yeoh's command of Sanskrit was no better than Lady Iris's command of Cat.

Bai examined the paper. It looked old, tattered, and dark. But it felt rubbery and smelled smoky. Although the notion of magic piracy was new to Bai, thanks to Lao and his many disreputable associates, the concept of forgery was not.

"What are you grinning at?" Shumeng demanded. "Master Sorcerer's gonna turn you into a toad."

"*Om mani padme hum! Om mani padme hum!*" Yeoh chanted.

"Not with that mantra, he's not," Bai said.

Shumeng's eyebrows drew together. "It's not a mantra! It's a spell. Tell him, Kuaisu."

The fox growled and shouldered the girl back.

"*Om mani padme hum! Om mani padme hum!* It is done," Yeoh intoned. "Dragon, you are bound to my service by the power of the Blood *Taijitu* and the great ninefold spell by which the monk Xuanzang commanded the Jade Dragon and the Monkey King on his journey to the West."

"See, I told you it was a spell," Shumeng taunted.

"It wouldn't matter if it was," Bai said. "The professor lacks the power to make it stick."

"Who needs magic powers when I can call upon the spiritual energy of Xuanzang and the force of his heavenly patron, Guanyin." Yeoh produced a chopstick-sized iron wand from his sleeve and pointed it at Bai. "Now you will be punished for addressing your master without permission. Kneel!"

Bai snorted. Chortles of white smoke dribbled down his chin. "How do you propose to make me?"

"You hold the instrument of your subjugation in your hand: Guanyin's sutra of binding, transcribed in Xuanzang's own hand. Now, kneel!"

"This?" Bai tossed the paper on the table.

Yeoh gasped and snatched the paper to his breast. He shook his wand like old Deng. "Guanyin herself will punish you for desecrating her relic."

"That's no relic."

"You're wrong. It's real. I've seen its power in action."

Bai chuckled. "Before or after you took possession? Trust me, your sutra doesn't work. I'd know."

"That's impossible! It's the same sutra its former owner used to bind his dragon servant. The beast was as tame as a kitten. You can't fake that."

"Sure you can." Bai nodded at the fox. "With the right partner, it's as easy as aging new paper in old tea. I recommend Lapsang Souchong for that distinctive, burnt monastery smell. Your relic is a fake, just like your other talismans."

Yeoh sputtered. The fox bristled. Shumeng shouted, "Liar! Show him, Master Sorcerer!"

"Much as I'd like to see him try, I need to speak to the prefect of police about a murdering counterfeiter with a sideline in *gu*. Have a nice death, Professor." Bai flicked his forehead in a rude left-handed salute.

And nearly lost an eye when Yeoh threw the wand at him. "Kuaisu, collar him!"

The fox jumped, transforming in midair into a naked woman with three bushy, white-tipped tails. She flung the papers on the table at Bai. The pages exploded in flight, folding themselves into dragonflies. They dove at his face. As he batted aside their razor-edged wings, she snatched something off a shelf and charged. A hinged iron collar with spikes on the inside yawned between her hands.

Using the kettle as a counterweight, Bai swerved and kicked her ribs. She fell into the print table. Her arm landed in the ink tray. It sizzled like meat on a griddle. Screaming, she jerked away. The dragonflies popped like firecrackers. Smoking orange cinders rained to the floor. Bai caught a whiff of bacon and a glimpse of blistered flesh before the fox dropped the collar and rolled. She landed in four-footed form and flung herself against his legs.

Yeoh shrieked and chucked printing blocks at his head. Dodging awkwardly because of the *gu*, Bai almost missed the flare of sun on silver. Yeoh was palming something. Bai swung the kettle to deflect the alchemist's throw. At the same instant, Xiaoliang dashed behind him. The boy tripped over Yeoh's skirts and stumbled into his sister. Yeoh fell forward.

The kettle crunched into his temple. A flash of disbelief crossed his face as he crashed to the floor. Blood soaked his cratered features and spread from under his scholar's hat. His left eye had burst from its socket, but the right continued to glare indignantly. Wisps of smoke unlike any Bai had ever smelled floated upward from the alchemist's *gu*- and powder-splotched robe.

"Master Sorcerer!" Shumeng cried.

"Stay back," Bai ordered as he set the kettle on the floor.

Xiaoliang hauled Shumeng into the tunnel. Bai dumped a bucket of sand on the body, hoping to smother any fire before it caught. It didn't work. Whatever unholy mix the alchemist had accidentally compounded was still reacting. To keep it from spreading, Bai needed to destroy Yeoh's clothes in a controlled burn. He grabbed the man's right shoulder to carry him outside. The fox snapped at his hand.

"Stop! I've got to get him out of here!"

She screamed like she had at the restaurant. He had time to say, "Not again," before foxfire bleached the world white, and a paper whirlwind spun around his head. So, he did the only thing he could. Shapeshifting blind, he fell upon the corpse with the full weight of his dragon form.

* * *

Blind shapeshifting was bad, but a forced molt in a confined space while he was still blinking spots from his eyes was worse. Bai couldn't even dry himself. There wasn't anything left fit to serve as a towel. There wasn't any pearl either. When he checked under his shed skin to ensure the chemical reaction had stopped, he found Yeoh's right hand. Its forefinger and the ring it wore were gone, vanished with the children and the fox.

A clatter of hoofbeats approached the kiln. Who could that be? And how in seven hundred hells did they get past the foreman and the dogs? Bai peeked through the shutters and groaned. Prancing up to the building astride a splendidly caparisoned white mare was the only person in the world equal to the task.

Bai flung open the shutters. A draconian growl rumbled from his human lips as he readied himself for a defensive shift. "*Laaaaooo.* What are you doing here?"

The mare shied. Lao stilled her with a click of his tongue and dismounted. The horse blinked out of existence. An equine silhouette no bigger than a saucer fluttered into the sorcerer's palm. He folded it into a perfect square and slipped it into the pouch at his belt.

"Checking my student's progress. Now where's my pirate?"

Bai gaped. "How did you know?"

"Because the entire conference was a cunning ploy devised by the Department of Rites' newest and—" Lao splayed bony fingers over the bright new Mandarin's badge pinned to his faded gown "—if I do say so myself, most perspicacious special consultant, to trap the biggest magic pirate in four provinces."

"How was I supposed to know that? You said you'd curse me vegetarian if I went anywhere near the place!"

"Works every time. Good thing, too, or those idiots at the Department of Justice would still be scrying for stolen talismans. After seven years, you'd think they would've realized the pirate had a magical creature capable of forging anything—no stealing required. But I deduced the truth, and I knew exactly how to flush the villain out of hiding. One magic servant is never enough for these people. They're always looking for a bigger score, and there's nothing bigger than a dragon. So, who was it?"

"You used me as bait!" Steam hissed out of Bai's mouth. "I could've been captured. Enslaved!"

Lao shot him a pitying look. "Don't be melodramatic. I had everything under control."

"You're as crazy as Deng! Half the scholars at that conference wanted a piece of me. Two of them crashed their sedan chairs trying to get to me. The rest are probably still hunting. I'll be forced into hiding—and I'm the hero here!"

"Details, details," Lao said blithely. "I knew you'd manage."

If Bai could've broken the spell that constrained him from harming his teacher, he would've ended his human education in a fiery instant. But he couldn't, leaving Lao free to commit still more crimes against his person and his self-respect. It was a shame Yeoh was dead. He would've loved to give Lao a taste of the professor's chemistry.

Inspiration blazed like a fire stick. Stifling the urge to grin, Bai heaved a dejected sigh. "Your pirate was the conference's keynote speaker, Professor Yeoh."

"Yeoh? The man is the top in his field. Why…?" Lao shook his head. "Never mind. With alchemists, it's always money. Turning lead into gold is an expensive proposition."

"Doesn't that defeat the purpose?"

"So does swallowing mercury to become immortal, but people do it all the time. Wait, you said 'was.' You didn't eat him, did you?"

Bai reared. "I wouldn't soil my fangs with him. He ran into a kettle of *gu*."

"A magic pirate, a shape-shifting fox, and *gu*?" Lao crowed. "This assignment just keeps getting better. Don't touch anything. It's all evidence. I'll be right there."

"Use the back door. The side room is booby-trapped," Bai said helpfully.

As soon as Lao vanished around the corner, Bai dragged his molted hide away from Yeoh's remains. The only identifiable parts were the extremities. A large fly rubbed its forelegs together over the raw stump of the Yeoh's ring finger. Bai scowled. The fly was having more fun than he was. *For now.*

Lao burst through the doors of the red-splattered wardrobe. Skidding on the gore, he grabbed the jamb to steady himself.

Bai would always treasure the moment when his teacher's indifferent human nose registered the rotten meat stench of aging blood and ruptured bowels, and his mind comprehended the nature of the mess on the workroom floor. The old sorcerer's eyebrows retreated under the edge of his scholar's cap. His wrinkled face paled. He lifted his hand from the doorjamb and stared at his bloodstained palm. He whimpered. Bai distinctly heard him whimper.

Lao tried to speak. He failed. His prominent Adam's apple traveled the length of his throat. He gulped and tried again.

"The fox?" he croaked.

"Gone. I think she was an unwilling accomplice. She must have smelled Yeoh's dragon-taming spell was a forgery, yet she said nothing." That much was certain. Everything else was surmise. "I suspect she was bound to his pearl ring. She took it with her when she left."

Bai tilted his head toward the alchemist's hand. A russet-hued dragonfly whizzed past and snatched the fly on the wing. A small shiver danced down his spine. *Could it be…?*

"Probably." Lao said faintly. "I suppose you'll burn all this."

"I wouldn't dream of it, Master Lao," Bai purred. "It's evidence."

Lao shouldn't have been able to blanch further, but he did.

"Actually, I have a better idea," Bai said.

Lao eyed him warily.

Bai scratched the drying mucus on his chest. "I need to wash, and the Yangtze isn't far as the dragon flies. Have your paper servants load the remains into my old skin. I'll dump them when I bathe.

"It's only fitting," he added. "The professor was a pirate. He deserves to sleep with the fishes."

Tatsu: Cryo Five

Gerald Brandt

Motion woke me from the darkness of slumber. Not the normal movement of distant things that I had become accustomed to, but a sharper reflection that betrayed something's presence.

It was far off yet, in this black I have called my home for longer than I care to remember. For longer than I can. But it was getting closer. I could *feel* it on my skin, despite the layers of protection covering me. I flexed, the movement small, only enough to know that I still existed, that my body had not disintegrated into dust as I slept. Too small for whoever was out there to see.

Next, I checked my treasures. There were not many, but I knew each one by its shape and smell. I knew the details of every imperfection. I knew them more than I knew myself.

They were perfect.

They were hidden.

They were safe.

And they were mine.

Each of my treasures lay safely inside my body, protected by my thick hide and layers of armor. The only way to get to them was to kill me, and that would not be an easy task. Or so I hoped.

The movement got closer.

I had more once. More treasures. Thousands of them. That memory, like so many others, has faded into the distance of time and age. It feels as though it was not really me, back then, like it was not my body or my soul that kept the treasures safe. If I concentrate, if I use some of the precious energy left to my failing shell, I do remember some of it.

There were twelve of us. Somehow, that was supposed to be lucky, supposed to help us find our new homes. I do not know how it helped. As soon as we left, we all went our separate ways, and the twelve became one. For years, I traveled, then for decades, then centuries. Constantly alone, looking for the place I could call home, the promised land. The place my treasures could be safe and flourish. I found only emptiness and desolation, my only consolation that perhaps the others had found what I could not, had succeeded where I had failed.

Now, I was old. I could feel parts of me decaying, dying off one piece at a time. There was not much left anymore, of me or my treasures. But I still had fight in me, still felt the furnace of heat and flame in my belly, still could protect what was mine. Even if it meant the end of me. Though it would mean the loss of everything I held so dear, at least I would no longer be around to feel that pain I knew so well.

The movement had stopped, yet I knew they were still out there. It was almost as if I could sense them, as though they had reached out and touched me. An impossibility, but it kept my mind on the task at hand, at least. Kept me aware that they were still there until they moved again. When they did, they were exactly where I knew they would be, and moved exactly as I thought. Closer to my treasures.

* * *

For a while, I could still sense my fellow travelers, until the distance between us became too great. I did not care back then. I was young and strong, at my peak. There was nothing that could stand in my way, that could stop me from finding a new home for my treasures, a place where I could trust they would never be found, where they would be safe and I could watch over them like a proud parent. But time has a way of tempering us all; of showing us our mortality and our weaknesses…our frailty against the vastness of what is out there.

The first storms I encountered were small. Still, I skirted around them as best I could. When a big one came, and there was no place for me to go, I hunkered down and weathered it out. That one did not leave me unscathed; I still bear the scars today. Despite that, my treasures were safe and my journey was still ahead of me. I was filled with optimism.

It took almost a century for the next big storm to find me. It put the first one to shame with its size and ferocity. I tried to go around it, over it, even under it, to no avail. I was pelted by rock and ice. Light reflected off my skin in tiny rainbows that inflicted a pain more intense than I had ever known. I could feel it cut deep, past my defenses. It was here I lost the first of my treasures. That was a pain worse than what the storm inflicted on me. When it was over, I had lost half of what I had tried to keep safe, half of the treasures that were more me than I was of myself.

What the storm took away, it also gave. I felt reborn. Even through my grief and pain, I knew I was not the same. My body hurt and my heart ached with loss, but my mind had strengthened. I was, I realized, complete. I swore, then, that nothing would take my treasures from me ever again, that I would die before I lost more.

I failed at that, too.

* * *

A sudden wave of clarity fluttered through me like the coldness of space. Of course I could feel whatever was out there. There was a reason I could sense it even when it no longer moved. It was like me, but not quite. Another dragon had entered my home, looking not for safety as I had, but for more to add to her horde. This was not one of the twelve seeking out its brethren, but an outsider, seeking only to take what did not rightfully belong to it.

She was young. I could tell from the way she moved. She was close enough now that I could see her hide was unmarked, smooth. That was a weakness. Though she was easily twice my size, I was battle ready. I had fought for my life before, protected my horde from the onslaught of others. She had not, and because of that, the advantage was mine.

I stopped. *I had fought before.* Where had that memory come from? It was not there a moment ago, but now that I felt it, I knew it to be true. I had fought before, and my presence here proved that I had won.

Or that I had managed to escape.

Time stripped everything away, and that one piece of memory, though seemingly sharp and clear, remained without detail. Whatever had happened back then, there would be no choice today. I would fight. Not because of ego or strength, but because of the lack of it. I was too old to run, and had no place to run to. I had made this place my refuge, knowing that I would die here. Whether that death came from age or from battle was a moot point. If fate had chosen battle, then who was I to argue? My only wish, my only dusting of vanity, was that I would at least put up a good fight. Maybe I would even win, and my treasures would remain safe a while longer. With that thought, I rose from my resting place, and spewed fire from my open maw.

If age was her fatal flaw, mine was time, for I had paused as memory had risen to the surface, and fire flew into empty space.

* * *

The battle did not last long, nor was it as violent as I had thought it would be. Neither had death come to take me. Instead, it was humiliation as

I lay crippled and unable to move. There was no pain. That surprised me. But then, she had not used fire against me. She had done something else… something more subtle. The touch I had felt earlier had strengthened, become a force I had no defense against. It was as though she had simply opened a door, and I no longer had the will or ability to fight.

But I did have one more weapon. Protecting my horde was so ingrained into who and what I was that nothing she could do would change it. No one, no *thing*, would get what was rightfully mine. No harm would come to my treasures from outside. I would destroy myself and what remained of my horde first.

I started the countdown.

I felt another tickle that turned into a command I could not deny, and the countdown stopped, my humiliation complete. I could not even complete my basic programming.

* * *

I let them in with the same ease. She pulled up beside me in the darkness and linked with me, creating a passage between my body and hers. I felt my horde increase. There were five of them, five treasures that now walked through me. Five treasures, the same, and yet…not. I monitored the beat of their hearts, felt their moist breath when they removed their helmets, heard them communicate by pushing waves through the air.

I realized then that she—they—were not here to steal from me, but to help.

One of them removed a glove and laid a warm hand against my wall.

"It's okay, old man. You've done a good job. It's time to go home."

I felt another tickle, another presence that was so like me, yet not, and then I was gone.

A King Arthur Dragon in Space Station 23's Court

Gini Koch & Bebe Bayliss

Cador was going about his ordinary tasks. Find a couple of goats for lunch—sheep were tasty but their wool got too stuck in the fangs for them to be anything but a last resort. See if any young women in the nearby villages might be acceptable to become his next official maiden. Ensure the home fire inside his belly was stoked—currently being handled by a dead tree. Mundane things for a dragon of this age.

And what an age it was. Arthur was on the throne, the greatest king the land had ever hoped to see, surrounded by noble knights, and Cador's last maiden, Guinevere, was his queen, meaning a job well done right there. In fact, after he found a goat, it was time to visit, at her request, to give her guidance with an issue she hadn't felt comfortable sharing via a messenger.

It was a time of peace and prosperity. And magic. Quite a lot of magic, and Merlin's experiments were getting wilder by the moment. Perhaps this was what Guinevere wanted to discuss.

Cador finished munching on the tree, his home fire now nicely filled up, and it was time to find those goats.

Only, instead of goats, he found a young man, brandishing a pitchfork. "I have you now, foul fiend!"

Cador heaved a sigh, which created a bit of smoke, which dribbled out of his nostrils. "You can't actually hurt me with that."

"I will not be swayed by your evil, forked tongue."

"Can't help how we're made, and less insults would do a lad of your stature, build, and looks wise, since you're basically an insult waiting to happen."

"I will destroy you as Saint George destroyed your forebear!"

"About that, not a relative of mine, though, as a dragon, I do take offense—"

"Silence! I, Lucius the Soon to be Great, have found a spell of Merlin's to destroy you utterly!"

"Merlin actually likes dragons. He's one of us, essentially."

But Lucius wasn't paying attention to Cador. He was, instead, busy scrunching up his face.

"Are you in pain?" Cador asked solicitously.

"No, I'm remembering the words that I heard!"

This did not bode good tidings. The lad clearly wasn't able to read. Sounds in spells mattered, but understanding what the sounds meant mattered more. Intention in spells was key.

"I think I'll just be on my way..." Cador started edging away.

But the boy began the incantation. "By the powers of the great mage Male-ifin-sentry—"

"That word or name cannot be right," Cador shared.

Lucius ignored him. "—I call upon the powers—"

"Isn't that a bit repetitive? I mean, most spells don't work like this."

"Shut up, fiend. I call upon the powers to destroy the drac-oh-nin-on-ian fiend in front of me."

"Just going to move behind you, don't mind me."

Lucius sped up. "I banish thee in space and time and send you from this year, the year...what year is it?"

"As you count it, five hundred and twenty-three anno Domini."

"Thank you. Five hundred and twenty-three anno Domini and send you far from me!"

They both waited. Nothing happened.

"Lovely effort, good try. Now, if you'll excuse me..." Cador kept on edging around the boy.

"It should have worked! I saw the lizard slain!" Lucius looked at his pitchfork. "Of course!"

"Well, while we do share some traits with lizards and such, we're really our own genus and—"

But Cador's explanation was cut short, because Lucius threw the pitchfork at him. "Die, foul fiend!"

Cador knocked it away with his right front leg. "Really, this is no way to behave. Does your mother know what you're about?"

Lucius reached into the pouch hanging around his waist. "This must be what it was for," he said, more to himself than Cador, as he pulled out a pulsing, glowing orb.

"That looks…almost alive," Cador said uneasily. "What is it?"

"Merlin called it a sie-in-tiffic device to move him through time and space."

"Stealing from great wizards is not a good thing for a boy your age to be doing."

Lucius took a deep breath. "Be far from me in five hundred and twenty-three!" Then he threw the orb directly at Cador.

Cador tried to dodge, but the lad had decent aim and the orb hit him square in the face. "Ow!" It felt as though something foreign was sliding all over him, encasing him in a substance like jelly. And he began to tingle. "Excuse me, is this supposed to be happening?"

Lucius stared at him, open-mouthed. Cador took this to mean the answer was "no." The rhyme of the boy's last sentence must have worked and activated whatever the orb really was. Somehow and in some way.

The tingling increased. He lifted and moved as everything around him went past in the blink of an eye. He kept floating up, higher and higher, still tingling, unable to move or speak, heading…somewhere. Somewhere dark, though there were pinpoints of light that moved far faster than he.

It seemed like forever and no time at all when he heard words again. A woman's voice, faint at first, then louder. "…in all of time and space, pretending that a young man doing his job had maleficent thoughts about anyone, let alone the Draconian ambassador is ludicrous. This case should be thrown out of Space Station Twenty-three's court never to return!"

The tingling increased and he felt he was moving faster. He wasn't sure where to, but perhaps it would be better than the nowhere he was right now.

* * * *

Paula was at a loss. She had a client who was going to be put to death because he'd tripped over a mop, and her main witness was late to court.

Her many-greats grandfather had probably never had issues like this. An Earth lawyer so famous he'd changed the way legal battles were fought, Super-Great-Grandfather Melvin would never have been in this situation. Then again, he hadn't had to take a job on a space station as a public defender, either. Things had definitely been better, and easier, a few centuries ago. She needed to channel his genetic genius, and she needed to do it now.

"Counselor Belli," Judge Matier said tiredly, "we're not at summation, so I assume you're stalling. I realize this is a time-honored maneuver for you, but are you calling another witness, or are you going to sit down and allow the prosecution some time?"

Paula shot a look over at Melissa Matthews, her legal clerk, who nodded emphatically. Good, her witness had finally made it. "Your honor, I'm not stalling, I'm merely sharing that, in the year two thousand five hundred and twenty-three, we shouldn't be dealing with this kind of an incident as a major crime when a sincere apology should be enough. But," she said quickly, before Aaron Franks, the prosecutor, could object, "we are not here to discuss Draconian laws, and I'm in no way insinuating the fine people of Draconia are overreaching their, as they call them, 'foul fiend laws,' but am merely sharing that I now call my witness to come to me in the court of Space Station Twenty-Three!"

Super-Great-Grandfather Melvin had always been a showman. Theatrics were important, you had to play to the jury or, in the case of how space stations operated, the judge and, because it was always wise, the spectators. So, as she said the last words, Paula flung her arms wide, lifting one arm towards the courtroom door, and the other towards the ceiling. She was not prepared for what came next.

There was a fizzing sound, and suddenly there was a dragon standing on the floor next to her, midway between the plaintiff's table and the judge's bench.

As with every other space station in the galaxy, the courtroom was intentionally huge, so the dragon didn't land on or break anything. The galaxy was filled with lifeforms of all shapes and sizes and they all ended up in court at some point.

Since this was a case dealing with Vesantolocryn, the Draconian ambassador, there were actually quite a lot of dragons in the courtroom. But they were from the planet Draconia, and this dragon didn't look much like them. Well, the general shape, yes. But it was clear he was far more animal-like than the Draconians were. He was on all fours, for one thing.

He also looked shocked. Paula imagined she looked shocked as well, in no small part because she'd been expecting the janitorial partner to her client to come through the doors, not a dragon to appear like magic.

"Theatrics are always appreciated, Counselor," Judge Matier said in a tone that indicated quite the opposite. "Could you please have your witness state their name and planet of origin?"

Paula and the dragon stared at each other. There was nothing for it—this time, she really *had* to stall. Hopefully he had animal-level hearing.

"Cough," she said under her breath, not moving her lips.

The dragon looked confused. "Ah…" he said just as quietly.

"*Cough.*"

He coughed. Smoked belched into the courtroom.

"Your honor, a thousand apologies!" Paula said, keeping the relief out of her voice. "But my witness clearly needs some water. Could we possibly adjourn for just a few minutes so I can relieve his distress?"

Judge Matier coughed. "Yes. Recess, back in fifteen or whenever the smoke clears."

Paula jerked her head at Melissa, who joined them. "Let's get our witness somewhere very private," Paula said quietly.

"I, ah, would like to partake of some water, actually." The dragon sounded nervous. "I have no idea where I am."

"Keep it down," Paula muttered, as she put her hand on the dragon's front leg and began to lead him after Melissa, who'd grabbed their client and headed to their private room attached to the court.

When the four of them were inside, Paula shut the door while examining the dragon. He was about twelve feet long, stood on all fours, had a horse-like head, and spikes running down his back to end in a spear-tipped tail. Unlike the Draconians she knew, his wings were on his back and looked powerful enough to achieve flight. He was red with golden highlights, and red wasn't a typical Draconian color. "I'm Paula Tryscha Belli. In court, please refer to me as P.T. though—it sounds stronger. And you are?"

"Not understanding your issues with your name, but I am Cador the Custodian. Feel free to merely call me Cador."

"That's what I do, too!" exclaimed their client. "I'm Dommo Anime, Cador, and it's really nice to meet you!"

"A pleasure," Cador replied.

"Stop speaking Dommo, I guarantee Cador isn't using the term in the same way you are." Paula took a deep breath. "Your planet of origin?"

He stared at her. "Earth."

Paula stared back. "Really," she said after a long while. "What year were you born, if you don't mind my asking?"

"I do not. I was born in the year, as humans count, four hundred and twenty-three anno Domini. I was attacked by a ruffian, Lucius the Supposedly Soon to be Great, in the year five-hundred and twenty-three, and then things went…strange."

"So, wait, you're over two thousand years old?" Dommo asked. "You look great! What's your secret?"

Cador shook his head. "No, I'm one hundred years of age. And I have no secrets I know of. Lucius threw something he'd stolen from Merlin at me which brought me here. I believe, at any rate."

"Merlin?" Paula asked. "As in *the* Merlin?"

Cador nodded. "Yes, the wizard of King Arthur's court. My last maiden is the queen, Guinevere."

Melissa cleared her throat. "Cador, when you, ah, left, were things going well between Arthur and Guinevere?"

"Yes, of course! Though my Guinevere did want to discuss a personal issue with me, though I have no idea what it was."

Melissa grimaced. "I do." She looked at Paula. "I'll bet our new friend is not going to enjoy my information."

"Probably not." Paula's hobbies related to courtroom theatrics and showmanship. Melissa's hobbies were far more interesting. Among other things, Melissa had an encyclopedic knowledge of all things Arthurian.

Cador coughed again and more smoke belched out. "I'm so sorry, but I truly would like that drink of water."

"Melissa, get Cador his water—use a bucket. Dommo, sit there and don't speak. Cador, once Melissa returns and you've had your drink, I think you may want to be in whatever position a dragon of your lineage would choose to be in for some very shocking news."

* * *

Cador considered insisting there was no way he'd moved two thousand years into the future and so far from Earth it would take weeks to return there on what Paula called a starship—two words which made no sense when said together—but decided that would be foolish, because he could tell she wasn't lying.

He definitely considered saying something truly nasty about Lucius, but, even if a miracle had happened and that boy hadn't been murdered by someone doing the world a favor, he'd been dead for just under two thousand years. Cador felt it was wrong to hold a grudge that long, so he let it go.

Per Melissa, who also was clearly telling the truth, Merlin and Arthur and Guinevere, and all the others, were considered myths. Popular myths, myths still spoken of two thousand years later, but myths, nonetheless. It hurt his heart, but that was the way of humans.

What hurt more was what had happened to Guinevere when Lucius had sent him out of place and time. She'd needed Cador's guidance regarding Lancelot, and he hadn't been there. He'd failed her, failed Arthur, too, in that sense. His reason for being, a *dragon's* reason for being, destroyed because of an idiot.

There were no longer any dragons left on Earth and they, too, were considered myths. Too many people like Lucius had killed them all. There was, per Melissa, some talk that dragons had been real, taken to the stars, and had founded Draconia. He could but hope.

What was going on had been explained as well and he took it in, internalized and accepted it, and moved on. Well, other than for one key question.

"But why am I here, in this place, now?" he asked, after Melissa had returned with more water and Cador had drunk it all in one gulp. "As opposed to still floating in space or landing elsewhere."

Paula shook her head. "I have no idea."

"My name sounds a lot like what you said after the year," Dommo said, ignoring Paula's repeated commands to stop speaking. "I'm Dommo Anime, like the art form."

"Yes, a dragon from Arthurian times certainly knows about anime," Paula said. She looked at Cador. "I just don't think someone should die because they tripped over their own mop and fell onto some dignitary's cape."

"That's a killing offense in this world?" Cador couldn't keep the horror from his tone.

"It is on Draconia. The space station courts have to acquiesce to planetary laws quite often, and since it happened to the Ambassador..." Paula shrugged. "I'm doing my best, but the witness I was expecting was not, to be honest, you, Cador."

His stomach grumbled. "What, if I may ask, is the goat situation on this—what did you call it—space station?"

She stared at him, then laughed. "Oh. You're hungry. We don't have live goats, but we'll get some food for you. Meat only, or do you eat grasses and grains?"

"Meat for preference."

Paula sent Melissa off to gather sustenance. Cador considered Dommo's name. "Anno Domini is something like the reverse of Dommo Anime."

"True. What was the full spell the kid used on you?" Paula asked.

"It was mostly incoherent." But he repeated the words and what Lucius had told him of the orb. "I truly believe Merlin's orb is more to blame than anything else."

"In the age you're speaking of, a scientist would be a wizard," Paula said. "And, if we take the legend of Merlin to be true—and you're here, insisting this is someone you knew personally, so we can take that to be rock solid—then he was probably the premiere scientist of his age. And that means his orb worked." She sighed. "Lucius must have stolen the original."

"Perhaps. Perhaps Merlin created another and moved himself forward but with accuracy."

"How does this help me?" Dommo asked plaintively as Melissa returned lugging what appeared to be half of a cow with her. She was a small girl but seemed to be able to carry heavy loads. Obviously from good peasant stock. Cador approved of good peasant stock—they were the people who kept the world working. Or, presumably in this case, the space station he was somehow now sitting in.

"It doesn't," Paula admitted.

"I hope it's okay that it's raw," Melissa said as she put the food down in front of Cador.

"Raw is just as I like it," Cador said happily. "It was kind of you to remove the hide and hooves, though they do add substance and crunch."

Paula and Melissa didn't say anything, though Cador was certain they both wanted to. However, he hadn't eaten for two thousand years—and a day—since Lucius had prevented him from finding any goats, so Cador chose to eat instead of question.

Which was fine, because Dommo was filling the silence. "So, I guess dragons eat things whole, huh? That's interesting, because sometimes I eat things whole, too. But usually only fruit or vegetables that have good-tasting skin and stuff."

"Dommo," Paula said tiredly, "please, by all that's holy, stop speaking."

"Are you going to put him on the stand?" Melissa asked her.

"Only if I have to." She shook herself. "Where is our actual witness?"

"No idea," Melissa said. "I took a look when I went to get water and then food for Cador. I was assured he'd arrived, but now there's no sign of him. However, there was one thing I heard that might help us—Vesantolocryn has it out for our client, but not because of the cape incident. That's just their excuse. There's more going on, but I couldn't catch what."

Paula looked at Dommo. "What else could you have done that would have upset the Draconians?"

"I have no idea! I mean, Aeronella always says I'm the nicest human she's ever met."

Silence filled the room. Cador stopped chewing and assessed the situation. Whatever Dommo had said, it was a shock to both women.

"Dommo," Paula said slowly and carefully, "are you saying you have a relationship with a female Draconian?"

"Yes," he said cheerfully. "Aeronella is the nicest person I've ever met. She and I don't see genus, we just see love."

This caused both Paula and Melissa to look more stunned than before.

"Excuse me," Cador said after he swallowed, "but do the Draconians follow the dragon-maiden relationship rules here, or do they follow something different?"

"Dragon-maiden relationship rules?" Paula asked, clearly for all three humans.

"A moment." Cador looked pointedly at the empty bucket and coughed discreetly.

Melissa took the hint, grabbed the bucket, and headed off for more water. She returned just as Cador finished his side of beef. He drank all the water, then nodded. "So much better, thank you. Now, am I to understand that you do not understand the dragon-maiden relationship?"

"Correct," Paula said. "We've never heard of it."

"Well, not exactly," Melissa said. "I've found references to it, but they were quite vague."

"Dragons ate maidens, that's what I've always been told," Dommo added. "The Draconians don't do that, but they aren't dragons from the stories."

"We absolutely do not!" Cador replied, horrified. "That was a foul accusation made by that heinous George person from ages ago. He wanted that dragon's maiden for his own, she did not want him, and he murdered her protector to get the 'woman he loved' or, as we think of it, his unwilling victim."

"History's a lot different when you talk to someone who was there," Melissa said to Paula.

"Exactly," Cador replied.

"I don't want to be rude," Melissa went on, "but you may need to tell us this quickly. The courtroom was almost cleared of smoke when I got back with your water, and all the Draconians are back in their seats."

"I can fix that." Cador went to the door they'd entered this room from and gave her an expectant look. "Just a crack should do the trick."

Paula groaned, but nodded, and Melissa dutifully trotted over and opened the door. Cador took a deep breath and let it out slowly, sending more smoke into the room. He noted the attendees in the stands.

These Draconians looked like combinations of all the Earth dragon clans. Interbreeding could be why, and would make some sense, especially if Merlin had moved more than himself in space and time. There were other differences, but the main ones were that they stood on their hind legs and used their fronts ones as humans did, and they all wore long, elaborate capes.

He backed away, and Melissa closed the door as he settled back down. All this had taken only a few seconds. "That should give us a bit of time. Now, the dragon-maiden relationship is an ancient one, created in the early days, when humans were finally smart enough to use weapons and have rudimentary language.

"Over time, an important part of our culture as dragons became finding a worthy maiden. We dragons select our maidens carefully—she must understand learning is of the utmost importance, being kind and fair to all is key, and a variety of other good qualities.

"Once a maiden has agreed to join with her dragon, the two go off to the dragon's home where all is peace and safety. The maiden is brought up with proper manners, a complete education including a variety of languages, and the ability to mingle with the highest nobility or the lowest serf and to make all around her feel at ease.

"Our maidens then go on to find suitable mates, or they stay with their dragon if no suitable mate is felt to be available. This choice is up to the maiden, though her dragon will, of course, do his or her best to encourage their maiden to be of service to the rest of humankind."

"So," Paula said, "I've never heard of this as a Draconian custom."

Cador shrugged. "It just means they've forgotten the old ways. If they're truly dragons, of course."

"Aeronella said their eternal leader's name is Merlin," Dommo shared. "They still follow his rules, though he tends to leave them alone unless they need him."

The others stared at him. "*The* Merlin?" Paula asked finally.

"I don't know, but she says he's wise and good and has lived for at least three thousand years."

"Merlin was a crossbreed," Cador said, "from the earliest of dragon-maiden times, when a maiden and her dragon fell in love. Because his birthing killed his poor mother, those relationships were forbidden ever after. But him being three thousand years old would be fairly accurate—dragons live long lives in the first place and if Merlin discovered the secret of longevity, I can guarantee he'd use it."

"Who wouldn't?" Melissa agreed.

"So that's part of why he has such magic and scientific genius," Paula mused. "Because he's a mixture of a long-lived race and a human, with the human drive of exploration and the talent to really explore." Paula pursed her lips. "Would you consider him an ally?"

Cador shrugged. "I have no idea. Two thousand years is a long time to remember someone."

"We all remember Arthur, Guinevere, and Merlin, and the rest of that court," Melissa pointed out. "I'd be willing to bet Merlin remembers the dragon who unwillingly got to test his transference system."

"Especially if he used it to save the rest of his relatives," Cador agreed. The women both shot him questioning looks. "I suspect the Draconians are likely to be descendants of Earth dragons rescued from extinction by Merlin. Clearly the orb was for movement over great distances with no risks of aging, seeing as I'm here and still the same age as when I was attacked. I would expect nothing less of Merlin, to be honest—he was the greatest sorcerer of any age."

Paula looked at Melissa. "You know who we need to find and call as a witness?"

Melissa nodded. "Since it's unlikely I can expect to get the Supreme Draconian Ruler here by request, the Draconian Aeronella." She grimaced. "Not that I have any idea where she is or how I get her into court."

"She's with the delegation," Dommo said helpfully. "Her father always likes her to be nearby."

The looks on Paula and Melissa's faces were almost identical—horrified expectation.

Cador cleared his throat. "Allow me to guess, since this situation seems to be going from poor to worse. She's the Draconian ambassador's daughter, correct?"

Dommo nodded and Paula groaned. "You're right, Cador," she said, "it's worse."

"Well, calling her to the stand will be easy," Melissa said. "Potentially deadly, but easy."

Cador reached out and patted both women's shoulders. "Fear not, good maidens. I believe I may have the solution. Now, allow me to share what I'm hoping you can determine before we re-enter the courtroom."

* * *

The judge's chambers weren't big enough for Cador to enter, but the hallways were thankfully wide, so he stuck his head through the doors and blocked the hall. Paula hoped the complaints would be overridden by Cador charming the judge.

She explained the situation as quickly as possible and the judge shook his head. "First of all, if you're telling the truth, we have an extremely ancient personage on our station, and I don't wish to be rude." He got up from behind his desk, went to the door, and put out his hand. "Judge Paul Matier."

Cador offered his front paw. "Cador the Custodian. It's a pleasure to meet you, Judge Matier. Paula—excuse me, P.T.—has told me great things about you."

Judge Matier snorted as their handshake finished. "I'm sure she has. You're taking all of this remarkably well. I'd normally expect some histrionics at the least."

"Dragon nature is to think versus react if at all possible." Cador described what had happened to send him into the future and to their space station.

"So, essentially, you're a British dragon, keeping calm and carrying on, right?"

"If you say so." Cador clearly didn't get the reference, but Paula had to admit the judge had called it correctly.

He gave her a wry smile as he returned to his seat. "Counselor, barring your becoming a galaxy-class magician since our case last week, your story seems more likely than any other option I can come up with. However, what bearing Cador's presence has on the case is the question, not who he is or where he's from."

"Untrue," Cador said. "Your acknowledgment of my being who I say I am, and where and when I say I'm from, will be of the utmost importance."

Judge Matier looked at him for a long moment. "Other than acceptance of scientific magic, there is no other proof you are who you say you are. I mean, as I said, I believe it, based on what you two have told me, but it's still an unproven fact."

"Your word is law, is it not?" Cador asked. "Your role has been explained and, for want of a better descriptor, you are the king of this space station. Not because you rule the others, but because your decisions are binding, and that means you, essentially, make the laws, just as Arthur made the laws."

"We have other judges," Judge Matier pointed out.

"True, but, per P.T., you are the main judge of this, I believe it's called, circuit."

Judge Matier shrugged. "True enough. So, you two want me to, what, acknowledge Cador as being a real dragon from Earth? To what end?"

"From what Melissa has shared, my being taken from my proper time and place doomed my last maiden, Guinevere, to fail. She needed my guidance and counsel and, lacking it, fell into an inappropriate relationship, which is why, ultimately, Camelot was destroyed, and the righteous path was left. The course of history was altered and not for the good. Right now, a perversion of justice is being attempted in your courtroom, and I simply cannot stand idly by and do nothing. I must make amends, even if those amends are two thousand years too late, to ensure good will triumph over evil."

"So," Judge Matier said slowly, "for the want of a dragon, the kingdom was lost."

"It could be," Cador admitted. "I haven't been here long enough to research, but I believe Melissa would agree with your assessment."

The judge cocked his head. "How well did you know Merlin?"

"Quite well. He's the reason the dragon-maiden relationship continued after his birth, and it was he who tutored all of us in how to choose our maidens and ensured we would be their counselors, mentors, tutors, and confidantes."

Judge Matier's brow furrowed. "Is it possible your being sent here was not accidental, but rather a choice Merlin made?"

Before either Paula or Cador could reply, there was a knock at the door and the court bailiff stuck his head in. "Your honor, the courtroom is cleared of smoke and we're ready for you."

* * *

News of Cador's arrival had spread throughout the space station and the courtroom was packed. So, not just any audience, but a big one. Exactly what Super-Great-Grandfather Melvin would have wanted. Time to live up to his memory.

Aeronella was indeed sitting right up front behind her father, who was next to the prosecutor. She radiated stress and worry. Which was good. If she was actually in love with Dommo—though the planetary gods alone knew why—then she would be willing to help. If she wasn't too afraid of her father's wrath. But then again, that was part of their plan.

Cador was in front of the door to their offices, sitting on his haunches, ramrod straight, tail wrapped around his feet, giving the Draconians some of the best side-eye Paula had ever seen. He looked imperious and just this side of furious.

Judge Matier nodded to her. "Counselor, you have a witness to be sworn in."

"I have two your honor. I would like to first call Aeronella from Draconia to the stand."

The courtroom started buzzing with gasps and people talking. "Silence," Judge Matier said calmly. The room quieted.

"This is an outrage!" Vesantolocryn shouted.

"Is it?" Judge Matier asked calmly. "Why would that be?"

"My daughter has nothing to do with this case!"

"Your honor," Paula said, "I believe Aeronella is considered of age in Draconia, which makes her an adult in your courtroom. And the defense does indeed believe she has much to do with this case."

"The witness will come to the bench, give her name, her planet of origin, and pledge to tell the truth, the whole truth, and nothing but the truth."

Aeronella stood and came forward. She had her father's regal posture, her head was elegantly shaped, and, as she arranged her silvery cape over her petite frame, her beautiful blue-green scales caught the light. She was trembling, and her tail twitched nervously, but she held her head high. "I am Aeronella, daughter of Vesantolocryn, Draconia's Ambassador to Sector Twenty-Three in the Milky Way Galaxy. I am a Daughter of Draconia, and I pledge to speak only truth."

She sat in the witness box, glanced nervously at Dommo, and gave him a little smile. He gave her a little wave back. Paula noted prosecutor Franks and Vesantolocryn both saw this. Vesantolocryn looked furious and Franks looked like he thought his client was about to breathe fire.

"Aeronella," Paula said in a friendly tone, "please describe your relationship with the accused, Dommo Anime."

Aeronella was silent for several beats. Paula didn't mind—this was theater and she could hear Super-Great-Grandfather Melvin telling her to allow the witness to draw this out.

Finally, Aeronella took a deep breath. "He is my boyfriend." The courtroom erupted in shouting. "And I'm not ashamed!" she shouted over the din. "Because we don't see genus, we only see love!"

"Quiet!" Judge Matier bellowed. "Anyone not remaining silent will be removed, including you, Ambassador."

Paula continued the moment she could be heard. "Aeronella, why, in your opinion, is your father trying to enforce an ancient 'foul fiend law' over what was, by all accounts, a simple accident where no actual harm was done other than a cape needing to be cleaned?"

"Because he doesn't want me to be with Dommo," Aeronella replied. "Because he's genist and doesn't believe in the mingling of species."

"Objection," Franks said. "Conjecture."

"No, it's not!" Aeronella said before the judge could respond. "Daddy doesn't want me to 'mingle' with humans, he's said so many times."

"Based on the witness' statement," the judge said, "overruled."

"Aeronella," Paula went on, "to your knowledge, is someone accidentally treading on a Draconian's cape a real 'foul fiend offense' or are those 'laws' arbitrary in any way?"

"I've never heard of one being enacted."

"Objection," Franks said. "The witness is not the authority on Draconian law."

"True enough," Paula said quickly. "My next witness, however, is."

"Are you done?" Judge Matier asked her. She nodded. "Counselor Franks, do you wish to cross-examine?"

"Not at this time." Franks looked like he was getting a headache.

Aeronella left the stand. "I now call my next witness." Paula nodded to Cador, who approached the bench.

Judge Matier looked at those in the court. "The removal for disruption stands, so I suggest you all remain quiet." He turned to Cador. "State your name, planet of origin, and pledge to tell the truth, the whole truth, and nothing but the truth."

"Your honor, I always tell the entire truth. Lying is a human trait, not a dragon one. At least, no *true* dragon would ever lie. I am Cador the Custodian from planet Earth."

"Welcome, Cador from Earth," Judge Matier said. "Counselor Belli, proceed."

Cador wasn't able to fit into the witness box, so he stayed where he was. "Cador, when were you born?" Paula asked.

"I was born in the year four-hundred-and-twenty-three anno Domini and was sent two thousand years into the future."

"Who sent you?"

"To my knowledge, the person who attacked me is not how I came to be here. Merlin's scientific magic is what sent me forth."

"It's our understanding that there are no dragons on Earth."

"Sadly, not anymore. I believe what could be called my descendants live on the planet you call Draconia, since their historical records share that Merlin took their ancestors from Earth to preserve the species and gave them their own planet, named Draconia."

"Do you, Cador, believe the separation of species is correct?"

"Objection," Franks said. "What bearing does this have on the case?"

"Overruled," the judge said, "but get to the point, Counselor Belli."

"I do not," Cador replied. "The dragon-maiden relationship is an ancient one and at the heart of our laws. That two thousand years have passed and there are now dragon-squire relationships seems, to me, to be the correct kind of progress. And one, I'm sure, Merlin would approve, were he here."

"How dare you insinuate you would know anything about our Supreme Draconian Ruler's thoughts!" Vesantolocryn shouted. "I'm the head of Draconia on this space station and my word is law!"

Cador sniffed. "Sir, I knew Merlin personally and you are no Merlin. And, quite frankly, as I understand it, the person whose word *is* law on this space station is not you but Judge Matier."

"Order in the court," Judge Matier said sternly. "Ambassador, if you again speak out of turn, I will find you in contempt, and if I do so, your case will be thrown out."

There was an audible gasp from the spectators. This was done, of course, many times, but rarely to a person of this high rank.

"Cador," Paula went on as Vesantolocryn sat down, smoke coming out of his nostrils, "from what you know of Merlin, would he find the relationship between Aeronella and Dommo to be allowable?"

"Objection," Franks said. "Seriously, what does this have to do with the case at hand?"

Here it was, all or nothing. "The defense believes the Draconian ambassador is overstepping his authority and has enacted an ancient and, frankly, heinous law in order to remove his daughter's human suitor from her life. This is a perversion of justice and should not be allowed to stand in this or any other court."

"Based on that accusation," the judge said, "I'll allow the question. And the answer."

"Merlin is the product of a human mother and dragon father," Cador shared. "And, as such, he would not be pro a female human and male dragon being wed, since his birth killed his mother, unless science and medicine have progressed far enough in this time that the mother's life would not be forfeit. However, there is little risk of a male human and female dragon pairing causing issues for the dragon mother. And, as Merlin himself shows, the offspring of such a pairing has the potential to be extremely powerful."

"Thank you. Your witness," Paula said to Franks.

Who looked resigned but gave it a shot anyway. "Cador, you claim to be from Earth, and sent here from two thousand years in the past. Can you prove this claim?"

"Why should I have to?" Cador asked politely.

"So we can be sure you are who you say you are."

"The judge, the highest office on this space station, has agreed I am Cador the Custodian from Earth, or he would have already called me on the charge of perjury." Cador looked at the Draconian delegation. "You shame all of dragon-kind for this embarrassment of a display. You should be leading humanity in the ways of arts, politics, deportment, and all other important facets of life. Instead, you sit on a planet far removed from them and try to destroy the one relationship that is actually adhering to our true ways. For shame. *For shame!*"

Vesantolocryn growled and looked ready to leap at Cador.

"Counselors, please approach the bench. And yes, Ambassador, you, too."

Paula jerked her head and Melissa joined her and the others as they clustered together in front of the judge. Cador leaned his head closer.

"Counselor Franks, I'm about ready to call out the Ambassador for contempt of court. But before I do, I have to ask—how much research did you conduct regarding Draconian 'foul fiend laws' before bringing this to trial?"

"All the information I was given came from the Draconian delegation," Franks admitted. "There was no indication they were lying." He turned to Vesantolocryn. "Ambassador, it will look very bad to your superiors on Draconia should the judge rule you in contempt or, worse, guilty of perjury."

Vesantolocryn shook his head. "We have those laws and they are within our rights to demand."

"You may," Paula said. "And you might even be able to convince the judge of your claim. However, you're not going to convince either your daughter or the spectators in this courtroom." Vesantolocryn looked trapped. Time to give him a way out. "But honestly, Your Excellency, the truth of the matter is you now have an Elder of your race explaining that your daughter's relationship is time-honored."

"Draconian law shares that the older the Draconian, the more revered and respected their words are," Melissa added. "Plus, based on Earth's now no-longer-legend information about Arthurian times, Cador is, realistically, the eldest of the elders, behind only Merlin in age and wisdom."

"But...her suitor is so...so *unworthy*," Vesantolocryn said miserably.

"No," Cador said, but gently. "Dommo is innocent and young, but his heart is pure. Yes, he is but a squire, but he is also a young man who, under your daughter's fine influence and tutelage, can become a knight, or even a king. This is our real purpose and, if you are truly descendants of dragons, you know this to be so."

Vesantolocryn didn't appear fully convinced.

"Do you want to be known as the person who condemned a young man to death for being slightly clumsy, when all will know you had him killed because he loved your daughter?" Paula asked. "Or would you prefer to be known as the Draconian who brought your planet into the future by embracing the old ways?"

Vesantolocryn looked over at his daughter, who had moved to sit next to Dommo and hold his hand in her paw. She looked very protective. Dommo merely looked smitten. "But...they want to marry," Vesantolocryn said finally.

"Well, as to that," Cador said cheerfully, "if they are to enact the dragon-squire relationship, much must be accomplished before that could be approved. I'm happy to share the lengthy list of achievements Dommo will need to accomplish before a wedding could be considered."

Vesantolocryn brightened up. "How long a list? How much time do you think will be needed?"

"Based on Dommo's openness and enthusiasm compared to his life experience, I would expect a decade before he would be considered ready," Cador said, far more diplomatically than Paula could have managed. "If not longer."

Vesantolocryn seemed to be giving this serious consideration.

"I'll waive contempt and perjury charges," Judge Matier said, "if you consent to drop the case and never try to utilize your 'foul fiend laws' in any court on any space station or planet."

"They are, as has been said, archaic," Vesantolocryn admitted. "And we now have an elder to whom we can look for guidance. I will withdraw the case, as long as Cador the Custodian agrees to help oversee Aeronella's... situation with Dommo."

"Agreed," Cador said. "Though I would prefer to oversee here, on the space station."

Vesantolocryn nodded. "Agreed. I'm posted here and am not due for a new mission for at least five space station years." He put out his paw. "Thank you."

Cador took the paw in his own. "It is, I believe, why Merlin sent me here."

* * *

They were back in the Defense chambers. "That went well," Cador said. He felt quite pleased with the outcome. "Though, once your king understood the situation, I never had a doubt."

"I don't believe Judge Matier wants you referring to him as a king," Paula said.

"He is as wise as Arthur was, at least before the troubles."

Melissa nodded. "Arthur was a good king until then. But Judge Matier is not in the same situation."

"We couldn't have done it without you, Cador, so thank you for all your help," Paula said. She looked a little lost. So did Melissa.

Cador cleared his throat. This was a huge thing, and he wanted to ensure he made his request properly. "This is an amazing new world I find myself in, and I would like to make a formal offer which, since we are in a new age, I can make to you both."

The two women gave him their full attention.

He took a deep breath. "Would you two do me the honor of becoming my maidens?"

"I can't speak for Paula," Melissa said, "but I cannot say yes fast enough."

Paula grinned. "Absolutely. I'm thrilled to help lead the galaxy back to the future."

"As," Cador said happily, "it should be."

Migration Season

Larry Ivkovich

Kor, member of the daxas Wyvern Guard, knew it was time. Orange and black-winged butterflies had begun the long voyage to their winter home. Kor watched the large cloud of insects fluttering overhead as they instinctively followed their ancient migration route. Various avifauna would soon follow, heralding a similar journey for the daxas—the once-a-century migration of the dragon Thunder to its southern breeding grounds.

Shaking his head, Kor shooed away two plovers picking among the fangs of his opened jaws. Eager for bits of Kor's most recent kill, the small birds fluttered above him, trilling angrily at having their meal interrupted. Kor ignored them and rose from beneath a grove of majestic redwood trees where he'd been resting. Arching his back, he stretched his thick neck, loosening the tightness of old muscles, popping aging joints, growling at the aches and pains of three-hundred years. He shook his horned, triangular head, spread and rustled the large, membraned wings against his blue, scaled flanks. His nostrils flared at the myriad smells of the vast Domicile forest, his still-sensitive hearing alert for the slightest sound. But it was more than those familiar sensations which struck him.

The burning in his blood, the thunderous beating of his great heart, beckoned him to join the migration. A migration, for the first time in his memory, Kor would miss. How could he answer that primal call? Daxas mated for life. There was no other for Kor than his beloved mate, Essa, dead these past three years. Perhaps if he was younger or…

If Essa were still here.

A loud whooshing noise startled Kor out of his saddened reverie. A nimbus of glowing blue light emanated from the location of the western Lumen, the wormhole connecting the human realm of Earth and the daxas Domicile. A flock of startled cotingas erupted from the foliage near the Lumen's human outpost. Kor chuffed, puzzled; such a sound and reaction by the avians indicated the Lumen must have been opened.

Kor growled softly. The Lumen had been monitored for almost two centuries by Earth humans. The wormhole was only activated thrice a year to allow human research monitors stationed at their outpost to be relieved by a new monitor. This was not such a time.

Alarmed, he unfurled his wings and lifted off the ground. Skimming the redwood crowns, he studied the Domicile landscape as he flew toward the outpost.

The autumnal season had begun stripping the redwood, *moakle*, and *lestus* trees of their foliage; the air had become cooler. The Domicile was a part of what humans called the *multiverse*, a planet "discovered" by human quantum-engineers over two centuries ago and accessible only through the Lumens located in parts of the Domicile. However, the Domicile had always been home to the daxas and other so-called mythical and endangered biota of Earth. The Lumens allowed Domicile life to travel to the Earth and back in ancient times to explore, to hunt, to mate.

To become the stuff of legends.

Ahead, stood the Lumen outpost. The two-storied, rectangular *Hub* building housed a laboratory, AI network, and communication station. The smaller *Admin* contained offices and lodging units for the monitors and researchers who made scientific forays into the Domicile. A generator/recharging station stood between the two buildings.

Several strides from the Hub, the opened Lumen shimmered in whirling spirals of blue and silver, its huge nimbus outlined by a human-constructed metal arch. Nothing looked untoward. But, before Kor's startled eyes, the outpost's protective energy barrier, invisible except for a thin, shimmering aura, crackled and popped. As if struck by an outside force, the barrier collapsed into quickly dissipating tendrils of blue arcs.

Kor hissed as he alit within a redwood grove. Crouching behind the enormous boles, he peered at the outpost through the surrounding forest undergrowth. The Hub's front entrance irised open. As Kor watched, a device called a *drone* flew out from the building interior.

Since Essa's death, Kor had roamed the Domicile alone, apart from his Thunder, despite entreaties by the daxas Queen and fellow Wyvern Guard to return. Curiosity overcoming his loneliness, he often observed the outpost while concealed. His "spying" enabled Kor to understand much of the humans' languages, customs, and certain concepts and technology. Such learning had filled his time. He'd seen drones before but the one he observed now was different than the others—larger, more disc-shaped and streamlined. Nodules, lights, and a segmented pincer-arm studded its gray, metallic surface.

Kor knew it wasn't here for any peaceful purpose.

The drone hovered in front of the Lumen, lights on its underbelly blinking. In a moment, two more drones and seven humans, five male and two female, emerged from the wormhole. Outfitted in what Kor intuited as military-style uniforms and helmets, they carried long and deadly-looking...*pulse-rifles* with supply packs slung on their backs.

Kor hissed. These humans were intruders.

A movement at the front of the Hub showed a fourth drone emerging from the building, prodding a human female roughly with its pincer-arm. The female stumbled onto the pavement. She was short and stocky, with long dark hair and tawny skin, wearing trousers, boots, and a short jacket. A small supply pack lay belted at her waist. Kor recognized her as the current outpost monitor.

A male intruder approached, his...*pistol* pointed at the monitor's head. The monitor shouted and gesticulated angrily. Kor listened carefully, concentrating. It was hard to decipher all that was said even with Kor's acute hearing but the monitor's stance, gestures, and expressions demonstrated her outrage.

One of the armed females joined them. By her commanding manner Kor sensed she was the leader of this group. He focused his attention on her as she spoke quietly to the male. She then pointed to the monitor.

The monitor stepped forward and cried out, making a gesture which seemed to anger the male. The leader silenced the two and spoke again to the male before walking back to the other intruders who had removed their supply packs and began to unload them.

The male motioned to the monitor with his weapon, directing her away from the Hub toward the Admin lodging units. A few strides from Kor's hiding spot the monitor turned and once more faced the male, her expression fierce, defiant, fists clenched at her sides. She spat on the ground in front of the male, who spoke in threatening tones.

Kor bristled. The male said a word which Kor heard clearly and understood all too well. *Hunt.*

These humans were hunters. This was an invasion of the Domicile, actions taken like those on ancient Earth when dragons became feared, demonized, and preyed upon, forcing them to retreat to their own world. Kor's mouth skinned back from his fangs; his claws dug into the ground, tail twitching. How had this happened?

Kor watched as the male moved closer, his weapon trained on the monitor's head. He pulled what appeared to be some kind of restraints attached to his belt. He motioned for the monitor to lower herself to her knees. He cursed as the monitor refused, pointing the pistol at her leg.

Kor launched himself from the undergrowth, springing toward the male. The male began to turn toward Kor, eyes wide, gunhand swinging in his direction. Kor's jaws clamped down onto the male's head and neck, crushing his helmet and the skull beneath. Flinging the body from him, Kor spat out blood, flesh, bone and helmet shards, and whirled toward the monitor.

She stood as if frozen, mouth agape, hands held protectively in front of her. Kor bowed his head to the ground, rumbling in his throat. The monitor wavered, unsure of what he wanted or, Kor reasoned, whether to fear him. She glanced at the *hovercycle* parked near the generator/recharging station.

No doubt thinking she could escape on it, the monitor sidestepped toward the single-seat, anti-grav, levitating vehicle. This close, her speech, though tentative, was more understandable. "Okay, okay, nice dragon..."

Kor stamped a foot on the ground, his tail twitching, raised and lowered his head again.

She stopped, brow furrowing. "You...you want me to get on your back? No, no, you can't possibly understand me."

Kor snorted and nodded fiercely.

Voices and footfalls approached. The hunters had heard Kor's attack.

"Spirits." The female's eyes widened. "You *can* understand." She pointed to the man's fallen weapon. "The beam-pistol?"

He growled, nodded and once more stamped his foot. She must hurry!

She moved, scooped up the pistol, and placed it in a jacket pocket. After a heartbeat's hesitation, she mounted Kor's back. She clamped her arms around his thick, short neck, her legs pressing against his flanks. Kor spread his wings and launched skyward.

"Oh!" the monitor cried. "Holy crap!" She was relatively small by human standards and easy to carry. Yet Kor felt her strong, and perhaps desperate, grip as she held onto him, her face buried against his neck. His wings cupping the air currents, Kor rose above the redwoods. He must get to the Aerie and warn the Thunder!

Shouts from below. They'd been spotted. The monitor raised her head from Kor's neck and cried, "A drone's after us! It's got lase-weapons! Spirits, I hope you understand *that*!"

Kor did. He roared and descended, looking for an opening in the treetops to drop through for cover. "Your left!" the monitor shouted, pounding that side of his neck. Kor banked, barely dodging a hissing lase-beam.

Rage empowered him. Who were these human filth to invade his land? To threaten and attack and wantonly hunt Domicile life? He couldn't, wouldn't, allow such a violation!

He whirled and faced the approaching drone. "Shit!" The female gripped him even harder, "A little warning, please!" Kor reached within his essence for his long-dormant FireBreath. Mustering his strength, he called on every bit of his inner strength, willing those numinous elements all Wyvern Guard dragons possessed to flare to life.

His FireBreath ignited, spreading throughout his body like a storm. He opened his mouth and spewed a column of concentrated flame at the drone. The fiery projectile struck the device, sending it flaming earthward. It exploded just above the redwoods. Crown-monkeys and striped lemurs scattered shrieking among the treetops.

"Yes!" the monitor shouted, smacking a hand against Kor's neck. "An honest-to-Spirits fire-breathing dragon. Oh, look out!"

Too late Kor sensed the second drone. He roared as a lase-beam sliced through his left wing. Forcing back the burning pain, he struggled to keep aloft.

"Hold still! One more second!" From the corner of his eye, Kor saw the monitor raise the male's beam-pistol as the drone moved in for the kill. Kor strained to hover in place to allow her a clear shot. A moment more…

She fired. The drone jerked erratically, tendrils of white sparks snaking over its surface. It plummeted, spiraling toward the trees. "Yeah!" the monitor shouted. "Hey, are you all ri—?"

Kor fell, his injured wing crumpling. He fought to keep balanced, to slow their descent. Folding his wings tightly against his flanks, tail outstretched behind him, he dropped through an opening in the redwood canopy. Branches tore at his body, some snapping under his weight. The monitor cried out, still clinging to him.

Kor angled his good wing, using his tail for balance, to keep from upending and crushing his human rider. The ground rose up. As if knowing his intentions, the monitor screamed, "I'm getting off!" Kor felt her release her hold and fall away.

Kor's feet hit the leaf-covered, hard-packed forest floor. He lurched forward, claws scrabbling for purchase, rolled, and slammed into a boulder.

* * *

A sensation Kor could only describe as *cool fire* surged through him. A panoply of images, concepts, of…*knowledge,* filled his essence—it was the Earth year 2734 A.C.E; the Wormhole Outpost Team at Earth Base Alpha, Cape of Good Hope, South Africa had been attacked…

Hey, hey! A voice in Kor's head, words tingling but clear. *Dragon, you all right?*

Kor snarled and lurched forward on the ground beneath him. *Easy, easy,* the voice intoned. His throat felt raw because of the long disuse of the FireBreath. He tasted blood. Groggily, he opened his eyes. The human monitor knelt in front of him, her expression worried, her hands hovering above him as if afraid to touch him. Blood spotted her forehead, dirt covered her clothes. *Can you hear me?* she asked, her words unspoken. *Understand me?*

Kor blinked. The strange, new knowledge filling his muddled mind started to...*coalesce. I...hear.*

It works! Thank the Spirits! The female blew out a breath. *My name's Nia Rodrigo and I'm this quarter's outpost monitor. I've attached one of our new psi-interface comm-discs to your forehead. It's technology that'll enable us to communicate.* She indicated a small, rectangular device belted next to her waist-pack. *I can control the disc with my control pad but you're the first dragon it's been tested on since two centuries ago and the interfaces at that time were pretty primitive.*

It was done with...my Queen. Kor noted the female Nia had no such disc on her forehead. She didn't need one because... *You...*hear *my thoughts because the...interface is...configured to your...neural-comm implant.*

Nia looked as if she'd been struck, touching the spot behind her right ear. *How'd you know that?*

The interface has given me...understanding.

Nia stared. *That's incredible. It must have amplified and shared my knowledge with you or something like that. Didn't know it would do that.* She frowned. *Wonder if it works both ways? From you to me?*

Kor didn't know the answer to that. He concentrated instead on this instantaneous and clear communication. The daxas could mind-speak with each other in a like fashion but to do so with a human was a wonder indeed! In the time of the outposts' creation, the communication of those humans who desired peace and stability with Queen Qera had been long and difficult though ultimately successful. An accord had finally been struck—humans built research outposts at select Lumens, sealing the rest to protect Domicile life, while the daxas never again set foot on Earth.

But things had changed. *I...am...Kor.*

I can't believe we're communicating! Nia's eyes lit up, then her expression sobered. *Okay, thankfully, Kor, you were unconscious for only a few seconds. Those shadow-guilders'll be looking for us. Luckily, this comm-disc is on its own special frequency so the guilders' can't track us that way. Do you feel like any bones are broken? Internal injuries? Your head?*

Kor blew out a breath. *Nothing broken. You?*

Nia grimaced. *Just freaking sore. My head feels like what that shadow-guilder's must have felt when you crushed it. Gotta say, you scared the crap out of me but I'm glad you showed up.*

Shadow-guilder?

Bad guys. Criminal organization. She rummaged in her waist-pack. *Okay, I'm going to give you something to jack up your metabolism and ease any pain.*

Before Kor could respond, Nia…*slapped* his neck. As she took her hand away, Kor felt something left behind, adhering to his flesh. She did it again, pressing a second object against his hide. A soothing warmth shot through him.

Kor took a deep, deep breath. The energy he'd expended with the FireBreath, his wounded wing, and the fall had left him sorely weakened. But now, incredibly, his strength returned, his senses alight.

He snorted and rose easily to his feet. *Yes. Feel better.*

Nia nodded. *Good! It's a medication patch designed for animal biology—combination pain neutralizer and—*

Energy booster, Kor finished.

Nia grinned. *That's right. They've been tested on a number of different beasties including reptiles, so I figured it'd work on a dragon.* She touched the side of her own neck. *I stuck a human-attuned one on me. We were lucky we weren't hurt more.*

*Yes. Fortunate you kept the interface and…*medication *on you.*

First rule of the monitors—gotta be prepared for anything. She made a frustrated sound. *Except we weren't prepared for this attack, damn it!*

She turned away, blinking back tears, not of sadness, Kor intuited, but of anger. *The guilders jimmied our AI security protocols which allowed them to invade our Base Alpha on Earth. We let down our guard, not thinking the South African headquarters could be breached. We were forced to open the wormhole into the Domicile. Those dung-eaters think they can bag a dragon or two or any of the other Domicile species. Evidently ancient Earth beasties and once-extinct critters are suddenly in great demand on the inter-solar black market.* Nia stepped back as Kor hissed. *Hey, what's wrong?*

Kor hunkered closer to the ground. *A drone and one other approach. Get behind me.* Nia scurried and crouched behind his left flank as the weaponized drone appeared above them. Following it was one of the hunters piloting the outpost's hovercycle. Both devices skimmed the forest canopy unerringly in their direction. *Can you shoot them?*

The trees are in the way, Nia answered. *Not sure. Hey look!*

Large flocks of mohos, cotingas, dartwings, and other avifuana appeared. The birds flew around, over, and below the drone, cawing, trilling, and squawking. The thick murmuration forced the drone below the treetops.

The device changed course, adjusting to fire at multiple avian targets, slowing and dropping beneath the canopy.

Nia Rodrigo! Kor thought-sent.

On it! Nia aimed the beam-pistol and fired. The drone jerked back at the beam's impact, its power source disrupted. It fell hissing to the ground.

Kor grunted in approval. *The hunter…*

He won't hurt me, Kor, Nia responded. *They need me. But you're a target!*

The hovercycle broke through the scattering throng of birds, listing to one side. Its rider attempted to get it under control, his pistol clutched in one hand. He fired wildly in Kor's general direction, the shots missing despite Kor's bulk.

Stand back, Kor thought-sent and leaped into the air. He clutched the cycle's undercarriage with his jaws and pulled the cycle to the ground. Kor violently shook his head from side-to-side as if the bike were some prey he'd caught and flung it into the underbrush. The hunter crashed onto the ground and lay still.

Kor snarled, his anger and bloodlust mounting. He turned toward the human Nia, his long tongue flicking from his mouth, his horns flattened against his head. She stood close. It would be so easy to take her.

Nia stepped back, eyes wide. "Kor!" she cried aloud. *Kor, please.*

Kor growled. What was he thinking? He closed his eyes until the anger passed. He coughed. *I am sorry, Nia Rodrigo. I promise you I will not harm you.*

It's okay. I'm pretty pissed off too. Nia still kept her distance, pointing to the fallen shadow-guilder. *Uh, good job there, big guy.*

Kor snorted. *And you. You too are a…good shot.*

I got lucky. Nia strode to the fallen hunter and knelt at his side. *Dead,* she thought-sent as she stood up. *Neck's broken.* She shot an anguished look at Kor, her manner changing. *I've never seen anyone killed right in front of me before and now I've seen two…*

Kor rumbled. *Again, I am sorry, but it was necessary.*

She waved a dismissive hand. *I know, I know. I'm not blaming you, Kor.*

But you have not killed, Nia Rodrigo. Be thankful for that. It is not always easy, even for a daxas.

Nia attempted a smile. *Oddly enough, despite your scary, uh,* episode *just now, I trust you, Kor. Where've you been hiding all this time?*

Kor ignored the question. *I sense nothing or no one else approaching.*

Nia looked up at the sky. *What's with those birds?*

They sense the danger the Domicile faces.

Well, I guess we could use all the help we can get.

What do you mean?

The guilders have some heavy-duty weaponry including two military-style transports back at Earth Base Alpha ready to come through the portal once they've scoped everything out on this side. They'll use the transports to pack up and deliver their freaking trophies!

A disturbing thought struck Kor. *Then they know of the daxas Aerie.*

Nia sighed and looked away. *Right. The coordinates of the Aerie aren't stored at Earth Base Alpha for security reasons, only here at the outpost AI. That's why the guilders caught me, to download the location of the Aerie for them. It's what I meant earlier when I said they needed me.*

Kor snorted in disgust. It seemed humans couldn't stop being wary of the daxas. *Why do you have those…*coordinates *at all?*

To her credit, Nia looked abashed. *I know, it sounds creepy, Kor, but we wanted to be able to find the daxas in case of any emergency.*

An emergency like this one? Kor angled his head, fixing Nia with a pointed gaze.

Yeah, we screwed that up, didn't we? She blew out a breath. *I'm really sorry, Kor. They threatened the rest of my team if I didn't do what they demanded. That shithead was going to tie me up until they needed me and then they would have probably killed me afterwards.*

Kor hissed, noticing Nia's hands were shaking. *I must warn my Thunder but I cannot fly now.* Queen Qera's HealingBreath could fix his wing, he knew. Her power helped the wounded, healed many of the sick. But the Queen wasn't here. *We need to reach the Aerie on foot.*

I know, your wing. I wish I could help you with that.

Kor grunted. *It could have been worse without your assistance.*

Nia snapped her fingers. *Wait a minute. Can you…is it possible to contact the other dragons* now*? From here? Don't you have that ability?*

Kor shook his head. *The daxas do possess a form of mind-speak, but the distance to the Aerie from here is too great to make contact. We must get closer for me to do so.*

But wouldn't your Thunder know something's wrong?

Kor paused. How much should he reveal to this human? Old suspicions arose in him. No, no, she'd proved herself an ally. He must trust her as she said she did him. *My dragon kindred immerse themselves within self-induced pre-migration…*trances, *readying for the long flight to our breeding grounds in the southern archipelagos. Including the Queen's Wyvern Guard.*

What's that?

A special daxas force which protects the Queen. Kor snarled. *I…was once one of them. But, like you humans, the daxas also let down their guard. The Wyverns, instead of guarding the Aerie during the migration trances as we have always done, now also participate in the trances instead of doing so when the Thunder emerges.*

Nia looked thoughtful. *So the guilders would have an easier time trapping or killing the dragons. They not only knew about the Aerie but must have hacked the data about the migration trances too.*

Indeed. Kor growled softly. *As such, the Thunder can be taken by surprise and only a daxas can interrupt the trances and warm them. No other…*alarm *would be effective.*

And that has to be you? Obviously, you're not preparing for the migration. Why not?

Kor chuffed. How could he explain *that*? Three years ago, Essa died of a wasting sickness. Even the Queen's HealingBreath couldn't save her. Essa and Kor had been broodless but, before she died, Essa told Kor to carry on after her. If only for Essa, Kor wanted, *needed*, to do so! He wasn't ready for the Final Sleep all Elder daxas initiated at the end of their days. Not yet. Surely he had more to do in life!

Perhaps that was why he was here now.

Okay, Nia thought-sent when Kor didn't answer her question. *None of my business. Got it.*

Kor's mind abruptly churned with strange thoughts, manifested, he was certain, by the human knowledge given him through the psi-interface. An idea formed.

The psi-interface cannot project without being connected to the sender, yes? he thought-sent. *Can its power and range be increased?*

A look of surprised understanding transformed Nia's features. *You think we* can *contact your* Thunder *from here by boosting the interface?*

Kor cocked his head to one side. *Can we?*

Kor sensed Nia's mind, like his, racing with possibilities. *Well, theoretically, yeah. It shouldn't be more difficult than amping up any other communication device.* She frowned. *I don't know, Kor. It means we'd have to get back to the outpost…*

Kor moved his great head to within a human hand's length from Nia. His face reflected from her brown eyes. *Nia Rodrigo, you are a monitor, yes? Trained in such things? Can you or can you not* boost *the interface?*

Nia started at Kor's closeness but then her expression turned to one of intense concentration. *I* could *modify the outpost's intra-comm system and link it with the comm-disc. It'd be good for one strong burst and I should be able to do it quickly. I think.*

We must try then. We will return to the outpost and I will keep the hunters at bay while you work. My FireBreath is spent and needs time to recharge but I have other skills I can use. You must enable contact with the Aerie. Kor paused. *Please, Nia Rodrigo. I need your help. All of the daxas do.*

Nia looked away, running a hand through her hair. She was young, perhaps of a human's third decade, strong and determined. Kor had seen those qualities in her at the outpost. Nia hadn't shown any fear in the face of death. But now, doubt clouded her features. *Uh, are you sure? I mean, the fall and everything...*

He snorted. *I am old but not infirm, especially with the medication.*

Okay! Nia once again clambered on his back after placing the beam-pistol in a jacket pocket. As soon as she settled, Kor turned and raced through the forest back toward the outpost. Kor's huge muscles moved smoothly beneath Nia's clutching body. Because of the medication's rejuvenating effects, he felt like a young daxas again!

The lush forest landscape rushed by in a blur, the tips of tall grasses brushing against Kor's flanks, the fallen leaves spiraling away in his rushing wake. Insects buzzed frantically alongside him. Small, agitated forest creatures scuttled out of his way. The questioning roars of felid prides and canid packs sounded from the distant mountains and shadowed depths of the forest. The varied life of the Domicile sensed something important about to happen.

Nia gripped Kor more tightly as he maneuvered through a boulder field. *Glad you're here, Kor. I've never been in a situation like this before.*

And I am glad you are here, Nia Rodrigo. And I trust you too. Surprised, Kor realized he meant it.

* * *

The outpost was in chaos. Droves of birds flew in a formation which blocked the Lumen in a whirlpool of circling avian bodies. Other birds attacked the hunters who seemed unsure what to do. A few harried a drone high above the outpost. Some flew around a very large, multi-wheeled vehicle. Kor's new knowledge sparked: the vehicle was one of the autonomous military transports Nia mentioned, powered by remote control. Equipped with a mounted lase-cannon, immobility webbing, and stasis cages for their "cargo."

Damn them, Nia thought-sent. *That leader must have gotten a signal back to Base to get the transport. But those assholes didn't expect the birds. Hell,* I *didn't expect it.*

Kor grunted. *In truth, neither did I. But we must take advantage of the avians' boldness.*

Right, get me to the back of the Hub. Any chance any of the other Domicile beasties can help us?

Doubtful. The avifauna and the daxas are kindred of the air and are so bonded.

Kor sprinted to the rear of the Hub building. The male guilder's mangled corpse still lay where Kor had tossed it. Kor stopped at the rear entry door where Nia jumped off of his back and pressed the surface of her belted control pad. The door irised open. Nia pressed the pad again and turned to Kor. *I just closed the front iris and will close this one once I'm inside. What are you going to do?*

Kor chuffed. *Join our avian comrades in dealing with the guilders.* He lowered his head to allow Nia to remove the interface comm-disc.

No keep it, Nia thought-sent. *Base has stored a few more inside the Hub for field-tests. I'll boost one of those.* She placed her palm against his snout. *Listen Kor. The guilders can power up the transport's lase-cannon so you be careful, you hear? You have to be able to use the boosted interface to contact the Aerie so get back here in one piece!*

Understood. Kor turned and raced around to the front of the building. He didn't hesitate. Because of the avians' diversion, the shadow-guilders didn't sense Kor until it was too late. He plowed into two of the hunters, sending one hurtling head-over-heels and trampling the other underfoot. Roaring a long unvoiced battle cry, Kor clawed one of the females, knocking her to the ground. The avians continued their aerial assault although many lay dead on the ground as the hunters regained their focus and found their targets.

Three of the five remaining guilders down. Two left. Kor had to stop them from not only interfering with Nia but from sending another message through the Lumen.

A lase-beam struck him in the hip. He roared in pain as the fourth drone dropped lower, breaking free of the birds' attempt to block it. Once again Kor grasped his FireBreath and desperately stoked it with his essence. This unnatural machine would not succeed! The fire sparked and streamed from his open mouth, striking the drone. It tumbled away and exploded.

Kor whirled, seeing one of the surviving hunters covered in mohos, enclosing him in a pecking and slashing cocoon. Screaming, the man fell as the mohos continued their ravaging assault.

Kor felt the burning pain of a *pulse-blast* sear his neck. He hissed, his breath rattling. "Die, you stupid, bloody animal!" The hunters' leader stumbled past him, her face covered in talon cuts, her uniform shredded. Her body glimmered in a wavering aura, some sort of protective force webbing she'd managed to activate to repel the birds. She fired her pulse-rifle again, grazing the side of Kor's head as she ran toward the transport. Kor reeled, fighting to stay conscious. If the leader had the remote control and powered up the transport…

The transport roared to life, its mounted lase-cannon coming online and swiveling toward him. Summoning his remaining strength, Kor charged the transport. He swerved at the last moment and rammed the side of the vehicle with his head and shoulder. Ignoring the pain shooting through him, he shoved his weight against his much-larger opponent. Whining and shrieking, its wheels spinning, the vehicle strained against Kor's bulk.

With a desperate roar, Kor heaved upward and overturned the transport, sending it crashing onto its side.

He turned, gasping, dizzy, one of his horns broken and bloody. The shadow-guild leader stood at the Lumen entrance, shooting her weapon at the avian wall blocking her way.

Kor pushed back the searing pain and charged the leader. She must not get access to the Lumen! The female turned and readied to fire another pulse at him. Kor lunged and brought his forelegs down upon her, crushing her and her protective aura to the ground.

Kor found his voice and roared, vision blurring with blood, body wracked with pain. He staggered to the outpost's closed front iris. *Nia Rodrigo!* he cried mentally through a haze of agony. He pawed weakly at the iris. *Open…*

The iris spiraled open and Nia rushed out. *Kor! Oh, Spirits, you're hurt.*

Never mind. Kor found it hard to breathe. *The boosted disc?*

I did it! I've modified the comm system and amped it up. Nia stepped back, eyes wide. *Wait a minute. Your comm-disc. It's gone! How could…how can we hear each other?*

Kor shook the blood out of his eyes. The disc must have detached when he rammed the transport. He panted, his breath quickening. There was no time to ponder impossibilities! He leaned his head toward Nia. *Attach!*

Nia reached up a trembling hand, wiping the blood from his forehead. She affixed the newly powered comm-disc, its surface glowing brightly, and fingered her control pad.

Kor hissed as an electrifying surge, much stronger than the effects he'd experienced with the regular psi-interface and medication patch, expanded through him. His thoughts shot outward like a bolt of lightning, *Queen Qera. Brother and Sister daxas. Danger at the Lumen. Come quickly…*

Kor felt his old heart swell as if ready to burst. His legs crumpled beneath him. Birds flew above, squawking and trilling in distress. Somewhere, far away, Nia Rodrigo cried out.

Kor dropped to the ground and plummeted into darkness.

* * *

Kor, beloved.

Essa stood in front of him, radiant, shining like the sun. Her head-crest glowed with a shimmering light. Her green eyes likewise shone. Her wings fluttered against green and yellow flanks, tail curled behind her.

So I have passed through the Veil. A landscape of brilliant light surrounded Kor. The AfterRealm. *We can finally be together again, Essa.*

Not yet. Essa's thoughts were so familiar, so beautiful, and so unexpected. *As much as I long for that, it is not yet your time.*

What do you mean?

You have more to do in life, Kor. Her eyes flashed. *You have an important part to play in both the daxas and human realms.*

But it's been so hard without you.

We will be together again. It is the way of things, yes? But first you must return and assist in the beginning of an important new time for both humans and daxas. Essa chortled, the gentle laugh she always used when chiding him. *Don't look so surprised. Look what you have already done.*

Kor felt as if he were falling. *I miss you.*

And I you. But I am so proud of you. And, as humans would say, I think you and Nia Rodrigo make a good team.

A good…team? Before Kor could make sense of that curious remark, he was gone.

* * *

Cold. Like ice. Frigid.

Burning. Heat scorching though him like…

Life!

Kor swayed to his feet, wings spread. He wavered, legs unsteady. A human female placed her hands against his neck. *Kor! You're back! Steady now.*

Nia Rodrigo. A great sense of relief, of *joy*, enveloped Kor. Other figures appeared in his blurry vision. Several of his Thunder moved peacefully among humans at the front of the outpost Hub. Kor knew the humans were members of Nia's Earth Base Alpha team. Dartwings and cotingas flew trilling above as if in celebration.

And standing before him…

My…my queen. Kor slowly bowed his head to Queen Qera of the daxas.

Slightly larger than Kor, the Queen's golden scales gleamed, eyes blazing like the sun, head-crest erect. Wisps of HealingBreath drifted from her mouth. Two of the Wyvern Guard stood on either side of her. *Elder Kor,* Qera thought-sent. *Courageous warrior. We are gratified to see you.*

Kor steadied himself, realizing he felt strong, alive. His heart beat soundly. He looked at his torn wing. The wound was gone.

My Queen, you've healed me.

Of course. Qera's wings fluttered. *How could we not? You and Nia Rodrigo have saved us. In turn, the daxas have helped Nia's people.*

As Kor's vision fully cleared, Kor saw the psi-interface comm-disc on Qera's forehead. Kor looked at Nia. She'd been communicating with the Queen!

Your message got through, Kor, and the Thunder got here so fast! Nia stood before him, hands on hips, face beaming. *And it's true. We went back through the portal and stopped those scuts! None of my team or any of the dragons were hurt, thank the Spirits.*

The guilders there had weapons.

They knew something was wrong. More were about to cross into the Domicile because of their leader's signal, but they were completely caught off-guard. Nia laughed. *You should have seen their faces when the Queen appeared like an old Earth bat-out-of-hell!* She stopped and bowed to Qera. *Um, my apologies, your...your majesty.*

Qera rumbled in amusement. *No need. Please continue.*

Well, we got the AI protocols for Earth Base and the outpost back online and held the guilders until government security arrived. They'll interrogate those scuts and track down the shadow-guild.

How long was I senseless?

Several hours of human time, Qera said. Y*our wounds were severe and, because of your age, it took time for you to mend. Nia Rodrigo's extraordinary intelligence and skills allowed us to overpower these vile hunters and save her people.*

Kor chuffed. *Well done, Nia Rodrigo.*

Nia blushed. *I couldn't have done it without you, Kor. You and those absolutely stellar birds gave me just enough time to boost the interface. Sorry you missed all the fun at Base. But we make a good team, huh?* She folded her arms across her chest, a mischievous look on her face. *Especially since you don't need the interface comm-disc anymore.*

Team. Kor remembered what Essa's spirit had said then grunted in surprise. The import of Nia's words struck him. The first disc had been torn away during his battle with the guilders and the boosted one was no longer attached to him. He'd been hearing Nia's thoughts and sending his own since then! *How can this be?*

Nia shrugged. *Something we'll have to investigate but a psychic connection was formed between us.* She grinned. *Maybe it's magic! Dragons are magical, right?*

Qera nodded, her eyes bright. *And we hope you and Nia Rodrigo will continue as a team, Elder Kor.* She angled her head toward Nia, who continued:

There's been a movement the last several years on Earth for more interaction with the daxas. Our government now finally agrees. There're benefits to both species in communicating more, knowledge to share. You're sentient, intelligent creatures, Kor, which is why the interfaces were updated, to see if we could communicate more efficiently with you. We finally figured out the wormhole network is why dragons were part of every Earth culture's mythos, because the daxas traveled the wormhole portals to and from your world and ours.

We too were explorers.

And that makes the daxas as much a part of Earth as humans. Our hope at Earth Base Alpha was to contact the daxas once testing of the new comm-

discs was completed. Nia shrugged. *Which, I'd say, we've done pretty damned successfully.*

And we agree, Elder Kor, Qera thought-sent. *Too long have the daxas remained apart except for the humans' occasional scientific foray. That must change if we are to guard both our worlds against further incursions. We need to help each other. One way is to appoint you as our official Domicile liaison between the humans and the daxas, Kor. But that is not a command. It is your choice.*

Nia placed a hand on Kor's neck. *Whattya say, big guy? Want to keep working together?*

Yes, Kor thought-sent, feelings of long-missed belonging and purpose enveloping him. Essa was right! His heart soared. *I do.*

Nia grinned. Qera rumbled approval.

Kor couldn't smile but in his heart and mind, he did.

Bone and Blood

Barbara Campbell

Long ago, people described their kind as touched by the gods: interpreters of dreams and healers of broken bodies. In this darker age, they called the women moon-calves, wild things, witches.

For most of the year, mother and daughter lived in the high meadow, tending their small herd of goats. The day they left the village for good, people spat into the footprints the pair left in the dust.

When the first snowdrop of spring pushed through the frozen ground, the young woman brought forth a daughter and died with screams and tears and blood. The old woman howled her grief to the mountain and whispered her curse against the man who had stolen her daughter's maidenhead.

Seasons came and went. She taught her granddaughter to harvest healing herbs, to make fishing lures, to turn milk into cheese. Most importantly, she warned her never to seek out other people and to flee if ever they ventured onto their mountain. The girl listened and learned and obeyed. And when death came for the old one, she was alone.

The people of the village were unaware of her existence. Even the man who planted the seed of life in her mother's womb did not realize that it had bloomed; he had been struck down with a mysterious disease that slowly ate away at him until he died with screams and tears and blood.

Sometimes, the villagers turned their gazes to the hills and wondered what had become of the women. But then they shrugged and returned to their fields and their homes, their children and their lives.

And so it might have remained if not for the bone flute.

* * *

She finds the bone in her treasure field, gleaming white among the loose scree of black rocks. The mountain had given her many treasures over the years: brightly-colored feathers, shards of flint, a bird's curved talon that she wears on a scrap of hide around her neck.

The hollow bone is as long as her hand from fingertip to wrist. Perhaps a wing bone from the same bird that gifted her the talon. She caresses the bone, wondering how to honor the mighty bird from which it came and the earth-spirit that revealed it to her.

With her flint scraper, she smooths the jagged edges and carves out a notch at one end. With the talon, she bores three holes.

By the time she completes her task, the red sun perches atop the mountain's peak. As the mountain devours it, the girl raises the bone flute to her lips.

The first notes tremble like her breath. As she continues to play, a steady vibration pulses inside of her like a second heartbeat. Her lips and fingertips buzz like bees among the mountain thyme. Molten heat flows through her body. And with it come visions. Of countless sunsets and sunrises. Of the slow unfolding of seasons. Of the eternal cycle of birth, death, and renewal.

She is unsure if these are memories or dreams. If she is making the music or only a vessel for it. Or if bone and girl are creating this miracle together.

Her eyes close as the bone flute sings. Wind and rain, it whispers, storm and sun. Snow-capped mountains and dark, tumbling streams. The freedom of soaring through the clouds. The sweet fragrance of wild mint. The shrill bleat of a newborn kid. The delicious nectar of blood.

Her eyes fly open. The flute falls from her nerveless fingers. But the vibration grows stronger. Only when she hears the maddened cries of the goats does she realize that the ground beneath her is shuddering.

A sharp crack draws her gaze upward. Rocks hurtle down the mountain's flank. Fir trees sway as if buffeted by a gale. As long as she has lived, the mountain has been a sure and unchanging part of her world. If it could crumble, what would stop the sky from falling or the sun from sinking into the west, never to rise again?

She pushes herself to her feet, only to stagger and fall to the earth again. She curls into a ball, covering her ears with her hands, waiting for the mountain to bury her under a shroud of rock.

The earth heaves a final time and falls still. The goats resume their grazing. The thrushes resume their warbling. Only the jumble of boulders and broken trees offer a mute testament to what occurred.

She swallows down the bitter taste of bile. She hoped to honor the earth-spirit with her song. Instead, she has angered it. It has rejected her gift of music. It has rejected her.

* * *

That night, she dreams. And in her dream, the flute sings.

Wind and rain, it croons, storm and sun. Snow-capped mountains and dark, tumbling streams. The fierce joy of diving into battle. The sour fragrance of fear. The shrill screams of dying men. The delicious nectar of blood.

She awakens, sweat-soaked and trembling. Pours an offering of water into the earth. Buries the flute under the dirt floor of the cavern in which she lives and vows never to play it again.

But still she dreams. And still the flute sings. Of deserted caves and empty skies. Of endless years of solitude. Of eternal darkness, buried alive within the earth.

She awakens with tears on her cheeks. But she smiles as she digs up the bone flute, gently wipes it clean, and carries it into the sunlight. At last, she understands what the earth-spirit wants.

The flute sings and the earth rumbles its response. She forces herself to play on, to stifle her fear, to ignore the distant crash of rocks and the cries of the goats. Only when the ground near her cracks open does her breath fail her.

The fissure snakes toward her, relentless as a lightning bolt. Her fingers encircle the talon at her breast. She whispers the prayer of protection her grandmother taught her.

The fissure stops an arm's length from where she sits. She creeps toward it and stares into its depths. Two yellow lights flicker in the darkness like miniature suns. And then they wink out.

The girl smiles. The earth-spirit has heard her call. Soon, she will be able to free it. And then neither of them will ever be lonely again.

* * *

A child betrays her. An impetuous boy who disobeyed his parents, climbed the mountain, and saw everything. Terrified, he scrambled down the mountainside to discover his village in ruins.

The people put aside their shock and sorrow long enough to listen to his hysterical babbling. That night, they bury their dead. And then they gather their weapons

* * *

The bleats of the goats jerk her from sleep. A narrow shaft of rosy light creeps past one edge of the hide that covers the cavern's opening. She pulls her shapeless tunic over her naked body. Around her waist she knots the hide belt holding the sheath for her knife. Wolves rarely venture near in summer, but something has disturbed the beasts. She pulls back the hide and peers outside, squinting against the brilliance of the newly-risen sun.

A gasp escapes her lips. She closes her eyes, wondering if she is still asleep, if this is another of the dreams sent to her by the bone flute. When she opens them again, they are still there.

Since her grandmother died, she has never seen another human being. Now, there are too many to count gathered before her.

She recalls her grandmother's warning that people are more dangerous than wolves, more cunning than foxes. But surely, these people are yet another gift from the earth-spirit, a reward for obeying its call. And the sight of them is sweeter to her than the honey she gathers from the bees.

An old man with flowing white hair pounds his staff three times on the ground. The milling crowd falls still. Some make signs over their chests. Others frown and whisper. She does not understand why they frown when all she can do is smile.

The old man says something, and unexpected tears blur her vision. How many years since she has heard a human voice other than her own? And how amazing to discover that the voice of a man is so much deeper than her grandmother's.

When he speaks again, she cocks her head, sifting through the unfamiliar words. She answers him in the tongue taught to her by her grandmother, the secret language of wise women. The old man's frown deepens, and the men and women in the crowd stir restively.

He points to the fissure and then down toward the valley. He shakes his staff and shouts. His anger steals the smile from her lips. She shrugs helplessly, her gaze darting from face to face. A careworn woman pushes a boy-child forward. His eyes hold the terror of a rabbit struggling to escape a snare.

The boy-child lifts his fingers in the air and wiggles them. She mimics the gesture uncertainly. Only when his childish voice begins crooning a melody does understanding dawn.

She nods and holds up one hand, bidding them to wait. Then she hurries back into the cavern and emerges, brandishing the flute. As one, the people suck in their breaths. Some stumble backwards, holding up their hands. A woman screams. A man shouts. The boy-child buries his face in his hands, sobbing. She tries to tell them that no harm can come to them, that her meadow is protected by the earth-spirit, but her words seem to have no meaning for them.

Again, the old man pounds his staff, silencing the commotion. Again, he points at the fissure and then to the flute in her hands.

Her grandmother had many rituals: prayers to offer when skinning a rabbit or pulling a kid from its mother's womb; herbs to gather only under a full moon; words to chant when brewing a healing tonic. Perhaps these people have such a ritual that governs the playing of music.

She so wants to please them, to replace their frowns with welcoming smiles. So she nods and walks to the fissure. Glancing over her shoulder, she sees the old man following her, but the others remain huddled together, watching them with narrowed eyes.

He thrusts his staff at the fissure. Obediently, she raises the flute to her lips. But he shakes his head and shouts. After a moment's hesitation, she offers the flute to him. His eyes widen, and he steps back, still shouting and shaking his head, still pointing at the fissure.

And then she realizes what he wants her to do. This time, she is the one to shake her head and edge away. She tries to explain that the flute is a treasured gift from the earth-spirit. How can she toss it away like a scrap of unwanted gristle?

Her words only seem to stoke his anger. With a final shout, he raises his staff and brings it down on her hand. She gasps as pain stabs her knuckles. Gasps again as the bone flute slips from her fingers.

She lunges for it, but already the flute has disappeared into the darkness of the abyss. She hears it clattering against the rocks—once, twice, three times—every echo fainter than the one before, until there is only silence.

Her breath catches on a sob. She feels as hollow as the bone flute. But when she lifts her head to gaze at the old man, he smiles. Smiles!

Her ears ring with the clatter of the flute. Her knuckles throb with the pounding of her heart. The emptiness inside her fills with molten heat. And with it come visions. Of noisy fledglings that nest in the trees and silent bones that sleep in the soil. Of the patient unfurling of leaves in spring and the sudden gust of wind that rips them from their twigs in autumn. Of sun-warmed earth in summer and the clack of bare tree branches in winter. Of countless dawns and innumerable dusks. Of the endless unfolding of seasons and the endless years of solitude.

She smiles at the old man. And when he turns toward the crowd, she draws her flint knife and plunges it into his back.

As he staggers and falls, she sings. Wind and rain, she chants, storm and sun. Snow-white hair and outflung hands. The ferocious delight of kneeling beside her prey. The sour fragrance of his fear. The shrill screams of the people. The delicious nectar of blood.

She sings as she seizes his hair and yanks his head up. She sings as she slits his throat. She sings as the crowd surges toward her

He gulps at the air like a fish she has landed. His eyes roll wildly, searching the sky for help that will never come. His blood drips into the fissure. She hears it pattering against the rocks—once, twice, three times—until it is drowned out by the baying of the crowd and the shrieks of her laughter.

* * *

Beneath the earth, the dragon stirs.

Long ago, people worshipped her kind as gods: bringers of the rain and heralds of the sun. In this darker age, they called her demon, monster, myth.

For years, she wandered the world, searching in vain for another of her kind. Until at last, old and exhausted, she fell to earth, flinging up stones and boulders that covered her like a shroud.

Centuries came and went while she slept and dreamed and waited. Until finally, her bone sang to her.

She senses it, tantalizingly close, and noses at the rocks until her snout touches the tiny lost piece of her. Her body trembles. She hardly dares to breathe for fear of dislodging it, of losing it yet again. With the infinite patience that has allowed her to survive so long beneath the earth, she nudges it closer until she can seize it in her jaws. Her fangs close upon it with a satisfying crunch that seems to reverberate through her lair.

She raises her snout to the narrow shaft of sunlight, listening to the shouts of the humans, the scream of the fledgling whose mind and dreams she knows as well as her own. She breathes in the freshness of the air, the gamey reek of goats and humans. And closer still, another scent.

Her nostrils flare. Her tongue flicks out to lick the rocks. After so many centuries, she has almost forgotten the taste of blood. The salty sweetness. The bitter tang. A rivulet of life coating her fangs and sliding down her throat.

The emptiness inside her fills with molten heat that penetrates her belly and her lungs, her heart and her limbs. She thrusts her mighty head skyward. She wants to bellow her power, but knows she must conserve her strength for this battle with the earth.

Her body heaves, but she remains trapped. Maddened by her helplessness, she struggles, measuring progress each time a rock shifts, each time a clod of earth falls away. Finally, she frees one front leg. She rests, savoring her victory, then returns to the battle and frees her other leg. Her hind claws scrabble at the earth, seeking a foothold. Her front claws rip away the rocks that imprison her. Close now, so close. Her muscles tense. And she hurls herself toward the sun.

Rocks bounce off her leathery scales as she surges upward. Only when she clears the earth does she unfurl her wings and finally give voice to her triumph. She hears her call resounding through the mountains, every echo fainter than the one before until only the screams of the humans shatter the silence.

She descends to earth and perches on a pyre of rocks, basking in the heat of the sun. Humans lie half-buried beneath the rubble. A twisted leg, an outflung arm, a hand clutching a long staff. The aroma of blood and flesh overwhelms her senses. She flings aside rocks to feast on the dead and dying. It feeds the body but lacks the thrill of the hunt.

Soon, she tells herself. Soon, she will know that pleasure again.

She pauses, mouth agape to devour, as she uncovers another body. Long, black hair covers one cheek, but she recognizes the face of the fledgling who peered down at her, the one who made music with her bone, the one whose dreams she shared. The dark eyes stare sightlessly at the sky. Blood glistens from the wound across her throat, a crooked red gash that mimics the snarl that twists her lips.

Poor little fledgling. Did she have no mother to warn her how easily humans turn against their own kind? No nest-mates to teach her that fleeing is sometimes better than fighting? How could she hope to battle so many?

For battle she did. Her fingers still grip a shard of flint that drips with the blood of her enemies. Fledgling she is and foolish she might have been, but this one was as fierce as any dragon.

She noses aside the remaining rocks. Her head draws back when she sees the talon on the fledgling's chest, the talon ripped from her wing tip when she fell to earth so long ago. She bares her fangs to take back what is hers, to be complete again after so many centuries.

And yet, she hesitates. She can feel the spirit of the fledgling hovering near her, anger and defiance now replaced by confusion.

The fledgling fought and died for her. Let her keep the talon in token of that battle.

Gently, she nudges the fledgling's body into the gaping hole in the earth. Her clawed foot sweeps rocks down—once, twice, three times—until the fledgling is lost from sight. Her body will sleep in the earth. Her spirit will soar through the clouds with the dragon she freed.

Come.

A shiver of wonder emanates from the fledgling's spirit as they ascend to the mountain's summit. Together, they watch the few surviving humans swarming down the slope, as small and insignificant as ants.

There are no other signs of humans or their rock dwelling places, only towering peaks overlooking vast heathland and patches of green forest. Her keen senses tell her that the land abounds with game. Streams offer fresh water. The mountains are pitted with caverns. One might be large enough to shelter her when the snows come.

Later, there will be time to explore. But first, she must honor the fledgling's sacrifice and her gift of freedom.

Wait.

A stab of panic from the fledgling's spirit.

Never fear, little one. I will return. And then neither of us will ever be lonely again.

The dragon throws back her head. A plume of fire streams from her mouth. The earth shudders as she races down the mountain. Her wings unfurl and lift her skyward to fly, to hunt, to feast.

Wind and rain, she bellows, storm and sun. Snow-capped mountains and dark, tumbling streams. The fierce joy of plummeting earthward toward her quarry. The snap of bones. The shrieks of the dying. And always, the delicious nectar of blood.

The Breeding Habits of Dragons

Journey Sloane

Today, I finish the last of my six-hour sessions with my artist, Jace McCray. Sessions could have been longer and I'd have been done much sooner, but I have to operate within the expected human tolerances. It's taken months to get to this point, but I cannot imagine doing it the old way with pigments on stretched canvas or chisel upon stone. The eagerness to be done has me entering McCray's Ink a half hour early, as usual. I finish up my bill with Challa and she gives me a cheeky wink, her bright blue human hair and ivory dimple studs not nearly as gorgeous as her natural elephant trunk and tusks. If everything goes as planned, it's not just my life that will change today.

Jace gives me a friendly smile as I turn to look for him. "'Sup, sweetheart?" he asks as he comes to take my sweater. I know I should wear a coat to better fit in with human expectations, but I hate the feeling of being restricted like that. Immediately, the pungent smell of his stress smacks into my senses. I resist the urge to wrinkle my nose and my heart drops a little bit in dismay.

"Bad day? We can reschedule." I start to tuck the e-reader I'd just pulled out back into my bag. I want this Scaling as free of temper as possible. I do not need his bad mood contaminating the process at this late stage.

"Not too bad." He looks puzzled for a moment, but then shrugs it off. "And working on you will be the ending this day needs." He wiggles the fingers of one hand at me. "Sweater, Dragon?"

I resist the temptation to roll my eyes as I shrug the oversize wrap sweater off my shoulders and hand it over. My human name is Ophelia, but he gave me the Dragon tag shortly after we started working on the piece that covers most of my back. It unsettled me at first, but I'm fine with it now. He knew nothing. I put my bag in one of the cubbies provided. He leads me over to one of his tables and hands me a towel before disappearing to engage in hygiene rituals. I slip off my top and fuss with the waist of my skirt, pulling it down low on my hips, then stretch out onto my side. I let myself slip back into the book I'm currently reading. The heroine has realized that even though she finally wants to live, she's going to have to sacrifice herself to save her family. I need to know how this ends, and Jace's "Jesus, woman!" is not a welcome interruption.

I sigh, reluctantly pulling my attention from the book to him. I have to admit, if in some alternate universe I actually did have the urge to mate, he'd check several of my boxes. Tall, muscled, covered in tattoos, with long brown hair and a beard he keeps braided at work but loose at home. (I confess to a bit of curiosity about my artist.) "Yes?"

"Boobs, Dragon, boobs." He's trying his best to keep his eyes on mine, but I can tell it's hard. He likes what he sees and his hormones are reacting.

I cannot imagine being at the mercy of my hormones on such a level. It would make life so uncomfortable. But this is on me, because I forgot the modesty covering he expected me to wear. "Oops," I say, reaching for the towel and pulling it across my chest, which I'd thought was covered enough by my emerald green bra. The human world seems to change so rapidly it sometimes takes me by surprise that modesty expectations still exist. I don't apologize, though. Talented artist or not, he is still only a human. I decide to tease him a bit to deflect the situation. "I forgot you've never seen boobs before."

He splutters. "I've seen plenty of boobs before, woman." A pause, then a wicked grin. "But yours are far nicer than average."

If I had been in True Form, I'd have preened. If he complimented me again, I might do so anyway. I watch him, wondering if he'll compliment my hair or my skin. I do love my compliments.

His face goes white and vaguely green with my silence. "I'm sorry, Dragon. That was out of line."

"No," I say, realizing he misinterpreted my silence. Apparently, I'd humaned wrong. Again. "I agree. They are far nicer than average."

There is a moment of tension in the air as he takes in my words, then he laughs. "All right, Dragon, we just finishing up the coloring or adding a new title?"

"One new title," I say, and tell him what it is. "Other than that, just finishing up." I twist a bit so I can look at my side, where the tail of my dragon comes in on my waist, dipping down across my hip bone. The tail lies across a spill of books with immaculately scripted titles in miniature font on them, though some are left blank for books yet to be read. There are more of these all across my back, ranging all across the genres. I want a well-read progeny.

He nods and readies his tattoo pen. "All right. You ready?"

"Yep." I pay attention only long enough for the first bite of the needle. As usual, it's nothing more than a tolerable annoyance. I turn my attention back to my book and lose myself within the pages. One of the things I appreciate about Jace is that he doesn't try to make small talk with me. He simply sets about doing his job to the best of his ability. Occasionally he pokes me with a finger to tell me he needs a break, but other than that, we're good.

* * *

I've finished the book I had come in with, and another besides, when Jace lets me know we are officially done. As soon as he says the words, a horde of skitterbugs scurry under my back scales. At least, that's what it feels like. I shiver, suppressing the instinctual urge to roll over and do a full body wiggle to crush those little assholes. I don't have long before I need to start the birthing process, but I know I can't run out either.

Jace leads me to a set of standing mirrors and steps away. I strip off my bra so there is no fabric hiding any affected skin and look. I'm able to see my tattoo in all of its glory for the first time. The tattoo takes up almost the entirety of my back, with the Scaling's large, whiskered head resting upon my left shoulder blade and the thick, winding body—all done in gorgeous blue and green jewel tones—resting upon a more than respectable pile of books. Not all dragons hoard gold for their treasure. Books are a treasure all their own.

I turn and lift my arm so I can see the edge of the book pile cascading over my side and the spiked tail that ends close to my supposed reproductive area.

Like me, my Scaling is in the style of dragons from Eastern lore. Germanic dragons are ill-suited for city survival. They're just too bitchy and inclined to violence.

The tattoo is perfect. My Scaling will be perfect. Jace is about to see a significant increase in Mythical Lores coming through his shop. Particularly Dragon Lores. The thought makes me proud of my artist. Each breed of Lores gravitate to those who represent them best. In return for their work, we pay exceedingly well and play protector when necessary. The skin on my back goes through a scrunch and release cycle which lets me know I need to go immediately. *Still*, I command the Scaling, as a knock sounds on the edge of the divider screen. A second later, Challa asks if she can pop in for a picture of the finished tattoo.

I let her in and she quickly takes a couple of pictures then bandages me up. I don't need the protective coverings, and she knows it, but human rules must be followed. Before she leaves the makeshift viewing room, she leans down and presses her cheek against mine, whispering, "Best wishes on your birthing."

I do not thank her, but I smile widely and let loose a short purr that rumbles in my chest.

Moments later, I'm fully dressed and heading out to the front of the shop to grab my stuff. Jace, who was calm as an old dragon sunning itself on a hot day while finishing up my piece, now vibrates with some sort of tension. I'm curious so I don't object when he steps inside my personal space and asks, "What are you going to do now that your dragon's done?"

I knew as soon as I'd seen the full finished tattoo that I would entrust this man to bring forth another of my lineage. "I was thinking about letting you cover me in something else."

The way his eyes go molten with heat makes me bite down on a smile. I know I shouldn't tease the poor human, but it's irresistible. I blame the shifter romance I just read cover to cover. I wait a beat, and clarify. "I've been considering a sternum tattoo." I hesitate, grinning at him. "But that would require you to see my boobs. So I might have Challa do it."

"Challa's got a while to go before she's ready for a large-scale sternum tattoo," he says, voice more than a little grumbly. Like the idea of Challa working on me made him mad. Like he owned my body. My Flame flares inside me. No human would ever claim ownership of me. Only his talent kept me from striking him.

"Think I belong to you, do you?"

His eyes widen and he clears his throat. He knows he's in dangerous territory. "No," he says. "No one can own a Dragon. Only appreciate and protect." The words are good. I understand appreciation and protection—I guard the city library for just that purpose—so I don't snap at him when he brushes his thumb against my jaw. "I want to make sure what goes on your body is perfect, and I don't trust anyone else but me."

Little did he know that, once Challa's training was complete, we were all hoping her human heritage would be enough to give her the magic she needed to breathe life into our progeny. She is a third generation Yali and a talented artist in her own right, and we need her. Because thus far two Lores cannot make a childling without some human in the mix, and Mythical Lores especially are damned tired of the need for human involvement. They make things so much more complicated. The skin on my back ripples again, reminding me I must hurry. "I'll call when I figure out what I want." With that, I mutter brief goodbyes to both and leave.

It is hard to resist the urge to change to True Form as soon as I'm in the alley, but I must maintain human form until the Scaling is birthed if I want it to have shifting ability. I do. Non-shifters do not survive long in this world. I mount my bicycle and, fast enough I know I'm risking getting flagged as unusual, bust ass to a small Safe House, one of many known to all Lores in the area. I knew from checking out a few of them that it was the only one in the area with a large kiln available. I'd come in last week to dust and prep the basement for tonight. Trial and error had proven ovens did not get hot enough for what I need.

The house is small, but the walls are thick and the multiple freezers are kept stuffed to the brim with all kinds of meat and frozen veg. I lock up behind me with shaking fingers, then shed my clothes as I dart through the house and down to the basement. There's a thick mattress covered with a fire retardant blanket lying on the floor and I toss the last piece of clothing to the side a second before flopping face first onto it. There are no books in this room. They are too precious.

My skin itches and burns as the magic burbles up within me, twining through my cells, searching for the foreign elements pushed inside my skin. My Flame twists restlessly inside, fanning of its own accord and sending heat to my pale extremities. I grab hold of the titanium alloy chains joined to two poles sunk deep in the concrete flooring on either side of the bed and wrap them around my hands, gripping as tight as I can. My core temp increases exponentially over sixty seconds, a nuclear explosion of heat inside of me, though it takes a few minutes longer for that heat to translate to the surface.

I've read the books, of course. I know to expect the birthing to be "most painful." Most painful doesn't come close to adequately describing the fiery torment that burns through my cells when Dragon Magic meets the sparks of life the artist had etched into me with his inks. Sparks which ignite into a fire on the surface of my back, searing heat tracing the bold lines the human had laid down on me.

I cannot pull up my True Form. Cannot seek shelter from the fire in the body which tolerates it so much better. But this is the fire of Magic and it is so much hotter than my own natural Flame. Still, my True Form is there, waiting, and it comforts me. Surrounds me. A groan of both pain and primal satisfaction starts deep inside, tears its way out of my chest and throat. I bury my face against the cover to muffle the sound. The Lore community has tried to make sure the area is friendly to us, but it's best to be safe.

The fire spreads from the outline to the color and I can feel it racing in dancing waves across my skin. I turn my face to the side, sucking in a lungful of air that had been faintly lavender-scented, but now reeks of burning flesh. I pull against the chains and feel the smallest amount of give to them that wasn't there before as the poles bend in toward me.

Shit. The poles were supposed to be strong enough to withstand this. I groan, this time in frustration, then force myself to take a few measured breaths. I throw myself into my own imagination, working to lose myself within the mental world I've populated with some of my favorite characters. The hold I get on that world is tenuous, but it's enough. I throw the pain I'm experiencing onto one of the characters, seeing how they react to it.

The pain recedes to a manageable level as I disassociate. Within moments I can even relax my grip on the chains, though I do not notice doing so.

The fire dies, the room going dark again.

I'm breathing hard, but I can't move. Now is the make-or-break point for my Scaling. Others have gotten to this point only for their progeny to be unable to take the final step of separation. I mentally reach out, finding the fledgling consciousness attached to me, and poke it.

The Scaling sends me flashes of reds and claws, letting me know it wants to be left alone.

"Tough," I say aloud, and wince from the pain. "Get off of me."

My skin ripples again, magic enabling it to stretch and fill. Triumph fills me. I did it. My first Scaling. But then, abruptly, it settles back down, my skin returning to normal.

No. The word is crystal clear inside my mind. The Scaling's mind is rapidly maturing.

"What do you mean, no? Get off of me!" Nobody warned me the Scaling might not want to leave.

No. Warm. Comfy. Will do later.

Oh, my god. I've created a lazy dragon. I'm horrified. Will I fail this birthing purely because the progeny I've created lacks the motivation to be born?

"Off!"

No.

I'm frustrated. Irritated. And trying to ignore the ridiculous amusement tickling at my insides. It's not funny. It really isn't.

"I have a book waiting for you." I'm not above bribery.

A stillness. The Scaling considering what I've said. Finally: *Which one?*

Books. Works every time. "Dawn by Octavia Butler." It was a great first book. It was time for my Scaling to part from my own impressions of what I'd read and start making their own.

Picture version?

It must have sensed my confusion, because it bombarded me with pages filled with bold color and white speech bubbles.

Graphic novels. My Scaling wanted graphic novels. The *one* type of book I hated to read. It was still reading, so I couldn't object, but STILL. Also, it wasn't something I had on hand. "No. The words only version."

Bah. There was a rustling feeling under my skin, like the Scaling was getting comfortable. A little ridiculous, considering the dragon existed in my skin at the moment, not underneath it.

I thump my head against the mattress. "I'll buy it for you. If they don't have it, I'll buy you whatever graphic novel you'd like. Just please get off of me." I'm whining by the end, definitely, but no one else is around to hear it, so I don't care.

Two.

That little shit. That absolute little shit. Indignation fills me, and the voice which comes out of me next is pure Birther Dragon, no human involved. "Remove yourself, Scaling or I will claw you from my skin."

There's that considering silence again, just for a heartbeat. And then: *Yes, Birther.*

My skin starts to swell and stretch again and I am thankful the fire has mostly numbed my nerve endings. There's a sudden sensation of too tight, too full, and I feel a dull itching I know would be so much worse at any other time. And then the prickle of tiny claws digging into the muscle right before the Scaling does a full body shake that tears my flesh open. It wastes no time in scurrying off my back and onto the bed beside me, nuzzling up against my side.

Cold.

Whoever said childbirth was beautiful was wrong. It's painful and the Scaling at my side is covered with what I think is blood and a type of protective membrane they are already shedding. Where it has ripped, I can see shades of blue and green. They are small, with whiskers like mine, and slightly bulbous silver eyes. They are the exact size of the tattoo they came from, and they will stay this way for as long as they are bound to me. Contentment washes through me. I have done my duty to my species. I let loose one of the chains completely and lightly cover the Scaling with my arm.

We both lie in the silence for a few moments, but when the little one shivers, I know what I have to do. Carefully getting to my feet, feeling like I've aged four hundred years, I scoop up the Scaling. My eyes have adjusted to the dark again and I can see that right now its scales are still so soft they are not protecting it at all. They need hardening up, and there's only one way to do that.

I wince my way over to the kiln and place it on the basking stone inside. Then, before they can register what's happening, I'm sliding into my True Form. I take a moment to revel in the relief as I heal from the trauma of the birth.

Birther?

I use the handholds on the outside of the kiln carefully; I don't want to puncture it. I raise up enough I can look into the opening.

My Scaling stares at me, absolute delight shining in their eyes. *You're beautiful.*

I know. I eye the fuel compartment and rear back as my Flame gathers in my stomach and chest. With a belch, I spew flames into the open kiln, igniting the fuel below and bathing my Scaling in a direct hit from my Flame.

I know in the human world this would be considered a horrible thing. But right now it is a moment between a Birther Dragon and her Scaling, and what I am doing will up the chances my progeny will survive. I draw a parallel to a human saying that makes me want to laugh. This truly is the Dragon version of a bun in the oven.

The Scaling—who I really must name soon—gives a happy little body wiggle, basking in the heat. When I run out of breath, I inhale again and repeat the process. I do this three more times before closing the door to keep the heat in. The Scaling will be safe in there, baking until its scales are hardened. And I will eat. Likely clean out one of the freezers in its entirety.

* * *

Three weeks later and it's time for my Scaling, now named Emrys, to lay eyes on the human who helped create them. The little one isn't ready for human form yet, but this should be enough to satisfy their curiosity. For now. These past three weeks have been enough to make me realize that if I was anything like Emrys as a young Scaling, I should find my Birther and apologize to them. Repeatedly.

I get us to the shop about an hour before closing. I am in my human form and Emrys is nestled in tattoo form across my back. It is a form they will only be able to take until they muster up the gumption to develop a human form. As unmotivated as my Scaling is, I have a feeling we'll be traveling like this for at least a few human years.

It's dark, so I quickly climb the rusted fire escape to the roof of Jace's building. Up there, I check once again to make sure he has installed no security cameras. Once I'm sure everything is clear, I kneel down and lift the back of my shirt over my head, baring my back.

Emrys stays where they are nestled and, since we are in public, I communicate with them mentally. *Off.*

For once there's no bitching about how they'd much rather stay where they are. My skin swells and splits as Emrys takes form. The process is, thankfully, no longer as painful as it once was. When they are beside me, I quickly shift into my True Form. I've enough years under my belt that I no longer have to take my clothes off to do so. Instead, the Lore magic binds their fibers to my form in some fashion. It's a trick I'm curious enough to wonder about, but not curious enough to ask one of the Old Crowd to explain.

Emrys scuttles around the roof, popping their head up over the ledge to look down below every ten feet or so. Their whiskers and tail flick with excitement as they take in the new sights. It is the first time I've let them explore a space not explicitly designated as safe.

A few minutes later, when the two of us are just getting into a game of tail tag, I hear belligerent voices below. You know how some humans have voices that set your teeth on edge? In True Form, they sound a hundred times worse. One of the two has a nasally voice which grates on my senses and arouses the urge to roast them with my Flame as penance for their mere existence. He probably tastes as bad as he sounds, but I'm willing to make that sacrifice.

Unfortunately, the consumption of humans for the crime of existing was outlawed before I was born. Which is a shame, because there is a horrible overpopulation issue many Lores would be happy to assist with.

I cannot block out his voice, no matter how much I try to focus on other things. But my attention is truly caught when I hear my artist mentioned. They don't say his name, but Jace is the only tattoo artist in this particular area. What they are saying is not complimentary, and what they are planning is even worse.

Listen, I command Emrys. They scurry up beside me and we both poke our heads over the ledge to look in the direction of the voices. The two are hidden in the shadows, but our eyesight is superior. The smaller one is wearing a black stocking over his face. The larger one looks like a football player wannabe. *They are planning to hurt our artist.*

Death, Emrys tells me, and the scales in the center of their body rise and rub against each other. *Death, Birther.*

Quiet, I tell them, placing my claw at the base of their neck and running it a short way down their spine. It forces their smaller scales to lay back down in a domino effect. *We cannot bring Death until we are sure they are attempting to harm him. Some humans are full of threats but have no Flame.*

What I leave unsaid is that I don't want to have to file the paperwork to account for the extinguishment of human life if there is no need for it. We settle in to listen. As much as the nasaled one repeats himself, I assume at first that I'm not getting the full story, but that he'll get around to it. Soon

I understand there is no story. My artist refused to place his inks upon this man and it pissed him off.

My Flame grows hot enough that my little one forgets they're supposed to be paying attention to the happenings below and tucks themselves along my underside. An artist has the right to choose their canvas and not all canvas is suitable. This egotistical hate-filled halfwit and his oversized goon will learn to respect my artist's boundaries.

The door to the shop opens, then closes again, and I hear Jace's familiar footsteps. My takeout withdraws further into the shadows. I give my Scaling a mental nudge and they resume their position beside me.

Death?

Patience, I counsel.

The two step out from the shadows; I see the orange light of the street lamp catch on the barrel of a gun.

Jace freezes, raising his hands. "Don't want any trouble."

"Then maybe you should just fucking do the tattoos like you're told," the nasally one says. The larger one is coming around to Jace's side, staying out of his sight. "I'm thinking maybe you should give me that bag by way of apology. Maybe then I won't give you another orifice in your face." The way he cackles, I know he thinks that was the most brilliant thing ever said.

"I'll give you the money," Jace tells him. His voice is too calm, like he's facing a rabid werewolf and knows it. It's smart. Humans as stupid and petty as these two are can be deadly. "No problem with that. Let me get in my bag and get it for you, okay?"

"Ain't so big and bad now, are you?" Another cackle. "Give me everything, ya fucking libtard. I'll make that bag my new goddamned toilet."

Libtard? Emrys asks.

The current political climate in America is such that people who believe in the values the country was supposedly founded upon are treated as though they are idiots who wouldn't be able to tell a tail scale from a belly scale even if they were clearly labeled, I say, watching as Jace tightens his grip on his bag and shifts his weight. The bag is obviously important to him, though I don't understand why. *It is a process of othering occurring on both sides of the divide which may eventually lead to a civil war within our lifetime.*

Are we libtards?

We're Lore. We'll exist after the human race stupids itself out of existence. Pay attention.

"Wouldn't if I were you." The big one finally makes his appearance. He's only a couple inches shorter than Jace. I don't see what he does, but whatever it is makes Jace stop his minute movements. "Think we'll take the jacket, too. Lose it, big man."

Over the side, I tell Emrys. *Keep up high. Silent claws.*

Should I be involving a Scaling as new as Emrys in this? Probably not. But if the little one has no fighting instinct, it's better for their life force to be released now before they continue to take up time and resources best spent on those who can help our species thrive.

I join my Scaling, going low enough that I'm no longer looking at the tops of their heads and can see my artist's face.

"Don't want any trouble," Jace says again. "Asking real nice you let me keep that messenger bag, though."

"Aww, him wants his bag? What, did Mummy get it for you?"

Jace's expression changes. Only for a split second, but it's enough.

The stupid one shrieks with laughter. "Holy shit, his Mummy did get it for him. Aw, that's so cute."

It is cute, actually. Attachment to a gift from your birther like that means there's a strong bond. That should be treasured. We dragons aren't the most sentimental, but even we know that. Also, at this point I'm determined to end Nasally's existence simply to ensure my ears never encounter his voice again.

A growl rumbles out of me, the sound bouncing off the buildings around us.

The two crane their necks around, trying to pinpoint where it came from. I flatten myself out as much as possible, pretending I'm graffiti on the side of the building.

"You didn't tell me dude had a dog," the larger of the two says. "You know I don't like dogs, Chad."

"Don't say my fucking name, you idiot," the other one snaps, looking back at his companion.

I gather myself, and send the ready signal to my Scaling.

"And he don't. I didn't see any sign of it in the shop. Probably just some guard dog going off somewhere." He turns his attention back to Jace. "Give me the fucking—"

I push off hard against the stone wall and slam into him, raking my claws against his jacket and spilling white fluff upon the ground. I twist around him so fast he'd have to be superhuman to identify what I am. My second and third strikes draw blood and the smell of disease hits me hard.

As I hear a girlish scream from the larger man, indicating the Scaling has charged into battle, I throw myself away from my target in disgust. I cannot be infected by human disease, but it makes the meat taste absolutely horrible. My takeout is spoiled, dammit.

The asshole doesn't stop to see what attacked him, or wonder why I stopped. He just clutches his middle and runs like the hounds of hell are after him. I turn back to the remaining man in time to see him fall to the ground as Jace tackles him.

Away, I command. The Scaling has proven itself. Also, I don't want Jace to break one of his precious hands on Emrys if they accidentally get in the way.

Emrys scuttles out of the way and I assume they're following me as I climb the side of the wall, melding myself against it. Only too late do I notice that my Scaling not only chose to stay, but is watching the human-on-human action with rapt curiosity.

Come here, I tell them, cursing myself for not picking them up and bringing them with me. It is a better world for us if we keep humans as unaware of our presence as possible. My Scaling chitters and their scales sing with the speed of their vibrations. Their back arches and they do a little hopping dance around the tussling humans.

You must hide, I send with a firm mental poke, but Emrys isn't paying attention because suddenly Jace is still. His eyes are locked on my Scaling, his mouth dropping open.

Shit.

The man on the ground raises his head and groans as he tries to push Jace off. The artist looks down, frowns as though he'd completely forgotten the man existed, and draws a fist back. The punch he delivers makes the asshole's head bounce off the concrete of the alleyway and I can't help the purr of pure pleasure that vibrates my chest.

Jace moves off of the now unconscious man, but doesn't stand up. Instead, he crouches directly in front of my Scaling, tentatively extending his hand. Emrys lowers their scales and raises a front claw to preen, but their eyes stay fastened on him. They are a happy little dragon who got treats of both unexpected violence and meeting the human who helped bring them to life. I'm surprised they're not purring.

There's nothing I can do at this point, and my instincts tell me Jace can be trusted, so I don't interfere as the two of them check each other out. After a long moment, the artist says something that surprises me. "Thanks for saving me…Ophelia?"

He recognizes the Scaling. I shouldn't be surprised, and huff in self-directed amusement. Jace's head snaps toward me. I go statue-still on pure instinct. His eyes narrow and he looks between Emrys and the shadow I'm cloaked in. "Well, I'm glad you're not alone. You're a tiny thing."

That *tiny thing* just took on a six-foot tall and wide thug. Something Jace seems to have forgotten already.

"I'm gonna go check out your friend, okay?"

Emrys tilts their head, considering, and then bobs it once.

Traitor, I send to them, but there's no venom in the thought. While I'll need to make sure later that Emrys understands the rules for keeping our species safe, they are too young to be faulted right now. They raise their head, small nostrils flaring, and make for a nearby dumpster.

Jace watches, clearly smiling underneath his face fur, and then comes my way. I'm okay with it right up until he slips his phone from his pocket. No pictures. No pictures, no video. It is getting harder every day to maintain our secrecy and, if it wasn't for a wide net of Lore and Lore-friendly people, we'd have already been exposed ten times over. Still, we can't depend on them. It is on each of us to keep hidden as much as we can. I growl at Jace. Not as loudly as I could, but it gets the point across.

His eyes widen and he holds up a hand, palm out. "Not gonna take pictures," he tells me. "Just going to put on the flashlight because I want to see you better, if that's all right?"

I do trust him, I realize. Truly. So, after waiting long enough to make it clear that it's not an instantaneous acceptance, I give a soft chirrup and turn my eyes away as he turns on the flashlight app on his phone.

"Oh," he says, and there is such pure wonder in his voice that I have to look at him. When I turn my head, our faces are inches apart. "You're gorgeous." He bites his lip and then raises a hand, gesturing at my back. "May I?"

I'm not a domesticated animal to be petted for human pleasure. But I understand why he wants to touch me. Just as I encourage my Scaling to use all their senses when experiencing something new, he clearly wants to do the same. I give a sliver of a nod. I don't want him to think I'm eager for this.

He places his hand on my back and gently strokes his palm down a short section of the center of it. "Scarlet, Liberachi, Dragon Breath, Ruby…" He's listing the colors he sees in my scales, voice reverent. "Sunflower, Lightning, and Ochre." Those aren't the exact colors. He's translating them into what he knows best: shades of ink.

My Birther was a traditionalist and I was conceived on canvas by an artist who adored the Fauvism technique. Luckily, my Birther managed to convince him to tone it down a bit. So my colors do at least blend well together.

I hear the sounds of the other human stumbling in the opposite direction, muttering something about never trusting Chad again. There was no indication he saw us, so I'm content to let it go.

Jace turns his head to face me and I observe him in return. In human form, he's aesthetically pleasing to me. In True Form, his lines and colors are a mix of soft and hard, dusky and vibrant, and I can see the art which went into his own creation. Looking at him, I can understand how humankind believes in gods. Because it is hard to believe he was not shaped from someone greater's imagination.

"I recognize your eyes," he says softly. "Ophelia?"

I taste his cheek with a flicker of my tongue in answer. He tastes of salt and wonder.

A high-pitch chirping sound interrupts us and I hear the familiar skitter of my Scaling's claws as it abandons the dumpster and races toward me. In a flash, they are splayed flat against my back, pressing their face against my scales.

What's wrong?

Trash. Panda. I can feel small vibrations against me and scent their fear underneath the smell of garbage from their excursion. *Creepy. Don't like. Go home.*

They're not trash pandas, I tell them. *The correct word is raccoon.* It's my fault, though. I played a video on YouTube for them that was supposed to list the animals most commonly found in the city while I took a shower. I took too long and came back to excited talk about Trash Pandas, Danger Noodles, Nope Ropes, and Murder Logs. Thanks, Internet.

"Your…baby?" Jace shines his phone light over Emrys and recognition dawns. "It's your tattoo," he breathes, and his brows draw together as he loses himself in the chicken or the egg question of what came first. My Scaling or the tattoo.

Distract. Say goodbye, I tell Emrys. I want to get out of here before Jace starts asking questions I'll have to refuse to answer.

Emrys comes through with a subdued little chirp and a nudge to the hand hovering inches away from my skin. Jace instantly focuses on them and gently strokes their head. "You're gorgeous, too," he says.

Emrys does a full-body shimmy at the compliment, making their scales rasp softly together. I can feel the pride radiating from them.

My artist looks at me, amusement shining in his eyes.

I roll my eyes, but then I can't help myself. All that adoration *is* shimmy worthy. I repeat Emrys' action, but before Jace can react, I'm up the side of the building and to the roof where we will wait for him to leave before we change back to a red-headed human and her tattoo.

It takes a while. I think I blew his mind.

* * *

It's summer, scorching hot and perfect. The humans are griping about the heat wave, but us Dragon Lores are in absolute heaven. And it's finally been long enough that I can start the process of giving Emrys a sibling. Because, oh gods, does Emrys need a sibling. It is rare for a Birther to take on two Scalings before the first has experienced at least their second year, but sometimes exceptions must be made. And if I don't find a way to keep this Scaling entertained, they're going to be the first recorded case of Death By Birther in the last three hundred years.

When I walk into the shop, thick red hair pulled up into a messy bun and wearing a bikini-style top that bares as much of my sternum as possible, Jace is waiting at the door, a wide smile on his face. He doesn't look at me with lust the way he had before, though. There's something different in his eyes. Reverence. "Dragon," he says. "How are…things?" He darts a quick glance at Challa as he says it, his voice guarded.

Challa had sent word all was well, but it reassures me to get confirmation he hadn't mentioned the encounter to her.

"Good," I say, and smile at him in return, turning briefly to show him my back.

He traces the tattoo's lines with a gentle finger. "Looks good."

I face him again, turning the conversation to the reason I'm here. "Are we ready to get started?"

"Yeah," he takes the hint. "Challa said you wanted another dragon, right?"

I nod in agreement, and his gaze drops to my belly for a split second. I can tell he's curious, but Challa's presence is keeping the questions at bay. Good.

My artist leads me back to his work station and excuses himself. He returns a moment later with a sketchbook he opens to show several dragon designs specifically worked to fit on my sternum.

I could almost kiss him. Instead, I let out a very quiet purr of pleasure and let him help me onto the table. Once I'm up there, he whispers in my ear. "Your baby's head is on the wrong shoulder."

Oops. I give Emrys a mental poke. I feel the burn of magic as they shift positions. It doesn't take long after that until I'm flat on my back, nose buried in my e-reader while my artist works his magic on me once more.

Gods in Chains

Em McDermott

At night, after the paddock gates locked and the slavers went to sleep, the psychic dampening field dropped to a low, irritating buzz in the backgrounds of our minds and we could merge. There was little to say to each other about the day that had just gone by. Each one was a mindless cycle of drudgery. Only the luckiest of us was allowed to taste the stars, or perhaps the least lucky, for slavers let only the most broken of us keep their wings, and fliers were punished with extra chains at night. No, there was nothing to replay from the day, and so we replayed memories passed to us by the Old Ones. Memories of the Time Before.

What do we want tonight? hummed Obsidian. Many of our best memories came from him. Once he had merged with a dragon who had actually flown in the Time Before.

Thermals on a hot day, I answered.

You always want thermals on a hot day, complained Tanzanite. *I want swim in a cool ocean.*

Other opinions chimed in, but it was all a bit silly, really. The night was long and contained time for many memories.

A flight above a warm ocean on a warm day, decided Obsidian, ever the compromiser.

Instantly, I was there. I did not even need to close the layers of lids over my eyes. I could stare at the barren stone of the paddock, at the curled-up bodies of my fellow slaves, at the traveling purple current of the buzzing dampening field, even up into the thin atmosphere of this planet's sky to the stars beyond, and smell the salt of the oceans of Earth.

The feel of the wind was my favorite thing. I shivered in pleasure at its cool caress on my sensitive belly. In this memory, the sky was cloudy and the sun was not hot enough to bake the scales of my back. Instead, mist rising off the sea tickled me and wet my tongue.

Around me, the sky was full of dragons. They were dragons long dead and they were us, my brothers and sisters from the paddock. The memory was not quite a memory, but a framework for a game we played called What Life Should Be Like. As in life, we each made our own way.

Tanzanite tucked her wings in tight to her sides and dove, spiraling her body until she was a blur. She cut into the water like an AK-DR Interstellar Missile. She was a beauty to behold, her scales sparkling violet, her wingspan enormous.

I was smaller, silver-white as a fish in the tropical sea beneath, my tight male body the perfect complement to her vast power. At least, I liked to imagine that's what might have been in the world that should have been. I followed her dive with my own.

My stomach jumped into my throat as I pulled my wings in tight and dropped like a stone. If I'd kept my wings out, I could've flown forever, but I made my choice and began to fall. I flipped face down, my long neck snaking out to kiss the water first. I began my own spin, lazy and slow. The water rushed like scale oil over my skin. The salt tingled pleasantly on my dry spots.

If this were my real body dropping into the sea, the salt would have felt like acid in all the cracks and tears between my dull, chipped scales, but there was no use thinking of that sort of thing.

I swam. Deeper and deeper, I plunged into the great vast sea. I did not worry about finding Tanzanite; distance did not exist inside the merge. If I reached out to touch the tendrils of our mind connection, I could feel that the sea around her was two degrees warmer than it was around me. She was closer to the surface and to shore. I made my own way.

Down, down, until the sea resembled the black emptiness of space. The pressure squeezing my body meant nothing to me; the air in my many lungs would last hours. With the channel to my lungs closed, I could not drown by swallowing water. Dragons were built for such extreme places. My scales glowed, lighting the darkness. I blocked the chit-chat of the others and imagined myself alone. I floated in the embryonic nowhere-space.

Are you here, too?

It was not a voice I knew, and I was startled. It was a child's voice, soft and tentative. A human female. I could sense this, although I did not understand how. Hundreds of years had passed since the last human had merged with one of my kind.

I'm here and I'm not here.

That describes me, too, the girl said, and a picture came along with her thought. A picture of a human girl, a few years shy of puberty. Her skin was the brown-black of smoky quartz and the coils of her hair were sun-gold. She stood alone in a cage—one of *their* cages, a white box with purple electricity crawling along the walls. *I am in this cage, and yet I sense you. I taste salt, and there is pressure squeezing my skin.*

Without giving it thought, I rose until I crowned the surface. *Is that better?*

Oh yes. Doesn't that sun feel nice? It was out from behind the clouds. I launched into the air and let the breeze and heat dry my scales.

Where are you? I asked.

Where you are.

What is happening?

I hope I've made a friend.

A thousand answers she might've given, answers laden with scientific postulation or fear or wonder. Instead, she answered with an innocence I thought lost from the world. My heart swelled at the tenderness of her simple hope, and a fierce primordial instinct filled it. In the Time Before, it was the honor of our kind to protect theirs, and the honor of theirs to merge with us. Gods are nothing without their mortals. Together, we made living worthwhile. Wonder and reason, mythic power and simple humanity. Merged, dragons and their riders wielded power once thought to be unconquerable.

Now, the old instincts, long dormant, rusty and stiff with disuse, rose from the rubbish pile in the deepest corners of my brain and shook off the dust. They charged to the forefront of my mind with shocking fervor and strength, surprising me with the forcefulness with which they asserted that the little girl was *mine* now.

Precious, we are more than friends. You feel it, too, don't you? A strange fear gripped me that she did not, that the possessiveness that dug its claws in me at my first picture of this golden child was not reciprocated.

Oh yes, Tungsten, she said.

She knows my name, I thought with a thrill. How does she know my name? My heart was aflame and I coasted towards the horizon, which retreated before me, always a little further ahead, a hazy promise of the future.

* * *

Morning dawned, and the rising pitch of the dampening field stole away the touch of the little girl. Silent with mourning, we came back to the husks of ourselves. Tanzanite lay curled in on herself, her scales the dull color of a murky tidal pool. Though she was young, some of her scales had baked to stone already. The sulfurous air shimmered with heat as I shook off the coating of ash that had settled on me overnight.

Tanzanite, did you sense a little girl in our merge last night? I spoke only to her, not entirely trusting that some of the others might not betray my secret for an extra ration of sheep or a paddock further from the volcano's fires.

What are you talking about, Tungsten? Tanzanite's sweet multi-tonal voice was melodic music. *Last night's merge was like all the others.*

I spoke no more on the subject, and she did not question me, but my gaze rose above the fence of our prison to the stark white buildings that pimpled the flat surfaces of the closest dormant mountain. My sharp eyes could easily pick out each window built into the base. Behind which of them was my little girl?

A horn blared and the doors of the gate opened. Their purpose was to cage dragons, and the doors dwarfed the human operators who came through them. Purple electricity sparked at the ends of the prods the slavers carried. They marched towards us in formation, like soldiers with heat suits for armor and prods for spears.

Like well-trained pups, my thunder and I shuffled slowly out. We were lumbering, awkward beasts when we walked. Tanzanite's wings trailed their tips in the ash as she walked before me. The horns along her tail had been cut brutally short. Her wings, so glorious in my mind-space made of memory, were a skeletal framework with a gaunt fabric of flesh coating. Holes had been deliberately torn in the hide between her metacarpals, leaving her wings a tattered mess of useless weight on either side of her.

How would I reach the base that the humans had built on that mountain when my wings were clipped, the same as Tanzanite's? And what would I do if I did reach the girl? The bitter truth was that I could not fly us away to safety. I could not save her in any way that I could imagine. I was a beast of burden, a fallen god, a discarded remnant of a time past. Even as I thought these things, I knew they did not matter to the possessive *ache* that had awakened in me at the first touch of the girl's mind. An instinct that I could not reason with told me that, if only she would touch her small hand to my parched hide, the whole world would right itself.

They brought us to the lava lake and the workday began. Into the lake I dove, my fellows beside me. Down, down we swam.

I was not fast, like in last night's memory. My tattered wings could not provide the same thrust through thick magma as they could through salty ocean. The magma burned as it burrowed into the cuts and tears in my dry hide. Pressure and heat such as this made diamonds, and it would make stone out of me, too, given enough time. Not much more time at all, actually.

The bottom of the lake was studded with tunnels. I swam into one I'd carved with my own claws. Sharp claws were the only weaponized part of our bodies *they* let us keep, for we needed them to carve the tunnels.

The tunnel burrowed towards the center of the primordial world. The surface of this planet was nothing but fields of active volcanoes divided by ocean. The atmosphere was white ash. In the mantle below the surface, diamonds awaited collection. Only dragons could reach them before they were ejected.

The tunnel went on for miles. I swam deeper than any human could have survived, even in one of their spaceships. Mini-quakes rumbled like a hungry stomach. When I was deep enough, I swept magma and stone into the receptacle I carried. I scraped my body along the stone as I executed a turn in the tight tunnel, and then I was ascending.

It was lonely down here. Though the magma and stone blocked the dampening field, they created one of their own, and I could not hear even the shallowest thoughts of the others.

Don't be lonely, said the voice of the girl. She startled me so much that I dropped my bucket and found myself glad it was tied to my tail.

How can we speak over such a distance?

What do you mean? I'm right here. And she was. I felt the warmth of her small body tucked right up beside me. It was a pleasant warmth, not like the intense heat of magma. A subtle scent of spiced milk replaced the acrid sulfur scent of my buried world. Her small arm wrapped around my leg and she pressed her hand against a crack in my hide. Her touch cooled me, as if her hand were coated in cream.

It wasn't real, of course. Not in the physical sense. The girl was in her cage and I swam up from the mantle in conditions she could never survive. The psychic power required to merge under these conditions was astounding.

You know my name, but what is yours?

I'm Genesis, the girl said.

We spoke as I ascended. When I reentered the lake, I could sense the nearby members of my thunder, too. The magma deadened the dampening field enough to allow us to speak, though we couldn't see each other through its thick angry redness.

I'm not in a good way today, Tungsten, Obsidian shared on a private thread. We both rose to surface for a breath, and to make our first drop of the day.

What's the matter?

I'm stiff.

A long moment of silence acknowledged the weight of his admission. *How stiff?*

Very stiff, old friend, said Obsidian.

It took too long to crest the surface of the lake. Magma dripped from my scales as I climbed laboriously out onto hardened stone. I looked around for Obsidian, but he hadn't surfaced yet. I made my drop and collected a fresh bucket. By the time I was ready to dive again, Obsidian had surfaced. He stumbled as he stepped away from the lake. He dropped his bucket, the magma and stone inside spilling out, making the slavers nearby jump away.

I stood frozen at the edge of the lake, watching him. He lifted a leg to take another step, and it locked in the air. His head swiveled towards me, the vertical slits of his pupils finding mine.

Freedom at last, said the old dragon, then he turned to stone.

The humans called it in, announcing it to each other in enthusiastic voices. "Yup, black," they said into the microphones inside their protective suits. "A nice big guy, too." They prodded him with their electric sticks, to be sure. They prodded me when I did not dive again. Electricity arced through my body. For a moment, I considered what might happen if I bit off one of their heads. I still had teeth, after all. But then what? As the third man thrust his prod against my skin, I slipped back into the lake.

I did not notice the heat, for it was not as hot as the anger that burned in my heart. Even Genesis' psychic touch could not comfort me. Though the oldest in our paddock, Obsidian had been only a hundred and fifty-two. In draconic years, he was a child. We all were. But the diamonds we harvested were only part of our value to the slavers. The other value was our bodies themselves. For when a dragon died, their scales transfigured into a gemstone harder and rarer than any diamond. It was our version of aging, a process that proceeded slowly while we were alive and ended with a dramatic finish, leaving nothing but a statue behind. The natural process took eons, but heat and pressure could bring it about in decades. Each evening, when I surveyed my own body, I assessed the time I had left by how many scales had already transfigured into solid, inflexible silver-white gemstone. They would grow no more, would flex no more when I twisted and turned. The hide that stretched between the hardened scales was the rawest for being exposed. Yes, only a few years left now.

* * *

That night, Obsidian was not there to call for the opening of the mind-space. The buzzing of the dampening field died down until I could feel the readiness of the others, but we sat together in an empty room, not speaking, no one opening a memory.

Finally, it occurred to me that I must speak. I was the next oldest. Obsidian had passed many of his memories to me over the years of our imprisonment together, and I contained others besides. I had never met an Old One myself, never received a memory of Earth directly from the source, but I had been given memories of flying over this world. The hot air rising off the volcanic fields made flying a game-like challenge.

I was about to initiate the picture when another image superseded it.

Hello, Tungsten. The girl's voice accompanied the image.

A thunder of dragons blotted out Earth's blue sky. The wingspans of the largest made Tanzanite look like a newborn. They flapped with massive, slow strokes, bobbing in place. It was a wonder they didn't cross with each other and tangle and fall—there were so many. And on each of their backs, a rider.

Awe filled me, and I opened the picture to the others without thinking. All memories as old as this had been lost. To see it now was a gift that must be shared and savored. If I were human, I would cry.

Don't cry, my friend. It is a thing of beauty.

It certainly is, I answered.

I was in the body of one of the gods in that sky. My gigantic wings swept up and down. A lazy power filled me. On my back, my saddle itched a little. Sitting in its seat was a human woman. She reached down to pat my well-oiled scales.

I stretched and twisted, exploring the feel of the body. Not a single scale on my back was hardened stone. No, I was lithe and smooth, slippery and powerful. And I was more than just myself. I knew suddenly how we did not fly into each other. We were one. Every dragon and rider in the sky had joined together in a single merge. What could we not conquer?

We can be this again, Genesis said.

How are you showing me this? How did you speak to me when I was a hundred miles below you?

Do you remember the day the field went down?

I did. It was over a year ago. There had been some problem with the generators and the psychic dampening field had gone down completely for several minutes. I still savored the memory of the power that surged through me as I slipped into full merge with my thunder, the bonds between us tighter and stronger than I'd ever felt before. But even that day, I had not felt the girl.

Yes.

On that day, I gained access to something blocked. Lifetimes of memories, but I knew it wouldn't last. I searched through them quickly for something I could use to stay strong once the field came back on. I've been practicing. I'm a little stronger than their dampening field now.

A little stronger seemed like an understatement. This girl contained lifetimes of memories, more like a dragon than one of *them.*

I don't understand what you are, my precious, but I love you the same. Still, we could not be this again. My wings are clipped and my kind is virtually extinct, and there is no way back.

No, but there is a way forward, Genesis said.

* * *

The girl (*my girl, mine)* whispered to me through the night. When I woke from the merge, I found the same dumbfounded amazement in the eyes of the others that was likely in my own. She'd been with all of us, touched each mind in my paddock. She had told us her plan and we'd agreed to try it.

We were not afraid. Even as the merge dulled with the rise of the dampening field, I could feel the others enough to know that. Death was not a scary end to a life of slavery. Soon, death would come for me whether I rose in rebellion or not. Over half my scales had turned to stone already.

The warning horn bleated and the paddock doors opened. *Their* technology engaged to pull the beastly things apart.

Act normal until it's time, I warned, for the excitement of the upcoming escape had made some of my thunder act jumpy and odd. We fell into line, shuffling through the gate.

This might be the last time I watch Tanzanite drag her wingtips through the ash, I thought. I might never again see her powerful tail sweep back and forth behind her to help her keep balanced.

They brought us to the lava lake. My hearts pounded as I scuffled along familiar ground.

One of Obsidian's memories had been of the sun rising into the sky of old Earth. The colors, unobscured by ash, rivaled the sparkling hides of the Old Ones. When I watched that sunrise, I felt the stirring excitement of a great adventure just beginning, rising with the dawning day, handed to me as the sun's rays stole their first kiss on my face. I felt that way now.

In the distance, fliers carried cargo to ships in orbit. Their wings, still intact, stirred the ash clouds. Raw hide circles around their ankles and necks spoke of the chains they wore at night, but they were not chained now. If only I could have called out to them. *Join us, glorious fliers,* I would say. But the dampening field prevented a call of that distance.

I dove as usual into the lake. I swam down to the bottom where I could hear the others if they called. I did not go into my tunnel. Instead, I did the thing that Genesis had told me to do, a thing that frightened me and all the others. I opened my mouth.

Magma flowed into me. My teeth were stalagmites in a world of liquid and solid stone. I felt sure that any moment, the heat of the pulsing liquid inside and out would turn me wholly to stone and I'd sink to the bottom to rest forever. No, not forever. Someday, the volcano itself would blow me out.

The magma slid to the back of my throat and I choked on it, but my breathing channel was closed and I was not truly choking. I was only panicking. I calmed myself and reached out my mind for the others.

It is in me, I said.

Me, too, Tanzanite answered.

Me, too, answered others.

It is in us, and we are in each other. We will live or we will have freedom, I said, thinking of Obsidian.

The magma flowed into my stomach and churned with my own acid. It burned me, inside and out, pressing at me like two magnets that longed to be together, and I was a barrier between them. I felt sure, still, that it would burn my insides or turn me to stone and I would die, but I hadn't died yet.

Do you have memories of how dragon eggs were hatched in the Time Before? Genesis had asked me last night.

I did not.

They were kept warm by the magma of volcanoes. They were hatched deep in the Earth's mantle, every newborn introduced to fire before air. Tungsten, fire cannot harm you. It only gives you life.

When I was so full of heat and fire and pressure that I could hardly tell myself apart from it, I swam up.

"Hey, what are you doing back so soon?" a slaver called. He marched forward in his diamond-coated boots, his prod held out before him. I climbed laboriously over the edge. I was heavy. I'd closed my mouth, and it was not until the slaver stood before my feet, purple arcs of electricity sparking at the end of his prod, which inched towards my underbelly, that I opened it.

I poured fire from my gut. The slaver did not even have time to scream before he melted. Others came running. But I'd only spit up what was in my mouth and I was full of fire. I *was* fire. I clenched my stomach and blew, and magma showered the slavers who ran to chain me. It melted through their suits and their skin. The prods fell from their hands and their screams satisfied a long-dormant part of me.

Even as my body emptied of magma, it filled up with something else. Power.

My thunder was rising from the lake. In each of their bellies was magma. They fanned out and moved forward in formations we'd learned from our captors.

A piercing alarm wailed and humans poured from their buildings like an avalanche of a thousand tiny pebbles. They brought bigger weapons than the prods used by the slavers who watched over long-broken workers; they brought tanks and machine guns. But the wheels of the tanks were not made of diamond. I trumpeted my triumph as they melted beneath my sulfurous breath.

I'd expended the fire in my belly. I dove back into the lake. *Fill me up,* I thought. *Fill me with liquid fire and I shall be reborn. Just as she said.* I opened myself to the magma. I let it flow into my mouth, my stomach, yes, but more than that. I arced back and spread my wings wide, stretching my body until the magma licked every inch of me, inside and out. I gave myself up to the primordial forces of creation. For all of my short life, the magma had meant pressure and heat and death, but now it meant power and fire and rebirth, and I filled myself until fire smoldered in my eyes and dripped out from them like tears.

I rose.

Now to take out the generators. That was the mission Genesis had charged us with. They were kept behind the building where Genesis worked with the other human slaves. It was built into the high ground on the side of a dormant mountain, away from the lava pits. Only days ago, I'd looked mournfully up at the place, wondering how I might ever reach it. Today it seemed not so far.

I ran and my thunder ran with me. The ground quaked with the stomping of our feet. I stepped on a man and felt him flatten. We swept attackers and their sticks away from us with our wings, we bit off their heads, we breathed fire to melt their machines.

Yes, Tanzanite! I said as she swept three men over with her tail. We were gaining ground.

I'd thought before the moment I reached the building that I would go around it, but up close it looked not tall at all. I jumped, wings spread. Was this what it would be like to soar? It only lasted for a moment, then I landed on the roof. It cracked under my weight, part of it collapsing. Screams rose up from below me as chunks of cement buried humans alive. I felt a purr of satisfaction before I remembered that Genesis was down there somewhere, too.

Genesis! Are you okay?

I'm fine. Keep going.

I raced across the rooftop, light on my feet. I kept my wings out, barely touching down before I sprang up again. The roof held below me as I leapt across.

I could see the generators now. They were not far, and few men stood guard around them; they'd all come running to the lava lake. I hopped off the roof and lumbered to the generators. There were rows and rows of them, just boxes standing side by side, each making a whirring noise.

Are you close? I called to my thunder. *I need help.*

On our way, they answered. Glancing back, I saw them swarm around the building.

The men before me panicked and ran.

Almost there, I said to Genesis.

Destroying the generators was a work of art. Each of us did it in their own way. Fire spewed from my mouth as Tanzanite whipped her tail. Her neighbor jumped and stomped while mine slashed with his claws. The smoke and sparks were wild as a rocket launch. Angry mechanical whines rose in volume before drooping and dying. I raised my eyes to the lines of fence wire above our heads, those lines that were walked always by a purple electric charge that stole our oneness away. I followed a charge with my eyes, trumpeting when it blinked out. Everywhere, the purple cast that daily lit the white ash sky was doused. Lights died in the buildings behind us, casting us into a foggy gloom. The alarm cut off. I perked up my ears, listening for that telltale sound, the buzzing of the fences and their dampening field.

But it had ceased completely. I'd heard it all my life and the air sounded strangely silent now, despite the shouts of the humans coming around the building and the background rumbling of the volcanoes.

The tenuous merge between the members of my thunder flared to full strength. Only once before had I felt the bonds so firm between us. And Genesis was there, too. I stood outside by the wreckage of generators and I stood inside, rising from a metal chair.

I did not wear a protective suit like the slavers who guarded the room's exits and paced up and down between the tables, clenching small prods tightly beneath strained knuckles. I wore only a loose cotton pantsuit and no shoes. The tips of my fingers hurt. The table before me was piled high with diamonds.

Around me, other workers rose from their seats, murmuring to each other in wonder. They were children and adults and old ones. They wore the same white pantsuit with no shoes.

"Back in your seats. Now!" a slaver said. He thrust his prod into the guts of those closest to him. They bent over, convulsing, but as soon as he stopped, they stood back up again and charged him, ripping the prod from his hands and the helmet from his head. He screamed and clutched his face, though he would not die of asphyxiation for some time. The diamonds on the tables were not thick with ash, as they would have been outside. But the slaves stomped their feet on him and punched him with their fists, and then one picked up a chunk of black dragonscale from her table. It had chipped during Obsidian's life, making a sharp edge, and she slashed with it. When she raised it back into the air, it was red with blood.

The other guards fell the same way.

"Come on, come on!" Genesis shouted to the other slaves. She ran, and my sight ran with her. Out through the double doors and down a long hall. She knew the twists and turns.

But a squadron of heavily armed guards formed up with machine guns at the end of the hall. I roared, the urge to *be with her, protect her* stronger than anything I'd ever felt. I charged towards the building, but coming around the sides were more tanks to face off against my thunder.

For a moment, I felt split in two. And then I heard her voice, hard-edged and clear as crystal. *We are one.*

The reminder echoed in the cavern of my mind. She'd shared the thought with each of us and I was in every mind she shared it with, hearing it over and over. The bonds of the merge swelled, fastening us into a single consciousness: Genesis and I, and all of my thunder, and all of the humans who were with her. We became like the vision I'd seen of a thousand dragons in the sky with riders on their backs, every one of them together in a single merge. I was Tanzanite, biting the head off a slaver and tasting liquid iron as I swallowed. I was Genesis, accessing the muscle memory of an ancient rider to kick and punch and destroy. I was myself, dousing a tank with liquid fire and feeling satisfied as it melted.

When *they* were all dead, inside and out, their shrieks having died with them and not even their machines left running to scream their outrage, Genesis came outside.

She shuffled towards me in a pair of diamond-coated boots that were too big for her. She wore no protective suit and helmet over her cotton pantsuit, and I felt instantly afraid that she'd die of breathing the toxic, sulfurous air.

She read the thought from my mind, although I hadn't meant to send it. "Fire cannot harm a dragonrider," she said. "Not like it can *them*, anyway."

Rider? At this word, I was filled with shame and disappointment, for I could not be ridden. Had she done all this because she thought I could be? Did she think to climb on my back now and be swept upwards towards the stars?

You cannot ride me, precious one. I will never fly. I hung my head so low, Genesis could touch it. My girl deserved a whole dragon.

Her laugh tinkled like a bell. "Have a look at yourself."

I did not know why she suggested this, but I obeyed. I saw the same old cracked, dry hide. Familiar scales of dull pale gray, over half already turned to gemstone. I spread my wings to peer at the holes that had been viciously cut into the membranes when I was barely hatched. My eyes snapped open wide. I spread my wings to their full span and stared.

Awe filled me. Greater than the memory of any dawning day, greater than the sight of the Earth from space, greater than watching a newborn tumble from an egg was the sight of my own wings. They were whole.

I flexed and turned them, as if it might be an optical illusion. *How?*

"You are reborn."

Dragons are hatched from volcanoes, she'd told me. Dip into the fire and you shall be reborn.

I'd been swimming in that magma every day for years, but I had been afraid and closed myself to its power. Until today.

The magma could not turn back time. It could not soften the scales it had hardened to gemstone. But it had returned the ancient power of flight and I would spend my last decades with Genesis on my back. My hearts soared.

"I will be your rider, Tungsten," Genesis said. "I will wear armor made from your scales, as riders did in the Time Before." She reached her arms up like a child wanting to be lifted. She could not even reach my underbelly, so I tucked in my wings and bent down until her small hands could touch the scales that ran along my side. She found one that had hardened and dug her fingers around the edges to hold it tight.

Her fingers felt cool and soothing, just as I'd imagined they would, but I still panicked when she pulled back hard and the scale ripped free. I trumpeted my consternation and stamped my feet.

"Shh," she said.

My hide will be bare!

"Oh no, no it won't." She pressed her cool hand to the newly bare patch of hide and I calmed beneath her touch, though I was still afraid. "So much your kind has forgotten. So few memories passed down. You see, I will rub you with oil and when your hide heals, a new scale will grow in place of this one. A soft scale, sparkling with health. I will make my armor from that which hurts you, and you will live forever."

I stared at the girl. My eyes alone were half the size of her, yet she was all I saw. *I'd imagined at best we'd have a few years.* I could hear my own wonder in the tones of my thoughts.

Tungsten, we have a lifetime, my little girl said.

Not far away, Tanzanite trumpeted in triumph. The others in our thunder followed and I, too, threw back my head and filled the sky with a roar of joy.

This place will one day be the memory, I thought, and Genesis threaded her hand around my leg, leaning into me. The smell of spiced milk wafted up from the coils of her hair.

"Oh yes, soon. But we have slavers to kill first."

Above our heads, the drone of an engine grew louder as a spaceship descended on our position.

Back to the lava lake, then.

Genesis climbed on my back. There was the promise of fire in her smile.

The Left Hand of Giordino

Auston Habershaw

I walked into Grodin's Auction House with a kind of swagger that was new to me. New as the blue suit I was wearing; new as the convertible roadster I was driving. The swagger that comes with waltzing into a new place with a new job and a magic ticket in your pocket that says you get what you want or they answer to the boss. I'd been wearing this suit for three months, driving the car for two, and I didn't think it would ever get old.

Grodin's was a place I never figured I'd visit, let alone become a regular. In my old life—the life before my job as a professional henchman—this place never would have popped up on my radar. A fancy auction house for fancy people to buy weird art. Not my scene. This, though, was going to be my third time here.

I passed a business card across the reception desk to a young attendant whose navy blazer was too big for her bony shoulders. The business card belonged to my boss. It contained no words, no symbols. It was not cardboard—it was a slender, lightweight wood, sanded to a perfect, silky texture. It was black, but not quite black—there were hints of other colors, too—purples and blues and reds and greens, depending on how you held it in the light. Each one of these cards, I was given to understand, cost about sixty-five dollars to make; the boss bought five hundred of them from some craftsman out in the Berkshires. Good work if you can get it.

The card hit the desk with a sharp *click.* The attendant saw it and all the color drained from her face. As there hadn't been too much color there to begin with, I was worried she might pass out.

"Oh," she said. "Is...she isn't..."

"No," I said, inferring her question. "I'm here as her surrogate. Name's Samuel Braun."

The young woman took a deep breath. "She...uh...*you* weren't expected. You're not on the list."

I smiled at her. "Should I just call her and tell her you turned me *away*?"

The young lady did a very quick risk analysis. "Welcome to Grodin's, Mr. Braun."

A bunch of rich people crowded the waiting room of the old Boston auction house, the dark hardwood of the colonial décor clashing harshly with the sharp modern suits and smartly-patterned dresses of the occupants. Two out of three people were on the phone with some kind of financial entity, lining up their bids in at least four languages. Given who I worked for, I had no such responsibilities—when a dragon paid for something, they paid in cash. This let me evade the notice of the crowd for a bit.

I went to the bar in the corner, where I asked another blazer in a nametag to pour me some of the good champagne he had on ice behind him. I could tell the guy in the blazer was a working man like me—he had the hard look of somebody used to lifting heavy objects to pay the bills; his fingernails were chipped and his hands thick with callouses. He saw the same in me, I guess, and gave me a look that told me what he thought about me sipping champagne with this particular brand of rich folk. "I'm with Angharad Stoneweaver," I said.

"The dragon?" He cocked his head. "Heard she liked art. Wondered how that worked."

"How what worked?"

"She pay well?"

I tugged on the lapels of my suit. "This wasn't cheap, brother."

The guy grunted. "She hiring?"

We grinned at each other, but before I could tell him about it, my phone rang. The boss. I answered it immediately.

Angharad's voice was quiet in the way a nuclear submarine is quiet—smooth, heavy, dark, and not to be messed with. She didn't bother saying hello. *"Find Grodin. Tell him you want to inspect Lot #686."*

"Work?" the bartender asked, still grinning. He handed me a champagne flute.

"Who was that? A servant?" Her advanced senses took some getting used to—she could probably overhear every conversation in the room at that moment, even filtered through the phone.

"Just a man looking for a job," I said.

She paused for a second. *"He works for Grodin? Does it look like he works with his hands?"*

I looked at the guy, who had frozen in place, realizing he was being talked about. I thought about those rough hands. "Probably."

"I wish to meet him. Give him my card."

This seemed weird, but stuff like this was my job. I relayed the message and handed him another sixty-five bucks in hand-sanded balsa wood. He picked up the blank card. "What does this mean?" he asked. "How do I even find you?"

"Come to the estate, present the card. That's it." "When?"

"Whenever."

The boss's breath rumbled in my ear. *"Grodin, Mr. Braun. Now."*

I knew Grodin by sight—he was always hard to miss. He was short and bald and glowing in a goldenrod suit, his fingers sparkling with a half-dozen decorative rings. He was on the opposite side of the room, surrounded by art brokers to whom he was probably hoping to sell the majority of today's lots. They were chatting, champagne flutes held absently in their moist and manicured hands, but when they saw me coming, they all stiffened and took a few last sips of their drinks. Grodin straightened his checkerboard tie and adjusted his thick-rimmed square glasses, as though the boss would know if he looked off his game. Knowing her, she probably would.

"Ah, Sam," Grodin said, his eyebrows leaping up as though just noticing me—letting me know I wasn't expected. "Very pleased to see you—"

"Tell him," the boss said in my ear.

"She wants me to inspect Lot #686," I told Grodin.

The brokers exchanged glances.

Grodin was standing very still, like a man who'd fallen into the bear enclosure at the zoo. "Angharad knows that inspecting the lots is a security concern. I can't just allow—"

"Tell him I will be a third-party guarantor for the work," the boss said.

This irked me. "Do you want me to just put him on the phone?" I asked.

"Don't be insolent."

I switched ears and turned away from Grodin, who still wasn't making sudden movements. My heart rate spiked. I heard myself snap, "Look, I'm not your puppet, understand?"

I'd always had a big mouth—I couldn't help it. I remembered, about ten seconds too late, the stories I'd heard about Angharad's *last* henchman. Rumor was he was an ash streak somewhere.

Silence on the other end of the phone. Maybe five seconds of it. In those seconds, I contemplated mortality.

Finally, the boss snorted. If I had been in her parlor, I suspected I would have seen a whorl of smoke puff out her nostrils. I heard my fellow henchman, Claudia—who was probably holding the phone for her—cough in the background. Angharad ignored the noise. *"Very well, if you are too proud to be a puppet, then a trained monkey will have to do. Listen carefully…"*

Angharad relayed to me my instructions. These were not the instructions she had relayed to me before I left for the auction, an hour or so ago. Something had happened. I hung up without saying goodbye, hopeful that the big dragon wasn't too pissed at me.

Grodin had gathered himself since I was on the phone. "I can't allow a pre-show inspection like you're asking. It's against the law."

"What about making her a guarantor. Five-hundred thousand."

"That's far too high. That piece will never sell for—"

"That's not her concern. Five-hundred thousand."

Grodin thought about it. He knew Angharad had the money—she was a dragon, which meant she was rich. During my first interview with her for the job, I'd asked where she got all that wealth. She answered with only two words: *Through violence.*

I let the subject drop after that. She had money—that was what mattered.

The dealers surrounding us were silent—this was a duel between Boston's biggest art auctioneer and its biggest private collector. They didn't want to miss a thrust.

Making Angharad a guarantor meant that, if the piece in question—"Virgin Rebuked," an Art Deco marble sculpture of the pregnant Virgin Mary clutching her robe to her chest, face turned away—were to sell for less than a half-million bucks, Angharad would pay the difference. If it didn't sell at all, it would revert to Angharad's possession for the agreed-upon fee, rather than returning to the owner. She was, in essence, setting a guaranteed minimum for the piece to sell for, even if she herself didn't win it. It was a weird move.

Grodin didn't bite. "It's too much. I can't accept it, particularly not on such short notice." He raised his champagne glass. "Enjoy the auction, Mr. Braun."

Angharad's instructions had been not to press him, so, obedient monkey that I am, I didn't press him. I returned his salute and moved off. The art dealers watched me go and didn't start talking until I was out of earshot. Grodin made his exit shortly thereafter. The auction was about to begin.

* * *

I wasn't the only henchman there—not by a long shot. Plenty of big wigs and millionaires and vampire lords and what-not sent their goons to Grodin's. We had our own special row, just behind the dealers, our little paddles in hand. As Angharad's designated goon, I attracted a lot of the attention, since dragons were the biggest fish in any given pond—everyone knew my boss could eat their boss. Were they scared of me? I don't know—this crowd played things close to the chest—but I'll tell you this: you've never seen rich men in good suits pop out of their seats faster for a janitor's son than they did when I politely asked to get by.

If you've got the money to throw around and you're a lover of the arts, I guess auctions might be a fun time. For me, they alternated between deadly dull and flamboyantly wasteful. I remember counting dimes on my dresser to buy bus fare when I was a kid and here, just across town, some guy is dropping five figures on a black-and-white painting of a subway turnstile.

The boss was on the phone with me the entire time—she wanted to hear everything. I think she would have given her right wing to be there, nestled in the third through fifteenth rows, waving her little paddle with the tips of her claws. She wasn't just a fan of the arts, she was obsessed as only a dragon can be. She produced a running commentary as the lots came up, no doubt having Claudia flip through the auction catalog for her as they did. *"That's a horrendous example of her work. I bet Pierce bids on it—he sells to all those tasteless luxury car dealers on the North Shore. See? I knew it. Two thousand is a good price, though. Nobody ever said Pierce was brainless. What's next? The Sperry piece? Hmph. Fine, if you like these latter-day impressionists. Embarrassing, frankly."*

"Boss," I whispered as a few men wheeled a big black stone carving to the front. "Wasn't I supposed to bid on this Mauyraka thing? The basalt cabbage?"

A low growl over the phone. *"Don't remind me. Stick to the plan."* I stuck, watching the piece that Angharad had been obsessing over for weeks sell for a cool $125,000 to that vampire lord who lives out on Nantucket. I wasn't really sure what game the boss was playing, but it would be a cold day in hell before she could buy it back from that guy—he had this whole castle he'd built around an old lighthouse to furnish, and he had a lot of wall space to fill.

Then, finally, Lot #686 came up—Giordino's "Virgin Rebuked." The actual sculpture was pretty large—just shy of life-sized. A far cry from a big basalt cabbage, this was almost human. Tender and judgmental at the same time—you got a sense of the virgin's embarrassment, but also she was just a little too smooth, too angular to look real. Stuff shaped like people wasn't really Angharad's tastes, but what do I know?

"Now," the boss whispered in my ear, *"we see if they know to stay away."*

Grodin was at the podium, requesting bids. "Do I hear ten thousand to begin? Ten?"

The paddles stayed down. Grodin cast his eyes across the room, even to the back rows where the casuals lurked—art lovers with real jobs and not as much money, just there looking for a bargain. Nobody took the bid.

I got the sense people were looking at me. I heard whispers. Then I got it—by offering the guarantee, even though turned down, Angharad had made it plain she was willing to pay way over the sticker price for this thing. Nobody had the stones to cross her. Ironically, this meant she was about to get it cheap.

"Proceed," she said.

I raised my paddle. "Ten thousand."

"Do I hear twelve? Twelve thousand? Anyone? Anyone?" Grodin searched the bidders—nothing. Nada. Go in on a bidding war against a dragon? For *this* piece of weird crap? Are you *nuts?*

Grodin dropped his gavel with a soft tap and wiped his brow with a silk handkerchief. "Sold, to Angharad Stoneweaver, for…for ten thousand."

"There," I said into the phone. "Happy now?"

"No," Angharad said. *"Not in the least."*

"Boss, what is this all about?"

"When the auction is over, find Grodin and bring him to me."

"What? Why?"

Angharad's voice was like the low rumble of a distant flatbed truck. *"Bring him."*

* * *

Part of being a dragon's henchman is finding people and bringing them to her. This is a practical kind of thing—Angharad can't exactly swing past your office for a chat, not unless you work in Gillette Stadium. She needed me because, unlike her, I can talk to people and go places and see things that nobody in their right mind would let a dragon talk to, visit, or see.

There are all kinds of ways this goes down. Sometimes people are excited to see her and they basically jump into my car. Sometimes I've got to bribe them with dinner or something. Sometimes it's a polite kind of kidnapping—me with a firm expression, door held open, telling them that if they don't get in the car, maybe the boss would have to come and *find* them.

When I came up to Grodin after the auction and explained that Angharad wanted to see him, he just hung his head like he'd been sentenced in court. "Should we bring 'Virgin Rebuked?'" he asked.

Anghard had left no explicit orders in that regard. I shrugged. "She bought it, right?"

"Yes," Grodin said, mopping his brow with a silk handkerchief. "She did, didn't she."

Of course, once I saw the size of the crate, it was pretty damned obvious it wasn't fitting in my roadster. I texted the boss (so, technically, I was texting Claudia to ask the boss) what to do. Usually, Grodin would just ship it to the house, but everything about this—from Angharad making me bid on this thing to Grodin's behavior—was off.

The message came back: SHE SAYS PUT IT ON THE ROOF - C

The roof. Meaning Angharad was going to pick it up *herself.* I knew she flew around town sometimes, but the thought of her and her wings sailing over Boston, blotting out the sun like an evil cloud, made me nervous.

We didn't hang around for her to arrive—I was told to bring a man and I aimed to bring him. Grodin sat in the passenger's seat of the roadster with his bowler in his hand and a cat firmly planted atop his tongue. I don't feel the need for small talk and didn't have any on tap that would probably fit the bill, so I let the silence draw out. For some reason I opted against the radio, since Grodin's attitude very much matched that of a man on death row.

That was it. He was convinced Angharad was going to kill him.

"It'll be okay," I said once, out of reflex. I did not, in fact, have any idea if it would be okay. Was I driving a man to his death?

"I'll give you ten thousand dollars if you drop me at the nearest train station," he said at last. "Cash. All I have on me."

The reason Grodin had that much cash on him was because I had very recently given it to him. If he thought I was going to take Angharad's money to let him go, he was nuts. If there was one thing *everyone* knew about dragons, it was that you didn't steal from them. *Did not.* It's right up there with fist-fighting a werewolf or necking with a vampire.

Grodin figured this out on his own. "Oh God, what have I done?"

"You ever met her?" I asked.

He shook his head, lips pressed tightly together.

"She isn't what you think." And that much was true—Angharad Stoneweaver was not your typical dragon. She'd hired me, for one thing—a long list of vicious lawyers and professional scary people lining up for the job, and she'd picked me. A down-on-his-luck nobody with a shitty career in insurance investigation and a juvenile record.

I told myself that meant something. What it meant changed, depending on the circumstances. Just then, I was hoping it meant she tried to see the good in people. I didn't know Grodin well and I didn't particularly care for his business or his snooty friends, but that didn't mean I wanted to watch my boss burn him alive in her parlor. I *also* didn't want to lose my job or do any burning myself.

This was gonna be a kind of test. A test I sort of knew had been coming as soon as I'd taken the job. I'd gotten a lot of questions from my friends, from my family, about what I was doing taking a dragon's money. I was asking for trouble. Asking to sell my soul or worse. I'd laughed it off at the time—Angharad wasn't like that. They didn't know her like I did.

Now? Now that bravado didn't seem so funny anymore. Maybe—very possibly—they'd all been right.

I kept my eyes on the road. Grodin didn't say anything else.

Angharad Stoneweaver's estate was nestled within the winding, wooded roads of Brookline, which sticks into Boston's side like a toothpick through a croissant. Once you got past the tall stone walls obscured by thick hedges, you found yourself on twenty acres of green pasture through which a single driveway wound up towards the main house—a gleaming, asymmetrical construction of white concrete that had more in common with spaceships than castles. Sheep dotted the hillside around the house—Angharad's future meals. I didn't mention this last bit to Grodin; he looked like he was ready to throw-up.

I pulled up under the portico and the two of us got out. I put a hand gently on Grodin's back and guided him inside.

In the entryway, I ran into Claudia Houseman, my fellow henchman. Claudia is sort of a personal assistant for the boss—she manages Angharad's social media, keeps track of her mail, and if there are things that need to be done on the computer, that's her department. If you have ever done tech support for your grandparents, it was kind of like that, except the granny in this case could lay waste to the countryside if you didn't get her Facebook sorted. Most of it was Claudia desperately attempting to explain the internet while the boss grumbled at her about the buttons all being so small. Claudia is short and stocky with big glasses and a mop of hair that looked able to eat a comb whole and spit out the teeth. She was wearing a cream blazer with jeans and combat boots and, under the blazer, a T-shirt with certain strong opinions about what should be done vis-à-vis the police. She was pushing a handcart stacked with glossy auction catalogs. She did not look happy.

That meant Angharad must have made it to the auction house and back in the time it took us to drive here. She was waiting for us.

"She's pretty close to spitting fire," Claudia said to me, ignoring Grodin's existence. "I have literally never seen her this pissed off. Watch it, Sam."

Grodin had stopped in his tracks. His eyes were fixed on the auction catalogs—every one of them bore his company's logo. He looked like he was about to run for it.

"You'll stick up for me, won't you, Sam?" Grodin asked suddenly. "We humans—we stick together, right?"

That didn't sound much like any humans I knew, but I tried to keep my tone gentle while I took him by the arm. "Come on, Mr. Grodin—let's go and figure out what it is you did."

In we went, through the big double doors.

Most dragons, I was given to believe, hoard gold. Or money, at least. There was a whole crop of dragons living in the tri-state area these days, making fortunes in the stock market. There were dragons that owned diamond mines in South Africa and dragons crouching over oil wells in the Middle East. If it was valuable, chances are there was a dragon out there that hoarded it.

My boss, Angharad Stoneweaver, hoarded art.

Her parlor was about two-hundred feet across, a kidney shape with little alcoves where the doors were located. The long, curved wall was dominated by a massive window that gave a view of the property to the west, overlooking Brookline. Interspersed throughout this massive space, on black plinths or hanging on the pristine white walls, was one of the largest and most expensive private collections of artwork on the east coast. Angharad had a little bit of everything, her tastes trending more towards the abstract and modern than representational or classical stuff, but there were a few Renaissance masters hanging on her wall in little out-of-the-way places. To an art aficionado like Grodin, this was like being given access to the holiest of holies—a treasure trove of masterpieces not seen by anybody but the dragon and her small cadre of flunkies, myself included.

Grodin, though, didn't have time to gape at them. He was, instead, being stared down by the dragon herself, and she was occupying his full attention.

Angharad Stoneweaver is about the size of a subway car, assuming the subway car had wings and spines and horns and scales and was as black as the surface of a lake at midnight. No, that simplifies it—the boss was the precise color of her expensive business cards. Black, but with highlights that seemed to reflect the rainbow. She was an oil slick on the ocean; jewels under tinted glass.

Her golden eyes were fixed on Grodin, each the size of a dinner plate with the vertical black pupil of a cat. She was not lying down, but standing up, her wings fluttering, smoke curling from her nostrils. "Mr. Grodin, I assume."

Grodin, frozen in place, nodded.

Angharad paced to one side and flicked her tail so that the large window behind her slid closed—she had just come in from outside. There, sitting just behind her on the floor, was the crate in which Giordino's "Virgin Rebuked" was contained.

Angharad turned around like a cat and laid down on the floor, her gaze still fixed on Grodin. She looked like she might eat him. I wondered again what I'd do if I saw the boss kill somebody. Could I stand up to her? What would happen? It didn't seem like it would end especially well for me. The sudden disappearance of my predecessor seemed strong evidence of that.

"Say boss," I said, trying to keep my voice steady. "What's this all about, anyway?"

Angharad spared me an irritated glance. "*That*," she said, pointing a foreclaw at the crate, "is a forgery."

"Nonsense!" Grodin cried. "You…you haven't even *looked* at it."

Angharad snarled, showing an acre of fangs. She reached over with her tail and gave the crate one good whack, which caused the wood to splinter and rocked the crate on its foundations. "Mr. Braun, if you please…"

I hustled over and pried the front of the box the rest of the way off. There, packed in wood-shavings, was the statue. It didn't look like a forgery to me, but then again, I had no idea what an original Giordino was *supposed* to look like.

"Are you familiar with the work of Ernesto Giordino, Mr Grodin?" the boss asked.

Grodin licked his lips. I could see the wheels turning in his head—he was looking for an out. "Ye-es. Yes, of course."

"Then you know Giordino was right-handed."

"Er, I suppose…"

"I will leave it to your own initiative to verify. *I* know he was right-handed and yet *this* statue was carved by a *left*-handed person."

Grodin's mouth fell open. "Wh…what?"

"A left-handed person—the chisel marks are different, from a different angle. Obscured by the sanding and polishing mostly, but not entirely. Not to *me*."

"How…how could you…" Grodin was trying to keep up. So was I, but I had the gist. Angharad was accusing somebody of fraud.

This was bad.

Angharad gestured to a small stack of catalogs left on an empty plinth, probably by Claudia. "Mr. Grodin, if you do not want people scrutinizing your artwork, then I suggest you print catalogs at a lower resolution."

After a second to collect himself, Grodin asked. "If you are so certain it's a forgery, then why buy it?"

This was a pretty good question. I looked at the boss to see what she said.

"I bought it because I could not stand the chance of it falling into someone else's hands—someone else who *would* discover its provenance in time, and whose outrage would shutter your auction house, possibly forever. This I could not allow—your auctions are delightful and your eye for good art is impeccable."

"I'm...I'm flattered, Ms...."

"Don't be!" Angharad said, fire puffing from her nostrils. "It only remains to be learned whether you are a fellow victim or a *perpetrator* of fraud. If the latter proves true, well then, Mr. Grodin, you will most certainly *not* be thankful I caught you. And do not call me 'Ms.' It is demeaning. Use my name or, barring that, use nothing at all."

I think Grodin probably realized what thin ice he was on. His mouth snapped shut. He flapped his hands at his sides for a minute, then said, "You have me at a loss—what would you have me do?"

"Where did you get this piece. Who sold it to you?"

"A confidential seller."

The dragon's eyes narrowed. "Confidential to *me* or confidential to *you*?"

Grodin sputtered. Finally, his hands found some kind of resolve somewhere, since he balled his fists. "I won't speak to you without my lawyer present."

I winced. Even I knew that was a bad call.

"This is not a matter of *law*, Mr. Grodin," Angharad said, baring her steak-knife teeth. "This is a matter of what I will be eating for dinner."

Well, *that* changed the mood. Grodin's knees looked about to give, so I took him by the arm. This he misinterpreted as me, I dunno, *feeding* him to the dragon, so he started screaming. Angharad's head, which had been hovering pretty close to the floor, lifted up, her eyes wide. She *hated* screaming. "Mr. Braun!" she barked at me. "Control him! Control this man!"

Grodin was flailing around, sort of trying to slap me and run at the same time, and I was holding on to him to keep him from leaving...or maybe protect him from the boss...or...or something. He was an older guy and not a regular visitor to the gym, so he wasn't going anywhere, in any case. He was definitely mussing my suit, though. Finally, when he tried to bite me, I had to throw him on the floor, where he curled up in a ball and started whimpering.

"Jesus, boss! What the hell do you think you're doing?" I shouted up at the dragon. That's right—shouted. Three months on the job and here I was, mouthing off to my boss, the apex predator, in her own lair.

My life flashed before my eyes. I wondered how much of a mess my corpse would make. I wondered whether Angharad would make Claudia scrub the scorch marks off the granite tile floor.

None of that happened, though. Instead, Angharad actually managed to look contrite. "I thought he would receive the threat rather more stoically."

I rubbed a shaking hand through my hair. Angharad Stoneweaver—people person.

Grodin was sobbing. "Don't...don't eat me. Please! Please! Don't!"

Angharad recoiled. "He is leaking on my floor. Make him stop."

"What do you want me to do? Knock him out?"

The dragon's nostrils crinkled. "Gah! Get some paper towels!"

I went and got a towel and a chair and brought Grodin out a bottle of water. I sat him down, gave him the water, and threw the towel over the little wet spot on the floor that none of us referred to the rest of our visit. Angharad watched me carefully as I worked—it was a hard thing, being the object of a dragon's gaze. There was something different to it now, though. I didn't feel like I was being watched by a predator. I didn't even feel like I was being watched by my boss.

She seemed...appreciative? No—that wasn't it. I felt like she and I were working *together*. She was watching me to see whose side I was on. I could probably stop this, I realized. Pick up a phone, call the cops. Angharad wasn't *technically* above the law—if she was legitimately killing people, well, even *dragons* can't get away with that. Or, well, weren't *supposed* to.

But that would mean an end to this job. No more nice suits. No more roadster. No more swagger. And *was* Angharad going to eat this guy? Would she? Was I gonna take Grodin's side over hers?

As Grodin was gathering himself, I made my decision. "You better cut out the lies," I whispered to him. "She's got you."

"Who is your forger?" the boss asked.

Grodin sipped his water with shaking hands. He wiped his forehead with his pocket square. "What makes you think I have one on retainer?"

Angharad again gestured to the books. "*Patterns*, Mr. Grodin. I looked through every one of your catalogs for the past year. In them, I found six forgeries—all of sculptures from the early modernist period made by a left-handed artist, all put up for auction at shows *I* was not scheduled to attend. Had I not decided to send Mr. Braun unannounced today, I likely would not have spotted this one, and your criminal enterprise would have continued."

Grodin deflated even more. He was a far cry from the polished art curator I had seen a few hours ago. He looked like a piece of sagging sausage in a rotten banana-peel suit. "I've had...inventory problems. I needed a solution. I know you don't care for Art Deco, so..."

The boss glared at him. "I *detest* liars, Mr. Gordin. I detest cowards even more so. I do not think at this juncture I could stomach you, even if I *did* eat you."

Grodin moaned.

I gave Angharad a sharp look.

The boss puffed a cloud of smoke. "Very well, I am being hyperbolic about eating you, Mr. Grodin. I am *not*, however, above delivering you to the police for fraud. One public statement and you would be ruined forever."

"What do you want?" Grodin asked. He was thoroughly beat, now. He'd probably never be able to look me in the eye again, poor guy.

"The *name* of your *forger*."

Grodin looked at his hands with their glittering rings. He probably thought giving up the forger was giving the guy to, well, to a *dragon*. A guy with integrity—a *good* boss—never would have done it. But I guess maybe I was being a little hard on poor old Grodin. Nobody ever trained art dealers to face down dragons.

In the end, he spilled everything. When it was over, I poured him into a cab and told the driver to find a good bar and leave him there for a while to steady his nerves.

* * *

Angharad Stoneweaver knew how to wait. Patience is the great virtue of dragons—they watch, they listen. The world moves in its cycles and the doings of human beings are no different. All things come in time. The forger would come to her. He was already summoned. He would not stay away. She had been alive fifteen centuries—what were a few hours?

Samuel Braun, her new henchman, was not so patient. She could hear him in the atrium, pacing and pecking at the glass-smooth face of his phone. She could smell his anxiety—sharp and thin, like fallen leaves beneath dew. He was afraid of what she might do.

His fears were justified. Angharad had done many terrible things in her long life. Things that would curdle the souls of such men as Samuel Braun—red days full of screams and the smell of cinders in the air. But such days were a long time behind her. She had learned much about humanity, about herself. The wild angers of her youth were far, far gone.

Once, she saw humans as feral scavengers—ignorant vermin, bent on corrupting the world around them to better suit their ephemeral moods. Like all dragons, she preferred things that lasted and a world that worked according to natural rules. She could not stomach their brief pointless wars, their nebulous industry, their incessant labor to mar the earth and, later, the sea and the sky. She had slept six centuries to escape it, in fact.

Now, though, she saw things differently. Humanity was not a plague, but a river. It bent the world around it, bringing both life and death, rising and falling with the seasons and the whims of chance. One had only to look at them—*really* look, as only a dragon's patient gaze could—and you would see wonders.

Take, for example, young Samuel Braun, fidgeting beneath the weight of time's passing, wondering if he had betrayed his species by taking

Angharad's money. Angharad could see in every crease of his face the cares he had worn against the harshness of the world. She could hear the creak in his fingers where old breaks had healed. She could smell his earnest ambition, his genuine nature. There was a man who had honor in a way that others lacked, learned in the presence of so many who had disappointed him. He was not content to sink with his fellows—he would rise. Angharad, who at times fancied herself something of a gardener, wished to tend to that rising. She wished to see him grow.

It was dusk when at last the forger's vehicle rattled into earshot—a deteriorating pickup truck that smelled too much of stone dust to be anything other than that of a sculptor. She waited for Samuel to note the approach as well (several minutes) and then for him realize that the vehicle was turning up the drive (still more waiting).

Samuel recognized the man behind the wheel as the self-same man who had served him champagne at the auction house that morning. Angharad heard his breath catch and his heartbeat quicken. He had liked this man, she knew. Felt a kinship with him. She knew he felt, in that moment, as though he might have betrayed him for luring him here, to her lair.

The engine stopped. The forger emerged. "Hey," he said, "what's this all about?"

Samuel Braun, his heart beating hard, merely said, "Right this way, please."

The forger paused. "I'm…I'm not in trouble, am I? You'd tell me if I was in trouble, right?"

Samuel Braun did not balk, did not shift, though his heart kept hammering. "Right this way, sir."

Angharad permitted herself a contented grumble. Her henchman had chosen her again—chosen to trust her and her judgement. It was gratifying, like new buds breaking the soil after spring rain.

She had chosen her henchman wisely. She lifted her head and opened her eyes and made ready to receive a new mortal into her lair—a forger and a liar and a cheat, but, also, an *artist.*

And artists, perhaps more than any other creature, required *patience.*

* * *

The forger reacted better to meeting Angharad than Gordin did, I give you that. He stood his ground, looked her in the face, and waited to see what the big dragon would do. I waited, too.

Angharad had his forged piece in front of her, examining it. "You carved this. Not Giordino—*you.*"

The forger swallowed. "I needed the money. I ain't sorry."

"I detest liars and thieves. You know this."

"I heard stories, but I'm not gonna beg. I got paid a commission. Gordin's the guy that put it up as an original. Not me. I didn't even want to do it, but a man has bills, you understand?"

Angharad took him in with her vast, predatory gaze. "Not anymore you don't."

The sculptor clenched his fists, closed his eyes. I almost did the same. Could I live with this? I could see myself maybe getting over Grodin, but this guy? Just another poor working stiff trying to hustle his way off the bottom floor?

I felt Angharad's eyes on me again—that same gaze. An evaluating gaze—whose side was I on?

I stood there, as a good henchman should. I'd picked the dragon's side, come what may. I'd decided as much with Grodin. I'd decided as much when I ushered the guy in here. Hell, I'd decided as much when I bought this suit. I gave myself up to trusting the boss.

Angharad breathed no flames. Instead, she said, "I would like you to work for me on permanent retainer. I will pay you a monthly stipend to support all your living requirements."

The sculptor opened his eyes. "Wh…what?

"You will sculpt what you wish—original work only—and I will buy it if I find it suitable. If I do not, you may sell it to others—enter it in shows, put it up for auction, whatever suits you."

"You're giving me a job?" The sculptor was gaping at the dragon. So was I.

"No," Angharad said. "I am giving you a *patron.* You are not my employee. You are your own, freed now from petty obligations to even pettier men."

"I…I don't know how to thank you!" the sculptor said.

"I do not want thanks," Angharad replied. "I want *art.* Go and make it." The boss turned away from the sculptor. "My assistant Ms. Houseman will make the arrangements. Mr. Braun will show you out."

I did.

Later, after Claudia had produced the legal documents for the sculptor to sign and gave him some deadlines by which the boss wanted to see some work, and after I saw him off in his pickup, him beaming at me and shaking my hand and telling me what I great guy I was for this, the opportunity of his lifetime, I went back in to see the boss.

She was lying by the window, the lights in her parlor turned down low, so that she was little more than a vast, rippling shadow. Too many visitors for her liking, I guessed—it had been a long day. "It's all set," I told her, even though she already knew—she had heard everything, I was sure of it.

One great golden eye opened like the blaze of a flashlight and fixed on me. "Did you *really* think I was going to kill those people today?"

I was standing attentively, hands behind my back. I thought about my answer. "Seemed possible."

"And yet you did not betray me, even to save one of your own kind from death?"

No point in denying it, right? "I guess not, boss."

Her eye narrowed. "And yet you *scolded* me. Here, in my own house!"

I took a deep breath. "You didn't hire a yes-man, boss. You hired me. I call things like I see them."

Angharad Stoneweaver snorted a thick, black cloud and made a rumbling noise at the back of her throat a little like a garbage truck on trash day. Coming from her, it sounded a bit like a laugh. "I take it back, Mr. Braun—you are no trained monkey."

"I got a question."

Her eye narrowed. "You want to know how I knew the man you spoke to at the bar was the sculptor."

"You invited him here way before Grodin ever spoke his name. There's no way you could have known. It was just a guess—blind luck."

"You didn't turn," she said.

"What?"

"When you speak on the phone, you put it to your right ear with your right hand, leaving your left hand free. When the bartender handed you your champagne, he handed you the glass to your left hand *from his right hand.* Bartenders are trained to pour with their dominant hand. The man you were speaking with was left-handed. Only ten percent of humans are left-handed, even fewer who have hands like a sculptor."

My mouth was hanging open. "How did you know I—"

"The fabric of your suit is fresh, crisp...very noisy. If you had turned to accept the wine, I would have heard." Angharad yawned. "It was not a blind guess, but an educated one. I took a risk. Risk is important, Mr. Braun. It keeps us grounded. We must always have something at stake."

"What do *you* have at stake, then?" I didn't know the answer—big dragon, big house, all the money she wants...what?

"My trust, Mr. Braun. My trust in you." She laid her head on the floor with a soft thump I felt in the soles of my feet. "I am most gratified by today. Most gratified."

The compliment hung around me like heady smoke. I didn't want it to feel good—to feel like her trained monkey for real, like a pet—but it *did* feel good. It felt good to have someone like Angharad in my corner—someone who had seen it all, judged it, and picked out the best for herself. Panning gold from the muck of humanity.

In the end, I liked that I'd been picked. "Thanks, boss."

She didn't answer. She merely closed her eye and sank into the darkness of her parlor. Me, I went out for a drive and thought about my job. About those sixty-five-dollar business cards and the art dealers I dragged before a dragon's jaws and the sculptor out there somewhere, carving a block of stone into something new and weird and amazing. I found myself smiling; I found that swagger hadn't left me.

It was good work if you could get it.

Reenactment

David B. Coe

You couldn't pronounce my true name.

The Old English runes used to spell it include fricatives and diphthongs that have long since been lost to time and laziness and the perversion of something powerful and glorious.

But the name meant "death flame on the wing."

Pretty cool, right?

Now they call me Blaze, like I'm a horse, or the lead singer in some boy band. Never mind that I'm not a boy.

You can call me Tana. That's what my agent calls me, and that's what she puts on my contracts. If it's good enough to get me paid, it's good enough for you.

I'm a cross-breed between a Scandinavian Ridgeback and a European Horntail, meaning that I have spikes at the end of my… I'm sorry. I'm laughing because the speciation crap you read about in stories is just that: crap. All of it. I'm a fucking dragon. Period. Full stop. Yes, I have ridges on my back and spikes on my tail. I also have wings, and teeth that could chomp through a firetruck, and serpentine eyes that can bind and mesmerize and seduce. I have a flameheart inside my chest that allows me to breathe fire. We all do. It comes standard, to use a phrase you might understand.

Few of us remain. Humans may be puny and dim-witted, but you are relentless. We have been hunted to the brink of extinction. Most of my kind have gone into hiding in remote mountain ranges and high deserts.

They prey on what beasts they can find, forsaking riches and comfort, leading lonely, desolate lives.

Not for me, such an existence. Some time ago, I chose a different lifestyle. Did I sell out, take the path of greed and expedience? Hell, yes. What part of "I'm a dragon" did you not understand? Altruism and noble poverty are the province of nuns and monks. And washed-up, virtue-signaling dragons. As I say, not for me.

I'm a reenactor. You thought humans were the only ones?

In the sixty-plus years since California hosted the first Renaissance Faire, such gatherings of history geeks, costuming nerds, and fantasy-reading freaks have spread across the country, becoming ever more popular and lucrative. They're a growth industry.

Let's be honest, though. How long can any festival hope to keep people engaged with jousting matches between *knights*—that puff of smoke was me throwing up a little in my mouth—who are too out-of-shape and clumsy to sit a horse? How long can they bank on drawing crowds by holding battle tournaments among "swordsmen" and "swordswomen" who move in slow motion and wield wooden blades that might bruise, but certainly won't kill? Not long at all.

But give them a dragon? Send out a knight to slay him? Now *that's* entertainment.

Yes, they all think I'm a male. So what? I can live with their ignorance. I mean I do flyovers; they can see I don't have the proper equipment. But humans know as little about dragons as they do about jousts and swords.

Dragon males are tiercels, like male birds of prey. They're smaller and weaker than we are. Slaying a male is no great accomplishment. I've done it plenty of times. Slaying a female… Well, I've been alive for eleven centuries.

I sacked plenty of cities in my youth, in Britain, France, Germany, even in Spain, though I didn't like the heat. Early on, when I first began to work the festivals, I harkened back to those experiences in medieval Europe. I thought this new line of work wasn't that different, except all the attacks were put-ons and all the treasure I stole was plastic. And in the end, the humans always won. Those endings were hard to stomach at times, but I figured it was a living, and not a bad one at that.

I agreed to my most recent contract, with Highland Forest Renaissance Faire, two years ago this past spring, after they won a bidding war with several of the big state festivals. They were willing to pay what I wanted: twenty-one and twenty-one. That's twenty-one head of cattle, and twenty-one pounds of silver weekly, plus whatever fee they negotiated with Rebecca, my agent. She usually works on a percentage, of course, but she didn't want beasts or metal. I would have preferred gold to silver—who wouldn't?—but the per-ounce value is through the roof. At first, I liked it here. They made me comfortable, allowed me to take up residence in a cave on the premises, in a mountain large enough to accommodate me and my hoard, with space just outside the cave where the beasts could graze until I was ready to eat them. More important, the festival organizers made me the centerpiece of the show, allowing me to fly and "pillage" to my heart's content. Other Ren Faires of which I'd been part had me do the same thing every damn day: a flyover, a gout of fire, and then an off-stage roar or two as the hero "slayed" me. Easy-peasy, but boring and demeaning. That's what I thought at least. Centuries old, and yet I was as naïve as a babe. Back then, I didn't know what demeaning was.

Highland Forest claimed their concept was innovative, a step forward. They sought, in their words, "to build a narrative." They didn't want me to do the same schtick over and over. They wanted a story, an evolving experience that would keep customers coming back week after week, month after month. Patrons bought weekend passes and had what the owners called "an immersive journey back through time." And I was the star. Every flyover, every jet of fire, drew *ooohs* and *aaahs* from the people below. I loved that.

I basked in the glory of it, savoring the attention, the creative freedom they granted me. I didn't abuse it, of course. I didn't hurt anyone. Not seriously, at least. Maybe I singed a few tresses, frightened a couple of the other reenactors. I did set one tent on fire, but those below managed to put out the flames before they spread, and the visitors reveled in the authenticity. Our crowds grew and grew.

I should have known it couldn't last. I might have been the headliner for the first half of the season, but all that changed when they brought on "Sir Philip," he of the shining armor and snow-white steed. He wasn't like the amateurs I'd worked with at other faires. He was tall, trim, athletic, good-looking, with a thousand-watt smile and a booming baritone. And he knew his way around a sword and a horse. He'd been trained, obviously, though I have no idea where or by whom. But that first day I understood my life was about to take a turn for the worse.

He rode into the Ren Faire's central square while I was still in the midst of my pillaging and announced himself to the spectators and festival actors.

"Fear not, fair ladies and fine gentlemen, for I, Sir Philip of Glastonbury, have arrived!"

Cheers erupted. I craned my neck, looking to see who this moron might be, and nearly flew into the crown of an oak.

He drew his sword, the blade gleaming in the sunlight, and pointed it at me. "This fiend, this monster, shall trouble you no more! And as God is my witness, I say to you that before the first snowfall, I shall dispatch the demon to the pits of Hell where it belongs!" More cheers from actor and fan alike.

Fickle bastards.

Rather than engage with the man, I flew off. The last I heard, he was mocking my cowardice, eliciting laughter and jeers from the throng. I had half a mind to roast every last one of them, but I didn't. An opportunity missed, I'm afraid.

That evening, after the gates closed, I flew back to the village and confronted the owners of Highland Forest, Sharon and Jack Hill. Jack, ruddy-faced and round, with thinning salt and pepper hair, couldn't have been happier to see me. You would have thought I'd brought him plunder from Vegas.

"Great job today, Blaze. Really great! Some of the others wanted to warn you about Phil's arrival, but I said, 'Hell, no! Blaze is a professional. She'll know just what to do.' And boy did you. That was perfect. The way you banked and flew off. I couldn't have scripted it better myself."

"Who. The hell. Is Phil?"

Jack appeared stunned. He blinked, glanced at Sharon, faced me again, though he took care not to look me directly in the eye. "He's our hero, our star. Wasn't that clear?"

I almost said it. I came within a scale's breadth of making myself a fool, a laughingstock. *I'm your star! I'm the hero!* The words were on the very tips of my tongue. Fortunately, I bit them back in time.

What an idiot I'd been. Somehow, I'd convinced myself the current state of the story would last forever. But the truth had been staring me in the face all along. "Building a narrative." "An evolving experience." It was all in the bloody contract.

Phil was the second act. I was the problem and he was the solution. All this time, I'd been the villain and I didn't even know it. What's the old cliché? Every villain is the hero of their own story? Phil was a bucket of cold water in my fire-breathing face.

"Here he comes now."

I turned in the direction Jack and Sharon stared and saw him emerge from the gloaming. He wore jeans and a white dress shirt, but he still had the look of a hero. His hair was blond, shoulder length, his chin dimpled and square. I thought I heard Sharon give the softest of sighs.

The man had the good grace to check his stride when he spotted me. But he continued on, greeted Jack with a handshake and Sharon with a peck on the cheek. Then he turned to me. His baby blues flicked to mine, but not for any length of time. He played a hero, but that didn't make him truly brave.

"You're Tana, right?" At least he had the decency to use my name. And apparently his British accent was legit. "I'm sorry we couldn't introduce ourselves properly earlier today. It's a pleasure to meet you. The others told me a lot about you, but you're even more impressive in person."

What the fuck was I supposed to do with that? I wanted to bite off his goddamned head, but here he was being charming and gracious.

"The pleasure is all mine," I said, grinding my teeth with a sound in my skull like an avalanche. "I could tell the moment I saw you that you were different from other knights I've 'battled.'" I waggled my foreclaws, indicating air-quotes.

Jack beamed. "Phil is trained in three martial arts, spent a year with the Royal Shakespeare Company, and grew up on a horse farm. He's the whole package."

Well, tally-fucking-ho.

I'm pretty sure Sharon sighed again. I wanted to bite off her head, too.

After an awkward silence, I stretched a wing, flexed a talon. Phil eyed me, but didn't seem intimidated.

"I should get going."

Jack's brow creased. "You just arrived. Did you have smething else you wanted to discuss?"

"It'll keep."

"All right. We'll get next week's script to you by Tuesday. You're going to love the way we're finishing the season."

I'll bet.

I said goodnight to Sharon and Jack, nodded to Phil, and flew off, pleased to see that the wind from my take-off staggered Mr. Whole Package.

I kept to my lair that Monday, ate only a single steer, took little comfort from the cold shine of my hoard. I dreaded the arrival of the coming weekend's script. With reason, as it turned out.

It was a shit show. Sure, I got to do a couple of flyovers, and spit some burn, but every time Phil showed his pearly whites, I was supposed to fly off in terror, bellowing like a frightened cow. Worse, I was supposed to drop my plunder. Drop. My. Plunder. Out of what? Fear? Stupidity? Early-onset dementia?

No dragon worth their salt would ever drop the stuff they'd already pillaged. Even if they *were* afraid of some pretty-boy knight, they would hold on to what they had. But not me. Not in this two-bit fantasy nightmare.

I thought about going back to Jack and Sharon, but quickly dismissed the idea. I wouldn't get anywhere with them, and chances were Phil would be lurking nearby, alert to any attempt on my part to change the storyline. It was time to bring in the big gun.

Rebecca once gave me a tablet—an oversized smart phone, essentially—no doubt hoping to forestall unexpected visits of the sort I paid her that day. The tablet was utterly useless. Though bigger than a phone, it was still too small for my talons, and the first time I tried to write a text, my claw punctured the glass.

I flew to her home in the suburbs of New York, arriving after dusk and settling in her ample backyard.

"Rebecca."

I spoke her name loudly enough to reach her inside, but not at a volume that rattled the windows. I thought this showed tremendous restraint, since I wanted to roar until the chimney masonry shattered.

She stepped onto the back patio a few moments later, a tumbler in hand. I smelled Scotch. As usual, she wore business clothes and had her dark hair in a tight bun. I had often wondered if she ever dressed down or allowed herself to appear anything less than immaculate.

"Tana, how lovely to see you."

"Skip the crap. I want out of my contract with Highland Forest."

She laughed, not kindly. "Too bad."

"I'm serious. What would it take?"

"And I'm serious. It can't be done, at least not unless you've changed your stripes in the last six months. What's the problem? I thought you loved it there."

"I did. Not anymore. How do I get out?"

She opened her hands in surrender. "Okay, all you have to do is pay them for the cattle you've eaten and return all the silver they've given you."

I stared at her, unable to form words. She might as well have told me to hack off both my wings. This will sound crazy, I'm sure, but I couldn't give them back my silver. No dragon could. Maybe you thought a hoard was merely something we collected for the fun of it. It's much, much more. It's an obsession, a compulsion—it took me years of therapy just to be able to say as much. We gather because it's in our nature. It's who and what we are. To give any of it back, even a single bauble or the thinnest coin, was to deny our very essence, to go against our most basic nature.

I tipped my face to the stars and bellowed. Rebecca dropped her drink and stumbled back, hands clapped to her ears.

My wail built, skirled, shaking the very foundations of every house around us, and still I didn't stop, until my throat was raw and my breath spent. When at last I fell silent, dogs barked and children wept. Out front, a car alarm whooped.

"Good to get that out of your system?" Rebecca glanced down at the shattered glass and whiskey stain on her deck. "That was an eighteen-year-old MacCallan, damnit."

"So, I'm trapped. That's what you're telling me."

"You're a prisoner of your own greed."

"It's not greed. It's...it's psychological. You wouldn't understand."

"I'm an agent; I make my living dealing with headcases. Of course I understand. But that changes nothing. Unless you have the wherewithal to give up the silver you've claimed, you're stuck." She canted her head. "Why don't you tell me what's going on and maybe we can find a solution. Jack and Sharon are reasonable people. They know how lucky they are to have you."

I shook my head, abruptly unable to face her. "There's a new guy. A knight. There's nothing to be done. I should have seen this coming." I inhaled, exhaled, straightened. "And I shouldn't have bothered you. I'm sorry—for the noise, for the whiskey, for the intrusion."

"Who's this knight?" Rebecca asked, and I had the distinct sense she was asking for herself, looking for a new client.

"No one worth worrying about. Good night."

I launched myself and began the long flight back to my lair. I didn't feel any better, but I knew I was on my own. I couldn't get out, and I couldn't change anything, not without creating problems I didn't want to face. Which meant sucking it up. Doing what my contract demanded.

So be it.

That should have been the end of it. I was resigned to being stuck with Highland Forest for another nine years, because when you've lived for eleven centuries, a ten-year contract doesn't seem like a big deal.

But the scripts kept getting worse. One week they had me stealing "virgins" from the village. Virgins! That old chestnut! One dragon—a tiercel in Scotland—did that for all of two harvests back in the fourteenth century and humans have never let it go! And even that horny old bastard only took one at a time. The script had me gather a dozen. I kid you not. And then, according to the storyline, rather than face Big Bad Phil, I just let them all go. Fucking unbelievable.

A couple of weeks later, I had to return stolen treasure, again as a desperate measure taken to avoid a fight with the Great Knight. Never mind the shame of having to feign terror of a human dressed in a tin can; they had no idea what they were asking of me. It wasn't real treasure, of course. Props all of it. And I hadn't actually stolen any of it. But deep-seated genetic compulsions don't give a crap about what's real and what's not, what's a prop and what's really treasure. Ceding back those gems and coins nearly broke me. It didn't matter that they were fake or that my real hoard was just fine. As soon as we were done for the day, I flew deep into the mountains and poured fire into a secluded lake until the water frothed and bubbled, and steam billowed into the twilight sky, and dead fish rose to the surface. Still, I trembled, aching to retrieve what the most primitive part of my brain believed was rightfully mine. The lake cooled and I boiled it again. And again. And again. Until most of the water was gone and the full moon shone on a desolate expanse of hot mud and blackened stone. Finally, I returned to my lair and slept for two days.

I awoke famished and convinced I had weathered the worst of what the new festival narrative might offer.

If only.

The next script was also the last of the season. The climax. The big finish. Which meant I had to die.

Not really, of course. They'd made an investment in me and they planned on having me around for years to come. But for the purposes of the fucking "narrative," this was to be the weekend of my demise, of my defeat at the hands of Sir Phil.

I had to read the script three times to convince myself this shit was real.

"The Dragon swoops in over the central square, intent on burning the entire village to the ground." I know: nothing wrong with that. Just wait.

"When the Dragon sees Sir Philip at the head of a rag-tag army of villagers, the Dragon checks his advance and hovers before the knight. He threatens to kill the knight and the villagers, but Sir Philip hurls his sword at the Dragon. The sword strikes the Dragon in the chest [Dragon will catch the blade with a forepaw and clutch it to his chest to make it seem the sword has stuck there] and the Dragon, after dramatic death throes in the air, including a fountain of flame, falls to earth, landing on his back and moving no more. The villagers cheer and celebrate Sir Philip's great victory with a banquet and fireworks."

Even after the third reading, I could barely speak for my outrage. First of all, no dragon with any sense hovers before a knight. Humans are slow, weak, earthbound, and — oh, did I mention? — slow! Hovering slows us to your speed, levels the playing field, to use a human phrase. Why would I hover when I could burn the little fucker to a crisp in a flyover?

And don't get me started about the way he was to "slay" me. A thrown sword? I could turn it to liquid before it covered half the distance. And even if I didn't, the odds against a spinning sword striking true, in my heart, for a killing blow, were astronomical. That's why they needed me to catch the damn thing and clutch it to my chest.

I flew to Rebecca's house again that night and read her the script.

"What do you want me to do?"

What *did* I want her to do? I honestly couldn't say. I read her snippets of it again.

"Yes," she said, "it's a pretty stupid script. I would have expected better from Jack and Sharon. But here's the thing, Tana, the people watching don't know anything about dragons. They won't know how inaccurate it is. They won't think any less of you for 'dying.' They'll just think this knight—what's his name?"

"Philip." I spat the name with such venom, a tendril of flame flickered in the darkness.

"Right, Philip. They'll just think he's a hero, which is the point. You knew going into this that you'd be the bad guy, that it would end with you pretend-dead and some knight dancing around your corpse. So, what's this about really?"

She watched me. Rebecca was the one human I dealt with who actually looked me in the eye. She wasn't afraid of me, and the truth was, she had no reason to be. I trusted her and I wanted her to trust me. Which was why I couldn't bullshit her.

"I don't know. This gig started so well, and it's gone to shit so quickly…I guess I've got whiplash, you know?"

"I'm sorry for that. Had I known it would turn out this way, I would have warned you. Truly. But you're in it now. You're under contract for nine more seasons after this one. You have to make peace with it. They're feeding you well, adding to your hoard weekly. Focus on that. The rest is just for show, right?"

She was no philosopher, but there was a certain mercenary wisdom to what she said. I agreed with her, half-heartedly, and left her, winging my way back to the mountain.

I spent the rest of the week making peace with the ignominy of the season's end, telling myself it would be over quickly enough, and then I would have the entire winter and spring to enjoy my wealth and my life of leisure before beginning another festival season.

The weekend went as scripted. I did all I was supposed to, and I have to say, my death was a sight to behold. Roars, flailing of wings and legs—though not the one pinning the sword to my chest—erratic flight, a ninety-foot jet of fire, and a convincingly dramatic plunge to earth, ending in a bone-rattling impact. People screamed with delight, then began to chant Philip's name. That pissed me off, but I lay still and kept my eyes closed. I was a professional. I'd done my part. Phil gave his victory speech, as scripted, and the actor who played the village friar led everyone in a prayer of thanks to the Christian god. At last, Phil led the spectators off toward the banquet tent for the close-of-season feast. I opened an eye, decided it was safe to move, and quietly tossed the sword aside. I rolled off my back, unfurled my wings, and bent my legs to leap into the darkening sky.

"I knew you weren't really dead."

I peered over my shoulder. A young human—a boy—stood a short distance away, a half-eaten turkey drumstick in one hand, a soda in the other. The turkey leg was nearly as big as his arm.

"No," I said with a sigh. "I'm not really dead. It's a show. It's not real."

He nodded, took a bite of turkey.

I hoped that marked the end of our conversation.

"So, why do you do it?" he asked before I could fly away.

"I get paid."

"A lot?"

"Enough." At that moment, I wasn't sure this was true, but I wasn't about to share my doubts with this child.

"I was rooting for you to win."

I hadn't expected that. "Against the knight? You were rooting for me?"

"I don't like the knight. He's too shiny."

I sensed he meant more than Phil's armor and I was taken with a rush of affection for the lad. "Well, thank you. It's nice to know at least one person in the audience was on my side."

"Next time, you should burn him."

I chuckled. "I think I'd get in trouble for that, but I appreciate the thought. What's your name?"

"Blaze."

I nearly laughed a second time. "That's what they call me, too."

"I know. That's the other reason I was rooting for you."

A woman called our name from the far end of the festival grounds. The boy glanced her way.

"That's my mom. I have to go."

"Thank you for speaking to me, Blaze. Take care of yourself."

"You, too. I hope you win next year."

He lifted the hand holding the turkey drumstick in a sort of wave and walked off. I took a moment to survey the square, the damage I'd done to some of the village landmarks with my death plummet. None of it was serious; surely Jack would tell me whatever was broken could be fixed, and it was worth it for the performance I'd given.

I'll admit, at that moment I felt okay about all of it—the moronic script, my defeat at the hands of "Sir Philip," and my place in the narrative. I'd gotten through the season and had given our paying customers their money's worth. As a professional was supposed to. Now I could enjoy the winter in peace and solitude.

If only that had been the end of it.

My second season with Highland Forest followed the path of the first. Early on, when I was free to fly and plunder as I wished, everything was great. Then Phil showed up, and I spent the rest of the season seething and gnashing my teeth. It helped a little—*a little*—to know what was coming. But returning the fake treasure was no easier the second time than it had been the first, and the disgrace of the final confrontation still rankled.

Worse, the second time around, in the aftermath, there was no admiring child to take the sting out of my defeat.

Nevertheless, I made it through the entire summer and fall without once bothering Rebecca. She and I got together socially shortly before the holidays, by which point any lingering resentments from the completed narrative had faded. She asked me how the season had gone and I answered with diplomatic aplomb.

"It was fine. Nothing unexpected."

We left it at that.

I came to this third season confident in my ability to muddle through. I'd endured two years, my hoard continued to grow, and the remaining years in my contract would be finished before I knew it. Next time I signed on with a festival I'd be a little wiser, a little more prudent. Even at my age, I could learn a lesson or two.

The first several weekends went as expected. Jack and Sharon had settled on a storyline for the faire, one that proved popular and engaging. They weren't about to change it now. That's what I told myself, and I was pretty convincing.

Fool.

Again, the summer weekends passed easily enough. I did my best to entertain and frighten—mildly, to be sure—and offer a spectacle. But I dreaded Phil's arrival, and I began to question how many more years I could endure in this hellhole.

Nothing, though, could have prepared me for Phil's companion.

Her name was Deirdre and, in her own way, she was every bit as captivating as Phil. Black hair, pale, icy blue eyes, oval face, the body of a dancer. Jack fell over himself trying to charm her, but I don't know why he bothered. Anyone with a brain could have told him she and Phil were mated.

She greeted me with courtesy, her voice treacly and her English accent refined. She told me how eager she was to work with me and, like Phil, she used my correct name, even after Jack had introduced us using "Blaze."

I could find no fault with her—she was charming, beautiful, and no doubt skilled with swords and horses, just like her knight. I hated her instantly and was certain adding her to the narrative would only serve to unleash new horrors.

The first several weeks of the season's second act came as a pleasant surprise. The new scripts made room for her, but only as a partner for Phil. The story didn't change, at least not in any way that affected me. The old indignities remained, but I could deal with those.

So it went. The festival sped toward its climactic weekend and I allowed myself to relax. I never would have dreamed I could be thankful for the embarrassment of dropping my plunder, or the directive to give back my fake treasure, but nothing got worse, and under the circumstances, I couldn't hope for more.

The final script arrived right on schedule and I read it through, resigned to the familiar ending. What I found was so much worse, so degrading, so utterly unacceptable, I melted a quarter of my hoard before I knew what I'd done.

I flew from my cave to Jack and Sharon's home and roared for Jack the moment I landed. I held the script crunched in my talons.

He stepped onto his porch, a flinty look in his eye.

"This is my home, Blaze. I don't like being—"

"My name is Tana."

He heard something in my voice then, or maybe he noticed the smoke leaking from my nostrils.

"What can I do for you?" He kept his voice level, his tone respectful.

I held up the script. "You've seen this?"

"I have. You have concerns?"

"I will not subject myself to what they've written here."

"What specifically?"

"If you've read it, you know!"

He didn't argue, but instead gave a small shrug. "It's a good ending. We all think so. It promises something new, something different for next season. A partnership, if you will."

"She. Rides. Me! She treats me like I'm a fucking mule!"

"You're making too much of this. You're not a mule. You're a dragon. You're glorious! And this way, our *three* stars, you, Deirdre, and Phil, are united. That's what we want! The promise of a new narrative will blow people's minds. Ticket sales for next year will explode. I guarantee it. And if I'm right, we'll be able to consider raises for all of you. More silver. You'd like that wouldn't you?"

"Now *you're* treating me like a mule."

"I'm trying to treat you like a professional. But if that's not going to work, I'll tell you what you already know. You signed a contract, and it says you will follow the script to the letter, no matter what. Refuse and you're in breach, which we both know you don't want."

I shrank from the thought of surrendering my silver, but I wasn't ready to give in. "This isn't over," I said, and took to the sky.

It was late when I reached Rebecca's house. I didn't care. I dropped to the ground in the backyard , scaring an owl into flight, and called her name. I had to wait several minutes, and when she emerged onto her back porch, she wore a robe. Her hair was uncharacteristically tousled. She looked furious.

I tossed the script up to the porch. It landed at her feet.

"Page 31."

She stared at me before stooping to pick up the papers. She smoothed them, opened the script, and began to read. After a few moments, she paused to regard me again, then continued reading.

When she finished, she heaved a sigh. "I'll admit, this is bad. But nothing's changed. You're still under contract and, unless I'm wrong, you're still unwilling to face the consequences of breaking that contract."

"I'd rather die than be domesticated. And I don't just mean in the act. I'd sooner be slain than humiliated in this way."

"I believe you. Have you spoken with Jack?"

"He says it's good for the festival, that it will boost ticket sales for next season. He offered me a raise."

She quirked an eyebrow.

"Some things are more important than treasure," I said. "Even for a dragon."

"Well, if you want out of the contract, and you're willing to give back the silver, I'll start the process in the morning. Just say the word."

I pondered this, a war raging within me over the very essence of myself, of what it meant to be a dragon. Pride, independence, compulsion, avarice—all were as much parts of me as my wings, as the fire in my chest. How could I deny any of them?

The answer came as an epiphany. Maybe I didn't have to.

"Don't start it yet. I'll…I'll let you know."

Her expression flattened. "Great. Next time, Tana, show up earlier or not at all."

She pivoted and went back inside, closing the door smartly behind her.

I started for home, my thoughts churning, possibilities blooming like spring poppies, and an image forming in my mind: a little boy holding a huge turkey leg, saying, "I hope you win next year."

I kept to myself until the weekend. I didn't go back to Jack and Sharon, nor did I speak again with Rebecca, although I did reread my contract, and I found what I needed. I was in the dragon business long before I entered show biz. I didn't need her. She would be angry with me, and at some point I would need to apologize. For now, none of that mattered.

I followed the script through all of Saturday and into Sunday. No doubt Jack figured he'd browbeaten me back into line. I was happy to let him believe it.

Late Sunday afternoon, I swooped in over the village, sending founts of flame in every direction, and thundering in rage in between eruptions. The crowd ate it up.

Sir Philip and Lady Deirdre strode forth to the central square to meet me. He bore his sword. She held a thick, braided rope with a lasso at its end. I flew to them and hovered before them, as the script said I should.

She twirled the noose over her head, more cowgirl than Renaissance warrior, but no one cared, I least of all. She spoke her lines—something about "taming the scaled beast"—and let the rope fly.

I opened my mouth and let out a burst of fire that turned the rope to ash. She watched, wide-eyed, as flakes of it settled to the ground before her. The spectators *ooohed* again, blissfully unaware of what was happening.

Phil and Deirdre stood motionless, clearly flummoxed. Then Phil took a step and threw the sword, perhaps thinking I'd decided to follow last year's script. Either that, or he actually thought he might kill me.

I aimed a second gout of fire at the blade. The steel twisted, deformed, liquified, the molten droplets raining down on the dirt and tents and people below. *Ooohs* turned to cries.

Phil glared at me, his face red—from anger or fear or the heat of my fire, I couldn't say. "What in God's name are you doing?" he demanded, in something louder than a stage whisper.

I trumpeted in answer and unleashed a torrent of flame that lit the treetops and tents ablaze. Cries turned to screams. The crowd scattered, people, spectators and reenactors alike, running in every direction. Phil and Deirdre led the way. I considered giving chase, but didn't. I had no desire to kill. We dragons were never as bloodthirsty as humans assumed. We wanted our riches, we hungered for meat, but we rarely killed for the sake of killing. Not over trifles. Not over a bad script. I didn't want blood.

I just wanted revenge, and satisfaction.

I soared over the festival grounds, raking tents with my talons, burning food stands, firing tree after tree. Soon, every structure was destroyed or aflame, the glow turning the sky orange. I hesitated over Jack and Sharon's house, but not for long. I was confident they weren't inside, and I knew they had another place in Vail. I roared, fire hitting the structure with such force the roof buckled and windows shattered. Within seconds, the entire building was engulfed, flames crackling and popping, heat rising to warm my belly and underwings. It was a feeling I remembered from my earliest years, plundering and burning my way across Europe. I spat burn again, into the sky this time. Not for show. Not for silver or a bloody cow, but for the sheer joy of it. I couldn't remember the last time I had given myself over to this feeling. I was alive. I was powerful. I was a fucking dragon. Again. Finally.

I still heard screams in the distance, and for an instant I *did* want to kill, to burn and rend. I hungered for that old life, for that sense of invincibility I recalled from my youth. I was famished. There were no beasts here for me to eat, but car horns bleated a cacophonous melody in the distance—people desperate to escape. As if they could drive to safety.

One figure ran toward me, hands fisted but empty. Jack, his face livid, firelight reflected in the tears coursing down his cheeks. I hovered—yes, I noted the irony—watching as he slowed and halted.

"Are you fucking crazy?"

"Do I look crazy to you?"

He looked around, both hands clutched in his thinning hair. "What the fuck were you thinking? You could have killed someone."

"I didn't. Not a soul. I've been doing this for a long time, Jack. I'm very good at it. That's why you hired me in the first place."

"I didn't hire you for this, you piece of shit!" He gestured toward his burning house, flinching at the sight of it, fresh tears streaming. "That was my home. This is my business. And you've fucking destroyed it all!"

"You're insured. You'll rebuild. With luck, you'll be ready in time for next year."

He faced me again, expression hardening. "Fuck you."

"Careful. As you can see, you really don't want to piss me off."

"What is it you want?"

"To renegotiate my contract."

"Your fucking contract? You've got to be kidding me! There's no contract after this! You're fucking fired!"

"Excellent! Then according to the existing contract, the silver is mine, and the cattle are forfeit."

"The silv— Bloody hell! You *are* crazy!"

"Maybe. I'll move on from your mountain when I'm ready. For now, come near me or my hoard and I'll fry your ass to a crisp. Understood?"

He curled his lip, tears still flowing. "You'll never work in this business again. I'll see to it."

I threw back my head and laughed, flames dancing over my cheeks and jaw. "That's fine," I told him. "I believe I'm done with reenactments. I've missed the real thing. But I'll tell you what. I'll help you out with next year. You want an ongoing narrative? An immersive journey? How's this: your guests will never know when they're safe. Not when they're driving in and out, or when they're walking to the grounds from the parking lot, or even when they're hitting the goddamned loo. They'll never know when I might show up. And neither will you." I bared my teeth in a grin and he took a step back. "Talk about immersive."

I wheeled and glided over the burning treetops toward my lair, leaving Jack to stare after me. He owed me beasts for the coming week, but I knew he wouldn't pay. I no longer cared. I didn't need his beasts or his silver.

Dragons are more than scales and wings and fire. We're hunters. We're built for stealth. We're built to kill. And it had been a long time since last I hunted for myself.

About the Authors

BEBE BAYLISS is a California-born Canadian author who writes in all lengths and genres. Upcoming work includes a story in the Immigrant Sci-Fi anthology from Flame Tree Publishing. As a child, Bebe created the imaginary world of Vicklevania, wrote its first constitution, and continues to escape there regularly. Being unsuited to working for other people led to her career as a design studio owner, where she met co-writer Gini Koch, bonding over a shared love of snark and sci-fi conventions. Bebe lives in British Columbia with a very tall husband and a very small dog. www.bebebayliss.com

GERALD BRANDT is an International Bestselling Author of Science Fiction and Fantasy. He is a member of the Science Fiction and Fantasy Writers of America. His current novel is *Threader God – Book Three of the Quantum Empirica*, published by DAW Books. His first novel, *The Courier*, in the San Angeles series, was listed by the Canadian Broadcasting Corporation as one of the ten Canadian science fiction books you need to read and was a finalist for the prestigious Aurora Award. Both *The Courier* and its sequel, *The Operative*, appeared on the Locus Bestsellers List. By day, Gerald is an IT professional. In his limited spare time, he enjoys off-roading, camping, and spending time with his family. He lives in Winnipeg with his wife Marnie, and their two sons Jared and Ryan. You can find Gerald online at http://www.geraldbrandt.com, on Facebook as Gerald Brandt – Author, and on Twitter @geraldbrandt.

BARBARA CAMPBELL is the author of five novels published by DAW Books: the dark fantasy trilogy *Trickster's Game (Heartwood, Bloodstone, Foxfire)* and the fantasy-romance *Spells at the Crossroads (Spellcast, Spellcrossed)*, written under the pseudonym Barbara Ashford. Her short stories have appeared in previous anthologies from ZNB. In addition to her fiction, Barbara has written book and lyrics for more than a dozen musicals. Barbara is also a developmental editor; her clients have won publishing contracts and awards, including Grand Prize in the Jim Baen Memorial Short Story Award. Visit her at barbara-ashford.com and barbara-campbell.com.

DAVID B. COE is the author of nearly thirty novels and as many short stories. He has written epic fantasy – including the Crawford Award-winning LonTobyn Chronicle – contemporary urban fantasy, and media tie-ins. As D.B. Jackson, he writes the Thieftaker Chronicles, a historical urban fantasy set in pre-Revolutionary Boston, as well as the Islevale Cycle, a time travel/epic fantasy trilogy. David has a Ph.D. in U.S. history from Stanford University. His books have been translated into a dozen languages. http://www.DavidBCoe.com; http://www.dbjackson-author.com; http://twitter.com/davidbcoe; http://twitter.com/dbjacksonauthor

With her background in healthcare, **MADELINE DAU** enjoys exploring characters that wield fantastical versions of medicine. When she's not writing, she's running, with grand plans to complete a half marathon in every state. Her short stories have appeared in anthologies by Air and Nothingness Press and Lost Boys Press. She has two more short stories coming out in 2023, but the year is young. She resides in Florida with her family and two of the laziest corgis in existence. She can be found online at www.madelinedau.com and on Twitter @Madeline_Dau.

GRACE ELIZA writes and reads fantasy and sci-fi and especially enjoys stories with quirky characters that have room for growth. In her free time, she likes complicated board games, noisy dinners with friends, and long, nature-filled walks. Grace lives in Utah with her husband and cat. You can read more at graceliza.com.

Nebula Award winning author **ESTHER FRIESNER** has seen the publication of forty-one novels, over two hundred short stories, nine anthologies, and three collections of her work. She created the popular Chicks in Chainmail series (Baen Books), and the Princesses of Myth series of YA novels (Random House). She keeps busy, these days while wearing a Lipsync Assassin mask.

AUSTON HABERSHAW is a scifi and fantasy author who lives in Boston, Massachusetts. His other short stories have appeared in *Analog*, *F&SF*, *Escape Pod*, *Galaxy's Edge*, and other places. He is also the author of four fantasy novels—*The Saga of the Redeemed*—published by Harper Voyager. You can find him online at aahabershaw.com, on Amazon or Goodreads, or on Twitter at @AustonHab.

LARRY IVKOVICH's speculative fiction has been published in over twenty online and print publications. He's been a finalist in the L. Ron Hubbard's Writers of the Future contest and was the 2010 recipient of the CZP/Rannu Fund award for fiction. His four-part urban fantasy series, *The Spirit Winds Quartet*, is published by IFWG Publishing. Forthcoming in 2024 is steampunk inspired SF novella, *Hope's Song*. Larry lives in Coraopolis, PA with his beautiful and talented wife Martha and wonder cat Milo.
www.larryivkovich.com
larryivkovichauthor@gmail.com
www.facebook.com/Larry Ivkovich/

GINI KOCH writes the fast, fresh, and funny Alien/Katherine "Kitty" Katt series for DAW Books, the Necropolis Enforcement Files, and the Martian Alliance Chronicles. She also has a humor collection, Random Musings from the Funny Girl. As G.J. Koch she writes the Alexander Outland series and she's made the most of multiple personality disorder by writing novels, novellas, novelettes, and short stories in all the genres out there and under a variety of other pen names as well, including Anita Ensal, Jemma Chase, A.E. Stanton, and J.C. Koch, and she now enjoys expanding the fun co-writing with Bebe Bayliss. www.ginikoch.com

RUSSELL HUGH McCONNELL hails originally from Toronto, Canada, but over the years his mad peregrinations have taken him to many strange lands, both real and phantasmal. Having been shipwrecked on the shores of Texas a few years ago, he now ekes out a living in the wild prairie by teaching writing, literature, and liberal arts to interested (and uninterested) passers-by. "Cold Fire of Manhattan" is his first professional publication.

EM McDERMOTT lives with a thunder of backyard chicken-dragons in the rural woods of upstate New York. It's probably because she read fantasy books every waking hour of her childhood that she grew into a woman who is always looking for magical adventures in real life. If epic, dark fantasy with romance is the kind of adventure you crave, check out Em's website, emmcdermott.com, where you can download an exclusive story for free by joining her newsletter community. Or, put off chores a little longer by saying hi at Facebook.com/emmcdermotts/.

JOURNEY SLOANE is a queer writer of speculative fiction with an unabashed love for puns, dad jokes, and spicy romance novels. You can find free stories on their website https://authorjsloane.wixsite.com/journey-sloane or hit them up on Mastodon at @journeysloane@wandering.shop to talk about almost anything except politics and drama.

PAUL D. SMITH lives in upstate New York with his wife and two sons, where he works with emotionally disturbed and mentally ill children. He earned a master's degree in social sciences from Binghamton University in 1999 and works for a large child-caring agency. A lifelong love of science fiction, fantasy, and superhero stories influences Paul's writing. His five-part, middle grade *Jason and the Draconauts* series was completed in late 2019.

NIALL SPAIN is an Irish writer currently living in Toronto, Canada. He co-hosts two podcasts (both award nominated, one award winning) and when he's not writing you can find him climbing rocks, drinking craft beer, or cooking meals that are maybe a little too fancy. Find him over on twitter at: @niallspain.

MIKE JACK STOUMBOS is an author and educator, living with his wife and their parrot in Richmond, VA. He is best known as a 1st-place winner of the Writers of the Future contest and for his space opera novel series *THIS FINE CREW*. His work appears in anthologies from Zombies Need Brains, WordFire Press, and Camden Park Press, among others. He is the lead editor of WonderBird Press, whose first anthology, *Murderbirds*, made 1st-day funding and was named a #ProjectWeLove on Kickstarter. Mike Jack teaches writing craft classes for teens and writing habits workshops for emerging authors.

JEAN MARIE WARD writes fiction, nonfiction, and everything in between. Her credits include a multi-award nominated novel, two popular art books, and editing CrescentBlues.com. Her short stories have appeared everywhere from *Asimov's* to the anthologies of Zombies Need Brains. She is a frequent contributor to Book Bale and Con-Tinual, the convention that never ends. Find her on the web at JeanMarieWard.com, Facebook.com/JeanMarieWardWriter, Twitter.com/Jean_Marie_Ward and ConTinualConvention.com.

About the Editors

S.C. BUTLER lives in New Hampshire with his wife and son. He is the author of the Stoneways trilogy: *Reiffen's Choice*, *Queen Ferris*, and *The Magician's Daughter*, originally published by Tor Books; the novel *The Risen*; and a contributor of short stories to several anthologies and magazines. All of his novels are available as ebooks at his very primitive website, mutablebooks.com, and several of his stories are posted there for free. He also posts regularly on Facebook as S.C Butler.

****

JOSHUA PALMATIER is a fantasy author with a PhD in mathematics. He currently teaches at SUNY Oneonta in upstate New York while writing in his "spare" time, editing anthologies, and running the anthology-producing small press Zombies Need Brains LLC. His most recent fantasy novel, *Reaping the Aurora*, concludes the fantasy series begun in *Shattering the Ley* and *Threading the Needle*, although you can also find his "Throne of Amenkor" series and the "Well of Sorrows" series still on the shelves. He is currently hard at work writing his next series and designing the Kickstarter for the next Zombies Need Brains anthology projects. You can find out more at www.joshuapalmatier.com or at the small press' site www.zombiesneedbrains.com. Or follow him on Twitter as @bentateauthor or @ZNBLLC.

Acknowledgments

This anthology would not have been possible without the tremendous support of those who pledged during the Kickstarter. Everyone who contributed not only helped create this anthology, they also helped support the small press Zombies Need Brains LLC, which I hope will be bringing SF&F themed anthologies to the reading public for years to come. I want to thank each and every one of them for helping to bring this small dream into reality. Thank you, my zombie horde.

The Zombie Horde: Raymond Lowell, Michael Feir, Michelle Johnson, Brandon Babcock, Michael Seth, Rick Smathers, Michael Steinberg, Paul & Laura Trinies, Eva Holmquist, Elektra Hammond, Christine Hanolsy, Mustela, Vicki Greer, Lula Laney, Leah Smith, Joe Hauser, Anna Fultz, Ari Officer, Beth Morris Tanner, Bruce G, Erin S, Angie Hogencamp, Reed Mingault, Ruth Ann Orlansky, Ruthenia, Robin Hill, Nicole Wooden, SusanB, Bethany Tomerlin Prince, Miranda Floyd, Richard O'Shea, Lizz Gable, Patricia Bray, Alan Mark Tong, George Mitchell, Frank Nissen, Sheryl Ehrlich, Carla B, Richard Leis, Bonnie Warford, Brendan Lonehawk, Mandy Stein, Katrina Knight, Helen Ellison, Jennifer Shelby, Jeff G, Brendan Burke, Lynn P, Jessica Enfante, Rachelle Wright, The other Yvonne, Tim Lewis, Lauren C. Teffeau, Stephanie Lucas, justloux2, Karen Fonville, Jo Miles, Juanita J Nesbitt, maileguy, Neil Clarke, Jim Anderson, jjmcgaffey, Dennis Smitt, Christopher Wheeling, Simone Pietro Spinozzi, Aramanth Dawe, Brynn, Mireille Theriault, Sheryl R, Hayes, A. Giddings, Andy F, Eric, Cara Mast, Mary Jo Rabe, Frank M Greco, Jan M Schroeder, Lawrence M. Schoen, Amanda Saville, Simon Dick, Ian Chung,

Misty Massey, Dave Hermann, krinsky, Sean Collins, Patti Short, Michael Ball, Michael Feldhusen, Céline Malgen, Jessica K. Meade, Aurora Nelson, Cassie A Stearns, Paula, Rowan Stone, Jim Gotaas, Robert Parks, Allan Kaster, Claire Sims, Clarissa C. S. Ryan, Kai Delmas, Morrigen Stoumbos, Accelerator Ray, Jörg Tremmel, Nathalie Debonville, Gary Phillips, Karen M, Duncan Shields, Kevin, Brad L. Kicklighter, Anonymous Reader, Kerry aka Trouble, Mike Rimar, Keith West, Future Potentate of the Solar System, Sarah Cornell, Ronnie Darling, Jeff Eppenbach, Kenneth Givens, Terry Williams, Piet Wenings, Nancy Blue Spider Tice, Julie Pitzel, Heidi Lambert, Jonathan Brown, Tania Clucas, Cathy Green, Bess Turner, Jaq Greenspon, Stephanie Cranford, Susanne Driessen, Deanna Zinn, Niall Gordon, Dr. Charles E. Norton III, Alicia Henness, Lee Dalzell, Jakub Narębski, Curtis Frye, Jason Swensen, Brian Burgoyne, Daniel Braunstein, Kimm Antell, Kent Pollard, Lark Cunningham, Beth LaClair, Alfred J. Bohne IV, Random Yarning, Dascha Paylor, L.C. Parfomak, Katherine S, Anne Burner, Sarah Brand, Lori Gildersleeve, David Lahner, Lavender, Michael Fedrowitz, David Futterrer, Carol J. Guess, Lace, Fred and Mimi Bailey, Caryn Cameron, Sarah Liberman, Shel Kennon, C.L. McCollum, Ronald H. Miller, E.M. Middel, Jerrie the filkferengi, Joshuah Kusnerz, Coleman bland, Elyse M Grasso, Evan Ladouceur, Larisa LaBrant, Conrad "Tuftears" Wong, Rebecca M, Rande Goodwin, Max Kaehn, Peter D Engebos, Cody L. Allen, Jeanne Talbourdet, Catherine Gross-Colten, Shawnee M, Owen and Jenny Blacker, Sylvia Wilson, Darrell Z. Grizzle, K Costain, Mervi Hamalainen, Gin Marner, Edward Ellis, Stephanie Wood Franklin, Geoffrey Allen Baum, Taia Hartman, Elaine McMillan, Helen Cameron, Joseph Cox, Scott Raun, Sian, Amelia Dudley, Connor Bliss, Cyn Wise, Ilene Tsuruoka, Caroline Westra, Colette Reap, Pete Smith, Al, Jenny Barber, Matt Celeskey, Nicholas Stephenson, Peregrine F., Cyn Armistead, Hoose Family, Aysha Rehm, Tris Lawrence, Tom Foster, Andy Tinkham, Kathy Shannon, John Senn, Debbie Matsuura, Trip Space-Parasite, Nicholle F. Beard, Cat Girczyc, Jamieson Cobleigh, Jennifer Dunne, Ashley Clouser Leonard, Andrea & Griffin, Katie Cavanagh, Kris W, Elise Power, Karen Brenchley, H Lynnea Johnson, Agnes Kormendi, Megan Struttmann, Shane Bevin, RJ Hopkinson, Jeremy Audet, Jennifer Flora Black, Michele Hall, Moonpuppy61, Sandra Bryant, Phil Huffsmith,, Steve Arensberg, Jen L, Robyn DeRocchis, Nicole Van Den Eng, Stephen Rubin, Bill Clarke, Jade C Wildy, Catherine Fitzsimmons, Mark Newman, Eric Stallsworth, Jacen Leonard, Michael Barbour, Jesse N. Klein, Michael Kohne, Jenn Whitworth, Millie Calistri-Yeh, C R Lisle, Stephen Wroth, Grace Spengler, Chad Bowden, Brenda Rezk, Andrew Hatchell, Jesse S, Anthony R. Cardno, Terry Ebaugh, Erik T Johnson, Mark Lukens, Gail Z. Martin, Olivia Montoya, David A Quist, Neil, Emily Wells, Robert Claney,

Sidney Whitaker, Ravenna, Aaron V, Eric "djotaku" Mesa, Ann Zhu, Laurel Lyon, Leah Webber, Brooks Moses, Kennyboy Huie, K. Hodghead, Greg Dawson, Craig Hackl, Margaret Bumby, R. Hunter, Tim Jordan, Kat Feete, Mark Hirschman, Elaine Tindill-Rohr, Megan Beauchemin, Joanne B Burrows, Mary Alice Wuerz, Meyari McFarland, Steve & Beckey Sanchez, Dione Basseri, Jeannie Brockman, Bruce Arthurs, Amelia Smith, Alice Bentley, Jacob Pérez, Nathan Turner, Kelly Snyder, Keith E. Hartman, Deborah A. Flores, William Rivera, Howard J. Bampton, Jonathan Adams, Yosen Lin, Nirven, Jen1701D, Yankton Robins, J.P. Goodwin, ChillieBrick, Joachim Verhagen, Craig "Stevo" Stephenson, dennis chambers, Brendam, Katy Manck - BooksYALove, rissatoo, Vana Smith, John T. Sapienza, Jr., E. C. Ambrose, Jason Sizemore, Kitty Cunningham, Martyn Smedley, Carolyn Rowland, John Markley, K Kisner, Bari Nerr, Chris McLaren, Austin Beeman, Dina S Willner, Leane Verhulst, David Zurek, Jennifer Della'Zanna, Vulpecula, Johanna Rothman, Christopher J. Burke, Konstanze Tants, Erik Grove, Mark Carter, Sharan Volin, Isaac 'Will It Work' Dansicker, Margo Hardyman, Phillip Spencer, Vee Luvian, Penny Ramirez, Chris Huning, Ane-Marte Mortensen, Tina Connell, Margaret M. St. John, Patrick Osbaldeston, Tanya K., Robert B Tharp, MGK, T.D. England, Lynn K, Kate Stuppy, Georgios "Tymoris" Fotopoulos, Benjamin A Brinkley, Ryan Power, Carver Rapp, Chantelle Wilson, Mark Slauter, R.J.H., Ian Harvey, Brita Hill, B. K. Wellman, Lorri-Lynne Brown, L.C., Steve Salem, Juli, Chris Gerrib, Pat Knuth, Michael Abbott, Samantha Sendele, Melissa "Yi" Yuan-Innes, Cherie Livingston, Stacey Kondla, Anne & Jack, Steinar Bang, Catherine Weaver, Michael Halverson, Kimberly Lucia, Sandra Ulbrich Almazan, Krystal Bohannan, Tory Shade, André "JohnnyCanuck" Lalonde, Art Hodges, Frank Pryor, Tania, Paul Sparks, Shayne Easson, Margaret Killeen, Kristin Evenson Hirst, Gretchen Persbacker, LetoTheTooth, David J Fortier, Sam Robb, Beth Lobdell, Rebecca Buchanan, Todd V. Ehrenfels & the SFSNNJ, Annette Agostini, AJ Haynes, Jean Foster Garner, Eric Choi, Luke Nieland, Writers Drinking Coffee, David Rowe, Emy Peters, Chip Houser, Karen Lytle Sumpter, Amanda Cook, Mark Kiraly, Charlie Russel, Axisor and Firestar, Quintin, MJ Silversmith, Andrew Foxx, Marc Long, Robert, John H. Bookwalter Jr., Tracy 'Rayhne' Fretwell, Duncan and Andrea Rittschof, John Winkelman, SometimesKate, Jamie FitzGerald, Michael Hanscom, Stephen Kotowych, Eleftherios Keramidas, Judith Waidlich, Holly Elliott, Jackie Waldfogel, Raina Alexander, Daniel DeVita, Vincent N. Darlage, Ph.D., Tina M Noe Good, Ashley McConnell, Fantastic Books, Laura Davidson, Darren Lipman, Kevin Niemczyk, Darrell Mast, Rob Riddell, Randall Brent Martin II, I Onse, Laurie Stewart, Jason Palmatier, themadcanner, Rotten Roger DM, Susan Simko, Rich 'Razmus' Weissler, BunRab, Shirley, Linda Pierce,

Samuel Lubell, RickyD, Thorsten Daniel, rickmghc@gmail.com, Henry W Schubert, Jarrod Coad, Erin Penn, Tiffany Thornton, Jennifer Crow, Kat Haines, Sonya Lawson, Marty Poling Tool, Meg Fielding, Rosanne Barona, Kathleen Hanrahan, Andrija Popovic, Allie Judge, Venessa Giunta, Michael Axe, Colleen Feeney, Elizabeth Kite, Ellen Kaye-Cheveldayoff, Destroyer of Worlds, Mark Odom, Steven Halter, Josie Ryan, Nancy, Kai Nikulainen, Cherise Papa, David Grenewetzki, Berta Platas, Jennifer Berk, Lorraine J. Anderson, KTee Magrowski, Cliff Winnig, Elizabeth Cobbe, Sasha, Aaron M. Roth, Deborah Blake, Tasha Turner, Rhonda Eudaly, Iain E. Davis, Alysha Herrmann,

Manufactured by Amazon.ca
Bolton, ON

39429383R00148